Praise for Forgiven Again

Another riveting story from Gina Holder. *Forgiven Again* kept me up 'til 2 a.m. with page-turning twists until The End.

~**Patricia Bradley**
Winner of an Inspirational Readers Choice Award
author of *Logan Point Series*
The Memphis Cold Case Novels
Natchez Trace Parkway Rangers Series

With a sweet romance, gripping suspense, and a spiritual journey I believe all of us can relate to, *Forgiven Again* pulled me in from the first page and didn't let me go until The End. "I am A.D. Lawrence and I approve this message."

~**A.D. Lawrence**, author of *The Purple Nightgown (True Colors Series)*

Which is harder? Forgiving someone? Or forgiving yourself? Compelling, engaging characters. Political corruption and murder. Gina Holder's latest explores the ripple effects of success at all costs. A moving story of mercy and second chance love—both divine and human—that will not let go.

~**Lisa Carter**, author of *The Sound of Falling Leaves*
Under a Turquoise Sky

Politics, a secret past, and someone willing to kill, author Gina Holder offers a tension filled story that'll have readers believing in the hope of redemption by the final page.

~**Natalie Walters**, author of Carol finalist, *Living Lies*,
and the *Harbored Secrets* series.

Praise for No Greater Love

No Greater Love captured my attention from the first page! Gina Holder has crafted a novel of love and intrigue that will leave the reader wanting more.

~**Patricia Bradley**, author of Justice Delivered

No Greater Love is a wonderful dive into tense family history that doesn't want to be unearthed. With a refreshingly imperfect heroine and a close-knit town hiding its secrets, Holder pits her characters against their worst fears and unseen dangers for a climactic redemption story. Readers needing a glimpse of our Savior's love, the hope He offers sinful people, will find it in the pages of this novel.

~**Joanna Davidson Politano**, author of Lady Jayne Disappears

No Greater Love will take you on a joyride you won't soon forget with its relatable characters, vivid storytelling, and pulse-pounding suspense.

~**Tabitha Bouldin**, author of Trial By Courage

I got hooked on Paige and Hamilton's story in the first five pages and as I read the last page less than 24 hours later, my heart wildly thumping, I didn't want it to stop! Gina has beautifully crafted a romantically suspenseful story that kept my imagination churning with clues and tying together loose threads. There's never a dull moment with plenty of intriguing twists and turns, and the bad guys get exactly what they deserve! The characters are complex yet down-to-earth. You feel their pain, want to heal their wounds, and seek answers to their impossible-to-answer questions. "No Greater Love" drives home the undisputable reality that heroes are fragile, human, and fears of tragic "what ifs" always hover over them and their loved ones.

~**Janell Butler Wojtowicz**, author of Embracing Hope

Books by Gina Holder

Historical Romance

Whither Shall I Go? (Standalone)

Contemporary Romantic Suspense

Shadows Over Whitman

No Greater Love
Forgiven Again

Shadows Over Whitman · 2

Forgiven Again

GINA HOLDER

Forgiven Again
Shadows Over Whitman · 2
Contemporary Romantic Suspense

ISBN-13: 979-8-6745-6398-3
Also available as an eBook ASIN: B08GZMF4W9

Scripture quotations are from the King James Version of the Bible.

Cover design by Daniel Holder

Dedicated to Mothers and Daughters Everywhere

For what shall it profit a man,
if he shall gain the whole world,
and lose his own soul?

Mark 8:36

And he arose, and came to his father.
But when he was yet a great way off,
his father saw him, and had compassion,
and ran, and fell on his neck, and kissed him.

Luke 15:20

1

Twenty-Five Years Ago

Her hands wouldn't stop shaking. Seventeen-year-old Annie Staten pressed the phone's receiver to her ear. The long, curly cord tethered her to Dad's massive desk in the study. She dialed the familiar number. It rang twice.

"Hello."

Ryan's deep voice sent shivers down her spine. They hadn't spoken all summer. How would he take her news? "Ryan. It's Annie." Her voice trembled. The knot in her stomach grew worse.

"Annie. Wow! How are you?"

"I'm fine." She pinned the receiver against her shoulder with her chin, then twisted the hair scrunchie around her wrist. "Can we meet somewhere and talk? There's something I need to tell you."

"Sure, Annie—"

The line went dead. Annie's heart skipped a beat. "Ryan? Ryan?" Her words took on a hint of panic. *What happened?* She lowered the receiver and spun on her heel.

Dad stood, legs spread, behind her. His meaty finger held down the hook. He wore a scowl. "What do you think you're doing?"

Annie swallowed. "Calling Ryan." She chewed her lip.

He let go of the button and crossed thick arms over his barreled chest. "The preacher's boy? I thought he was in Texas with his grandparents?"

"Ryan got home last night. I decided to tell him about the baby."

"Why?"

"He has a right to know."

"Why?"

Was he really going to make her say it out loud? Her cheeks warmed. "He's the father."

"So?" Was that a snort? He certainly wasn't making this easy. "While you were in labor, he was sipping sweet tea and watching prairie grass in the wind."

"He didn't know." *Because I lied to him. I should have told him months ago.*

"He's never going to know."

"But Daddy?"

Dad's eyes narrowed. Annie cleared her throat. *I can do this.* If she were going to prove she could raise her child, she had to act like an adult. "I want to keep her. If Ryan wants to. We can get married and raise our baby together. Like a real family."

Dad snorted again. "What do two teenagers know about raising a child?"

Not much. Not anything. The very thought terrified Annie. "We could—"

With a sigh, Dad took the receiver from her hand and returned it to the cradle, then stepped closer and clasped onto her stooped shoulders. His scowl softened to a sad smile. "I thought we talked about this."

"We did, but—"

"There's no 'but,' Annie. You can't keep the baby. I won't let you throw your life away. You've been accepted to Stanford, and you have a bright future ahead of you. You're smart, and you're passionate. Keep your eyes on the prize. Don't let anyone distract you from your dream."

Only Richard Staten could compliment and scold in the same breath. "But Daddy…" The high-pitched whine slipped out again.

The grip on her shoulder tightened. "This isn't open for discussion."

Annie swallowed against the lump forming in her throat and blinked back her tears. She wouldn't cry. Not in front of her father. She straightened her shoulders and lifted her chin. He was right, of course, but she had never known a pain like this. It was even worse than the physical discomfort of giving birth. *How can I give her up?*

A beep broke the silence. Dad released her shoulders and removed the pager from his waistband. He frowned at the number on the screen.

"What is it, Daddy?"

"Nothing for you to worry about."

"Is it about the election?"

He didn't answer. Instead, he checked his wristwatch. A throat cleared in the open doorway. Matilda, the housekeeper, held a baby carrier. "She's ready, sir."

Annie's eyes widened. She choked, trying to speak. "You're leaving now?" *No. Stop. Don't take my baby.*

"Yes." Dad took the car seat from the housekeeper.

"I haven't said goodbye." *Please. Don't go.*

He rotated the carrier so she couldn't see inside. "It's better this way."

"Wait!" Annie rushed to her bedroom. She threw open the door, snatched her Bible from off her nightstand, then grabbed a pen. While she walked, she scribbled inside the front cover: *To my baby girl. I love you. I'm sorry. Annie.*

Dad was already leaving through the front door when she

closed the book and held it toward him. "Please. Give this to her new family."

Dad took the Bible, then, without another word, shut the door between them. The sound echoed through the house and slammed like a prison gate in her heart. In the parlor, she pressed her nose to the glass window, watching as he buckled the car seat into the back of the vehicle.

Moments later, he drove around the circular driveway and out of sight. Annie charged up the stairs to her bedroom, gulping back sobs. *What have I done?*

In the dark of night, Richard squinted, trying to distinguish the steel crossbeams of the bridge through the thick fog that had descended over the city of Portland. As he walked, the bundle in his arms grew heavier with each step. A rattle sounded behind him. He paused. Listened. Nothing. Maybe he was just paranoid.

He couldn't let his daughter's mistake haunt them both for the rest of their lives. *It has to be done. It's better this way.* Maybe if he repeated those words, he'd eventually believe them. Guilt smothered him until he could barely breathe.

His eyes cut to the Bible under his arm. Why did Annie hand that to him? Now, he had to dispose of it, too. He didn't know much about the Bible, but he was aware it contained the words: Thou shalt not kill.

Was he any better than King Herod or the Egyptian Pharaoh who'd murdered all those babies so they could stay in power? How was this any different?

I lied to my daughter. This little one is my own grandchild. He shoved the convicting voice from his thoughts, stopped at the metal railing, and peeled back the soft blanket. A tiny face stared back at him. Awake. The baby blinked and yawned. Their eyes met.

At that moment, his stony heart crumbled. How could he destroy this beautiful child? He lifted his head, leaned forward, and gazed at the rushing water far below. The severity of what he had been contemplating shook his being. He shoved his hand into his pants pocket and fingered the crinkled piece of paper it held. He'd memorized every threatening word meant to intimidate him and bend him to the blackmailer's will.

But, he couldn't go through with it. He wouldn't add murder to his list of sins.

While thinking through his next move, he continued on foot with no destination in mind. The city streets blurred through his tears. *What am I going to do? What am I looking for?*

The thick fog parted. A brick building materialized on the street corner. The streetlight slanted across the space.

Fire Station #9. In the window, a sticker depicted a baby.

He scanned his surroundings and spotted an empty apple crate next to the dumpster in the alley. He fetched the container and placed the Bible in the bottom, hoping to make a more comfortable base. Then, he laid the newborn on top, still wrapped in her warm blanket.

He jogged up the steps and deposited the crate with its precious cargo at the front door. Shame stabbed at his chest, but he reasoned it away. *It's a balmy night. She'll be fine.*

2

Present Day

Thursday evening, supporters and dissenters alike filled the crammed folding chairs, eagerly anticipating the Oregon Gubernatorial Debate. The blinding spotlights overhead forced Anna Kathleen Staten Phillips to squint as she waited on the auditorium platform of Roosevelt High School in Portland. The incumbent governor's voice echoed as she gave her opening statements.

Kathleen straightened a crease in the lapel of her black suit jacket and tugged at the hem of her skirt, where her knees peeked out from the edge of the fabric. She raised her eyes and surveyed her competition. To her left sat Dr. Kalvin Bale, a brain surgeon. His gray hair, glasses, and expensive suit exuded wisdom and distinction.

A newcomer, Isaiah Orozco, fidgeting with his notecards, sat to her right. He looked to be ten years her junior, giving him a disadvantage with the older generations but an advantage with the younger.

Kathleen's fingers brushed the crow's feet and frown lines marring her own face. Time had been kind, but still, these marks of her age and the gray hairs she regularly dyed crept faster than she'd like.

She shifted her gaze to the front of the stage. The governor wore a dark pantsuit and red slingbacks, with her hair styled in a short pixie cut. She'd been governor for the past four years and was advocating for a second term.

Do I have a chance to beat her? Many Oregonians agreed with her policies and appreciated the changes she'd made in this state. Others did not. Would the voters choose the familiar or opt for a change? *Do I have what it takes to win their confidence?*

I can do this. Kathleen eyed the notecards clutched in her trembling hands. *I know what I want to say. Just say it. Don't worry about the outcome.* But how could she not? This campaign was a culmination of childhood dreams and plans. Her current position as mayor of Whitman was merely a steppingstone on her climb to greater things.

With every breath in her body, Kathleen longed to erase the events of the past few months and forget she'd ever met Brooklyn Paige McDonald. Back in April, Paige arrived in Whitman, looking for her birth mother. At first, Kathleen believed it was a political stunt to coerce her into withdrawing from the election. But soon, she was unable to deny reality. Paige was the child she'd given up for adoption. Kathleen's father, Richard Staten, had abandoned the baby at a fire station rather than turn her over to an adoption agency.

Her father's betrayal had blindsided Kathleen, but she also understood his motive. A scandal would have devastated his campaign for governor back in the early 90s. She now faced the same dilemma.

Kathleen's line of sight flickered to the pack of journalists lying in wait, licking their bloodthirsty lips like wolves. If they caught a whiff of the undiscovered dirt, they'd stop at nothing to expose her as a fraud.

Kathleen had asserted that Paige maintain her distance to

prevent the exposure of the secret that could be detrimental to Kathleen's campaign. So far, Paige had respected her wishes.

Kathleen and Joe Donahue, her campaign manager and press agent, overcame the damage done by Kathleen's brother, Erik Staten, the head of a notorious crime ring. He was in prison now, but not before attempting to steal thousands of dollars' worth of artwork and nearly murdering Kathleen for witnessing his crimes. Another scandal would eradicate the respect she'd worked to achieve.

Over the incumbent's shoulder, Kathleen made eye contact with one of the journalists. He narrowed his eyes to slivers over his high cheekbones and pursed lips. His press pass was unreadable from the stage, but everything about him screamed professional. This was no mere freelancer. She'd have to watch out for him—one wrong answer to his questions could lead to slander and disgrace, something she couldn't and wouldn't risk.

She took a deep breath to calm her nerves, her chest rising and falling with the motion. Tonight, she had one goal—dodge their questions and escape the evening with nothing surfacing that could endanger her campaign as a gubernatorial candidate.

The reporters don't know anything about what happened. Why would they even ask? Besides, everyone makes mistakes. That happened years ago. No one's going to find out.

Dad's voice rumbled through her head like thunder echoing through the Wallowa Mountains. *Never apologize. Simply move on.* Move on. That's what she had been doing until her biggest mistake boomeranged back into her life.

"Thank you for listening." The incumbent governor finished her speech and returned to her chair. A smug smile tinted her face. *That woman believes she has this election in the bag.*

The official moderator, a middle-aged woman with the looks and demeanor of a stereotypical sitcom high school principal, stepped to the microphone. All she was missing was the wooden ruler to crack across her palm. "If the candidates will step to their podiums, we will commence with questions at this time."

Each candidate took their place behind the polished wood podiums. "This first question is for Kathleen Phillips. Ms. Phillips, what is your plan to deal with the lack of rural internet connectivity in our state?"

Easy question. I've got this. Kathleen opened her mouth to answer, but a piercing scream split her eardrums. *What's going on?*

"He's got a gun!" A male voice shouted.

The room erupted with chaos. The crowd split, exposing a wild-looking man aiming a handgun at the stage. His eyes flamed with rage.

An authoritative voice shouted out orders. Instinctively, Kathleen dropped to the stage, shielding her head with her arms. A shot rang out.

Footfalls and chairs slamming into one another joined the attendees' screams of terror. Steps thundered across the hollow stage, passing her, and headed for the incumbent governor.

Kathleen slowly raised her head. Was it safe to look?

Uniformed officers wrestled the gun from the shooter's tight-fisted hands, then pinned him facedown on the floor. Handcuffs snapped around his wrists. The shooter spat curses that made Kathleen's ears bleed.

An officer leaped onto the stage. "Is everyone all right?"

"I'm fine." The governor answered, an uneasy quiver in her voice. The male candidates stood, brushed off their trousers, and responded to the affirmative.

Kathleen rocked back on her haunches and nodded. Her voice lodged in her throat, and her pulse pounded in her chest. Adrenaline surged through her veins. Had someone tried to assassinate the governor?

A security officer nearby motioned to another. "Sir, you'll want to see this." What were they looking at?

Kathleen fixated on the light passing through a splintered hole in the back of her podium. She couldn't tear her eyes from the ragged-edged crater. Nausea roiled her stomach. Blood drained from her face, and she dug her fingernails into her palms. The second officer lifted his radio to his lips and spoke, but his words didn't register.

The gunman hadn't been aiming for the governor. She was the target. Someone had tried to kill her.

Iago stepped into the sunshine and shivered. The side exit door slammed shut. Whirling sirens and flashing lights drew his attention to the school's front entrance. The corners of his lips tugged downward. The hired gunman had missed his mark. Kathleen might just be the luckiest woman in the world. His phone vibrated his pocket. The name on the screen made him swallow. He tapped the screen and held it to his ear.

"You're a bungling idiot."

Senator Chatham spat a stream of curses. Loudly. Iago grimaced and pulled the phone away.

He knew he'd messed up. Senator Chatham didn't need to remind him. But it wasn't Iago's fault. Who would have thought Kathleen would survive two threats on her life? He had to give her props for that.

"She'll quit any day now." Iago took a cigarette from his pocket, lit it, and took a long draw.

"You're sure?"

Of course. Iago exhaled and watched the smoke curl toward the clouds. *If* everything went according to plan. "I honestly thought threatening her life the first time would do it. How was I to know she was such an ice cube?"

"Have you met the woman? She could freeze a rupturing volcano." Kathleen was relentless… and stubborn. Very stubborn.

"She won't win, so why is this so important to you?"

"My motives are none of your concern."

Silence. Chatham had hung up. Iago straightened his tie

and headed for his pickup truck. He opened the door, then paused to watch the frantic police through the tinted window. They scrambled around like ants during a rainstorm.

Well, if nothing else, at least he had her attention. His revenge would have to wait a little while longer. A slow smile spread across his face.

Yes, he most certainly had her attention.

The empty house echoed in a way it never had before. Brooklyn Paige McDonald took one last look around before closing the front door of the foursquare in the Hawthorne District of Southeast Portland.

With a sigh, she squared her shoulders and turned from the porch, letting the screen door slam behind her. Paige's gaze swept over the house and street. Her adoptive grandfather, firefighter Benjamin McDonald, had purchased the place long before Paige had been born. When he passed away, his sister, Hattie, moved from Seattle to care for her. A bittersweet sense of loss encompassed Paige. The home held so many memories—not all of them good ones, but still, this was the only home she'd ever known. *On to new adventures. And a new home.*

A series of grunts and groans emanated from the station wagon at the curb, as Aunt Hattie struggled to settle her pets in the rear seat. She pushed and prodded while Lancelot and Galahad, the Dalmatians, were having none of it. The big dogs preferred to race around the front yard rather than being squished between the suitcases and Delilah's cat carrier. It appeared that Gerald's birdcage got to ride shotgun. *Lucky parrot.*

In front of the station wagon was the moving truck that Paige would drive to Whitman loaded with everything the two women owned. A smile tugged at Paige's lips—thankful she wouldn't have to share space with the animals but sorry for Aunt Hattie and the long drive ahead of them.

Most of their belongings would go into storage. They possessed more than Paige realized, and far more had been considered "essential to life" than she'd anticipated. *I really thought Aunt Hattie would be willing to part with more of her stuff.* Instead, Aunt Hattie had insisted it *all* had sentimental value.

Paige clomped down the concrete steps, circled the twenty-six-foot truck, and opened the driver's door needing a good spray of WD-40. She hopped onto the faux leather seat and dropped her phone into the cupholder, after ensuring the GPS was set with directions to Whitman, a five-hour drive—at least.

She glanced in the side-view mirror. Holding a 64-ounce bottle of water, Aunt Hattie settled into the driver's seat. *Between Aunt Hattie and the pets, how many stops will we have to make?*

Paige checked the clock on her phone. It was already mid-afternoon, several hours later than she'd hoped to get on the road. *Looks like we'll be stopping for the night. I wonder how far we'll actually get.* Butterflies fluttered in her stomach at the thought of her new life in Whitman. Had it only been a month since she'd left to sell her house here in Portland and return?

Back in April, she'd found an old Bible in her attic containing a message from a woman named Annie, allowing Paige to uncover the truth about her adoption. Her entire identity had been based on a lie, and that realization had shaken her to her core.

With the Bible's message and the name of the town found on a bookmark, she had visited Whitman, hoping to locate her birth mother. Once in town, she took a job renovating an antiquated bookstore. Jessie Faye, the owner, set Paige on a path that had changed Paige's life. In the space of six weeks, she'd found a home, bought the bookstore, gained a boyfriend… and found her mother… who still didn't want anything to do with her, even though it was now the end of July.

Melancholy mixed with her apprehension. Would

Kathleen ever accept her as her daughter? The woman had made it clear she wanted nothing to do with Paige, and the public was not to know of their connection. Paige could only assume it had to do with her mother's campaign for governor and the fear that any skeletons in her closet would hinder that goal. *Maybe someday she'll claim me as her daughter. At least for now, I have my dad and half-sister.*

As Paige's cell played the theme to the sitcom *Happy Days*, Caller ID displayed the name, *Ryan Whitestone.* The corner of Paige's mouth twitched. *Speaking of my dad.* She snatched the phone from the holder, tapped the screen, then held it to her ear. "Hi."

"Have you seen the news?"

Paige's smile faded. That wasn't the greeting she was expecting. Ryan's voice sounded tense and uptight. A knot formed in Paige's stomach. "No, I haven't. What's going on?"

Ryan breathed heavily like he'd been running. "There was a shooter at the debate last night. Portland PD believes your mother was the target."

Paige sucked in a sharp breath. Fear sank like a rock in her stomach. "Is she OK?"

"According to the news, no one was injured. The police tackled the gunman before he could get off a second shot."

Relief rolled over her shoulders. What if Kathleen had been killed before they even had a chance at reconciliation? "Why do they think she was the target? Why not the governor?"

"The only evidence they have is that the bullet tore a hole in Kathleen's podium. That's all I know. I just wanted to alert you before you found out later through the grapevine. How's the move going?"

Paige blinked several times, pulling her thoughts away from her mother and back to the move. "It's going fine, I guess. We're a couple hours behind schedule, but we're just about to head out now. I'm not sure how far we'll get tonight, but barring any other detours, we should arrive at Jessie's house sometime tomorrow."

My house, not Jessie's. The house and bookstore now belong to me. Aunt Hattie and Jessie Faye will be living with me, not the other way around.

"That sounds great. Love you, Paige. We'll get together as soon as possible, all right?"

"Sounds great. Thanks for calling." *I love you, too. Dad.*

3

The next morning, just outside the Wallowa County Courthouse and City Hall, vehicle brakes screeched. Kathleen rose from her chair and moved to the window behind her desk. She touched the soft fabric of the sheer panels and pulled it to the side. A rented box-shaped moving truck parked parallel to the curb.

The driver's side door swung open, and Paige emerged. Spry, full of vitality, and with a skip in her step, she hustled to the back of the truck and raised the rolling door, then proceeded to unload cardboard boxes and haul them into the storefront.

Kathleen's breath hitched. Anxiety compacted her lungs like a boa constrictor squeezing the life out of her. The warmth of the summer sun through the pane didn't penetrate her skin. Her entire being was frozen from her fingertips to her toes.

Wind gusted down the street, swinging the old-fashioned wooden shingle on the bookstore. The wood-burned letters—Paige's Second Chance Books—mocked Kathleen's resentment. *Why did Paige have to come back? Why couldn't she have stayed in Portland? I don't want her here.*

Hadn't Kathleen made it clear she wanted nothing to do with Paige? Was her daughter a glutton for punishment? Did she think by moving into town, she could somehow change Kathleen's mind?

The rolling door on the back of the truck slammed. Before climbing into the cab, Paige paused and lifted her eyes to the second story window where Kathleen stood.

With a gasp, Kathleen leaped back, bumping something behind her. The standing lamp wobbled then crashed to the floor. Glass shattered. Fragments shot in all directions.

The office door burst open, slamming against the wall. Officer Cody Stone filled her doorway with his weapon drawn. Of course, he'd heard the noise and thought she was in mortal danger. She'd forgotten he was keeping guard in the hallway.

Within seconds, he'd swept the room and holstered his gun. "Are you all right, Mayor Phillips?" Nervous tension pinched the officer's forehead.

Physically, yes. Emotionally, Kathleen was a wreck. The night Dad had driven away with the baby in the back seat, she'd thought she'd left her mistakes behind her. Gone. A thing of the past. What a fool she'd been to believe this wouldn't catch up with her someday. "I'm fine, Officer Stone. I simply knocked over a lamp." She gestured to the pieces of glass scattered on the floorboards. Hopefully, he wouldn't notice the slight tremor in her outstretched hand.

"I'll alert the janitor." He reached for the two-way on his shoulder.

Kathleen waved her hand. "I'll do it myself." Frustration fumed in her gut. She was a tried-and-true Staten, and Staten's didn't need bodyguards. The entire thing was just a waste of time and money—for the officers and the taxpayers. The door closed behind the officer as he departed.

Kathleen righted the lamp, then stooped to retrieve the

broken glass pieces. A sharp point pierced her finger. Hissing, she stuck the bleeding appendage into her mouth. With a groan, she stood, straightened her back, then turned and dropped the chunks of glass into the nearby trashcan.

She flipped the switch on her tabletop fountain, then sat at her desk and logged into her computer. An emailed invoice for replacing the worn, faded, or missing street signs around town filled her screen. Her eyes scanned the electronic document.

20 signs. Official Flat Blade Street Name Signs (double-sided MUTCD Compliant, .080" thick Aluminum, reflective sheeting, 6" tall with 4" text). $40 each. Total cost: $800.00.

Just as she was preparing to electronically sign, a knock sounded on the interior door to her assistant's office. Kathleen raised her chin. "Come in." *What is it now?*

Her new assistant, Dennis Driscoll, poked his head around the door. "Madam Mayor?" His voice quivered. He fidgeted with a pen in his shirt pocket. "The campaign committee is here for your meeting."

Kathleen took a deep breath. Dennis's nervousness got under her skin, but he was far more competent than her last assistant. If this one didn't lose speeches or forget to book hotel reservations, he was already one step ahead.

She pushed her chair from the desk, stood, then wiped her palms down her slacks and straightened her navy blazer. "Thank you, Dennis. Please show them to the conference room. I'll be there in a minute." She leaned forward and added her signature to the document and hit *Send.* Picking a piece of fuzz from her cuff, she stepped to the mirror on the wall and checked her appearance, combing her fingers through her hair to fix a wayward strand. *Perfect.*

The election was only three months away, and she needed to be at the top of her game. *Don't let these distractions get the better of you.*

Dennis cleared his throat. He fidgeted with the end of his tie and wouldn't make eye contact. Kathleen cocked an eyebrow. Why was he still standing in the doorway? Hadn't she dismissed him? This went deeper than his usual mousy behavior. "What is it, Dennis? Spit it out."

He wiped beads of perspiration from his forehead with his sleeve. His Adam's apple bulged as he swallowed. "The police chief is with them."

I'm home. Paige shut off the ignition and set the parking brake. She unbuckled her seatbelt and eyed the small bungalow at the edge of town that she'd be sharing with Jessie Faye and Aunt Hattie. It wasn't the best arrangement, but it was the least she could do for the two women who'd impacted her life. Aunt Hattie had cared for her after the death of Grandpa McDonald. Jessie Faye had shown her the way to God and had sold Paige this house and the bookstore.

Paige rotated her midsection to stretch out the sore muscles in her back, then swung open the truck door and hopped from the driver's seat, slamming the door behind her. She turned as a police cruiser parked across the street. The officer gave a small wave. Inwardly, Paige squealed like an adolescent teenager. *Hamilton. He's here.*

After glancing both directions, she dashed across the blacktop. Patrol Officer Hamilton Bryant opened the car door and stepped out. Audible laughter bubbled from her chest. She threw her arms around his neck, digging her fingers into his dark hair. His arms encircled her, making her feel safe and wanted. Tipping back her chin, she raised her gaze to his. Her image reflected in his sunglasses.

Paige removed the glasses and held them behind his neck. Delight twinkled in his cornflower-blue eyes. He tilted his head toward her making her pulse increase. His lips covered hers, and a deep sigh lifted her chest. If only this moment never had to end.

He released her, leaving her breathless. "You're here." His husky tone sent shivers down her spine. The kiss had clearly affected him, too.

"I'm here." Paige's neck grew warm. Her hands trembled as she tucked her hair behind her ears. "That was quite the welcome." He could kiss her like that anytime.

Hamilton tucked her into his side and draped his arm over her shoulders. "Missed you." He planted a quick peck on her cheek. Together, they crossed the street. "Sorry I couldn't help you move. Get everything loaded, okay?"

"We had plenty of help." Her gaze traveled his face as they approached the moving truck. He hid a yawn with his palm, and his eyelids drooped. "You look tired."

"Graveyard shift. I couldn't fall asleep without seeing you first."

She tucked her hand in his and intertwined their fingers, then lowered her head to his shoulder. The material of his navy uniform brushed against her cheek.

Aunt Hattie's station wagon rounded the curve, then turned onto the gravel driveway and parked. The driver's side door flew open. "Yoo-hoo!" She waved.

Aunt Hattie climbed out of the car, dragging a purse and a giant tote bag. She dropped her bags on the sidewalk and threw her arms in the air like a cheerleader. "We made it, Paigey!" Aunt Hattie embraced Hamilton, pecking him with a loud smack on both cheeks while Paige retrieved the discarded things.

A screen door squeaked and slammed. Jessie appeared on the porch. As the elderly woman broke into a grin and waved, the morning sun highlighted her snow-white hair. "Welcome back to Whitman." The aroma of gingersnaps, Jessie's signature cookie, drifted from the house.

Paige raised the arm holding Aunt Hattie's purse and wiggled her fingers in response. Hamilton greeted her with a "Morning, Jessie," that was as hardy as he could muster in his exhausted state.

Jessie's focus shifted to Aunt Hattie. "You must be Paige's aunt. Welcome to your new home."

"That's me." Aunt Hattie grinned from ear to ear, then opened the back door to her vehicle. Galahad and Lancelot bounded from the seat and hurtled toward the house, barking and springing into the air. Paige passed Aunt Hattie's purse and tote bag to Hamilton then held out her arms for Delilah's cat carrier.

Jessie screeched. Paige swiveled toward the house. The two lovable pups had pinned the poor woman against the yellow siding. "Galahad. Lancelot. Stop that." Paige scolded. The dogs trampled down the porch stairs, raced across the yard, and jumped against Paige, knocking her into the car. She chuckled and accepted their energetic licks. "You guys were so ready to be out."

Aunt Hattie pulled Gerald's birdcage from the vehicle, then set it in the grass while she closed the door.

"Hello," Gerald squawked.

Hamilton squatted in front of the cage. "Who's this?"

"This is Gerald. He's an African Gray Parrot, and he's forty years old." Aunt Hattie answered. "He loves to be petted. It's okay. You can touch him."

Hamilton stuck his finger between the bars. Gerald rubbed his feathers against Hamilton's fingertip. Hamilton gestured toward the carrier in Paige's arms. "And who's that?"

"Delilah. She's a Persian." Paige answered while Aunt Hattie picked up Gerald's metal cage.

Hamilton's eyes flickered from one pet to another, then he rubbed the back of his neck and shook his head. "Wouldn't have wanted to be in that car on the ride down. Two dogs, a cat, and a talking parrot. These all belong to your aunt?"

Paige shifted Delilah's carrier to the other hand and started toward the house. "Yes, they do." Aunt Hattie loved her animals like family, even if sometimes they could be overwhelming.

When they arrived at the porch, Jessie blocked the front door, arms akimbo. Her lips were twisted in a deep frown. "I don't allow animals inside. I never have."

I should have asked about the pets, but it never crossed my mind that it'd be a problem.

Aunt Hattie set Gerald's cage down with a huff and planted her hands on her hips, mirroring the other woman's stance. "Why ever not?"

"Aunt Hattie—"

Jessie cut her off. "They smell. They pee on the floor. And they destroy things."

"Jessie, please—"

Paige was interrupted a second time. Back and forth, the two women bickered. Jessie's aversion surprised Paige. Who didn't like cuddly dogs and cats? What was she going to do? She didn't want to hurt either woman's feelings. "Stop. Both of you." She spoke harsher than she'd intended, but her sharp tone got their attention.

Both women stared at her with wide eyes.

"For now, let's leave Gerald and Delilah in their carriers. Hamilton, would you put the dogs in the backyard, please? Let's all go inside and talk about this like rational human beings."

Aunt Hattie nearly fainted at her suggestion, but several minutes later, Paige had managed to get both ladies settled in the living room—Jessie with a cup of tea and Aunt Hattie with a mug of black coffee. The two women scowled at each other like alley cats protecting their territory.

Hamilton squeezed her shoulder. "I'm so tired, I can barely stand up." He glanced at the two elderly women. "Though, I'd love to stay and see how this turns out."

Paige play-punched him in the upper arm. "Chicken," she whispered in his ear. "I love you, anyway."

"Love you, too. Give me a call later." Paige nodded as he grinned like the Cheshire cat, then hurried outside as if a vicious Chihuahua were at his heels.

When the front door closed behind him, Paige turned her attention to the two stubborn women. "I'm sure if we work together, we can come to a compromise—"

Aunt Hattie snorted. Paige pinned her with a reprimanding look, silencing her. "… and figure something out that fits everyone's needs." *Goodness. This is worse than dealing with toddlers.*

Jessie opened her mouth as if to speak, then closed it again. She took a deep breath, held it, then groaned. "I guess the cat and bird can stay in the house as long as the dogs remain outside, and Hattie cleans up any messes they make."

We're getting somewhere. "Aunt Hattie? What do you think?" *Please agree. It'll be easier for everyone.*

Aunt Hattie's lower lip quivered. "Alright, Paigey, I can do that, but what if Galahad and Lancelot get cold?"

Cold? Really? "It's summer. They'll be fine." Paige kept her voice low and even. "When winter comes, I'll get them a nice heated doghouse."

Aunt Hattie conceded with an "Oh, all right."

Success. OK. One fiasco avoided.

Through the front window, in the vacant lot across the street, Paige caught sight of a billboard promoting Kathleen's campaign, with the words: A Vote for Phillips is a Vote for Family. *My mother's slogan. Will we ever be a family?*

4

"What exactly are you saying?" Kathleen bit back the overwhelming urge to fire someone. She wasn't sure who yet, but someone was responsible for this mess, and when she found out who it was, they'd regret getting in her way. The members of her campaign team surrounded the circular conference table like King Arthur's knights. Each one had a specific domain, but someone had let her down. She just needed to figure out whom.

Joe, her campaign manager, paused his pacing. Sunlight silhouetted his figure—she couldn't see his face. "It's gone. Vanished."

"How? When?" Her heartbeat pulsated in her throat, and she pulled at her collar. Why was the room so warm? Wasn't the A/C on? "Would someone please open a window?" Out of the corner of her eye, someone moved to do as she asked. *Get control of yourself. You're stronger than this.*

"All that money couldn't have just disappeared." She turned toward Police Chief Mark House. "We're talking about millions of dollars here." A soft breeze blustered through the open window, rustling papers on the table.

Mark shifted in his chair and cleared his throat. "Someone hacked the account, then transferred the funds to an unknown location. This has all the signs of an inside job." A beam of light slanted through the window and bounced off his badge.

As the glare hit her pupil, she flinched. *Ouch.* Hacked the account? Inside job? She scrutinized the room, moving from face to face. Had one of them betrayed her trust? *Impossible. Mark is wrong. Someone else did this.*

She thought through her possible enemies—not a short list by any means. During her time as a lawyer, she'd made plenty of adversaries—basically, any client she'd ever represented who had lost or the opposing side if she had won. She had not made many friends among her own colleagues, either. Her drive and fortitude had intimidated them, and she hadn't much time for a social life.

However, none of them hated her enough to ruin her chances of becoming governor. As far as she knew. This seemed like the work of an experienced thief. Someone like her brother. But Erik was still under lock and key. Or someone like—

"What about Paige McDonald?"

Kathleen gasped. *Who said that?*

Everyone was looking at Joe. He leaned over a chair, white knuckles grasping the top, and pursed his lips together. Still in his early fifties, his hair was a little gray around the edges, but he wore it with class. His Armani suit and the gold watch on his wrist must have cost a pretty penny.

Her eyes flickered from one person to the next. They all looked equally shocked at his suggestion. He was treading on dangerous ground. She couldn't have anyone digging into Paige's past, and he knew Paige was her daughter. And a reformed thief, but the probability that she had committed this crime was slim to none. No petty thief could be this ingenious or gain access to secure accounts. *Leave it alone.*

"Why Miss McDonald?" Patti Hayes, her volunteer coordinator, spoke up. A pencil held Patti's silver hair in a knot on the back of her head. "She seems like such a nice girl."

"She—" Joe glanced Kathleen's direction. She gritted her teeth and narrowed her eyes. *Don't you dare.* "It was an unsubstantiated accusation. Forgive me." His hands relaxed and released the chair.

Kathleen blew out a breath. But a dark look crossed Mark's face. Kathleen attempted to read his body language, but it was difficult to determine if Joe had just prompted the chief to add Paige to his person of interest list. Or, if he were simply wondering why Joe would have thought to suspect her?

Mark shifted his weight and uncrossed his legs. "Be careful whom you accuse." His eyebrows tipped toward his nose.

Lance Ryder, the finance director, leaned back in his chair. "Sounds like the work of Erik Staten." He cracked his knuckles, then ran his fingers through his snow-white comb-over.

"How is that possible? Mayor Phillips's brother is in prison." Patti chewed her lower lip and wrung her hands. "How could he do any damage when he's behind bars?"

Mark scoffed. "Do you know how many crime rings are run out of American prisons?" He mirrored Lance's position and crossed his arms over his chest. "What about you, Lance? Aren't you the head of finances for this circus?"

Lance frowned. "I don't like what you're insinuating. Unless you have evidence, I suggest you shut up before I call my lawyer and sue you for tarnishing my reputation."

The two men stared at each other. Who would break first? "I'm not accusing you of anything. Just making an observation." Mark shook his head and turned his attention to Kathleen. "I'll need any computers that have accessed that account. We'll get someone on the money trail and see what we can uncover."

A phone buzzed. Mark answered. "Yeah… Right… Okay… I'm on my way." He hit the end call button, then pushed back his chair, and stood. "I'm needed at the station. I'll have my IT guy get in touch as soon as possible."

As he headed for the door, he paused. "Oh, before I leave, the debate shooter confessed to putting the sleeping pills in your beverage, Mayor Phillips. Apparently, he followed you from the rally in Salem. I suggest you maintain some type of security, but I'll reassign my officer to his regular duties."

Relief rolled over Kathleen. After ingesting the sedative that creep had dropped into her pop, she'd ended up with a broken nose and two black eyes from slamming her face into the steering wheel. *Hopefully, the judge will punish him to the fullest extent of the law. He deserves everything he gets.*

Chief House returned his peaked cap to his head and left the room. No one moved or spoke. He wasn't a large man, but his aura of authority was intimidating.

Joe cleared his throat. People turned his direction. "On another note, we've received the results from the polling agency…"

His mouth moved, but Kathleen didn't hear another word. Her thoughts returned to the missing campaign funds. She'd had her suspicions regarding the account for several months. Money was still flowing in, and the total had been growing—just not as quickly as she would have liked. Maybe she should have mentioned her concerns sooner.

According to Mark, the thief left no tracks. Two words flashed in her mind like a neon sign—c*ampaign fraud.* Shivers ran down her spine. Did Mark suspect her? Could she be a person of interest? Surely not. What possible reason could she have for stealing her own campaign money?

"Where's Roy?" Lance inquired.

Kathleen glanced around the room. Roy Nelson wasn't in attendance. The treasurer was late; this had never happened before.

"Kathleen?"

She hadn't even noticed his absence. When everyone else looked in her direction, she shrugged. "How should I know?"

Without warning, the conference room door swung open and bounced off the wall with a bang. Roy Nelson scrambled into the room, carrying a laptop and a power plug. He plopped the computer onto the tabletop, then thrashed back and forth, his eyes sweeping the walls.

What is he looking for?

Roy growled, then plugged the cord into an electrical outlet. With an exaggerated sigh, he dropped into an empty chair. "Sorry. Dead battery. What did I miss?"

Too much. Kathleen tapped her pen on the table, drawing everyone's attention. "Where were we?" She scanned the agenda and shook her head. Why bother? This train had derailed a half-hour ago with Joe's announcement, but she needed to get things back on track. "Patti. Update on the volunteer situation."

The tiny woman pushed her glasses up her nose. "We finished stuffing the available mailing advertisements this past week. We need a second printing, but without the campaign funds…" She let the sentence drop. Her eyes lowered to her hands.

There's no money for a second printing—Kathleen finished the thought. *This campaign is falling apart at its most crucial moments.*

"We had a good run, but I guess that's it." Joe pulled a chair away from the table and took a seat.

Kathleen raised an eyebrow. "What do you mean?" *Is he giving up?*

"The campaign's broke."

"So?" She splayed her hands on the table and leaned forward.

"Come on, Kathleen. You know what this means. We're done. Kaput. It's over."

She wouldn't quit. Couldn't quit. "It's not over. I'll support the campaign with my own money if I have to." *I am not sure where that idea came from, but I like it.*

Joe's eyes widened. "You've got to be kidding me. You

can't do that."

Kathleen stood. Her chair rolled back and hit the wall. "Why not?" She raised her voice. Who did he think he was? He might be her manager, but she was in charge. He couldn't tell her when to quit—only she could decide that. And Staten's didn't throw in the towel just because things got challenging.

Joe approached her. "Seriously, Kathleen. Admit defeat. Someone doesn't want you elected. Can't you take a hint? You're going to get yourself killed."

The others remained silent in their seats.

She pivoted on her heel and stood nose to nose with her campaign manager. She *was* going to fire someone. Him. "You're through."

His face blanched. "You can't fire me. You need me."

She didn't need him. She didn't need anyone. "I'll do whatever it takes to win this race. And I dare anyone to stand in my way. Even you. Get out." She wouldn't admit defeat. Quitters were weak, and she wasn't weak or a quitter. She was strong enough to face this. To quit was to fail. And failure was not an option.

5

Senator Kenneth Chatham signed his name with a dramatic flourish to the bottom of the printed document and handed it to his assistant. "Is that all of them?"

"Yes, sir. That's it. I'll get these filed right away. Let me be the first to congratulate you."

"Thank you, Bridge."

As soon as the door clicked shut behind Bridge, Kenneth pushed back from his desk, stood, and opened the curtains. A view of the Capitol Building in Washington, DC, filled the window, but in his mind's eye, he pictured another well-known white building. A smile tugged at his lips. The press conference was scheduled. His papers were being filed at this very moment. Soon, he would announce his intentions to run for President of the United States. *President Chatham.*

And for the first time in my life, Richard Staten can't pull the rug out from under me.

Someone knocked. Kenneth turned from the window. Bridge stuck his head around the door jamb. "I'm sorry to bother you again, sir, but—"

An enthusiastic, ear-splitting squeal cut him off. The door swung open, banging against the wall. Probably leaving a dent in the plaster.

"Daddy!"

His rosy-cheeked angel flew into the room and jumped into his arms. A silver tiara topped her raven black curls, and a puffy green dress contrasted beautifully with her almond skin. The five-year-old was the light of his life. Kenneth and his wife, Patricia, had adopted the little one from South Korea as an infant.

"Hello, sugar." He buried his face in her neck. She giggled and squirmed. "What are you doing here?"

His wife appeared in the doorway, wearing jeans and a tank top, and leaned against the door frame. "Sorry, Ken. She got away from me. We just returned from the zoo, and our little princess couldn't wait to tell you all about it." Her voice drooped with exhaustion. She stepped across the threshold and dropped into a cushioned chair.

"Daddy. Daddy. We saw tigers and lions and elephants and hippos and zebras and ate ice cream and pizza and petted the llamas and…" She paused and sucked in an audible breath. "And rode the carousel and the choo-choo train and—"

"Did you see the pandas?"

"Yes, we did. Oh, Daddy, they were so cute. I wanted one so bad, but Mommy said no, and that they belong to China. Who's China, Daddy? Can you ask her to give me a panda?"

He'd move heaven and earth to get his little girl a panda if he could. He glanced at his wife half-asleep in the chair. "Well, Patricia, it's done." He'd flown his family in from Oregon so they could stand beside him during this momentous occasion.

Patricia lifted her head. Understanding registered in her eyes. She stood and crossed to his side. "The papers are all signed?"

He nodded.

"I'm so happy for you." She raised on her tiptoes and kissed him on the cheek.

"Are you going to be president, Daddy?"

"We're going to try."

"You're going to win, Daddy." *Out of the mouth of babes.*

"Sir?" Bridge's voice came through the intercom speaker.

Kenneth set his daughter on her feet, then crossed to his desk, and pressed the button. "Yes, Bridge?"

"Someone is here to see you."

Someone? "Who is it?" Irritation tightened his chest. Who was interrupting his time with his family?

"He says you're expecting him."

Kenneth's eyes grew large. Oh, *that* someone. He looked at his wife and daughter. He hated to shoo them out so quickly, but they couldn't stay. "Give me two minutes, then send him in."

Paige set a cardboard box on the bedroom floor with a thump, groaned, and stretched her muscles. Her back and arms ached from unloading the truck. And that box was a lot heavier than the others.

"Thank you, Paigey." Aunt Hattie's voice carried from the other side of the room.

Paige squeezed between the piles until she reached an antique dresser where her aunt unpacked a suitcase. "Are you sure all of this is essential? It's getting crowded in here." *We were supposed to share this room. Where am I going to put my bed?*

"They're absolutely essential." Tears brimmed Aunt Hattie's lower eyelids. "This move is hard for me."

Paige's heart melted. *Poor Aunt Hattie. She gave up her last connection with her brother to move here with me.* While Paige looked forward to a new beginning, for the 80-odd-year-old woman, this move had to be more earth-shattering than life-altering. "I'm sorry, Aunt Hattie. I know you miss Grandpa McDonald. I'll keep doing what I can to make this transition easier on you." *Even if it means sleeping on the couch.*

"Thank you, Paigey. I do miss my brother. Living in his house kept his memory alive. It's hard to let go." Aunt Hattie brushed away her tears, kissed Paige on the cheek, then returned to her unpacking.

Paige's eyes flickered over the haphazard pile of T-shirts and undergarments in the drawer. Inwardly, she cringed. "Are you sure you don't want me to do that for you?" Her fingers itched. *Please, it's so disorganized.*

"I've got it."

Paige's shoulders dropped. *Ugh. How does she live like this?*

Aunt Hattie looked up. "I'm still missing a box. Have you seen my sock collection? I can't find it anywhere."

Of course. The "essential to life" eclectic sock collection. The socks had overflowed the box, requiring Paige to push down on the flaps while Aunt Hattie taped it closed.

Paige went outside to search the truck and spotted the missing box in the mom's attic. At least it was on top. She climbed onto the dining room table bound for storage, and with a flick of her hand, flipped the box down from the stack. *At least it's light.* The box tumbled down and landed on the ramp. *And not fragile.*

She carried Aunt Hattie's sock collection inside, then went to the kitchen and poured a glass of cold lemonade. The cool liquid was both sour and sweet on her tongue. She leaned against the counter, taking a few minutes to rest. A trail of sweat tickled her ear. *I'm so glad Dad and Hamilton said they'd move the rest into the storage unit tonight. I'm about worn out.*

A knock sounded on the front door. Paige set her glass on the counter, then walked to the door and pulled it open, only to be met by a high-pitched squeal and a hug with the strength of a python. "You're here!"

"Kylie!" Her energy lifted at the sight of her teenaged half-sister. Kylie Phillips had the same blond hair and piercing blue eyes as Paige, but that's where their similarities ended. They were opposites in every sense of the word, but Paige loved Kylie as much as any sister could. Her only wish was that Kylie could be told they were sisters, not just friends.

Kylie chattered without taking a breath, still holding Paige in her iron grasp.

Paige put her palms against Kylie's shoulders. "I'm glad to see you, too. Can you let go?"

"Oh, sure. Sorry." Kylie released her with one last squeeze. "I'm just so excited to have you back home. You're here to stay, aren't you? I mean, with you buying the bookstore and Mrs. Faye's house, you don't have any plans to move again, right?"

"Take a breath, Kylie." Paige closed the front door. "No, I don't plan to move anytime soon." Hamilton's face flashed through her thoughts. Would they get married someday? Her neck grew warm. She coughed and cleared her throat. "Anyway, how's work?"

"Great. I love working at the café. Can you believe a little cup of coffee makes someone's whole day better? Mrs. Jenn is so nice, and the coffee smells so good. Every day when I get home, I smell like coffee. Isn't that funny?"

"I'm glad you're enjoying your job." *I wonder how Kathleen is doing.* Should she ask? Paige took a breath. "How's your mom?" *Your mom?* How's my mom? That's what she wanted to ask. Better yet, she shouldn't have to ask Kylie; she and Kathleen should catch up over a cup of coffee. *Is that something mothers and daughters do?* Paige didn't know. How could she? She'd never had a mother.

"Fine."

Kylie's clipped answer caught her attention. *Fine. That's it?* Kylie turned from Paige. Something glistened on her cheek. Were those tears? "Kylie, what's wrong?" *I thought the news said Kathleen wasn't injured the other night. Were they mistaken?*

"Can we go outside? I need to talk."

"Sure."

They stepped onto the front porch and settled on the swing. "What's going on? Are you sick?"

"Sort of."

That's a strange answer. "What do you mean sort of?" *What if she's…* "Kylie, you're not…" She couldn't bring herself to finish. What if Kylie was pregnant?

Kylie read the intimate question in Paige's eyes. She blushed, and furiously shook her head. "Oh. No. Paige. No. I'm not. I wouldn't. I made a vow to wait until I get married, and I'm committed to keeping it. It's just that…"

"What's bothering you?"

Kylie picked at her chipped nail polish. "There's something I need to tell Mom. But I don't know how." She paused. "I don't want to go back to college."

"Oh." Paige's eyes widened. "I'm guessing she's not going to take it very well."

"She's not, and I've made myself sick with worry. I don't know what she's going to do when she finds out I don't want to be a politician. She's always wanted to go into politics like her father, and she's convinced it's what I want too. But it's not for me. I hate arguing, and I'm terrible at making decisions. I'm a follower, not a leader."

Paige used her toes to rock the swing into motion. "What *do* you want to do?"

Kylie jutted her chin. "I love my job at the Rustic Cup. I want to be a barista."

A barista? Paige's mouth dropped open. She snapped it closed before Kylie noticed. Her little sister could be anything she wanted, and instead, she chose to serve coffee. *To each their own, I guess.* "You'll have to tell her eventually, and if politics aren't your thing, your mom should respect that."

"I know." Kylie dabbed her eyes. "Will you come with me when I do? I'll feel better having you there."

Come with you? "I don't think I'll be much help."

Kylie shifted on the bench. "My mom doesn't like you very much. Why is that? Did you do something to make her mad?"

What a way to change the subject! Paige opened her mouth, but no words came out. What could she say? Her throat constricted. Kathleen didn't like her. So much so that it was surprising she hadn't forbidden Paige from befriending

Kylie. *It's getting harder and harder to keep this a secret.*

"It's probably because she thinks you'll be a bad influence on me," Kylie answered her own question.

Paige coughed. A bad influence? What did Kylie know? "Why would she think I was a bad influence?"

"You got arrested when the pawnshop was robbed. Everyone knows the police arrested you, but then they found out you didn't do it or something and let you go."

Oh, right. The pawnshop robbery. "I was innocent." She affirmed.

"I'm glad you were. I don't think I could be friends with a criminal."

Kylie's comment knotted Paige's stomach. "Kylie, there's something I need—"

A melody drifted from Kylie's cell. "That's Mom. I've got to get this." Kylie took the phone from her pocket and held it to her ear. "Yeah… Okay… I'm coming… Bye." Kylie frowned and lowered the phone. "Sorry. I've gotta go. Thanks for listening, Paige. You're a good friend." Her little sister skipped down the stairs, climbed into her car, and drove off.

Paige swallowed the lump in her throat. Would Kylie still think so if she knew the truth?

6

Sunday morning, after a bowl of cereal for breakfast, Iago paced the living room of his tiny apartment. The stench of mildew drifted from the carpet fibers. He paused when Tchaikovsky's 1810 Overture ended on the record player. He moved the needle, and the scratching sound ceased. Something brushed his bare feet. He looked down at the gray-striped, three-legged tabby. "Hungry, Tybalt?" The cat meowed in response and followed him into the kitchen where Iago retrieved a can of cat food from the cabinet and placed it under the electric can opener. A whirling hum filled the air.

Getting Kathleen to drop out of the election was proving difficult. The woman was as stubborn and pigheaded as her father before her. What next? What would make Kathleen quit? What was she most afraid of? Maybe he hadn't made it clear that the threats on her life had to do with the election. Maybe she needed an ultimatum.

Insistent meowing broke into his thoughts. The can opener had stopped. He plopped the cat food into the bowl on the floor, then dropped the can and lid into the garbage. Tybalt's noisy eating grated on his nerves.

Iago moved down the hall into his bedroom, then sat at the desk, joggled the mouse, entered his password, and logged in. He stood and moved to the opposite side of the room, where he squatted and removed the fake electrical outlet from the wall, then popped the micro SD card out of the hidden camera. As he straightened, his knees cracked. He inserted the card into his computer, then sat in the chair to wait for the files to download.

Tybalt, licking his chops, jumped onto the desk and curled up behind the keyboard. Soon, soft purring and the clicking of the keys filled the otherwise silent abode. The smell of a neighbor's dinner seeped through the thin walls and turned his stomach. He wouldn't have to stay in this rat hole much longer.

Iago leaned back in his swivel chair and focused on the news article taped to the wall. She'd slipped his grasp too many times, but she wouldn't escape again. He would take her down.

No one would stand in his way. No matter what it took.

Kathleen settled into a booth at The Rustic Cup Café and Bakery, resting her purse beside her on the leather cushion. A deer antler lamp hung over the table, and paintings by local artists decorated the brick interior walls. The aroma of freshly brewed coffee wafted in the air mixing with the scent of homemade pastries. Motor vehicles and pedestrians passed by the glass window front.

She relaxed her shoulders and rested against the back of the booth. The café was busy, but no more than usual at this hour. The Rustic Cup was a hotspot for the townspeople of Whitman.

Jenn, the owner, approached the table, check pad in hand. "Good afternoon, Mayor Phillips. What can I get for you?"

She removed a pencil from behind her ear and licked the lead tip. A layer of white flour coated the woman's black apron and sensible shoes.

She'd suggested several times that Jenn open additional cafés in other towns, but Jenn wasn't interested in "diluting its uniqueness," as she put it. But why cap your dreams? How could anyone be content with mediocrity?

"A chicken Caesar wrap and a black coffee. Thank you." Her stomach rumbled, agreeing with her choice for lunch.

Jenn scribbled on the check pad. "Anything else? I made a fresh batch of oatmeal raisin cookies. They're hot out of the oven."

Jenn's oatmeal raisin cookies sounded delicious. *Too many calories.* "No. Thank you. Just the sandwich and coffee."

"Coming right up." Jenn moved to the next table and began clearing the leftover dishes and trash.

Kathleen glanced around the café. Where was her daughter? Was she working today? "Is Kylie here?" She raised her voice, hoping Jenn heard her over the café noise.

Jenn paused, hands loaded with plates and coffee mugs. "She's not on the schedule. I haven't seen her. She's probably hanging out with Paige." Jenn turned and headed through the kitchen doors.

Kathleen's gut twisted. Kylie and Paige were spending time together? The girls had interacted a few times, but had they grown closer than superficial acquaintances? Would Paige reveal their familial ties? Was it smart to trust a former thief with such a volatile secret?

Kathleen rubbed her forehead, then picked up her cell phone, and checked her email. Her thumb scrolled down the screen. Her eyes flickered back and forth as she ran through the incoming messages. *Nothing important.*

"Kathleen. We need to talk."

Joe's voice startled her, causing Kathleen to nearly drop her phone. She laid it on the table and raised her face. His cheeks were flushed, and his eyes narrowed to slivers. His lips were pursed together, and his jaw clenched tight. Sunglasses hung in the collar of his polo shirt.

"I have nothing more to say." She mirrored his expression and folded her arms in front of her chest. What was there to talk about? He didn't believe in her. She'd fired him. End of discussion.

He dropped onto the bench across from her without permission. "What *was* that? An animalistic power display? You know you can't do this without me."

Kathleen's pulse throbbed in her neck. "I know no such thing. I don't need you or your *counsel*." For emphasis, she air-quoted around the word *counsel*.

Jenn appeared at the edge of the table with Kathleen's lunch order. Leaning forward, Jenn set the plate and coffee mug down, then pulled a small stack of napkins from her apron pocket and laid them on the table with the bill. "Can I get anything for your friend?" She turned and addressed Joe. "I don't think we've met, but I've seen you around town. Welcome to my café."

Joe opened his mouth to speak, but Kathleen beat him to the punch. "He's not staying. Thank you, Jenn." With a frown and a final glance in Joe's direction, Jenn walked away.

"That was rude. I could have used a cup of coffee."

He was perturbed. Who cared? Not her. "If you don't mind, I'd like to enjoy my lunch. Leave."

"I want my job back."

Was that supposed to shock her? Of course, he wanted his job back. Didn't mean he was going to get it. Kathleen took a bite of her sandwich. She chewed, swallowed, then dabbed her lips with her napkin. "I'm surprised."

"At what?"

She looked him square in the eye. "You don't seem like the type to beg."

He jerked back like she'd slapped him. "I'm not. I've never begged for anything in my life."

She picked a tomato slice out of the corner of her wrap. She'd forgotten to ask Jenn to eighty-six the tomatoes. "Why not move on? You said yourself the campaign was finished."

She wiped mayo off her fingers onto a disposable napkin.

"The campaign *is* broke. Someone has tried to kill you. Twice, I might add."

"What makes you think that had anything to do with the election? It's not like they left a note. Maybe they have a vendetta against me. Or maybe they just don't like me. Maybe it was supposed to be a harmless prank."

She took a sip of coffee. "If you believe my campaign is sinking, why go down with the ship?"

"I—" Joe stopped speaking. His eyes lifted to something over her shoulder. What was he looking at?

"It's for you."

Kathleen jerked around. Jenn stood behind her, carrying the handset to a cordless telephone. Who knew Kathleen was at the café, and why didn't they call Kathleen's cell phone?

Jenn held out the handset. Kathleen took it. "Hello?"

Silence.

"I think they hung up."

No dial tone. They couldn't have. She started to hand it back when a muffled voice came through the speaker. She pressed the phone to her ear. "Hello? Who is this?"

"Annie Staten." The voice warbled like it came through a voice changer.

Annie Staten? Annie was dead as far as she was concerned. It would be a strange coincidence, but could the caller's name be Annie Staten? "Are you Annie Staten?" She felt stupid even asking, but she had to clarify.

There was a long pause. "No. You are."

How did he know that? Few people knew her nickname. She hadn't been Annie for more than ten years and hadn't been a Staten for even longer. "Who is this? What do you want?"

"The money's missing, isn't it?"

"How do you know that? Who are you?"

"That's not important. Withdraw. Or pay the consequences."

Withdraw? From the election? "Are you threatening me? I'm

not afraid of you."

"You should be."

The dial tone buzzed in her ear. Fear and anger warred in her chest. Who was threatening her, and why? Was this the same person who'd tried to kill her before? She lowered the handset and handed it back to Jenn.

"Are you okay? You're whiter than my pie dough."

She couldn't answer. Instead, she took slow, measured breaths. Her heartbeat raced. Goosebumps formed on her arms. "It's nothing. Just a prank call." Her gaze lowered to the sandwich on her plate. Suddenly, she'd lost her appetite. *Someone wants me out of this race. To what lengths will they go to accomplish their goal?* She swallowed and raised her head to meet Joe's eyes. He was right. She needed him, but she wouldn't admit that. Not to his face. "Fine. You can have your job back." *I hope I don't regret this.*

7

The next morning, Kathleen's eyes shot open wide. A cold sweat drenched her hair and pillow. *Deep breaths. In. Out. It was only a nightmare.* But it wasn't. A sense of dread paralyzed Kathleen's body. The caller's words kept ringing through her mind. "*Withdraw. Or pay the consequences.*"

He can threaten all he wants. I'm not afraid.

She rolled over and sat on the edge of the bed, adjusted the shoulder strap of her negligee, then ran her fingers through her hair, shooing the wet strands from her face. With a heavy sigh, she moved into the private bathroom where a steamy shower relaxed her muscles and calmed her anxious spirit. When she turned the knob, the stream of water clicked off, then she wrapped herself in a towel and stepped onto the cold tile floor.

Several minutes later, she stood in front of the bedroom mirror wearing a navy-blue pantsuit, pearl necklace, and matching earrings. She applied her makeup, then strode down the massive staircase and entered the spotless kitchen where her right-hand woman prepared breakfast. The aroma of fresh coffee and sizzling bacon filled the room. "Good morning, Matilda." Kathleen poured herself a cup of java.

"Morning to you, Madam Mayor. I fix your breakfast." Matilda turned with a twinkle in her eye. "I know you have been mayor of Whitman for three years, but I still remember the little girl who brought me muddy water trying to convince me it was chocolate milk. You were good politician, even then."

Kathleen allowed the memory to bring a smile to her lips. Matilda had been the Staten's housekeeper since her arrival in America from Colombia over thirty-five years ago. She was as loyal as the day is long but would retire soon. Kathleen's chest tightened. What would life look like without Matilda?

The toaster popped, and Matilda spread butter and strawberry preserves on the hot toast, then served Kathleen a plate of two sunny-side-up eggs, toast, and bacon.

Kathleen took a sip of coffee before opening the local newspaper, The Wallowa County Chieftain, to catch the news. She shuffled through the pages—news articles mixed with advertisements and classifieds. Withdrawing the comics, she set them aside for Kylie to read later. *Where is Kylie?* "Has Kylie been down yet?"

Her daughter was a late sleeper, so probably not, but it didn't hurt to ask. Her eyes flickered to the wall clock. What time did Kylie have to be at work? The barista job kept her daughter occupied and out of trouble, and for that, she was grateful. She'd be more grateful when Kylie finished her political science degree and could begin making a difference in the world.

Kathleen placed a bite of eggs into her mouth, following it with a chunk of toast.

"No." Matilda laid her dishcloth on the counter. "I will wake her."

Footsteps clopped on the tile floor. "I'm up." Kylie entered the kitchen. Her face was pale, and blue marks marred the ivory skin under her eyes. Dragging her feet across the floor, she poured a cup of coffee, then added enough cream and sugar to make dessert.

"Are you all right?" What had happened to her perky daughter? Did she get any sleep last night?

"I'm okay. Just tired." Kylie leaned heavily against the counter as if to emphasize her point.

"I fix you breakfast." Matilda scooped an egg onto a plate and held it toward Kylie.

Kylie laid her hand on her stomach. "No thank you, Matilda. My stomach doesn't feel well."

Kathleen's eyebrows slanted toward her nose. Something was wrong. She rose from her chair and laid the back of her hand on her daughter's forehead. "No fever."

Kylie shook her head. "I'll be all right. See you later." She kissed Kathleen and Matilda on their cheeks then disappeared down the hall.

Kathleen returned to her chair, filled with concern for her daughter's wellbeing. Obviously, Kylie wasn't feeling well. Maybe she was coming down with a cold or a flu bug. Kathleen should have insisted that Kylie stay home from work, but her daughter was a grown woman and made her own decisions, and she was growing up much faster than Kathleen would like.

After finishing breakfast and her morning routine, Kathleen drove into town, parked in the *reserved for mayor* space, gathered her belongings, and entered the impressive gray stone building in the middle of the town square. Her heels clicked on the marble floors as she walked to the elevator and rode it to the second floor.

The moment she came through the office door, Dennis rose. "Good morning, Mayor Phillips." He wore an eclectic Micky Mouse necktie with his green dress shirt and tan slacks.

"Morning, Dennis. Any calls?"

"Yes, ma'am. Mr. Wallis called to confirm you will be attending the gala at the Treasury Ballroom."

He followed her into her office, where she set her purse and attaché on a chair in the corner. "You confirmed for me?" He'd already turned on the light and opened the curtains.

"Yes, ma'am."

"Anything else?" Kathleen took a seat at her executive desk.

"Mail. And fresh coffee."

"Thank you, Dennis." He set everything on the corner of her desk, then left the room.

Kathleen checked her email, then reached for the manila folder in the inbox. Planning and Zoning had sent up a proposal from a developer wanting to tear down the old airport and build a new golf course. She read through the proposed budget and a list of benefits the developer believed the golf course would bring to the town of Whitman and Wallowa County as a whole.

The tantalizing aroma of the Colombian Dark Roast filled her nose and made her mouth water. While examining the forms in front of her, she reached for and contacted the disposable cup. A splash jerked her attention, and like watching a movie in slow motion, liquid poured across her desk. In a stream, it ran to the edge and dripped onto the floor.

She shoved back her chair and sprang to her feet. What a mess! Finding nothing to clean up the spill, she opened the door between her office and her assistant's. He sat at his desk, his fingers flying over the keys at lightning speed. He looked up, saw her, then stood. "Yes, mayor?"

"I need towels. The coffee spilled all over my desk."

"Yes, ma'am. Right away." Dennis sprinted down the hallway to get paper towels.

Kathleen left the door open and returned to her desk. A puddle had formed on the right side. *Oh no. The mail.* She grabbed the soggy mess and held it in the air. Dark liquid dripped onto the hardwood floor. Dennis entered the room, carrying a roll of paper towels under his arm. He tore off a large wad and mopped the desktop.

Kathleen laid a long section of towels on the floor, then

separated the envelopes and dried them off, arranging them in neat rows. She paused when a bright orange square caught her attention. It was addressed to her in care of City Hall but no return address. No stamp. No postmark. Interest piqued, she fetched a letter opener and sliced through the top. The envelope tore effortlessly.

When she removed a single sheet of folded paper, something slipped and fell to the floor. She picked it up and turned it over—a photograph?

Kathleen held the picture closer. Golden letters—N L Y apostrophe S. *Heavenly's.* The photograph had been taken from outside the restaurant, through the window. She and Paige sat at a booth inside. She'd only been to Heavenly's with Paige once—the day she'd requested Paige keep their familial connection confidential.

Someone had been watching them. But who? And why?

Kathleen turned to the accompanying note. The coffee had browned the page and smeared the ink. Goosebumps rose on her forearms. Two large words were written in the center: I KNOW.

Ryan Whitestone could kick himself in the rear if his legs were long enough. He closed the study guide he had been perusing, removed his reading glasses, and pinched the bridge of his nose. Sunday's sermon would have to wait. *I can't get her out of my mind.*

He pushed away from his desk and stood. The rickety desk occupied the center of the small, crowded room along with a copier, metal filing cabinet, and several loaded bookshelves. Well-worn carpet covered the floor. He paced to the single window and back, scrubbing his calloused hand over the nape of his neck.

What *was* he going to do about Annie? *Kathleen.* He corrected himself. *Mayor Phillips.* He corrected himself a second time. She'd asked him not to call her anything but

Mayor Phillips.

Like that was possible.

She would always be his Annie. His high school sweetheart—the love of his life. But Annie had made it clear she had no desire to rekindle their relationship, no matter how he felt about her. Did his beloved still exist inside of the stoic Madam Mayor?

He pivoted and smacked his palm against the wall. The stinging did nothing to distract his thoughts. He was a pastor—a man of God—he shouldn't feel this way. He'd prayed for years that God would take away these emotions. *Why do I still love her after all these years?*

He lowered into his chair and dropped his head into his hands. *You've forgiven me, Lord. You've washed away the stain of my foolishness, but whenever I look at Annie, the weight of my past decisions crash down upon my soul.*

She'd lied to him. Kept his child from him. He should hate her. And by man's standards, he had every right. But what did God expect of him?

He'd made so many foolish mistakes. He shouldn't have—but he had, and he'd accepted the blame for his sin. Still, if he could get a do-over… but… a picture of his beautiful daughter formed in his mind. *Thank you, Father, for the beauty that comes from ashes.*

With a sigh, Ryan rose from his chair and returned to the window. A gentle breeze shook the pine needles of the juniper trees that surrounded the church. Clouds floated lazily through the sky that reached to the peak of the Wallowa Mountains. Mayor Phillips's car was parked in the paved lot.

Was he hallucinating? He blinked. No, Annie marched toward the church building. A determined expression scrunched her face, and her hasty strides traversed the space between the parking lot and the front door.

He hurried to the foyer and opened the door. Kathleen's eyes widened in surprise, but she recovered quickly. "Annie—Mayor Phillips. What are you doing here? I mean, how can I help?"

"Who have you told about Paige?" Annie crossed the threshold into the church.

His brow furrowed. "No one," he answered. Annie glared at him, eyes blazing. "What's this all about?"

Annie shoved past him and headed for his office. He followed. She shut the door behind him, even though they were alone in the building. "Please have a seat."

"I'd rather stand." She slapped a photograph onto the desk. "Look at this."

Ryan stepped forward, leaned over, and lifted the snapshot. *Looks like Heavenly's.* "What's—"

"Someone took this photo and sent it to me with this note." She extended the paper toward him. He read the cryptic message.

"'I know.' What does that mean?" As soon as the words left his lips, he understood. "You think this is my fault?"

She placed her hands on her hips. "Someone blabbed. It wasn't me."

"I assure you I didn't tell anyone about you and Paige." *But I did tell Paige about you and me.* He'd done the right thing. His daughter deserved to know her father.

"Don't tell Paige you're her father."

"Excuse me?" Air wheezed from his chest.

Annie eyed him oddly and cleared her throat. "I've given this a lot of thought. It's best for everyone if we keep this private. No one needs to be informed of our indiscretion. Paige has agreed to honor my wishes regarding my relationship with her."

Her monologue gave him a second to catch his breath. "Best for everyone or best for you? Don't I get a say in this?" *Paige is my daughter, too.*

She shifted her purse to her other shoulder and brushed her hair back with a slight flourish. "I don't see why. You've had no part in her life for the past twenty-five years, and there's no need to begin now. It's not like you've ever been a father to her."

As his blood pressure rose, Ryan prayed for strength. His

neck grew warm. A pang started in his temples. "You've never been her mother. What gives you the right to make this decision?"

Annie's eyes enlarged. Did she expect him not to argue with her? "This is in the best interest of all parties involved. Do you want your congregation to know you have a non-marital child? Would you put your position at risk?"

He blinked. How *would* his congregation respond? What would the pulpit committee do if… when he told them? The church had been desperate to find a new pastor after their last one retired. It was challenging to find someone willing to shepherd a small country church.

And he'd been thankful for the opportunity. Not many churches were willing to hire a convicted felon. However, it was a one-time event, and he'd paid his debt to society. He'd assured the pulpit committee that they had no further need for concern. Of course, he hadn't known about Paige at the time.

Was he willing to jeopardize his career and calling? "What others think of me is none of my business. I hope that in time, they will acknowledge that I am a sinner, just like them, and they will offer me the same grace and mercy that God extends when they fail Him."

As Annie swallowed, her throat moved. His response seemed to knock some of the wind out of her sails. "Be that as it may, this is the most beneficial course of action. For all parties involved. At least allow Paige a few months to adjust."

He crossed his arms. "A few months? As in, after the election?"

Annie's face paled. "That's none of your concern. Please just do as I ask." Her voice cracked. She turned and took hold of the door handle.

"I already told her." Ryan mentally slapped himself. *I could have handled that with more tact.*

Annie released the knob as if it burnt her hand. "You what?" She hissed and pivoted to face him. Daggers shot from her eyes. If looks could kill, he'd be a dead man.

"I told Paige I'm her father."

"How could you be so stupid? When?"

"Couple of weeks ago."

Annie closed the distance between them. "Information like this could ruin everything. How dare you… without asking me first?"

Ryan bristled. "Annie—" He shook his head. "Kathleen. You may be the mayor of this town, but I don't answer to you. I made this decision in the best interest of *my* relationship with *my* daughter. It sickens me to know I missed out on the first twenty-five years of her life. I'm not going to miss out on the next twenty-five because of public opinion."

Annie clenched her fists at her sides. Was she going to speak or punch him in the gut? Without a word, she stormed out of the room, slamming the door behind her. A picture frame fell to the floor and shattered.

How will I ever win her back?

8

Shock. Betrayal. Fear. A myriad of emotions surged through Kathleen as she drove home from the church. He'd told Paige that he was her father. He'd promised to wait until Kathleen was ready, but he'd reneged on that promise. How could he do that to her? Ryan Whitestone was a liar and a Benedict Arnold.

Kathleen parked the car in her garage, then trudged inside the house, head throbbing. She checked the time on her phone. It was only mid-morning. *I'll take some pain medicine and lie down.*

In the kitchen, she filled a glass with tap water then ascended the stairs to her bedroom. She retrieved pain pills from the bathroom and swallowed them with the water. Sitting on her bed, she kicked off her shoes. With a sigh, she laid on the mattress, head on her pillow, then set her eyeglasses on the nightstand next to the half-empty glass.

She shifted to her side and shut her eyes, then flopped back the other way and pulled an afghan up to her chin. The urge to scream welled inside her chest. How would she get any rest if she couldn't stop thinking?

Kathleen jerked, gasped, and sat up, groggy and disoriented. What had awakened her? How long was she out? Her head whirled, and her vision blurred. *Glasses.* Groping at the nightstand, she found the lenses and set them on her face. A melodious chime echoed through the house. *The doorbell. Someone's at the door.*

Kathleen padded down the stairs, and as she passed the mirror over the sideboard, she caught sight of her reflection. Mussed hair. Smeared makeup. Wrinkled slacks. Bare feet. *I'm a disaster. I can't answer the door like this.* They'd just have to go away. Her car was in the garage—no one would know she was home.

The doorbell rang again. *If I peek out the curtains, they might see me and know I'm ignoring them.*

Then a knock.

"Mayor Phillips. Are you home?"

She recognized the voice that carried through the door. Patti Hayes. The volunteer coordinator. What if the campaign had encountered another setback? *I have to answer. This could be vital to the election.*

Kathleen ran her fingers through her hair, then wet her fingertip and wiped away the smudged eyeliner. She straightened her shoulders and opened the door. The woman on the front stoop wore hot pink sweats and held a plate of muffins covered in plastic wrap. "Patti? What can I do for you?"

"I whipped up these muffins for breakfast this morning and thought I'd bring some over before I head to headquarters."

Muffins? That was it? "So thoughtful. Thank you." Would Patti notice her sarcasm? She accepted the plate.

Patti blushed and waved her hands. "Nonsense. I just wanted to make sure you were okay after that dreadful meeting. It was intense. Do you need a shoulder to cry on?"

A shoulder to cry on. What kind of sap does Patti think I am? "I'm fine. It was all a big misunderstanding. I've given Joe his job back."

Patti's face blanched. "You rehired Joe Donahue?"

"I did. Do you have a problem with that?" When Patti didn't respond, Kathleen narrowed her eyes.

"Anything else?" Kathleen snapped.

Patti's eyes widened. "No. I just wanted to make sure you were okay"—she gestured toward the plate of muffins—"and bring over the muffins. I'll—I'll let you get back to whatever you were doing." Patti walked to her car.

Kathleen shut the door and carried the plate into the kitchen. Setting it on the counter, she peeled back the plastic and sniffed. The aroma of peaches and brown sugar awakened her senses. Her stomach rumbled.

She picked up one of the baked goods and peeled off the paper wrapper, then split the bottom from the muffin top. She took a bite. Moist. Sweet. And oh, so delicious. She finished the muffin in just a few bites and licked her lips. Patti was an excellent baker. These muffins gave Jenn down at the Rustic Cup a run for her money. As she dropped the wrapper into the trashcan, Kathleen eyed a second one. No. One was enough for now.

Her cell phone buzzed in her back pocket. She answered. "Hello."

"It's Patti. Again. I'm on my way to headquarters. Are you coming out today?"

She hadn't planned on it. "Am I needed?"

"I'm sorry. I should have mentioned this when I was at your door. We have several items that need your approval. We're trying to move forward despite the recent setbacks."

Move on. Move forward. "I'll be there as soon as I can."

Kathleen drove to the campaign headquarters in La Grande, parked in the strip mall parking lot, then entered through the glass door decorated with *Vote for Phillips* stickers. Volunteers bustled about the storefront, making phone calls, stuffing envelopes, and soliciting donations. The consistent murmur of voices and typing on keyboards was the soundtrack to her campaigning efforts. The energy renewed her zeal. These people must believe in her, or else they wouldn't be here.

Patti approached. "Thanks for coming. Let me show you the proofs for the new mailouts."

Kathleen followed Patti between the tables, chairs, and volunteers. She approved the new mailouts, then watched the final draft of a TV advertisement that was set to run next week.

"Hi, Mom."

Kylie? Kathleen looked up and paused the video. "What are you doing here? Are you feeling any better?" She moved to Kylie's side and touched her forehead. Still no fever.

Kylie stuffed her hands into her khaki shorts pockets. "Can we talk?"

Talk? Now? "I'm busy." *If elected governor, I'll be busier than ever.* A twinge of guilt niggled her conscience. "Is it important?"

Kylie shifted from one foot to the other. "Nah, we can talk later. Is there anything I can do to help?"

Kathleen barely kept her mouth from dropping open. Kylie hadn't expressed any interest in what went on inside headquarters before. Her heart skipped. "What would you like to do?" She gestured around the room.

On one side, a row of volunteers worked the phones—some taking inbound and some making outbound calls. Facing them, others used laptops to interact with social media.

Kylie shrugged. "I don't know."

What could Kylie do without a lot of training? A stack of envelopes laid on one of the folding tables. Kathleen snapped her fingers. Kylie was a wiz at math.

Kathleen walked to the table, and Kylie followed. "Here.

These are contribution pledges. Open them, then stack them according to how much the individuals pledged. If it's marked other, just set it in a pile on its own. Then add up the totals, record them, and give it to…" She looked around. Where was Roy? Not in the building. "Give it to Lance." She pointed out the finance director. "He'll make sure Roy gets the information."

With the rest of the finances missing, these were more essential than ever. Kathleen made a mental note to call the bank and open a new account. One with tighter security measures, if possible.

"Okay. Thanks, Mom." Kylie plopped onto the folding chair and tucked her legs underneath the table.

"Mayor Phillips, may I have your assistance?" An Asian college student waved his hand from two tables over.

She walked to his side and leaned over his shoulder. "Yes?"

"Your social media ads expire tomorrow. Do you want them renewed?"

"Yes. Thank—" The lights went out, and the room fell silent. Those on the phones pulled their headsets away from their ears. The laptops remained lit.

"Did someone forget to pay the electric bill?" Someone joked. Scattered chuckles came from the volunteers. As a variety of conversations ensued, a buzz filled the room.

Kathleen's eyes adjusted to the dim light. She raised her voice to be heard over the noise. "Would someone go check the electrical breakers in the panel?" Would she need to call the electric company?

Minutes later, the lights flickered, then turned on. A volunteer reentered the room with a shrug. "None of the breakers were off. I guess it had something to do with the power lines. It seems to be working now."

How odd. Kathleen surveyed the room—everything seemed to be in order. The Asian student began speaking again and pointed at something on the screen. She started to turn her attention back on him, then paused.

Kylie's chair was empty.

Kathleen turned from discussing design options with the graphics artist and caught sight of a lime-green T-shirt. Piles of paper surrounded Kylie on the tabletop, and she had her head down, writing on a notepad. Her long, blond hair slipped forward, shielding her face from view. Kathleen moved between the tables and stopped behind Kylie's chair. "What happened? Where were you?"

"Mom! You scared me." Kylie swiveled in the chair and brushed her hair out of her face. "You're like a ninja!"

"When the lights came on, you weren't in your seat. What happened to you?"

"I've been right here." Kylie's pencil twirled on her fingers like a baton.

"No, you weren't. Where did you go?"

Kylie turned away and moved her pencil over the notepad. A small scribble appeared on the paper. "I—I went to the bathroom."

Kathleen folded her arms. "In the dark?" Her daughter was lying. But why? What about? Kylie had never lied to her before.

Kylie shrugged.

"Are you almost finished? We close up at four."

"Yes." Kylie picked up the notepad. "I just have to add the totals. Did you still want me to give it to Mr. Nelson? He just came in." She pointed at the short, bald man speaking with Patti.

Roy held up one finger, then approached Kathleen. "We've got a new problem."

"What's wrong now?" Kathleen swallowed the lump that formed in her throat.

Roy handed her a piece of paper—the strip mall owner's company stationery. "The owner has decided not to lease us this building any longer. We have thirty days to vacate."

Iago drove to the meeting point, checked his watch, then peeked around the corner of the abandoned warehouse. He breathed in the sickening smell of standing water, asphalt, and the refuse from the dumpster farther down the alley. Where was Nelson? Late. Again. He'd been patient, but his patience wouldn't last forever. Not with Nelson. And not with Kathleen.

Footsteps on the pavement drew Iago's attention. Without warning, he snaked out his arm and grabbed Nelson by the collar, slamming him against the exterior stone wall. A gasp of shock and dismay shot from his quarry's throat.

The element of surprise was a beautiful thing.

"Why is Kathleen still in the running for governor? You were supposed to put a stop to it months ago."

"I'm trying. She's stubborn."

Trying? He wouldn't call Nelson's feeble efforts trying. Iago tightened his grip on Nelson's neck. "You're not trying hard enough."

"I've done everything you've asked."

"What about the municipal funds? Why wasn't there an investigation? She should have been ruined." The police should have traced the stolen city funds to Mayor Phillips by now and arrested her for fraud, but it hadn't happened. What was the holdup?

"I'm fairly sure Mayor Phillips reinstated the stolen amount herself. Maybe she bribed the city treasurer. I don't know. But it's not my fault." Nelson shrugged and squirmed like a worm on a hook.

Really? Bribed the treasurer? Iago's smile returned. Kathleen was becoming more like her father every day. "You need to convince her to drop out of the election. Do whatever you have to."

"What if I can't?" The words choked from Nelson's throat.

"I'll tell the police what I know." He clicked his tongue.

"You'll go away for a long time."

"I won't have to worry about prison. My wife will kill me if she finds out."

A second later, a woman's piercing scream slammed against his eardrums. As Iago's head swiveled toward the sound, he released Nelson's throat. She'd seen them.

Iago made eye contact with the woman, then her footsteps pounded the pavement as she ran out of sight. What was she doing in the industrial district? No matter. He would have to deal with her sooner rather than later.

9

Tuesday morning, Paige woke to a bitter, acrid smell permeating the air. Sunlight slanted through the window, highlighting a smoky haze that hung over the living room. Loud whispers carried from the kitchen to the living room. "You're burning the bacon."

"I am not. Paigey likes it this way. Don't put milk in those eggs. They'll be all runny."

"Will not. I've been making them this way for sixty-five years."

"Be quiet, you old goose. You'll wake Paigey."

"She's a grown woman. You shouldn't call her Paigey anymore."

"What do you know? I've raised her since she was twelve…"

Ignoring the bickering, Paige rolled off the couch, grabbed her clothes, then headed for the bathroom where she showered and dressed. Her hair was still wrapped in a towel when Aunt Hattie called, "Paigey, breakfast is ready."

Paige sat at the table and bowed her head while Jessie said the blessing. She scooped up a bite of the perfectly scrambled eggs and savored the buttery taste on her tongue. *Yum.*

Aunt Hattie stared at her with a wide-eyed, expectant gaze. Paige snapped off the brittle end of a piece of bacon and put it in her mouth, careful not to grimace as the charcoal-like flavor seeped into her taste buds. She washed it down with apple juice. She'd digested Aunt Hattie's burnt bacon more times than she could count, but it never got any more delectable.

Fighting the urge to stick out her tongue at the aftertaste, Paige's eyes flickered back and forth between the two women who ate only what they'd cooked. "Aunt Hattie, won't you have some eggs?" She picked up the spoon from the serving bowl.

Aunt Hattie snorted. "Not if *she* won't eat any of my bacon. I worked hard on it."

"No, thank you." Jessie crossed her arms. "I haven't acquired a taste for coal."

Paige rolled her eyes and went back to eating in silence. She took another bite of burnt bacon and held back a mischievous smile. Aunt Hattie really was the worst cook she'd ever met. But the woman had a good heart. Out of love, she tried her best, even if her best barely passed for edible.

What was Paige going to do with those two? They fought like cats. Sometimes, she wanted to declare this was her house and kick them both out.

"Jessie." She paused, and Jessie looked up from her plate of eggs. "I'd like to go over the bookstore's books. Where can I find them?"

Jessie's wrinkled forehead furrowed. "We have lots of books. What kind do you want?"

Oh no. That doesn't sound good. A knot formed in Paige's stomach. "Accounting books. You know, logs of the income, expenses, payroll…your husband kept books, right?"

Jessie shrugged. "I don't know."

"How do you not know?" A small pain started in Paige's temple.

"Lawrence and I never discussed business. Our conversations consisted of 'How was your day, honey?' 'Just fine. How was yours?' I talked while I prepared dinner, and he relaxed from a hard day at work. Don't get me wrong, Lawrence was a good husband. It was just the way things were back then."

"How have you been keeping track since his death?"

Jessie rubbed her wrinkled cheek. "Keeping track of…"

"Income, expenses, payroll, taxes." Paige flinched, and the pain in her head doubled. Would the IRS get involved?

When she first met Jessie, the woman was still using an adding machine and handwritten receipts. Paige had created a digital point-of-sale system for the store. Drawers full of carbon copies came to mind. Paige shuddered.

"Oh, taxes. The city sends me a bill for my property taxes each year."

"What about federal taxes on the business?" *Oh boy.* Jessie's face went blank again. *Looks like I might have my work cut out for me.*

"My records are in the filing cabinet in the office."

Paige swallowed the last of her juice, wiped her lips clean, then put her dishes in the sink. "I'll see you two later." She kissed them both on the cheek, then headed into town on her bicycle. After arriving at the bookstore, she locked her bicycle into the bike rack, went inside, and switched on the electronic OPEN sign. She then went back to the office where she locked her purse inside the desk drawer and pinned her name tag to her collared shirt.

Turning to the filing cabinet, she tried the handle. Locked. Paige rummaged through the desk and found a set of small keys. She unlocked the filing cabinet, then opened the top drawer. A nightmare stared back at her, just like she'd suspected. The drawer was full of receipt books. The second held invoices with receipts stapled to them.

The bell on the front door jingled. *Someone's an early*

shopper. "I'll be out in a minute."

Becky Thorne, Hamilton's sister, poked her head around the door jamb. "Good morning."

"Morning."

"Nice to see you, too." Becky grinned with a toothy charismatic smile, then stepped into the office. She wore a light blue T-shirt and jean skirt, and her lengthy, black hair was pinned on the back of her head. Becky was the principal of the Whitman school, a Real Estate Agent, and the mom of three boys. Sometimes, Paige thought she might be Wonder Woman's alter ego.

"Sorry. I'm in the middle of something."

"That's fine. I just brought this extra pie I baked last night. I thought you and Nori might enjoy it later, or you can take it home for Jessie and Hattie." She set the pie on the corner of the desk. "What are you looking at?"

Paige met Becky's eyes, so much like Hamilton's, and gestured toward the open drawer. "I want to go over the books for the store, but I'm having trouble finding any."

Becky propped her hip on top of Paige's desk. "Dad is Jessie's accountant. He should have what you need."

Wade Bryant? Paige jerked around. "Really?" She'd met Hamilton and Becky's parents at the Thorne's Memorial Day picnic.

"He's a CPA. He's handled Jessie's finances for years, including filing her taxes."

Relief flooded over Paige. She chuckled. "Does Jessie know that?"

"I should think so. You should see the pile of paperwork Jessie puts on Dad's desk each January. All you'll need to worry about is the current year, which is probably what all these things are for." She picked up one of the carbon books, then tossed it back in the drawer. "I could call and get you an appointment."

"Thanks."

After Becky left, Paige turned her attention from the bookstore's financial situation. She headed for one of the boxes moved from the house in Portland. Using a box cutter, she sliced through the tape on one of the thirty-five boxes of books that crowded the small office space. A musty scent filled her lungs, and a feeling of calm traveled over her body. She took a small stack of books from the box and rubbed her fingertips over the embossed hardcovers. "Welcome to your new home."

Tears blurred her vision. Her dream of owning a bookstore was finally a reality.

Paige sat down at her desk and began the difficult task of inventorying her personal collection into the bookstore's database. It took several minutes per book, as she researched the history of each one and determined a competitive price point based on their rarity and condition. Then took photos and printed barcodes from the POS system. She'd add them to the website later.

When she finished a small stack, she carried them to the front room, set them on the checkout desk, then picked up the top one and tucked it onto a shelf in the classics section like she was tucking an infant into their crib.

The bell on the front door jingled, and the door opened. A second later, the air around Paige moved as someone stepped close and planted a kiss on her cheek. She flinched, startled by the sudden touch. A squeak escaped her lips.

"Good morning." Hamilton laughed. "Didn't mean to scare you."

As she turned into his arms, her cheeks flushed warm. "Good morning to you, too." Her eyes scanned his rumpled uniform. "Are you on duty?"

Hamilton rubbed calloused hands over her forearms. "Just finished. Graveyard. Thought I'd stop in and see how you're doing before I go home."

"I'm good."

"Hattie and Jessie getting along any better?"

"Um," Paige chuckled awkwardly. "Not really."

He shuffled his dusty shoe on the carpet. "Might have been a better idea to get your own place."

Paige's shoulders raised and lowered. She blew out a breath. "I keep hoping they'll settle down and make this work. Those two could be good friends if they stopped bickering over every little thing."

"What was it this time?" Hamilton leaned against the metal bookshelf and crossed his legs.

"This morning, Aunt Hattie burnt the bacon. Yesterday, it was cows."

He looked at Paige like she was crazy. "Cows?"

"Yes, cows. Aunt Hattie doesn't like the cow-themed kitchen, and she throws a fit every time Jessie's cookie jar moos. Jessie says that's to let her know when Aunt Hattie is stealing cookies again." She paused. "I just wish they'd *try* to get along."

Hamilton squeezed her arm. "They'll figure it out. Give them time. You'll see." He hid a yawn behind his hand and blinked. "Sorry. I gotta get some sleep, so I'm ready for my big date tonight."

"What date?" She waggled her eyebrows. "Who's the lucky girl?"

He leaned close. His breath smelt minty like he chewed a mint before coming in. Probably covering stale coffee breath since he was on duty all night. "You are. Did I forget to ask?"

Paige stuffed her hands in her pockets and rocked on her heels. "I'd love to go on a date with you." Butterflies fluttered in her stomach. *It'll be our first date since I moved back.*

"Great. Pick you up at seven." He jerked his chin toward the shelves. "Have fun."

"Oh, I will." Nothing made her happier than her books.

As the door shut behind him and the police cruiser pulled away from the curb, Paige turned, scanning the blue walls, yellow trim, and rows of well-organized bookshelves. The bookstore had a cozy yet modern feel. Geometric artwork decorated the walls. The upstairs loft had a reading corner with eclectic chairs and a media center with outlets and wifi.

Before she had come to work here, the store had been in absolute disarray. Jessie Faye had allowed the place to run down over the years. But Paige had brought it into the twenty-first century and created a profitable business out of the nearly bankrupt bookstore.

Her back pocket vibrated. Paige pulled her cell phone from her pants. *Kylie.* She tapped the screen and put the phone to her ear. "Hey, Kylie. What's up?"

"Can I come over and talk?"

Her sister sounded… odd. "Sure. I'm at the bookstore." Paige frowned and ended the call.

10

Twenty minutes later, Kylie blew inside the bookstore like a summer storm. "You'll never believe what happened to me yesterday."

Paige chuckled. Who needed pleasantries? "Hello to you, too."

Kylie froze and blinked rapidly. "Oh, sorry. Hello." She hugged Paige, then took a deep breath, not staying sidetracked for long. "Yesterday, I went to Mom's headquarters to talk about not going back to college. She was busy as usual, but I stayed around to help. Mom asked me to add up the contribution cards that people had mailed in. Did you know I'm good at math?"

Paige shook her head and picked up a stack of discarded books, walking down the rows. Might as well work while Kylie jabbered.

"Suddenly, the power goes out. And when the lights come back on, there was a note lying on the table in front of me."

Paige paused. "A note? From whom?"

"I don't know." Kylie shrugged. "That was the weird thing. It wasn't signed or anything. It just appeared."

"What did it say?" Paige pulled a book from the wrong shelf. Customers left books on tables, chairs, and on top of other publications. Others tried to help put the books away, but they often ended up in the wrong places.

"I looked around for whoever might have left it. When I came back to my seat, Mom was all like 'Where were you?' I was only gone a couple minutes." Kylie rolled her eyes.

Paige picked up another stack of books left on one of the cushioned chairs and walked to the cookbook section. "You didn't answer my other question. What did the note say?"

"I'm getting to that." Kylie grabbed another cookbook lying by itself and handed it to Paige. She then pulled a crumpled paper out of her jean's pocket. "You can read it for yourself."

Paige put the cookbooks away. Then took the scrap of paper from Kylie's hand. The piece was torn from a sheet of paper, and the words were typed. "False face must hide what the false heart doth know."

Kylie sighed loudly and cupped her chin in her hand. "What do you think it means?"

Paige read over the message again. *How strange.* "It's a quote from *Macbeth*."

"Who's Macbeth?"

Paige smiled at Kylie's question. "*Macbeth* is a tragedy written by William Shakespeare in the sixteen hundreds. It's also the name of the lead character. Macbeth was foretold that he would be king, so he murdered the real king and took his place, but then kept killing people out of paranoia."

Kylie scrunched her face. "Ugh, who'd watch that?"

"Apparently, a lot of people."

"What does it mean?"

Paige tapped her finger to her lip. "It's talking about secrets. Putting on a false face to hide what's in the heart."

"But I'm not hiding anything. Unless you count not

wanting to go back to college."

Was Kylie the intended recipient? Should they show the police? But it wasn't a threat. Just an odd message. *What is the writer trying to say? Who has a secret?* Paige handed the paper back to Kylie, then walked to her office and plopped down in the chair. *Me. Kathleen. Dad… Does this have to do with us? Or is it completely unrelated?*

Kylie's voice carried down the hall, growing louder. She appeared in the doorway and skidded to a stop. "Whoa! What are all these boxes?"

"Books. Some of them belonged to my grandpa, and some of them I bought myself. I've been collecting for a long time. It's always been my dream to open my own bookstore."

Kylie's eyes widened. Her mouth formed an O. "That's a lot of books."

"You should have seen my bedroom before they were packed."

Kylie stepped into the room and over a box. "Can I help?"

"Help? With the books?" Kylie nodded. Paige bit down on her lip. While she loved her little sister, Paige was rather fastidious and maybe just a little particular when it came to her books. Very particular. "It involves a lot of historical research and information comparison. The rarer the book, the more it's worth. Personally, I love it, but I'm afraid you won't find it very exciting." *Sorry, Kylie. I'm too obsessive over how it's done. Please don't feel rejected.*

"Oh," Kylie said. But instead of looking disappointed, she giggled. "That does sound boring." She perched on the top of a step stool and fell silent. Paige glanced at her out of the corner of her eye. What was Kylie thinking about? Paige picked up her water bottle and took a swig. "Paige?"

"Hmm?"

"Were your parents sad when you moved all the way across the state?"

Paige choked on the water. Little dribbles ran down her chin. *My parents?* She grabbed a tissue and wiped her chin.

Ryan was happy to have her close. Kathleen, on the other hand, would rather never see Paige again. But Paige couldn't tell Kylie that. *How can I answer Kylie's question truthfully?*

"...would have a heart attack if I wanted to move that far away. Which I don't."

Kylie hadn't stopped speaking—Paige had missed the first part. As her sister continued chattering in the background, Paige picked up a stack of books from the corner of her desk and carried them to the fiction section. Kylie followed and held back the row while Paige added the new books to the shelf. "You should invest in some bookends, but they're hard to find. I looked for some for my bookcase at home. I ended up using a block of wood."

Paige pinched her lips to keep from laughing aloud. Leave it to Kylie to change subjects so quickly. "Let me know if you find any good ones."

"Thanks, Paige."

"For what?"

"For being the sister I never had."

Paige's stomach twisted. Her heart ached to tell Kylie the truth. Kathleen was forcing her to live a lie. *I don't know how long I can do this.*

"I didn't eat breakfast. I'm hungry." With Kylie's random proclamation, the moment slipped away.

"Do you want to get something from the Rustic Cup?" She could use some coffee. And maybe one of Jenn's scones. Her mouth watered at the thought.

"Yes, please."

Paige grabbed her purse and slipped the strap over her shoulder. As they headed to the front entrance, Paige confirmed Nori's presence behind the register. Jessie had hired Nori Pham during the time Paige returned to Portland to sell her house. Nori was a good employee. Paige planned to keep her on. She waved her hand and got Nori's attention. "I'll be down at the café. Call if you need anything."

The woman in the booth kitty-corner to theirs hadn't taken her eyes off them since they sat down. Something about her seemed familiar. Where had Paige seen her before? The stranger had a silver chin-length bob with no bangs. Her skin was nearly flawless, but smile lines punctuated her eyes. She sat with her shoulders squared. Her outfit was a classy twofer midi dress with nautical vibes. Why was she staring at them?

"Who's that woman?"

Kylie stuffed a chunk of cinnamon roll into her mouth, then glanced over her shoulder. "I don't know." She said with her mouth full.

Paige tried to ignore the stranger. She finished her lemon scone, then sucked the last of her iced coffee through a straw. Kylie said something and laughed. Paige smiled like she'd heard. Her eyes lifted and carried her gaze over Kylie's shoulder. When they made eye contact, the woman's face flushed. She averted her eyes, then hastily opened her purse, laid a few bills on the table, and scurried out of the restaurant.

"That was weird."

"What's weird?" Kylie brushed crumbs from the front of her vintage T-shirt.

Did I say that out loud? "It's nothing." Paige waved her hand. "When I made eye contact with the woman, she left."

Kylie took a sip of her coffee, then licked her lips. "She was probably embarrassed you caught her staring."

"You're right. That was probably it." Tiny hairs prickled on the back of Paige's neck at the thought of being watched. Ever since her uncle had nearly killed her, she was a little leery when things seemed suspicious. She touched the deep scar in the palm of her right hand. OK, maybe more than a *little* leery. Paige checked the time on her phone. "I should get back to the store."

Kylie nodded. "My shift starts now, anyway. See you later?"

"Sure." Paige slung her purse strap over her shoulder and walked back to the bookstore. As she entered, the bell jingled.

Nori Pham turned from her place behind the counter. "Morning." The middle-aged woman greeted her warmly.

"Good morning. How's it going?" She set a disposable coffee cup on the counter. "I brought this for you. It's Jenn's new iced mocha."

"Thank you. I wasn't expecting anything." Nori brushed her long, black hair over her shoulder and took a sip of the cold drink. She licked the remnants off her upper lip. "That's delicious."

"No problem." Paige shrugged and leaned her elbow on the counter. A frequent customer stepped forward. Nori turned her attention to the elderly man. "Did you find everything you were looking for?"

"Yes. Thank you. I've been looking for Edward Garnachelli's debut novel for about forty years. I can't believe you had it, Paige."

"You're welcome. Anything for my favorite customer."

Nori took care of the transaction, then they waved and sent him on his way. "You're so good with the customers. I enjoy working here, and I appreciate the job."

"Of course. You're very welcome." Paige smiled. "You do good work. I'm happy to have you. I'm going to work on inventory. Just holler if you need anything."

"Will do."

Paige closed the office door, then maneuvered through the stacks of boxes and sat at her desk. She scanned the store email for anything important and answered a few questions, then checked for new orders on the website.

But no matter how hard she tried, Kylie's weird note and the strange woman at the cafe wouldn't leave her thoughts. Who left Kylie that note? What did it mean? Who was that woman? Why did she look familiar, and why was she watching them? Were the two connected? *Of course not. Right?* Paige sighed. Might as well see what was happening on the floor—she wasn't getting any work done here.

She left the office and climbed the stairs to the loft. Several visitors rested in the cushioned armchairs, reading.

Others worked on their computers in the media center. A teenage boy sat in the last plastic stack chair with a game interface on his laptop screen—Tyler Thorne—his mop of blond hair was a dead giveaway.

She walked up behind him and grabbed his shoulders. Hamilton's nephew screamed and spun around in his chair. The other customers wagged their heads, annoyed at the outburst. Tyler clapped his hands over his mouth, then took off his headphones. "Miss McDonald. You scared me to death. Why'd you do that?"

"Sorry, Tyler. I didn't know it would startle you so bad. What are you up to?"

"Tony started violin lessons. I asked Mom if I could come down here to get away from the noise."

"Knock yourself out, but don't play anything your mother doesn't approve of, or I'll get in trouble."

"I won't." Tyler put his headphones back on. He returned to his game, and the animated character started swinging a sword at a strange-looking creature. Paige shivered at the weird sight, then moved to the wooden railing and laid her arms on top. Like an aristocrat from ancient times, she surveyed her kingdom below. This was her domain. She was responsible for everything that went on inside these walls. And she loved making sure every one of her denizens left happy.

A flash of silver drew her attention to the far side of the store. Was that the woman from the café? What was she doing in the bookstore? Paige chucked at herself. *Probably looking for a book. This is a bookstore.* But something still bothered her about the woman.

Paige strolled to the front counter and shimmied to Nori's side. Nori finished an over-the-phone request, laid the receiver in its cradle, and handed Paige an order form. "Hannah Keith wants to know if you have any books for toddlers. She wants to start encouraging her little boy to read. Something about a thousand books before kindergarten."

"I'll take care of it." Paige took the paper. "Hey, have you ever seen her before?" She jutted her chin toward the stranger perusing the do-it-yourself section.

Nori blew her dark bangs out of her eyes. "Maybe. Why?"

Paige frowned. "I saw her earlier at the Rustic Cup. She was staring at Kylie and me."

"She looks familiar—don't you think?"

Does she? "I don't know. Maybe."

"She looks like you."

Paige rolled her eyes. "She does not." She playfully punched Nori on the shoulder.

"Come to think of it, she looks like Dawn Winters."

"The actress? What would she be doing in Whitman?" Ms. Winters had stared in a wide variety of movies and sitcoms and had won at least one Oscar. Why would a celebrity visit such a small town in the middle of nowhere? No one visited Whitman, Oregon, on accident.

"Hold on, she's coming this way," Nori whispered. "Can we help you find anything?" She raised her voice to address the approaching woman.

"I've got everything I need. Thank you, though." The possible celebrity laid a first English edition copy of West Side Story on the counter.

Nori picked up the book and rang up the sale. "Is this everything?"

The woman nodded, but her gaze stayed on Paige. Nori was right. The actress did resemble Paige, something about the shape of her nose and cheekbones, but that was impossible. "I don't mean to pry, but are you Dawn Winters?"

"I am." Ms. Winter's smoky voice held only a hint of her age. "You're a beautiful young woman."

"Thank you." Paige squeaked. She cleared her throat while Nori finished the transaction. Ms. Winters paid in cash—for a $500 book. Paige was intrigued. What business brought Dawn Winters to their corner of the world? It certainly couldn't be to buy a copy of West Side Story from her little bookstore.

"Thank you, and come again." Nori handed the woman a brown paper bag containing her purchase. Her hand trembled.

Ms. Winters turned to leave, then paused and looked over her shoulder, meeting Paige's eyes. "You have a lovely bookstore, Paige." Before Paige could answer, she'd pivoted on her heel and sashayed out of the store.

How did she know my name?

Later that afternoon, Paige locked her bike in front of Bryant Accounting, LLC, then entered the office. Wade's secretary greeted her. Wade rounded the corner from another room. "Welcome back to Whitman, Paige. What can I do for you?" Hamilton's father, with gray hair and dark eyes, stood head and shoulders taller than Paige. The siblings got their blue eyes from their mother, Jessica.

"I'm sure Hamilton told you that I own Jessie's bookstore now. I'd like to review the books so I can create a financial forecast for this next year. Becky said you've been responsible for Jessie's finances."

"Sure. Congratulations, by the way. Follow me and have a seat." Paige followed Wade into his office. He left the door open. She took a seat across from the imposing desk in the center of the room. He sat in the other chair and folded his hands on the desk calendar. "Unfortunately, I can't share any of that information without a signed affidavit from Ms. Faye, giving permission for you to view her finances. Just being the new owner of the store doesn't give you permission to see historical records."

"I really just want to make sure there are no surprises like unpaid taxes or a huge mountain of debt."

"I'm sorry. I can't disclose information without Ms. Faye's approval."

Paige sighed. This felt like a total waste of her time. "Can you at least tell me how long Jessie's been your client?"

"Yes. About twenty years. Ms. Faye retained my services

after her husband's passing. The poor woman was in over her head. Now that you own the store, do you plan to continue using my services?"

Paige rubbed her arms. The air conditioner was making her chilled. "I don't know. You can imagine my surprise when I opened her cabinet to find all those loose receipts and carbon books."

Wade let out a boisterous belly laugh. "I've had to face that pile every year for the past twenty years. Please tell me you're going to employ an electronic database."

"Absolutely. In respect to your client privileges, can you at least tell me if I should expect calls from collections or receive an eviction notice tomorrow?"

"You will not receive an eviction notice tomorrow. The next day, however…" Wade laughed. "Just kidding. The building has been long paid for. As soon as you bring me that affidavit, we can take a look at the records. Though I must warn you, I only have the past seven years on site. If you want farther back, you'll have to ask Jessie where she put them."

11

The sun was beginning to set when Kathleen changed into jogging clothes and stepped outside. After she checked her shoelaces, she popped earbuds in and set off at a slow pace. The blacktop pounded beneath her sneakers. She picked up speed. Her pulse increased, and her breaths came in shorter spurts. A slight burn began in her calves. How long had it been since she last exercised? Too long, if the numbers on the scale were any indication.

What was she going to do about her headquarters? She'd wanted to charge into the landlord's office and demand they renew her lease, but she'd called six times yesterday, and no one answered. She'd called Joe, and he'd looked over the contract again.

According to the papers she'd signed, the landlord had the right to cancel the lease with thirty days' notice. Why hadn't she seen that before? Or maybe she had but hadn't considered it to be a problem. Now, she had a month to find a new location, and the sooner, the better. But why the sudden change? As far as she knew, they hadn't missed a payment.

Running on the open road, Kathleen moved to the left side to face oncoming traffic. It wasn't long before she left the residential area of town and entered the commercial district. The traffic light turned red, and the crosswalk sign indicated *do not walk*. While she waited, she jogged in place to keep her heart rate elevated.

Out of habit, she glanced toward the town square. The courthouse stood like an imposing giant in the middle of the grassy yard. Her eyes traveled over the well-attended concrete walks and flowerbeds, and the white-washed gazebo standing closer to the cross street. Paige sat inside the pavilion, talking with someone. Who was that with her? Her companion looked female.

The light turned. Kathleen jogged a few steps closer, turned off her music, and stuffed her earbuds into her pocket. She squinted and slowed her stride. A Black woman with curly hair, wearing dark slacks and a pink top sat across from Paige. Was that the reporter from the Wallowa County Chieftain? What was her name? *Carmela Carlson.* But why would Paige be talking to Carmela? Was she telling the journalist about Kathleen? *No, Paige promised. She wouldn't… would she?*

Kathleen ducked behind a parked car and watched until the pair stood and shook hands. After Carmela climbed into a vehicle on the other side of the square and drove away, Paige picked up her purse and walked in Kathleen's direction. Kathleen straightened, then stepped in front of her, arms akimbo. "What were you doing with that reporter?"

Paige jerked to a stop to keep from running into Kathleen. "Oh, goodness. I didn't see you. Please excuse me." Paige wore a knee-length, sleeveless dress with pumps and accessories. When Kathleen didn't move out of the way, Paige shifted her purse to the other shoulder. "Is there something I can do for you?"

"Why were you talking to Carmela?" Annoyance laced

her tone.

"Carmela?" Paige looked over her shoulder at the journalist's vehicle turning the corner out of sight. "I don't see how that's any of your business."

Kathleen's blood pressure rose. How dare she? "It is my business if you're going to tarnish my reputation by spreading lies about me."

"Who's spreading lies? You didn't even come up in the conversation."

What? Kathleen stumbled. *I didn't?* "Then what were you talking about?"

"We ran into each other. Carmela asked about interviewing me for a human interest piece. I said no."

She turned Carmela's offer down? How can I be sure? "If you *accidentally* ran into each other, why are you so dressed up?"

"I met Hamilton—Officer Bryant—at Heavenly's. We had a date."

A date. Paige was dressed for an evening out. "Oh." It was all Kathleen could say. When had she become so paranoid? "So, you weren't giving her the scoop about us?"

"I said I wouldn't."

"I've gotten so used to people stabbing me in the back, I just assumed you would, too. Eventually." Why had she said that? She wasn't looking for sympathy. She didn't need Paige feeling sorry for her. Her past was none of Paige's business. "Forget I said that. Have a nice evening." She jogged off before Paige could see the warmth climbing her cheeks. Which was more embarrassing? The fact she'd assumed Paige was spilling secrets or that she'd spilled one of her own?

Kathleen turned off Main Street and headed north on Harwood toward the post office, big-box grocery store, and hospital. The sun dipped behind the mountains making the sky glow a golden hue with streaks of rosy pink. The evening air cooled. Goosebumps raised on her arms.

A dark vehicle with tinted windows came over the hill. The driver had plenty of time to notice her, but the pickup truck scooted closer to the solid white line. A brick barrier loomed ahead with no space for her to pass between the wall and the truck. *They've got to move over.* The vehicle drifted nearer to the wall.

Kathleen waved her hand. *What are you doing?* She stopped running and waited, planting her hands on her hips and breathing heavily. The vehicle passed the wall, then moved farther to the left, crossing over the white line—heading straight toward her.

"Hey," she shouted and waved, blinded by their headlights. They obviously weren't looking where they were going. No time. They were going to hit her. She sprang back into the bushes—prickers stabbed tender skin. She shielded her eyes as the truck sped past, shooting dirt and gravel into her face, then swerved back into the lane.

Kathleen coughed and spit debris from her mouth. *What was that? They didn't even slow down.* She sat paralyzed, trying to catch her breath. *Did that really just happen?*

Brakes squealed, and an engine idled. A car door slammed shut. Running footsteps echoed on the pavement. "Ann—Kathleen, are you all right?" Ryan Whitestone stood over her. Of all people to be driving by, why did it have to be him? It could have been anyone else.

Literally, anyone else would do.

"Can you stand?"

When she nodded, he stuck out his hand. With great reluctance, she grasped it and allowed him to pull her to her feet. Pain shot through her leg. Stickers and leaves stuck to her clothes and lower limbs. It was too dark to see how much damage had been done, but she swiped something wet—blood. "Thank you. I'm fine. I appreciate your concern." She took a step and hissed. "Irresponsible driver. That's all it was."

She'd twisted her ankle. The pain sent a wave of lightheadedness rolling over her.

Ryan's hand touched her arm. Warmth radiated through his fingers. "Are you sure you're okay?"

No. I'm not. "I'm fine." She took a step and tumbled

forward. Ryan caught her before she hit the ground.

"Whoa! You should go to the hospital and let them check you over. I can take you."

"I'm fine. It's just a sprain." How many times did she have to say she was okay? She didn't need help. Especially not *his* help. She jerked out of his hands. "Thank you for stopping." She took a few hobbled steps forward. *Leave. Go away.*

Ryan didn't move. "If you won't go to the hospital, at least let me drive you home. You can't walk all that way in your condition."

Another shooting pain. Another wave of lightheadedness. Her stomach rolled. "Fine. Take me home."

As Ryan pulled back onto the road, tension hung like a dense cloud inside the vehicle. What could they possibly say to each other? He had to be angry with her. Why had he even stopped to help? He could have just left her there. No one would've blamed him.

He is a pastor. Maybe he's sworn to lend aid like medical personnel. Do preachers take a vow like the Hippocratic Oath? Perhaps it was like that Bible story of the good Samaritan who helped his enemy.

Were they enemies? A knot formed in her chest. Why did that thought make her sad? They might not be enemies, but they certainly weren't friends. Not anymore. That ship had sailed.

Ryan cleared his throat. "Kathleen." He kept his eyes on the road. "I want to apologize for breaking my promise. I was only thinking of myself, and I'm sorry."

Kathleen looked at him out of the corner of her eye. Was he serious? What did he expect her to say? That it didn't matter? That she was okay with it? Both of those answers would be a lie. She shifted uncomfortably.

He continued when she didn't answer. "I'm hoping you'll forgive me."

Forgive him? As in, pretend it never happened? How could she do that? The damage had been done—Paige knew.

"Ryan…"

She couldn't finish her thought. Ryan's sad puppy dog eyes made a smile quirk the corner of her lips. He'd used that look on her so many times when they were teenagers. "I'm still mad, but thank you for apologizing." That was more than the rest of the men in her life had ever done.

"You won't mind if I spend time with our daughter?"

Kathleen's breath hitched. Spend time together? He and Paige. As father and daughter? "I don't know…" A tightness gripped her chest. What was this feeling? It wasn't anger. Was it… jealousy? Was she jealous that Ryan would be able to build something with their daughter, while she could not? *Certainly not. What do I care?* She chewed on her lower lip. *I do care.*

Instead of answering his question, she asked, "What will you tell your church? You don't want rumors to spread." How could he spend time in public with Paige and his congregation not become suspicious? Would they assume he was dating a woman half his age? "Everyone knows you're not married. How will you explain without flat out lying or involving me?"

She stared at his ringless left hand. He had claimed he never married because he was still waiting for her. But why? She'd been clear that she wasn't interested in continuing their romantic relationship when she went off to college at Stanford.

She'd hoped they would have remained friends. It was he who had cut off their friendship completely.

Kathleen mentally slapped herself. How could they have remained friends when she'd kept a massive secret from him? But of course, he hadn't known that. So, why had he never contacted her?

Then suddenly, he showed up in her life again at Dad's funeral in April. Where had he been all those years?

"I don't know what I'm going to tell the church or the pulpit committee about Paige. I'm still seeking wisdom and direction." The turn signal clicked as he pulled into the turn lane. He waited for a couple cars to pass, then turned onto her street.

Still seeking direction? From whom? God? Her old self, Annie, had believed that God cared, but Kathleen knew better. God wasn't interested in what took place down here.

Ryan maneuvered his car between the entrance pillars and onto her driveway. As they approached the house, Kathleen noticed that Kylie's car was gone.

"Thank you for the ride." As soon as the car came to a stop, Kathleen opened the door. "Have a nice evening." She stood, clinging to the door frame, and carefully put weight on her ankle.

Ryan's door slammed shut, and he rounded the car. "Let me help."

She didn't want his help, but what other choice did she have? The pain had worsened, and her ankle had grown stiff—she'd never make it up the stairs on her own.

His arm slipped around her waist, and the soft touch brought a myriad of memories with it. Kathleen pushed them away, then cupped her hand around his neck, trying to ignore the feeling of his skin under her fingers. The sooner he got her inside and left, the better.

Ryan helped her to the front door, keeping the weight off her ankle. "My keys are in my pocket." She removed her arm from around his neck and dug into the pocket of her jogging shorts.

He unlocked the door and helped her into the foyer. She balanced on one leg while he flipped the light switch—the place where his hand had been on her back felt oddly empty. "Thank you again for stopping. And for the ride home. I can take it from here."

Ryan moved to lay his hand on her shoulder, then pulled away. What had changed his mind? "You're welcome. I'm glad I came by when I did. Are you sure you'll be okay?"

She nodded. "I'll wait down here until Kylie gets home. She can help me climb the stairs." Had his eyes always been that blue?

Ryan opened his mouth, then closed it again. His lips pinched in a straight line, and he rubbed his palm across his facial hair. *Twenty-five years ago, he only had peach fuzz.* Her eyes traveled to where his bulging biceps met his sleeves… *those are new too.* A lot of things had changed since they last dated. Warmth climbed her cheeks. Had he noticed her staring? "Good night." She turned to hobble into the living room to wait for Kylie's return.

"We need to talk."

Why wouldn't he just leave? "There's nothing to talk about." She hopped on one foot until she was facing him. What did he want? If he were foolish enough to believe they could ever get back together… she'd burned that bridge a long time ago.

He closed the distance between them and took hold of her hand. She tried to pull away, but he held firmly. "My feelings haven't changed. I still love you. I will always love you."

Kathleen lifted her chin to look into his eyes. *Just like Paige's.* He gazed into her soul like he was trying to read her thoughts. "We can't go back." A burning sensation pinched her nose. *Do I still love him? Do some emotions never die?*

"Annie—"

Hardness entered her heart. She jerked her hand back. Why couldn't she get Ryan to understand?

He didn't love her. He wanted Annie—a girl she could never be again. He would never love Kathleen. He could never love the woman she had become. Annie had been a bright-eyed cream puff who let anyone, and everyone, push her around. But life changed all that. Annie was gone—she wasn't coming back.

In her place remained a strong, determined woman, bent and bruised but not broken. "You should go."

"Please, just listen—"

A loud sneeze came from the other side of the house, then the sound of tin hitting the floor. Kathleen's heart raced. "Someone's here."

"Kylie's—"

"...car is not outside. Someone is in my house." Her blood chilled in her veins. Kathleen tried to rush forward, but sharp pangs shot through her ankle. She stumbled and put her hand on the wall.

"I'll call the police." Ryan took his cell phone from his back pocket. "We should wait outside until they get here."

"That'll take too long. Whoever it is might get away before the police arrive." She hopped closer to the sideboard and pulled open one of the shallow drawers. Her pistol lay inside.

"What are you going to do with that?"

She ignored Ryan and disengaged the safety. Using the wall for balance, she crept down the hallway, her weapon cocked. At the end of the wall, just before the open area, Ryan held out his arm and blocked her path. With a quick jerk, he took the gun from her hands and shook his head. He made some silly hand motions like he was military, then stepped into the open, gun aimed toward the kitchen. "Put your hands up."

A woman screamed.

"Dawn?" Ryan's voice changed. As he lowered the gun, Kathleen stepped forward. A silver-haired woman, wearing a nautical twofer stood in the kitchen. On the floor lay the metal coffee tin. Loose grounds were strewn about the counter and the floor.

"Mother?"

"Hello, Kathleen. It's been a long time."

12

Kathleen's mouth fell open in shock. *Mother?*

Mother's eyes flickered back to Ryan. "Hello, Ryan." Her eyes traveled the length of his body. "My, what a handsome man you turned out to be. How have you been since you… it's been what—fifteen years—" Ryan interrupted her with a cough.

Kathleen ignored him and turned her attention to the intruder. "What are you doing here?"

"I can't believe that in all these years, you haven't changed the locks."

That's how she got in. Note to self: change the locks. But as usual, Mother avoided her question. "How did you get here? There isn't a car parked outside."

"I took a taxi."

Mother hasn't changed much since I last saw her. She's grayer and has more wrinkles, I guess. How many years ago has that been?

She approached Kathleen. Mother's eyes widened. "What happened to *you*?"

She pulled something from Kathleen's hair. A leaf. Kathleen looked down. Her jogging clothes were grimy and torn. Dried blood streaked from her knees to her red-stained socks. "It's nothing."

"Nothing!" Ryan's voice exploded. *I forgot he was here.* "Someone tried to run her over. She barely got out of the way in time."

"Goodness. I'm glad you're all right." Mother moved to the sink and turned on the tap, then tore a paper towel from the roll and wet it. "Why don't you sit, and I'll get you cleaned up?"

"I'm fine. I don't need your help. You haven't answered *my* question. What are you doing here?"

"Can't a woman visit her daughter and granddaughters without such scrutiny?" Mother spun with her hands extended. Ever the drama queen. Water droplets sprinkled the floor.

"We haven't spoken in years. You couldn't even bother to attend Dad's funeral." *Wait? Daughters? How did Mother know I have more than one daughter? Who told her? How long has she known?* "Did you say granddaughters?" She placed emphasis on the *s*.

Mother tossed the wet towel into the trash. A smirk spread across her face. "I did."

Something touched Kathleen's shoulder. Ryan. "I'm going to go. It was good to see you again, Ms. Staten. Take care. Bye, Mayor Phillips." He left the room. The drawer in the hallway opened and closed—he'd put the gun back. Neither woman spoke until the front door clicked shut.

"Does he know?"

"He does."

"I'm sorry about the mess." Mother gestured toward the coffee grounds. "I startled when I heard voices. Would you like a cup?"

Mother had made coffee. Acted like she owned the place, which she didn't, not since the divorce. "No, thank you. I want to know how you found out about her."

Mother poured a cup of coffee, then sat at the table, crossing one leg over the other. "Her? Oh, you mean Paige. Beautiful name, by the way. Did you pick it out?"

Kathleen didn't respond.

"I received a phone call informing me of her existence. Something you failed to do."

"It was none of your business. Dad took care of it."

Mother yawned dramatically, patting her delicate hand to her plump lips. "Yes, leaving the baby at a fire station is exactly the kind of thing your father would do. He never cared about anyone but himself."

"How dare you speak about Dad like that. You don't have the right to criticize him in my home. At least he was *here*. That's more than I can say for you."

"I was only a phone call away."

"He may not have been the best father in the world, but he always did right by his children."

A tinny laugh erupted from her mother's lips. "Sure, he did. Did you even cry when he died?"

Kathleen wanted to lie—to say she'd wept over the loss, but she hadn't. She missed Dad, that was true, but weep over him? How could you mourn the man who'd told you never to cry?

"I see. Of course, you didn't."

Awkward silence stretched on for several minutes. Mother cleared her throat. "I guess the question is—are you going to let me stay here, or do I need to get a hotel room in town?"

Everything in Kathleen demanded she throw her mother out on her ear. What *was* she doing in Whitman? Dawn Winters was a masterful actress, and Kathleen had no doubt there was more up her mother's sleeve than she let on. "Are you here to contest Dad's will? It's too late for that."

Mother waved her hand, dismissively. "I have plenty of my own money. I don't need any of his ill-gotten gains."

Friction impregnated the room. Kathleen's blood pressure rose. She hated Mother's jabs at Dad's character.

Dad was tough and ruthless, but he'd never done anything illegal. *As far as I know.*

"I saw your brother last week."

"How is the convicted criminal?"

"His spirits are high. He's hoping to get the whole case thrown out on a technicality."

What technicality? He's as guilty as El Chapo.

Erik had stolen millions of dollars in antiques in two countries, headed up the leading crime ring in the Pacific Northwest, and threatened both Kathleen and Paige with their lives. Who knew what other crimes he'd committed? "He's a bad man, Mother. He deserves to be in prison." Erik had always been her mother's favorite. Of course, she would think he was innocent. Her baby boy could do no wrong in her eyes.

"When do I get to meet my granddaughters?"

"Never."

"I'm their grandmother. They're both grown women. They have the right to decide for themselves."

"I'm their mother. I know what's best, and what's best is that they stay away from you."

Their gazes clashed like mountain goats. "You can stay here tonight, but I want you to go in the morning." When Mother went to move past her, Kathleen reached out and snagged her arm. "Stay away from my daughters."

The next morning, Kathleen stood at the top of the stairs, desperately trying to figure out how to get down independently. Overnight, the pain in her ankle had grown unbearable, and the ankle itself had swelled to the size of a tennis ball. Her stomach knotted at the thought of needing help, but how else would she get down the staircase to go see a doctor? As much as she didn't want to admit it, this was more than a simple sprain.

It had been hard enough to swallow her pride and allow Mother to help her upstairs last night, especially after arguing about Kylie and Paige. Part of her wished Mother had refused to honor her request, but Kathleen had heard the front door around six, and she'd already checked the guest room. Empty, except for Mother's perfume lingering in the air.

She wasn't sure what time Kylie had gotten home last night, but it was after Kathleen had gone to bed, and she could only hope Mother and Kylie hadn't made contact while Kathleen slept. If Kathleen inquired, Mother would probably lie. And she couldn't ask Kylie without making her suspicious or confused.

Since Mother was no longer in the house, her only choice was to wake her late sleeper. "Kylie?" She called down the hall toward her daughter's closed bedroom door.

She waited. The door didn't budge. Using the wall as a brace, she hopped to the room and opened the door. Kylie's bedding lay in a tousled mess, but no Kylie. Where was she? The bathroom?

Kathleen maneuvered herself to the bathroom door and knocked. "Kylie, are you in there?" No answer. She twisted the handle, and the door opened. Dark and empty. Had Kylie left for work already? She never worked the early shift.

Matilda had taken the day off, so her housekeeper wouldn't be in at all. Kathleen returned to the stairs and called out as loud as she could muster. "Kylie Michelle, are you down there?"

When she received no reply, she sat on the top step and slowly scooted down each one. She'd never felt more undignified in her life. By the time she reached the bottom level, she was breathing heavily, but at least she was down. Using the stair rail to stand, she hobbled to the door in the foyer and peeked out the window. Kylie's car was not in the driveway. Where had she gone so early?

Kathleen stuck her hand in her pocket. No phone. She'd left it upstairs. With a groan, she maneuvered to the landline in the kitchen, picked up the receiver, and held it to her ear. The dial tone buzzed. She dialed Kylie's number. It rang, but no answer. When the voicemail message began, Kathleen hung up. Who else could she call?

Joe? She looked down at the numbered buttons—what was his phone number? Did she know anyone's? 911 seemed a little excessive. It wasn't an emergency. How about a phone book?

Kathleen eyed the drawer below the phone. What were the odds the phone book was kept near the telephone? She pulled open the drawer. *Bingo.* She laid the book on the counter.

Who should she call? Who would be willing to help her? Opening to the yellow pages, she had two options—Paige at the bookstore or try Ryan at the church. Her stomach sank, and her throat tightened.

When she shifted, a searing pain shot up her leg. She had to get to the hospital as soon as possible. After flipping to the correct page, she dialed the listed number. Relief flooded her when a voice answered.

"Whitman Baptist Church. This is Pastor Whitestone. How may I help?"

Ryan checked his watch. 10:30. Half an hour since they took Annie back. He walked to the triage desk and cleared his throat. "Excuse me?"

"May I help you?" The nurse, wearing a Winnie the Pooh scrub top, raised her head. "Oh, Pastor Whitestone, what are you doing here? I thought you had chaplain duty on Mondays and Thursdays."

"I do. I brought Mayor Phillips in. I'm hoping to find out how she's doing."

"Let me check." The nurse rose from her stool and disappeared around the corner. Minutes passed. When she returned, she reported, "Mayor Phillips just went back for X-rays. Doc wants to make sure her ankle isn't fractured."

"Thank you." Ryan walked to his chair, sat, leaned his head against the wall, and closed his eyes. He couldn't have been more surprised when he'd received Annie's call than if God himself had been on the other end of that line. She'd *wanted* his help? But it had been clear once he'd arrived at her house that she'd considered him the last resort, though it still felt like a step in the right direction.

Sitting on her front porch in shorts and a T-shirt with hair bound in a playful ponytail, she appeared more youthful, vulnerable, and reminiscent of the girl he remembered.

He'd helped her into the car. They held a semi-civil conversation on the way to the hospital. Mostly, he'd just distracted her from the pain. Her face was sheet white for most of the drive, and she'd kept her eyes closed. When they'd arrived, the waiting room was empty. Annie had told him he could leave, but he chose to wait.

The ambulance siren whirled outside. Medics rushed into the building, rolling a patient on a gurney between them, then disappeared behind the automatic doors. Ryan bowed his head and closed his eyes, lifting a prayer to Heaven's throne for whatever the need.

Fifteen minutes more and the hard-plastic chair he occupied had grown unbearable. Ryan stood, stretched his back, then followed the corridor from the emergency department to the hospital's gift shop. He pulled on the handle, and the glass door opened.

The aroma of fresh flowers permeated the air, and the shelves overflowed with teddies, cards, and balloons. An old metal helium tank stood next to the checkout register. Ryan scanned the merchandise. What would Ann—Kathleen like? His only frame of reference was her teenage interests. *Does she still like the same things?*

He spotted a stuffed giraffe with large tear-drop shaped eyes. Annie had loved Precious Moment collectibles. He grabbed the giraffe, then moved to the flower display. White daisies had been her favorites. Did they have any? One small bouquet hid behind a vase of carnations near the back. *Perfect.*

She'll love these, and she'll know how much I care for her.

He carried the flowers and the stuffed animal to the counter. The cashier scanned the barcodes. "That'll be fifteen seventy-five. Pastor Whitestone, right?"

"That's me." He stuck his debit card into the chip reader. When it beeped, he took it out and returned it to his wallet. "How are you today?"

"I'm okay. Thanks for asking. Do you want these in a bag?"

"No, thank you. I've got it." Ryan picked up the gifts and returned to the waiting area.

The nurse at the desk flagged him down. "Pastor Whitestone, Mayor Phillips is back from X-rays, but it'll take a while for the radiologist to look at them. Sorry about the wait." Her eyes cut to the gifts in his arms. "Aww, are those for Ms. Phillips?"

Ryan nodded. Warmth gathered under his collar.

The nurse held out her hand. "Do you want me to take them back for you?"

"Thank you for the offer, but I'd rather wait to give them to her myself."

She raised her eyebrow as a look of understanding dawned in her expression. "Aww. How sweet. Does someone have a little crush on the mayor?"

How could he answer that? He cleared his throat and ran his finger between his shirt and neck. The nurse turned back to her computer screen, clearly not expecting him to respond.

Ryan walked to his chair by the window, placing the gifts in his lap. *Little crush? Make that a lifelong obsession.* Annie had meant everything to him, but she'd broken his heart. He'd made himself as vulnerable as a man possibly could, put everything on the line, and in return, she'd treated him like dirt.

So, why sit here like a lovesick fool with a stuffed giraffe?

Because no matter how hard he tried to move on, he couldn't. He still loved Annie with every fiber of his being, and somehow, he was going to win her back.

The sliding glass doors opened, and a hot breeze blew inside. Ryan looked in that direction. An elderly gentleman plodded across the threshold. He made his way to the desk and spoke softly with the nurse.

How much longer would this take? Not that he minded waiting, but he had work to get to at the church. His sermon wouldn't write itself.

The old man shuffled between the rows of chairs and took a seat nearby. Tears stained his weathered face. Sympathy smote Ryan's heart. Maybe he could help or offer comfort. Ryan placed the gifts on a chair beside him, then scooted toward the gentleman and touched him on the shoulder. "Sir, are you all right?"

The old man lifted teary eyes and shook his head. "I checked on my neighbor this morning, and she was unconscious on the floor. I have a key to her house, see." His gravelly voice cracked as he pulled a key from his pocket and held it up. "I called nine-one-one. The ambulance brought her in. I'm worried about her. I just wanted to see how she was, but they won't tell me because I'm not family."

"What is your neighbor's name?" As a clergy, he could ask.

"Patti Hayes. Do you know her?"

Patti? "I do. She's a member of my church. I'll see what I can find out."

Concern sank like a stone in his stomach. What had happened to Patti? After her husband had died from a heart attack several months ago, the retiree lived alone.

Ryan approached the desk. The nurse raised her head. "I haven't heard anything about Mayor Phillips, Pastor. Sorry."

Ryan shook his head and cleared the lump in his throat. A drop of sweat trickled down his temple. A sense of dread had settled on his shoulders. "This isn't about Kathleen. My congregant, Patti Hayes, was brought in by ambulance. I'm hoping to find out how she's doing."

The nurse typed something on her keyboard. "Yes, Patti Hayes is here."

"Is she all right? What happened?" His pulse thrummed in his neck.

"I don't know. Um, let me ask."

It only took a few minutes for the nurse to return. Her sad expression stilled his heart. "I'm sorry, Pastor Whitestone. Patti Hayes is dead."

13

Crutches pinching her underarms, Kathleen swung through the emergency doors, keeping her booted foot raised behind her, discharge papers in hand. Ryan sat alone by the window with his head propped in his hands. Butterflies fluttered in her stomach. *He waited?*

As she approached, he lifted his head. Tears streaked his cheeks. Goodness, it was only a sprained ankle. "What's wrong with you? I'm fine. I just have to wear this stupid boot for a few weeks." Doctor Zimmerman had said six weeks. Not hardly.

Ryan stood. His knees crackled with the motion. He looked like he'd aged ten years in the past two hours. "It's Patti. Patti Hayes."

She wrinkled her forehead. Patti? Her volunteer coordinator? "What's wrong with Patti?"

"She's dead, Kathleen."

As his words registered in her drug-scrambled brain, Kathleen blinked. "What?" She must have heard him wrong.

"Patti's neighbor found her unconscious on the floor this morning. He called the ambulance. The medics did everything they could, but she was declared dead on arrival."

Kathleen's pulse pounded. Her muscles quivered. "How—how did she die?" Patti had been so kind bringing over the muffins the other morning. And Kathleen had acted so cold. Almost rude. Guilt pressed on her chest. She should have treated Patti better.

"They're not sure yet, but the doctor believes it to be a stress-induced heart attack."

Patti Hayes was the kindest person in Whitman. *And now she's dead.* Did this have something to do with the campaign? Flashbacks slammed through Kathleen's mind. The shooter. The bullet hole in her podium. The realization that someone had tried to murder her. What if Patti had died because of her? Kathleen swallowed and took a deep breath. Things were getting out of hand. Was Joe correct? Was she taking too high a risk?

Kathleen rolled her shoulders back. Until there was proof that Patti's death had anything to do with her political campaign, she shouldn't connect the dots without concrete evidence. Kathleen felt sorry for Patti's family, but life must go on. Once governor, she could memorialize a library or hospital ward in Patti's honor. "Are you ready to go?"

"Yes, I need to get back to the church and call Patti's kids in Boise to give them the bad news. May I help you with anything?"

"No. I've got it." She turned toward the exit. Ryan picked up a bouquet of daisies and a stuffed giraffe from a chair. Was that a Precious Moment? *Please don't let them be for me.* She must be dreaming. Or hallucinating from the pain pills. Would it disappear if she closed her eyes? She lowered her lids, then reopened.

Ryan was eying her oddly, still clutching the giraffe. "Is something wrong?"

"Are those…?" She tipped her chin. *Please say no.*

"I remembered how much you liked daisies and Precious

Moments when we were teenagers."

He made eye contact and wore his heart on his sleeve. Hope shined in his eyes. There was no way to break it to him gently—she didn't want those things. Annie *had* loved them, but Kathleen couldn't stomach the sight.

"Please. Give the gifts to someone else. Anyone else. I don't want them."

They exited the hospital. Shoulders stooped, Ryan dropped the unwanted gifts into the trunk of his Kia, then helped her into the compact SUV. Awkwardness shrouded the ride home. Ryan parked in her driveway, then gave her a hand into the house and upstairs to her bedroom.

She paused. Turned. Ryan's lips pinched together. She'd hurt his feelings. He'd already been upset about Patti, then she'd rejected his roman—no, not romantic—gestures; there was nothing romantic between them. Kindness. Compassion. Those were the right words.

"Look, Ryan, I'm sorry about the gifts. I wasn't trying to be unkind or ungrateful, it's just..." How could she explain without telling him the truth? "I used to love those things, but not anymore. Now, they just..."

Remind her why she wasn't called Annie anymore.

Why she'd completely reinvented herself.

Why she could never be that girl again.

Too many painful memories. Too much... failure. "I don't expect you to understand."

Ryan opened his mouth, then closed it again. He took a deep breath. "Kathleen." Had he been about to call her Annie again? "I wish you would confide in me. I can tell you're hurting. Something happened to you. Why won't you let me in?"

She shook her head. She could never let him into her heart. If he knew the truth, he would hate her. He could never know how weak she truly was.

Paige maneuvered the squeaky buggy down the breakfast cereal aisle. A 1980's power ballad played in the background. Why had she volunteered for this again? Oh, right, because Jessie and Aunt Hattie couldn't decide which one of them should do the shopping. This was easier. Even if it meant squeezing something else into her already bursting schedule. She scanned the shelves loaded with corn, rice, wheat, and sugar-coated varieties. *What kind does Jessie want?*

She dialed Jessie's number, then put the cell phone to her ear. When no one answered, she tried Aunt Hattie.

"Hello? Who is it?" Aunt Hattie's whispered voice traveled through the airwaves.

Paige rolled her eyes and shifted the cell phone to her other ear. "It's Paige. Why are you whispering?"

"I have to be quiet."

What was that about? Never mind. She wouldn't bother asking. "Would you ask Jessie which type of cereal she wants? The list doesn't specify, and there's like two hundred different kinds."

"I can't."

"Why not?" What were those two up to now?

"She's praying again, Paigey. Jessie said to stop interrupting her when she's praying. I'm not sure who she's praying to, though, because she sits on the couch with her eyes closed and doesn't make a sound."

Paige parked her cart next to the boxes of corn flakes and out of the way of another shopper. "She's praying to the Christian God, Aunt Hattie. He hears the prayers of His people wherever they are. Don't bother her now, but when she's finished, will you ask her to call me back?"

"Okay. I can do that. Bye, Paigey."

The line disconnected, leaving Paige standing in the aisle, trying to decide what to do. Should she wait here? Or continue shopping? *I'll come back*. She still had to get yogurt, bread, and eggs.

She put her hands on the cart handle and started forward when the theme song from *Happy Days* played from the phone in her hand. *That was quick.* An unfamiliar number appeared on the screen. *Not Jessie.* Paige put the phone to her ear. "Hello. This is Paige."

"Good afternoon, Paige. This is Pastor Whitestone. Um, Ryan. Your—um, Dad."

Her heart fluttered. *My dad.* Would she ever tire of hearing those words? "Sorry. I didn't recognize the number. How are you?"

"I'm fine, thank you. I'm calling from the church. Anyway, would you meet me at El Bajio's for dinner tonight? We need to talk."

He sounded serious. Was something wrong? "I can do that. What time?" *Dinner with my dad and I get to skip out on a meal with Jessie and Aunt Hattie? Absolutely.*

"How about seven?"

"See you then."

Paige stepped inside El Bajio's a few minutes before seven o'clock. The restaurant was crowded. Was this normal for a weekday? As the host approached the stand, movement near the back of the room grabbed her attention. Her father eagerly waved his arm. *My father. Ryan Whitestone is my father.* She nodded at the host and pointed. "I'm joining someone."

The host grinned. His white teeth stood out against his tan skin. "Sí, señorita. Have a seat."

Giddy with excitement, her legs trembled, and her stomach bubbled. Paige wended between the tables to where her father waited. "Pastor—Ryan. Thanks for inviting me." She tucked loose hair behind her ear. "I'm sorry. I don't really know what to call you." Was it too soon to call him *Dad*?

He stood, shoving his hands into his pockets. "For now, you can call me Ryan. I know it's still a lot to take in. I hope someday you will be able to call me dad." He chuckled. "Dad. I always wanted to be a father."

"You didn't have any other children?" Paige's interest piqued. She slid onto one chair and set her purse on the other beside her.

Ryan returned to his seat and shook his head. "I never married."

"Never?"

He picked up the menu. "Do you know what you want to eat?"

He was avoiding her question. Why hadn't he married? What had happened between him and her mother? "The last time I was here, I had fajitas, but I'm thinking about trying their sour cream enchiladas."

"I'm not a fan of sour cream, but if that's what you want, go ahead." He laid the menu down on the table.

The server approached. "Drinks?"

"Water, please."

Ryan nodded. "Water for me as well."

"Are you ready to order?" The server spoke with a heavy Spanish accent.

Ryan ordered first. "I'll have the El Bajio burrito, and my d—friend would like…" He looked at Paige.

"Sour cream enchiladas, please, and thank you."

The server wrote on his check pad. "One El Bajio burrito and one sour cream enchiladas. We'll have it ready soon." He collected the menus and walked away.

An awkward silence settled. What could they talk about? Should she ask about his work? He was pastor of Whitman Baptist Church. A weight pressed on her chest. Did he know that she'd been a thief? Were there certain expectations for pastors' children? Even adult ones? Would he be disappointed in her?

In her nervousness, she fiddled with the sugar packets, sorting them by color and size. Some of her anxiety eased.

"You remind me so much of your mother. She organized sugar packets, too."

Paige looked at Ryan, opened her mouth, then closed it again. Her thoughts were so mixed up; it seemed impossible to put them into words. What should she say? Thank you? That's nice? She pulled her hands back into her lap. "I can't help it."

"I know."

They grew quiet once again. The server delivered the waters. Ryan took a drink, then set the glass on the corkboard coaster.

"I'm sorry. I don't know what to say." Paige fiddled with her straw.

"I understand. There's so much to talk about—it's difficult to know where to start."

"Exactly." Ryan understood where she was coming from. That was a relief. "What happened between you and my mother?"

He looked down at the carpet and appeared to study an old stain. At long last, he raised his head and made eye contact. "The summer after high school graduation, I visited my grandparents in Texas. They had moved there to get away from Oregon's cold winters. When I returned, I received a phone call from Annie—Kathleen—uh, Mayor Phillips. She was trying to tell me something, but the call dropped. I tried calling back, but no one answered. I left messages. I dropped by the house. All my attempts to contact Annie were thwarted one way or another. We argued the night of her going-away party. She left for college, and I didn't see her again until this year."

Paige let it all sink in. "Did you leave Whitman too?"

"Oh, I…" He scrubbed his hand over his chin. His face flushed again. Was he embarrassed? "I did. I've only been back in Whitman since April."

He was going to explain, right? He didn't. "If Kathleen broke your heart, why did you wait for her?"

Ryan's shoulders raised and lowered as he expelled a breath. "Charity suffereth long."

"I don't know what that means." Paige wrinkled her forehead. Was that from the Bible?

"It means love is patient."

"Oh. What did you do after my mother left? Is that when you went to seminary?"

"Uh, no. Not quite." Ryan shifted and fiddled with the silverware. "I don't like to talk about it, and it's not something I'm ready to share." He cleared his throat, and his skin flushed along his jaw. "I was a foolish young man who allowed emotion to control his actions. I was in rebellion to my parents, and I did a lot of things I'm not proud of."

That was something she could relate to. She'd done a lot of things she wasn't proud of either. Maybe she had more in common with her father than she'd realized.

"When you first came to town, you had your mother's Bible with you. Do you still have it?"

Paige shook her head. "I don't."

"What happened to it?"

"It's gone. I'm sorry. Why do you ask?"

"I considered returning it to Kathleen. I had hoped it might remind her of who she used to be."

What did he mean, who Kathleen used to be? Had she changed that much after Paige was born? "On the phone earlier, you said we needed to talk."

"Yes, we do. Just a minute." He shifted his gaze to something behind her.

The server stepped beside the table with their plates and set them down. Steam rose from each one. Paige took a deep breath—the tantalizing aroma made her mouth water and her stomach grumble.

"Can I get you anything else?"

Ryan looked at Paige, and she shook her head. "Thank you. We're good." The server walked away. "Would you mind if I say grace?"

"Please do." As he started praying, Paige bowed her head. The melodic tones of his voice rose and fell, and she found her heart joining his in giving thanks. She'd never get over the unconditional love that God gave her each day. She used to believe she was unlovable, and that even God himself didn't want someone like her, but He had used her father to show her the truth.

She recalled the Bible verse that had been highlighted in

her mother's Bible. *But God commendeth his love for us in that while we were yet sinners, Christ died for us.* Who had highlighted the verse? Had it been Kathleen?

"In Jesus' name. Amen." Ryan ended his prayer.

Paige raised her head with a soft "amen" of her own. She stuck her fork into her enchiladas and then put a bite into her mouth. *Delicious.* Spicy chicken and creamy sauce danced on her tongue. She dabbed her lips with a paper napkin.

"Kathleen, your mother, stopped by my office the other day."

Paige stuffed another bite into her mouth, then swallowed. "What did she want?"

"She told me not to tell you I'm your father."

Her hand froze on the way to her mouth. "But you already did."

"Yes, and that's what I told her." Ryan took a bite of his burrito. A string of cheese stuck to his chin. He wiped it off with the napkin. "As you can imagine, she was not happy. I broke a promise when I told you. I apologized for betraying her trust but clarified that I want to get to know you."

His words warmed Paige's heart. She wanted to get to know her father, too. They'd missed out on twenty-five years' worth of memories. She didn't want to lose another moment. "What did she say to that? Did she forbid you to see me?"

"No." He picked up his glass and took a long drink. He wouldn't look at her.

"What is it? What's wrong?"

"Paige. There are still some things we have to work out. Unfortunately, we need to limit our contact for the foreseeable future."

He'd mumbled the last sentence, but she'd heard him. Her heart dropped to her toes. She frowned and furrowed her forehead. "Why can't—I mean—I thought…" Tears stung her eyes, and a burning sensation started in her sinuses. How could this be happening? What did her mother say to him? "You just said Kathleen didn't forbid us from spending time together. I don't understand."

Ryan fiddled with his watch, then raised his chin. His gaze captured hers. "This has nothing to do with your mother. I mean, it does, but not in the way you think. Please, hear me out."

She nodded consent, and he continued. "Whitman Baptist Church hired a single man as their pastor. Not a single father. Only the Thorne's and Jessie know about you. Rumors could start."

"Rumors. What…?"

"When I candidated for the church, the pulpit committee was well-aware of some things I did in the past. They were willing to overlook my shortcomings due to their desperation to fill the pulpit as soon as possible. They don't know that I have a daughter. *I* didn't know I had a daughter. I need to speak with the pulpit committee, but I haven't figured out how to do that without bringing your mother into it. I need to tell them the truth, but I'm also trying to respect your mother's wishes. Do you see my dilemma?"

Did she? Maybe. The bite of enchilada in her mouth turned to sawdust. Even her father was more concerned with how people saw him than getting to know his daughter. "Are you embarrassed by me?"

"No, of course not." He reached across the table and took hold of her hand. His thumb rubbed over her knuckles. "I want nothing more than the whole world to know that I am a father. I have a beautiful, intelligent, charming daughter, and I don't care who knows. But God called me to be a pastor, and when I tell the pulpit committee about you, I may…" He took a deep breath. His breath shuttered as he slowly exhaled. "I may lose my job."

Paige chewed on her lower lip. Ryan kept his eyes on his plate. What now? Was this how it would be? Always one more obstacle to prevent Paige from having the family she dreamed of. How could she expect her father to choose her over… God?

Moments later, the silence broke. "Pastor Whitestone, is that you?" A shrill voice called from across the restaurant.

Diners turned as the sound disrupted their dinners. A tall, middle-aged, heavyset woman squeezed between the tables, heading straight toward them.

Ryan's face blanched.

The woman's arm waved like a pinwheel, and her purse swung like a pendulum with the motion. She wore a calf-length gray-checkered smock dress. "I just heard the news. Can you believe it? Poor Patti. A heart attack, my foot! I bet it was all the stress she was under working for Mayor Phillips. A slave driver, she is." The woman's voice carried across the restaurant. Ryan flinched.

Paige scrunched her eyebrows. *What is she talking about? Who's Patti?*

When she paused, Ryan opened his mouth to speak, but she cut in and kept talking. "Have you notified her poor children? Of course, you have. The poor dears. Have they decided on a date for the funeral? Let me know if I can help in any way. You know how I love to arrange meals for loved ones. Did you know Kathleen has to find a new headquarters? Mrs. Keith heard it from Mrs. Nelson herself. The landlords decided not to renew her lease. Good for them, I say."

The woman stopped talking long enough to draw a breath. Her eyes fell on Paige. Her entire face brightened as if she was just now noticing her. "Why, Pastor, I don't believe I've met this young lady before. Will you introduce us?"

14

"In other news, this morning at a press conference at the National Mall, United States Senator Kenneth Chatham of Oregon announced his candidacy for President of the United States. Chatham has served in the Senate since nineteen ninety-six. His first public appearance will be the gala at the Treasury Ballroom in Portland, Oregon this coming Wednesday. Senator Chatham stated his…"

Kathleen turned down the volume and stared at the news anchor on the flat-screen TV. Chatham was running for President? While she had slept, the world had gone mad. She shifted on the leather sofa and winced as pain sliced through her foot propped up on a footstool. Was it time for another dose of pain medicine? She checked her phone lying on the cushion beside her. *Not quite.* Kathleen groaned, laid her head against the back of the couch, and fixed her eyes on the textured spackle on the ceiling of the study.

Chatham for President.

Bile rose in her throat, and her stomach knotted. Dad had

despised the man, but she'd never been told his reasons. He'd simply warned her to stay away from Chatham and to avoid him like the devil himself. He'd claimed the senator was a liar and not to be trusted. Still, the man had attended Dad's funeral and offered his condolences. Was he as evil as Dad had claimed? And if he was, was he fit for the highest office in America?

Kathleen closed her eyes, letting her thoughts drift back in time.

One afternoon, she'd entered this very room, hoping to have a word with Dad. He'd stood, silhouetted by sunlight through the large window. At his side was another gentleman, one she'd never seen before. He'd handed Dad a legal envelope and said, "Here's your proof."

"Kenneth Chatham doesn't stand a chance." Dad had answered.

She took a step closer and stepped on a dog toy left by Dad's bulldog, Hank. The shrill squeal alerted the two men to her presence, and as he turned, Dad hid the envelope behind his back. "Annie, what are you doing in here?" Though she couldn't see his face, his tone rang with displeasure.

"What's that behind your back?"

The other man glared at her, and she stiffened. "You need to leave."

Dad growled then, but not at her. At the other man. "You will not speak to my daughter that way." He looked at her. "But he's right, Annie, you need to leave."

"But—"

"Move along."

She'd left the room then, and over time had forgotten all about that envelope. What had been in it? How had it affected Chatham?

Kathleen sat forward and lowered her leg from the stool. Nerves tingled as the numbness wore off. She pushed from the couch, stumbled toward Dad's massive executive desk, then grabbed the edge and maneuvered around to the armed chair. The computer booted up with a click of a button, bringing a peaceful forest scene to the screen.

Kathleen opened the web browser and typed Kenneth Chatham's name into the search bar of Wikipedia. She scanned the page, stopping when she spotted Dad's name.

Kenneth Chatham ran against Richard Staten and Melvin Carter in the 1992 Oregon Gubernatorial Election. Weeks before the election, Chatham withdrew, even though he held a substantial lead over the other candidates. No specific motive was given.

Kenneth Chatham ran against Dad? *How did I not know this?*

What had made Chatham back down even though he was in the lead? Did Chatham's withdrawal have anything to do with the envelope Dad had been given? Kathleen slouched in the chair, arms at her sides. If it did, did that mean Dad had blackmailed Chatham into quitting the race? *At least Dad hadn't had a member of his campaign committee murdered. Or possibly murdered. The rumor mill was probably already working overtime.* How would the media portray Patti Hayes's death? Blood thrummed in her temples. Would it all point back to her? Would she be held responsible for Patti's death? At least socially? If she were even suspected, what would that do to her campaign? What if Patti's family sued her in court?

"Dad?" She spoke to the vacant chair across from her. "What would you do in a case like this?"

Kathleen waited, but he didn't answer. Not that she'd really expected him to—she didn't put stock in ghost stories, but she ached to hear his advice.

He'd been her hero. She'd spent her life aspiring to be just like him. To make him proud of her. *Do whatever it takes to win, Annie. Whatever it takes.* His deep voice echoed through her thoughts. Sometimes she could still feel the weight of his hand on her shoulder.

Whenever they'd talked politics, Dad would stop what he was doing and listen to whatever she had to say. They'd watched debates on the television, then discussed the pros and cons of each candidates' platform. By the time she was twelve, she knew more about politics than any other subject.

She'd learned how to walk, talk, and stand with confidence. They'd practiced giving speeches, and he had taught her how to remain calm under pressure.

Now he was gone, and she felt so alone. *What can I do to soothe this over?*

She pulled a piece of notepaper from the drawer and penned a letter of condolence to Patti's family. Ryan would have their address. Then, she took out the checkbook. After deliberating only momentarily, Kathleen wrote a five-digit number, then signed the check. She tore it from the book and folded it inside the letter. There. That should satisfy Patti's family. Why should they sue her now?

She drummed her fingernails on the desktop. She picked up her cell phone and dialed Bob Lockhart, the coroner. "Hello, Kathleen. What can I do for you?" Bob's voice came over the line.

"Hi, Bob. I was just wondering what it would take to..."—she paused, looking for the right word— "...expedite the process and allow Patti Hayes's family to bury her as soon as possible."

The other end was silent. Had Bob hung up at her suggestion?

"What do you have in mind?"

Kathleen hung up the phone several minutes later, satisfied with the agreement. It was a win-win, really. Patti's family could have the funeral as soon as they wanted, and no one could accuse her of murder. Guilt gripped her stomach—she hadn't done anything illegal, not really... Doubt plagued her thoughts.

Well, it's too late to take it back. What's done is done. Kathleen shook her shoulders and opened the desk drawer to return the checkbook. A white legal envelope stuck out from under Dad's old address book. *What's this?*

She withdrew the letter and stared at her name scrawled across the front in Dad's handwriting. *What in the world?* She turned it, then slit through the flap with the letter opener. Her pulse raced. Why had he never given this to her while he was alive?

"Mom!" Kylie's voice traveled through the house, carrying a sense of panic with it.

"In here," Kathleen called back. She hid the envelope in the drawer. Pounding footsteps echoed on the stairs. A flash of denim and fluorescent pink passed the doorway, then doubled back. Kylie skidded to a stop and froze at the threshold. Her eyes widened as her gaze landed on the walker boot at the end of Kathleen's leg.

"Mom! What happened?" Kylie paused to catch her breath. Her chest rose and fell rapidly. "One of the nurses came in for coffee this morning and asked how you were doing. I didn't even know you got hurt."

"I'm fine. It's just a sprain."

"Can I get you anything?"

Kathleen shook her head. She braced herself as she stood and hopped back to the couch, flopping onto the cushion like a fish out of water, then used the remote to turn off the TV. She picked up a book, hoping to take her mind off Senator Chatham, Patti Hayes, and the pain in her ankle.

"Mom? Do you have a minute?"

Kathleen lowered her book. Kylie hadn't left? "Do you need something?"

"I need to talk to you." Kylie clasped her hands behind her back and chewed her lip—a nervous trait she'd picked up from Kathleen.

"Is it important?"

Kylie nodded. Kathleen gestured toward the chair opposite the couch. "Have a seat."

Kylie shook her head vehemently.

Dad's study was just another room in their home. *Not Dad's study—it is my study now. Will I ever think of this room as anything but his?* Kylie may not have liked the political side of her grandfather, and he had died in this very room, but she needed to get over it and move on. "I won't talk to you while you stand in the doorway. Come in. Sit down."

"Won't you come out here?"

Kathleen folded her hands in her lap. Kylie was acting ridiculous. "I'm too tired to play these games. If you can't act like—"

"Please," Kylie begged.

With a sigh, Kathleen stood, combed out her hair with her fingers, straightened her clothes, then picked up her phone and dropped it in her pocket. She wouldn't be caught without it again. Fixing the crutches under her arms, she swung a few steps forward.

Kylie blocked the doorway. "May we sit in the kitchen?" She whispered timidly.

Kathleen paused. Their eyes met. Kathleen blew out a breath. *Patience, Kathleen.* Kylie stepped out of the way, and Kathleen headed for the stairs. The going was slow, but she made it down, Kylie at her heels.

Kathleen maneuvered to the kitchen counter, poured herself a cup of coffee from the still-warm pot, then sat at the table, leaning the crutches against the edge. She took a sip of the black liquid. "Hmm,"—her tongue ran over her lips—"what is this all about?" Kylie paced back and forth, wringing her hands. The constant motion made Kathleen seasick. "Sit."

Kylie dropped into the chair across from her, continuing to tear at the skin around her fingernails. "It's about college." She bit her lip. "I don't want to go back."

Didn't want to go back? Had she misheard? Kathleen furrowed her brow, confused. "What do you mean? Do you want to change your major? You won't get into politics without a political science degree."

"I don't want to change my major. I want to quit."

Kathleen pushed away from the table, barely noticing the coffee that spilled over the edge of her mug. "I don't think so. Explain yourself."

Kylie quit picking at her fingers and cracked her knuckles like she was preparing for a wrestling match. "I'm going to quit school. I'm not like you and grandfather. I don't want to be a politician, and I'm old enough to decide for myself. It's my life."

Kathleen's nails bit into her palms. "It's been humiliating enough that you couldn't get into an Ivy League college because of your grades. Now you want to quit altogether? How could you do this?"

Tears brimmed Kylie's eyes. Her shoulders drooped. "Humiliating for you? It's always about you." Her voice quivered.

Kathleen flinched as if struck, but she ignored the guilt that poked at her stomach, and instead crossed her arms. Did Kylie not realize how much pressure she was under? "That's not fair. As mayor of this town and a candidate for governor, the media scrutinizes everything I do and everyone I encounter. My reputation is everything right now."

Kylie popped from her chair. "That's why I don't want to be a politician. I'd like to live my life how I want to and not worry about what everyone else thinks."

Kathleen slowed her breathing—shouting wasn't getting them anywhere. She could at least hear Kylie out… and look for a loophole to talk sense into the girl. "What is it you want to do?" A nurse? A teacher? A police officer? All noble professions and they still required higher education.

Kylie drew herself up to her full height and raised her chin. "I want to be a barista." Her gaze met her mother's as if challenging her to contradict.

A barista? Kathleen's body shook. She clamped her lips together and smirked. Seriously? "There are a million professions out there for you to choose from, and you pick barista? Why don't you do something important?"

"It is important. I've seen people's entire outlook change with a simple cup of coffee."

Kathleen gave an unladylike snort. "Who put this idea into your head?"

"No one. It's what I want to do with my life. Why is that so wrong? If it makes me happy, why is it so important to you that I be something else? I'm old enough to make my own decisions."

"Obviously not. Or you would know better than to throw your life away serving scones." She wasn't having this conversation—Kylie wasn't mature enough to understand—success was critical. Being a barista was *not* success. Working in a coffee shop was not a career option. "You can't quit school. That's final. This conversation is over."

Kathleen stood awkwardly and carried her mug to the sink. The liquid inside had grown cold. She poured the coffee down the drain and left the cup to be washed later. Exhaustion settled in. Flames licked her ankle under the boot—she needed another pain pill as soon as possible.

"Why don't you like Paige?"

Kylie's question sucker-punched Kathleen in the stomach. A heavy silence dropped like barometric pressure in the room. Kathleen struggled to catch her breath. What happened to the oxygen? "E—excuse me?"

Kylie stood in the middle of the kitchen floor, feet apart, arms akimbo. "Why don't you like Paige?"

Kathleen pinched her lips. She didn't have to explain herself. Not to Kylie. It was none of her business. She turned to put her crutches under her arms.

"Is it because she was arrested? She said she was innocent. She didn't rob the pawnshop."

Kathleen paused. "I know she didn't. But that doesn't mean we're going to be BFFs."

"Why not? Maybe you could if you got to know her."

"Kylie. I don't want to get to know her. I have better things to do than—"

"Couldn't you at least try? You don't have any friends."

"I have friends."

"Those are your coworkers and your employees. They don't count."

Kathleen had had enough. "This conversation is over."

"Just one more question?"

Kathleen groaned and pinched her eyes closed. A throb in her forehead joined the pain in her leg. *I can handle one more.* "What is it, Kylie?"

"Would you drop out of the election if I asked?"

Her chest clenched tight, and she was struck speechless. How could she possibly answer that? The cell phone in her pocket vibrated. Relief flooded her. Kylie's question put her between a rock and a hard place, and an unfair one at that. She'd lose either way. Now, she wouldn't have to answer. At least for the moment.

Dad's attorney, Don Wall's name flashed on the screen. "Afternoon, Don."

"The bank released Richard's safety deposit box. I can meet you to sort through it whenever you're available."

Kathleen turned her wrist and checked the time on her watch. "I'm available now." She'd do anything if it got her out of this conversation.

"I can meet you at the bank in a half hour. I'm already in Whitman meeting another client."

"Will do." Kathleen laid her cell phone on the counter. "That was Don Wall, your grandfather's lawyer. The bank has released the safety deposit box."

"Can I come with you?"

Kathleen froze. She couldn't say no. *I can't drive to the bank alone.* Her busted ankle had put a kink in everything. "Fine." As if she really had a choice.

Kylie pulled the car onto the road and turned in the bank's direction. Kathleen stared out the window, avoiding eye contact, hoping Kylie wouldn't bring up the subject of the election again.

"You didn't answer my question yet."

So much for hoping. Kathleen angled to face her daughter's profile. "Kylie…" She started, then stopped. What could she say? Kylie would not like her answer. "Maybe it's best not to talk about it."

Kylie cut her eyes at Kathleen, then faced the road. "You can't just ignore me like that. I want the truth. Would you drop out of the election if I asked?"

The truth? Would she withdraw if Kylie asked? "Kylie, why would you want me to quit? You know this has always been my dream."

"Mother. You're still avoiding the question." Kylie spoke through clenched teeth.

"Kylie Michelle, you've taken this too far."

"Tell me."

"You won't like my answer."

"Tell me."

Kathleen took a deep breath, steeling herself against Kylie's wrath. "I wouldn't withdraw from this election if God himself asked me to."

The next ten minutes were the quietest and longest of Kathleen's life. Kylie parked in the bank's lot and stopped the engine. "Do you want me to come in with you?" She sounded like a whipped puppy.

"No. Wait in the car, please." She couldn't risk Kylie seeing or reading something she shouldn't. She'd let Kylie think it was because she was mad at her. It was better than the truth. If Dad was guilty of blackmail, who knew what he might have kept in that box?

Kathleen fumbled with her crutches, then gathered her purse, and exited the car. The bank lobby was quiet and empty, except for a few clerks behind the counter. Don rose from one of the cushioned armchairs. "What happened to you?"

"Don't ask. Let's just get this over with."

"I'll let the manager know you're here, and we'll get to it."

Several minutes later, Kathleen and Don followed the bank manager to the open vault. Once inside, the two men stuck keys into the locks on box 314 and turned them. The locks popped open, and the manager removed the box from the slot in the wall and carried it to a private room. He set it on the table. "Just let me know when you're finished, and I'll return the box."

"Thank you." Don and Kathleen spoke at the same time. The manager left.

Was she ready for this? Kathleen removed the lid and looked inside—legal documents—ones that Don probably had copies of in his files. Kathleen flipped through the papers. Birth certificates, marriage license, divorce papers, the deed to the mansion. Dad had quitclaimed the house over to her before his death, so it wasn't part of the will. She'd need the deed if she decided to sell before moving to Salem. *If I win, that is.*

She set the documents aside in a neat stack, then turned her attention to the rest of the items. A necklace box, probably belonging to her mother. Should she return it to her?

Kathleen opened the lid. Inside, on blue satin, lay a diamond necklace. Expensive. Exquisite. Was it overlooked in the divorce, or did her father get it as part of his settlement?

She set it on the table, then took out a black film canister. Something rattled. She popped the lid and dumped a roll of plastic film negatives into her hand. *What were the images of? Why keep them locked in a bank vault?* She set them aside with the necklace, then reached back into the box—a key with a card attached by a string. An address was written on the tag. 100 Creek Road. Followed by the numbers 5 28 17. *That's Dad's handwriting.*

"Don." She showed it to the lawyer. "Do you recognize this address?"

"Doesn't ring a bell."

The deposit box sat empty. "I'll take the film, the necklace, and the keys. The rest of this can stay here." She returned the papers and closed the lid, then placed the other items into her purse. "I'm ready."

"I'll let the bank manager know."

Several minutes later, Kathleen put her crutches and purse in the back seat, then slid into the car. Kylie started the engine. "How'd it go?"

"Fine."

"Did you find anything interesting?"

"Not really. Just some boring documents." Lying to her daughter caused a pang in her temples. *It's for the best.*

As Kylie pulled onto the main road, Kathleen thought about the tag. *100 Creek Road.* Was that an Oregon address? Or somewhere else in the country? Was it a residence or business? Why keep the keys in a safety deposit box? What was Dad trying to hide?

15

Ryan pulled his car onto the dirt drive, unloaded the back seat, then stepped through the door of his family's farmhouse. The fresh country air wafted through the open doorway. He took a deep breath and dropped his suitcase on the rustic wood floor with a thud. After he shut the front door, he moved into the kitchen, then unloaded the groceries into the cabinets.

Once the few food staples were stored, he hauled his suitcase into the primary bedroom—the same one his parents had used during his growing-up years. He filled the empty dresser drawers with his clothes—jeans and T-shirts, with not a suit or tie in sight, then tossed his suitcase into the closet with a frustrated grunt.

Like an idiot, he'd been dumbstruck by Mrs. Pendleton's question last night at El Bajio's. *If that was supposed to be a test, Lord, I failed miserably.*

Reagan Pendleton was the biggest gossip in town, second only to her husband, Alexander, the museum curator. Paige had answered in his stead, introducing herself as the new owner of Paige's Second Chance Books, Jessie Faye's old store, The Bookshelf. Paige and Mrs. Pendleton had chatted briefly about their favorite books, then Mrs. Pendleton had moved on, while he sat staring like an owl blinded by headlights. When Paige made no mention of being his daughter, guilt had struck him in the stomach. He should have proudly introduced his beautiful daughter. Instead, he'd cowered and let her do all the talking.

Lord. I'm such a fool. What am I going to do?

His stomach growled. The grandfather clock in the hall struck noon. This would be his last meal for the next twelve hours. Prayer and fasting were two of his objectives for the next few days. Ryan returned to the kitchen to warm a frozen sandwich, unwrapping the plastic and sticking it in the microwave.

What did God want him to do about Paige? About Annie? Would she give him another chance? He'd shot himself in the foot with the daisies and giraffe, but he'd never expected her to outright reject his gifts? But then again, should he really be surprised? His forehead tightened. *There was something strange in her reaction, though, like her revulsion had nothing to do with me. What changed her so much that even her likes and dislikes are altered?*

Thinking about his time at the hospital yesterday with Annie brought his thoughts around to Patti Hayes. *Poor Patti.*

He shook his head. *No, not poor Patti.* Patti Hayes was strolling the streets of glory with her beloved husband, but her family's grief weighed on Ryan's shoulders. It had not been an easy phone call to make. Their suffering was like a knife to his heart, and losing a congregant hurt like losing a member of his own family.

With a sigh, he pushed away from the counter, then took his Bible, notebook, and pen, and sat on the couch. The springs squeaked. He set his stuff on the cushion beside him, then turned and knelt on the floor. The hardwood bothered his knees, but he ignored the discomfort. *Dear God. I'm so confused. What do you want me to do? How do I honor your calling in my life? I'm just a man with human emotions and desires. I'm so tired of living alone. But I don't know how to move on without Annie. I still love her.*

And what do I do about Paige? I love my daughter, and I want her in my life. I don't want to drive Annie away or ruin any chance we have of being together, but I don't want to choose between them.

And what's going to happen when I tell the pulpit committee I have a daughter? I can't expect them to overlook this. They were so gracious to forgive my other mistakes. They trusted me, and I gave them my word. But how can I choose my position as a pastor over my daughter?

The microwave beeped.

A groan slipped from his lips. Warm tears stung his eyes. He bent forward, pressing his face against the cool wood floor. He pounded his fist against the boards. *Help me!*

After he prayed for a while and his knees ached from kneeling, he moved to sit on the couch, then picked up his large Bible and opened it to the book of Proverbs. *Maybe Solomon will impart some of his wisdom on my befuddled brain.*

Beads of sweat dripped down his cheek. The farmhouse didn't have an A/C unit, and the room had grown warm in the afternoon sun. Ryan stood, stretched his sore legs, opened a window, and went into the kitchen to pour a glass of water. His gaze stopped on the microwave. His lunch—he'd forgotten about it. He opened the microwave door. The sandwich had grown cold, and the cheese congealed. Not appetizing at all. He took the sandwich from the microwave and dropped it into the garbage.

Through the open window, the tinkling sound of a wind chime and the wind whistling through the tree branches caught his attention. A cloud moved across the sun, casting a shadow over the backyard. A bluebird landed on the porch railing with a worm hanging from his beak.

He left the house through the back door. As the screen snapped behind him, his mother's voice echoed in his memories. "Don't let that door slam." A smile raised his lips. This had been his parent's home until they moved to Texas to take care of his grandparents back in March. He kept an apartment in town to be close to the church but loved coming out to the old place whenever he needed a getaway.

The farm stood secluded beyond a row of trees and was bordered by the Little Hurricane Creek. To the east, the former wheat fields had been reclaimed by the land. A large barn, now empty, stood at the back of the property surrounded by a split rail fence. As he headed toward it, he kicked his boots through the overgrown grass. As he came to the paddock fence, he leaned forward, propped one foot on the lower rung, and crossed his arms over the top.

The years melted away, and the pasture was once again filled with the lowing of Mom's prize-winning bulls. A teenaged Annie appeared behind him, and with one hop, she perched on the top rail, wearing jean overalls with one strap unbuttoned. Her hair was pulled up into a ponytail on top of her head. She held a piece of paper in her hand so tightly, the edge crumpled under her fingers. "I finished a new song yesterday."

He picked a daisy from the grass and tucked it behind her ear. "Yeah? You gonna sing it for me."

Annie's cheeks flushed, and she ducked her head against her shoulder. "I don't know."

"Please."

Annie's soft soprano voice had descended over the farm like spring rain. He'd never forget the beauty of it.

"No matter who I am. No matter what I've done. Your mercy calls for me to find you there. Your grace is ever new. Your love is ever true. Who am I, but what you see in me? I'm forgiven. Forgiven again."

As the memories faded and his thoughts returned to the present, Ryan dropped his foot from the fence rail to the ground. The Holy Spirit nudged his heart. Did he still have his copy somewhere?

Ryan eyed the barn on the other side of the paddock. His mom hadn't had animals in years. Last he'd heard, his parents used it for storage. Maybe Annie's sheet music was in there.

He strolled across the open area to the massive barn

doors. He pulled on the handle, and they opened. Not even locked. Apparently, there was nothing of value left inside. The smell of must, hay, and animal slapped him in the face, and he coughed. A layer of dirt and straw littered the cement flooring. Sunlight streamed through the upper window, highlighting dust mites in the air.

He surveyed the metal shelving units that lined the walls—loaded with dust-coated boxes, sleeping bags, an old fish tank, and a plastic potty chair. The cardboard boxes were well-labeled. His own name, written in black permanent marker, caught his attention. Might as well start looking there.

He crossed the barn and took the box from the shelf, then tore off the packing tape and opened the flaps. The papers on top looked like old school papers. This was going to take a while.

Ryan stepped back and canvassed the old place. An idea formed in his head. What was it Mrs. Pendleton had said? Kathleen needed to find a new home for her campaign headquarters.

What would work better than a big empty barn? There was plenty of room. It needed some cleaning, but if he got help, it wouldn't take long. Besides, it might be a good chance for him and Paige to spend some quality time together. His heart suddenly felt lighter than it had in days.

"I had dinner with my dad last night." Paige tried hard to keep her voice from drooping, but confusion and hurt seeped into her words.

Hamilton raised an eyebrow. "That's a good thing, right?" He took a drink of his coffee from the ceramic mug, then set it on the table. The Red Rooster Café special sat half-eaten on the plate in front of him.

Paige shrugged. "I honestly don't know right now." She pushed her spoon around aimlessly in her bowl of soup. Her heart weighed heavily after Ryan's revelation. What would he decide to do? It wasn't right for him to deceive the pulpit committee, but he might lose his job if he told them the truth.

As much as she longed to be a part of her father's life, she didn't want him to lose his position as pastor of the church. And what would Kathleen say when she found out? Should they go through with informing the committee without concern for Kathleen? Was she unfair to even ask this of them? Should her political designs play any part in their decisions? "He said we have to limit our contact."

Hamilton leaned against the back of the booth and furrowed his brow. "What? Why?"

"The pulpit committee doesn't know I exist."

"I'm not following."

"When he was hired as the pastor, they didn't know he had a—" she swallowed— "non-marital child. He thinks if he tells them about me, he'll lose his job."

A garbled voice came over the radio on Hamilton's belt.

"Do you need to go?"

Hamilton shook his head. "It's fine." He dipped a bite of meatloaf in the mashed potatoes, then stuck it in his mouth. "You're concerned that he might choose his career over you just like your mother has?"

Tears formed in her eyes. That's exactly how she felt, but she hadn't been able to put it into words. What if her father decided that being a pastor was more important? Would he ask her to keep their relationship a permanent secret? What if he decided she wasn't worth the risk?

Hamilton took her hands and squeezed. "Pastor Whitestone—your father—is a wise man. He'll do the right thing. Trust him. And trust your Heavenly Father. Doesn't He know what's best for you?"

Paige cracked a smile and wiped her tears. "Thanks, I needed that. I love you."

"I love you too." He stood, leaned over, and kissed her on the cheek. "Wish I could stay, but I need to head back to the station."

"I understand."

He picked up the bill, carried it to the cashier, paid for their lunch, then left. Paige watched as he climbed into the patrol unit and drove away. She turned her attention back to her bowl of soup and took one bite and grimaced. Cold. Pushing it aside, she took her phone from her pocket and opened the note she'd left herself.

"False face must hide what the false heart doth know," Paige muttered the phrase. She'd been contemplating the odd message since yesterday. Did the sender intend for this to fall into Kylie's hands, or was it meant for someone else in the headquarters? Did it have something to do with the election? Was it about Kathleen and herself? Or was Kathleen keeping other secrets?

Maybe I am way off base. Perhaps it had nothing to do with Paige or Kathleen. But if that was the case, why give the note to Kylie Phillips?

"Are you in conference? Or is this seat open?"

Paige jolted, then looked into the face of the actress Dawn Winters. Nori had been right. They did look a lot alike. "I was talking to myself. You're welcome to sit there." Her melancholy turned to giddiness. *A famous actress is sitting at my table!*

"Is this something you frequently do? Talk to yourself, I mean?" The elegant woman glided onto the bench, setting her drink on the table. The dark liquid in her glass smelled like root beer—Paige's favorite pop. She wore a bright orange floral scarf on her head, and sunglasses hung on the collar of her blouse.

"Only when I need expert advice."

How foolish Paige had felt the other day in the bookstore when she'd discovered she'd been wearing her name tag. Maybe the woman wasn't as mysterious as she seemed, but why had she been staring at Paige and Kylie in the Rustic Cup? And why had she fled the moment they made eye contact? Was it possible it was all in Paige's imagination?

"I know who you are." Dawn paused. A beat passed.

What does she mean by that?

"You own the bookstore, Paige's Second Chance Books. Well, I assume you are the owner since you share the same name. Is the bookstore your second chance, or is that simply a witty play-on-words because you sell used books?"

Paige squirmed. What a strange question. Was Ms. Winters prying into her personal life? Or innocently curious about the name? Paige chose not to answer the question. "What brings *you* to our town? Have you visited before? Do you have family in the area?"

As pink splotches formed behind the woman's jaws, she lowered her eyes, then picked up her glass and took a long drink. When she finished, she set down the glass and dabbed her lips with a napkin. "What were you mumbling to yourself?"

The evasive move piqued Paige's curiosity. "A line from *Macbeth*."

"I'm familiar with the play. What line?"

"False face must hide what false heart doth know."

The woman reclined against the back of the booth, running long fingers through her silvery hair. "I remember that one. Any particular reason you're contemplating *that* line?"

Paige eyed the woman across from her. Could she trust her with the information? The woman, while a celebrity, was still a stranger. "No reason. I just like Shakespeare."

"So do I. It's what first sparked my interest in the theater."

"So, what is a celebrity like you doing in a Podunk town like Whitman?"

The stranger searched Paige's eyes, then as a sad smile tilted her full lips, she touched Paige's cheek. Their eyes locked. Goosebumps prickled Paige's skin. Ms. Winters dropped her hand, slipped from the bench, and left the restaurant.

That was creepy. Why did she do that?

16

Paige left the cafe and returned to the bookstore, intending to research Ms. Dawn Winters, but when she stepped inside, chaos greeted her. Preschoolers ran amok. Books flew from the shelves and lay sprawled across the floor like dying soldiers. The children screamed, hollered, and chased each other in circles. Where had all these kids come from?

"What is going on?" Paige called over the noise.

Frazzled, Nori looked ready to pull her hair out. "You remember those posters announcing a preschool storytime."

"Yes." Paige had hoped a storytime would introduce the bookstore to a younger clientele.

Without a word, Nori swept her hand around the room.

Paige's mouth dropped. "What? So many?" Where were the parents? She scanned the room—no adult in sight. This was storytime, not a babysitting service. She'd intended for parents to remain inside the building, not run errands or grab a coffee break.

"Yep." Nori ducked behind the cash register. "Have fun."

With a sigh, Paige brushed her hair back, straightened her shoulders, and rushed to corral the children.

By the time the last child had been picked up, Paige was exhausted. As she surveyed the shambles, her shoulders sank. What a mess! A hand touched her shoulder. Paige turned to face Nori.

"I'll stay and help you clean up."

"I appreciate the offer, but I've got it. Thank you for your help. I couldn't have done it without you."

"You're welcome." Nori disappeared into the office in the back, then returned with her purse over her shoulder. She glanced around the battlefield and gave Paige a sad smile. "Are you sure you don't want me to stay?"

"I can't ask you to do that. You've already worked past your shift."

Nori shrugged. "I've got nothing else going on."

"OK. Thank you. If you don't mind starting down here, I'll check the mayhem in the loft."

Nori nodded, setting her purse on the checkout desk. Paige jogged up the stairs and surveyed the area. Not as bad as she expected. Most of the children must have stayed downstairs. It could still use a quick pick up, then she'd help Nori.

As Paige moved around the area, she spotted something sticking up between the cushions of one of the lounge chairs. She pulled it out and turned the thumb-sized stick in her fingers. *A flash drive?*

The USB was green on one side and yellow on the other, and the metal cover was stamped with the word, Oregon. *Someone's a Ducks fan.*

She cast a glance around the loft, even though she knew there was no one remaining in the store. *Who left this?* Paige wrinkled her brow and bit her lip. Would someone return for it? She tucked the drive into her pocket, then finished straightening up.

When she was done, Paige looked over the rail. Nori worked in the children's section on her hands and knees, scrubbing cupcake icing from the carpet threads. Maybe Nori knew who the drive belonged to?

Paige jogged down the stairs and reached Nori's side just as she stood, rag full of vanilla cake and blue frosting. Paige pulled the flash drive from her pocket and held it up. "Did you see anyone using this in one of our computers today?"

Nori shook her head and headed for the sink in the bathroom. Paige followed.

"No, I don't think so." Nori left the door open while she washed out the rag. "Did someone lose it?"

"Seems like it. I found it stuck in the cushion upstairs."

Nori twisted the cloth. Water dripped into the sink. "That's too bad. Hopefully, they'll come back looking for it."

Paige looked at the drive. Should she toss it in the lost and found or check it for clues to the owner's identity?

Nori cleared her throat. Paige raised her chin. "Don't tell me you're thinking of sticking that thing into your computer?"

"Why not?"

"I read an article about hackers leaving flash drives around loaded with viruses. People put them into their computers and end up with a virus." Nori gestured toward the device. "That could be one of those."

Really? How accurate was the information Nori had read? Would Paige be putting their system at risk if she examined the drive? Maybe it would be better to put it with the rest of the lost and found and hope the owner turned up. However, if this wasn't a virus and instead contained critical files, she shouldn't just leave it out in the open.

I'll put it somewhere safe until the owner shows up. Paige carried the drive back to her office, stowed it in a desk drawer, and locked it with the key on her keyring. It would be just as easy to get it from her desk when asked, as it would be to dig through the overflowing lost and found. When she returned to the front, Nori was slinging her purse strap over her shoulder. "Headed out?"

"I'll come in early and finish cleaning before we open. My

mom just texted. I forgot I was supposed to be having dinner with her tonight." Nori headed for the front door.

Paige locked it behind her, then turned and surveyed the remaining mess. She cracked her knuckles and went back to work.

An hour later, Paige walked through the front door of the bungalow and discovered she'd gone from screaming preschoolers to screaming octogenarians. Jessie and Aunt Hattie stood nose to nose in the middle of the living room. Paige tossed her purse in the closet and hung her keys on the wall rack. What were those two fighting about now?

Gerald caught sight of her. "Paige home." He squawked. The two women didn't seem to notice.

Jessie scowled and pursued her lips. "Why are you so loud? Can't you do anything without making so much noise?"

Aunt Hattie was quick to defend herself. "I have to make noise. You're too quiet. It's creepy."

"It's not creepy. It's peaceful. All you do is talk. You and that parrot." Jessie pointed at Gerald.

"Talk. Talk." Gerald mimicked and whistled.

Paige put her hand to her lips. *Silly bird.* She edged closer to the couch and cleared her throat. Both women jumped, clutching their chests.

"Paige. I didn't see you. When did you get here?" Jessie spoke first.

"Just a few minutes ago."

"Hello, Paigey." Aunt Hattie kissed her on the cheek. "Did you have a good day?" She looked like a child caught with hands in the cookie jar.

Nice try. "What are you two fighting about?"

Aunt Hattie pooched out her lower lip. "Jessie says I'm loud, and I talk too much."

You are loud. Paige would never say that to her aunt's face. But Hattie McDonald had a flamboyant personality, and Jessie was her complete opposite.

Jessie folded her arms. "She *is* loud. And she talks too much. I like my peace and quiet. It's refreshing, and it allows me to pray without ceasing."

Aunt Hattie rolled her eyes. "I may be loud, but at least I don't talk to invisible beings."

"He may be invisible, but at least He listens when I talk to Him."

This is getting interesting. What went on in this house today? Paige ignored the sudden urge to pop a bag of popcorn.

"I'm sorry I didn't get you a new roll of toilet paper. I couldn't hear you over the TV." Aunt Hattie pointed to her ears.

Toilet paper? Oh boy.

"That's another thing. I can't abide daytime television. The Dumb and the Senseless has to be the worst show ever made."

"It is not. It's better than that music you play on iGlow Radio. It puts me to sleep."

"My music is soothing. You wouldn't be so tired if you opened the curtains and let the sunshine in." To make her point, Jessie grabbed the curtain and yanked it back. The evening sunlight streamed through the glass.

Aunt Hattie covered her eyes and howled. "I'm melting. I'm melting. What a world." She sagged toward the floor, imitating the Wicked Witch of the West.

Paige couldn't hold back any longer. Laughter bubbled from her chest. "Aunt Hattie, water melted the Wicked Witch, not sunlight."

"Oh, all right." Aunt Hattie straightened, then flopped onto the couch with an audible exhale. "I'll try to be quieter."

Good for you. Aunt Hattie was extending the proverbial olive branch. Paige looked at Jessie, whose chest raised, then lowered.

"I appreciate that. I'll try to not let things bother me so much."

"There. That's better." *Crisis averted.* Paige's stomach grumbled. "What's for dinner?" The doorbell chimed. "Are you expecting anyone?"

Aunt Hattie shook her head. "Not me."

"Me either. Go. See what they want."

Paige opened the front door. A man wearing an expensive three-piece suit and sunglasses stood on the porch. He shoved a manila envelope in her direction. Paige took it. "Thank—"

Without a word, the man spun on his heel and left. He jumped into a black sedan stopped along the curb, then drove away. *Strange. What is this?* Paige closed the door and turned the envelope in her hands. The outside was blank. Who sent it? The sender obviously intended for one of them to open it. Who was it for?

"Who was that, Paigey?" Aunt Hattie's voice broke into her stupor.

Paige shook her head. Blinked. "I don't know. He didn't say."

Jessie narrowed her eyes. "Something doesn't seem right about this. I don't think you should open it. We should call the police."

Aunt Hattie paled. Her hands clapped over her mouth. "Do you think it's dangerous? What if it contains anthrax or something?"

Paige picked at the clasp with her fingernail. She could at least peek inside before bothering the authorities. What if it were nothing and she got the police involved over something silly? She opened the clasp and slid her finger under the flap to break the glue.

"Be careful, Paigey."

Paige pulled out a single sheet of paper. *That's it? No puff of powder. No flashing light or ticking. See, nothing to be afraid of.*

As she set the envelope on the coffee table, then scanned the short note, a knot formed in her throat. Blood drained from her face leaving her dizzy and nauseous.

"What is it, Paigey? Anthrax?"

"No, it's not anthrax. It's a quote from one of Shakespeare's plays."

All the world's a stage, And all the men and women merely players; They have their exits and their entrances, And one man in his time plays many parts.

17

Patti's funeral, Friday morning, had drained Kathleen of every bit of her energy. The looks. The whispers. She knew what they were thinking—this was all her fault. Well, it wasn't. She'd had nothing to do with Patti's death. Patti Hayes couldn't be dead because of her.

Kathleen kicked off her one dress shoe and sent it sailing across the foyer. It hit the wall and bounced back. How ridiculous she'd looked with only one pump. This boot was a nail in her tire in every way. But the hospital had called first thing this morning to let her know her scooter had come in—something to be thankful for. She would never have made it across the cemetery's water-logged grass with her crutches. She picked up the shoe and returned it to the shoe rack.

Kylie moved past her and headed for the stairs. "I'm going to change my clothes."

"Kylie. Wait. We need to talk."

Without a word, Kylie skittered up the stairs like a frightened mouse. Kathleen shook her head and removed her suit jacket with a sigh. Was she still mad because Kathleen wouldn't let her quit college? Or about Kathleen's answer to Kylie's question about withdrawing from the election? If that were the case, Kylie could pity party until the cows came home. Kathleen wasn't going to change her mind.

Why didn't Kylie want to follow in her footsteps? Being a civil leader or even a politician was satisfying work. A person in a position of authority could make a real difference in the world. But if Kylie didn't want to go into politics, as much as it would pain Kathleen, she'd allow her daughter to change her major. However, no child of hers would make a living serving coffee.

Kathleen's mouth watered at the thought of coffee. A mug of liquid caffeine was just the shot in the arm she needed to face the rest of the day. "I'm making coffee if you want some," she called. Maybe that would lure her daughter downstairs.

Not waiting for an answer, Kathleen wheeled her scooter down the hall to the kitchen. The aroma of Matilda's Columbian Chili Con Carne heating in the slow cooker permeated the room. She rolled to the counter where the coffee maker waited to work its magic. Kathleen paused. A manila envelope lay on the counter next to the appliance. Where had that come from? Had it been there when she'd left for the funeral this morning?

Kathleen picked it up. No name on the front. She shrugged and picked at the metal clasp with her fingernail until it opened, then she pulled out a single sheet of paper. Her gaze traveled over the lyrics and notes on the page. Memories flooded her mind, drawing her into the living room where she found herself seated on the rickety old piano bench.

Her fingers glided over the ivory keys. The words slipped through her lips, fragile and broken at first, but gaining strength with each phrase. When she came to the chorus, the soprano timbre of her voice rose and fell. The music filled the house with a long-forgotten melody.

"…No matter who I am. No matter what I've done. Your mercy calls for me to find you there. Your grace is ever new. Your love is ever true. Who am I, but what you see in me? I'm forgiven. Forgiven again."

As the last notes floated from her lips, the song came to an end. Her hands slid from the keys and lay tangled in her lap. She'd forgotten this song—penned by her own hand. She'd written it as a teenager back when God had felt so close. How long had it been since she'd felt that way? He seemed so far out of reach. The words she'd written floated through her thoughts.

No matter who I am. No matter what I've done. Kathleen had believed it then, but not anymore. How could God forgive her? She couldn't even forgive herself.

Who am I, but what you see in me? What did God see in her? Nothing. How could He? He hadn't paid attention to her in a long time. If He had, He never would have let those things happen to her. She'd disappointed Him, just like she had her father, and neither of them could stand the sight of her after that. She'd had to pull herself up by her bootstraps or fail miserably. God didn't get a say in her life. Not anymore.

If He didn't want anything to do with her, she didn't need Him. She was strong enough to handle it all herself. He'd see. She'd show them all. God, Dad, Lionel…

Kathleen glanced at the sheet music. Where had it come from, and how did it get in her house? She'd thought she'd trashed the only copy a long time ago.

A sniffling noise came from the doorway. Kathleen turned. Kylie stood at the threshold to the living room, wearing shorts and a T-shirt, tears glistening in her eyes. "Kylie." How long had she been standing there? How much had she heard?

"I didn't know you could sing. Or play the piano. I thought it was just a decoration. I've never heard anything so beautiful. What song was that? I haven't heard it before."

"And you won't again. At least not from me." Kathleen snatched the sheet music off the piano and crumbled it in her fist, then dropped it into the wastebasket as she passed. That part of her life was long gone. The girl she'd once been wasn't ever coming back.

Ryan swept the dust and straw remnants from the barn floor into the dustpan that Paige held against the cement. "I appreciate you girls helping me with this. We'll get it cleaned up a lot faster this way."

"No, problem. It's kind of fun."

Ryan smiled down at his daughter. She tilted her head and smiled back. His heart skipped a beat—his little girl had her mother's smile.

"Look what I found," Kylie called from across the barn.

"What is it?" Ryan helped Paige to her feet. She dumped the dustpan contents into the metal barrel and leaned the pan against the side. They walked together to where Kylie had opened a cardboard box.

"It looks like some kind of scrapbook." Kylie pulled a red binder from the box and handed it to Ryan.

"I'm surprised Mom didn't take that with her when she moved to Texas." He opened the book. "It *is* a scrapbook." As he turned the pages, memories flashed through his mind. "I remember this." He rotated the book so the girls could see the photo. He pointed at a chubby girl with brown pigtails, wearing a T-shirt with colorful bears on the front. "That's your mom, P—Kylie." He caught himself before it was too late. "These photos are from Vacation Bible School." He made eye contact with Paige over the book. She knew what he'd almost done.

Kylie was too busy looking at the photo to notice. Her mouth dropped open. She snapped her jaw shut, then spoke. "My mom went to VBS at our church?"

Ryan frowned. Kylie didn't know her mom had gone to church? Did she know her mom was a believer? Why hadn't Annie told her daughter? "Your Mom and her brother attended church every Sunday when they were growing up. Your grandfather wouldn't come with them, but the bus picked them up every week." *It's how she and I met.* He wanted to add, but better to leave that part out.

Kylie pulled the scrapbook closer and turned the page. She rubbed her finger over a smiling Annie holding a certificate for memorizing the most verses during the week. "I had no idea. She hasn't been to church for as long as I can remember."

"An—Kathleen was a devoted Christian back then. She loved the Lord and even wrote songs to express how much He meant to her."

Kylie's eyes widened. "Mom used to write songs? I wonder if she wrote the one she was singing this morning."

"Kathleen was singing?" He could hear the surprise in Paige's voice. "What was she singing?"

Kylie closed the scrapbook and handed it back to Ryan.

"I came downstairs after changing from the funeral, and she was sitting at the piano and singing a song I'd never heard before. I only caught the end of it, but it was so beautiful."

A smile quirked the corner of Ryan's mouth. *So, she got the song. And apparently had sung it.*

"But when I asked her about it, she threw it in the garbage and said something about never hearing it again. It made me sad. She played and sang so beautifully. I didn't even know she could do that."

A pang struck Ryan in the chest. Annie had thrown the music in the trash? Good thing he'd made a copy before dropping off the other with Matilda on his way to Patti's funeral.

Why had she thrown it away? Were the memories that painful for her? Ryan swallowed. He'd thought she was avoiding church because of him, not that she'd given up on God altogether. Somewhere along the way, Annie had lost her faith. But why?

"Kylie, when did you start attending church?" Paige asked.

"I'd never been to a church service before my dad died. But I'm not sure he would have let us even if Mom had wanted to. When we moved to Whitman, I started attending with my grandfather."

Ryan's curiosity was piqued. Richard Staten had had no interest in church back when Annie and Ryan were growing up. Ryan had been bowled over when he'd discovered Richard had become a Christian during the last couple of years before his death. "I was surprised when I heard Richard Staten was going to church. When did that happen?"

"I don't know. Maybe right before we moved. Or maybe after. I don't remember. Grandfather had cancer—that's why we moved here. It was hard to leave my school and my friends and come live with a stranger. I'd never even met him before that."

So, Annie hadn't come back to Whitman—even for a visit. Not until her father's diagnosis with cancer.

"Why is that?" Paige asked.

Kylie shrugged. "I don't think my mom and her dad got along very well. I mean, they were always arguing about something. They stopped whenever I came into the room, but I think it had to do with something that happened a long time ago."

Had they been arguing about Paige? Richard obviously had never told Annie what he'd done with her baby, or she wouldn't have been so shocked to learn her newborn had been abandoned. When Richard became a Christian, why didn't he tell her the truth? Why did he continue to lie to her? What kept Annie and Richard apart all those years? *Was he so angry with her—with us—that he didn't talk to his daughter for twenty years?* Why was Annie then willing to move back to Whitman?

So many unanswered questions.

"How did Mom hurt her foot?"

Ryan's thoughts jerked back to the present—Kylie was talking to him. He swallowed. "What did your mother tell you?"

"She avoided the question when I asked. I think she's

hiding something from me. I know someone gave her sleeping pills, and I know someone tried to shoot her at the debate..." Kylie's words hung thick like fog. "Do you know why I want to quit college?" The conversation jumped subjects in true Kylie fashion. "I don't want to be like her."

Ryan squeezed the teen's shoulder. "She's just trying to protect you. She wants what's best for you."

"Everyone thinks I'm naive and need protecting." Kylie held up her pointer finger—it bent at an awkward angle. "My father broke it. I know there are bad people in this world."

Ryan swallowed. He hadn't noticed Kylie's finger before. "I'm so sorry, Kylie. No one should..."

Kylie cut him off with a shake of her head. Tears brimmed her eyes. "Just tell me how Mom hurt her foot. You took her to the hospital. I know you know."

It was wrong of Kathleen to keep the truth from Kylie, but was it really his place to tell her? "Kylie, you should ask your mom?"

"Please, tell me the truth. I know Mom's lying to me."

"Someone tried to run her over while she was jogging. She jumped out of the way but twisted her ankle in the process."

Paige gasped, and a sob escaped Kylie's lips. Paige dropped her arm around Kylie's shoulders and brushed her hair behind her ear. Kylie sniffled. "Did Patti Hayes really die of a heart attack?"

Ryan shrugged. "We can only assume that's the case. I'm sure the police looked into it, and if that's the official cause of death, then..."

Assume was right. Doubt niggled Ryan's thoughts. *Could someone have killed Patti?*

He'd officiated the service. The chapel had been packed with those wanting to say their last goodbyes and support the family. Patti was loved by everyone who met her. She was the kindest, most generous woman he had known. Why would anyone want to kill her? And how could they have induced a heart attack and it not be picked up on a tox screen? Had the coroner done a tox screen? They may never know the truth. And he knew better than anyone to let God be the judge.

"I have a hard time believing my mom ever believed in God. You know what she told me the other day, she said she wouldn't drop out of the election even if God asked her to."

Harsh.

The two girls moved toward the entrance, but Ryan stayed back. His hand rested on top of the scrapbook. *What happened to you, Annie? How did you get like this?*

18

The grandfather clock in the hall chimed six times. *How did it get to be so late?* She'd lost track of time. Kathleen shifted in the chair, the back of her legs sticking to the leather cushion. She removed her glasses, rubbed her tired eyes, then put her glasses back on. She had temporarily moved her office to the study in her home. Stacks of papers and manila folders covered Dad's massive executive desk. *My desk—it is my desk now.*

Dennis worked at a makeshift desk in the attached meeting room. He kept the door between them closed and maintained a proper distance when he entered her space.

She stretched. Her ankle ached. It had been long enough. She could take another dose of medicine. She took two pills from the bottle on the corner of the desk with a drink from her water glass. At least, the pain would lessen soon.

Kathleen pushed the files aside, then picked up the jewelry case from the desk. She opened the lid and ran her fingers over the diamond necklace. She'd need to keep it somewhere safe until she could decide what to do with it; leaving it out in the open wasn't an ideal plan. She snapped the lid closed, then carried the necklace to the safe, put in the combination, then set the case inside, and closed the door. After returning to her chair, Kathleen added the strange key to her keyring. She'd given Dennis the address tag earlier to see what he could find out about the location of the address. She then picked up the film canister, opened the lid, and dumped the roll of negatives into her palm. *What are these photos of?*

She unrolled one of the strips and held it in the light. The background was dark like it had been taken outside in the bright sunlight. Three people stood in the foreground. Two of the men shook hands. Several wore long tunics and head coverings. *Odd.* She didn't recognize anyone in the photos. Why did Dad have them? When were they taken?

Kathleen rolled them back up, returned them to the canister, then tossed the whole thing into the desk drawer.

The door creaked. Dennis stepped inside, carrying a bouquet of wild roses. Her favorite. How did he know? Her heart skipped, and her mouth dropped open. She slammed it shut before he noticed. "Are those for me?"

Dennis nodded. "Yes, ma'am. They just arrived." He set them on the desk.

Arrived? So, they weren't from Dennis but delivered. Kathleen stared at the bouquet. "Who sent them?"

"I'm sorry, ma'am. I don't know."

Didn't look like the sender had included a card. She caressed one of the soft petals. *They are beautiful, that's for sure.* She touched the stem. A thorn punctured her finger—a droplet of blood formed on the surface of her skin. Maybe that was why she liked roses; they reminded her of herself. Thorns kept people from getting too close.

"If that's everything, I'm going to head home."

Kathleen jerked. "What? Did you say something?"

Dennis cleared his throat and straightened his tie. "I'm going home unless you need me for anything else. Do—do you need me for anything else?"

"Did you find out anything about that address?"

"No, ma'am. It's a widespread address, so I'm not sure if this particular location is in Oregon or another state. I'll keep working on it tomorrow. Good night, ma'am."

"Good night. And thanks for working here at the house. It's easier for me than trying to come into the office with this bum leg." She gave the plastic boot a tap.

"Of course, Mayor Phillips. Whatever you need."

The study door closed behind him. Kathleen propped her chin into her hand and stared at the roses. Who could have sent them? Ryan?

No. Ryan had tried to give her daisies at the hospital. He still thought of her as the teenager she'd been. With a sigh, she tore her gaze from the bouquet, opened the internet browser, and logged into her social media account. She set up the live video like she'd done once a week since the beginning of her campaign.

Within seconds, several thousand viewers had hopped on. "Good evening, my fellow Oregonians. Kathleen Phillips here, your candidate for governor. November is only a few months away. Remember—a vote for Phillips is a vote for family. I want to do my best to put *your* family first. Let's take some questions."

The comment line scrolled with questions and comments. Not all of them were polite.

"Here's a good question from LlamaLover2000. It reads, 'Ms. Phillips, what is your position on tax breaks for farmers? Are you for or against?'"

Before she could answer, her computer dinged, and a message popped up in the private chatbox.

WHAT WOULD YOU KNOW ABOUT FAMILY?

The user's name was simply a nondescript collection of random letters and numbers. And no photo.

Kathleen swallowed. *Who is this?* She kept a smile pasted on her face and began speaking about her desire to lend aid to Oregonian farmers in the form of tax breaks and subsidies during times of low yield.

The computer chimed a second time.

YOU DON'T BELONG IN OFFICE.

I have as much right as anyone. "Let's take another question. MountainMan64 asks, 'Do you plan to designate funds to fix the road damage on I-84?' Road damage is a genuine concern for the owners of motor vehicles, and I plan to address the need for repairing the flood damage as soon as it is feasible."

Another sound from the computer captured her attention.

WHY DO YOU WANT TO BE GOVERNOR?

That's none of your business. "My desire as governor of Oregon is to help give Oregonians a future we can be proud of. HikerBabe asks, 'Do you plan to address the growing homeless population in our major cities?'"

HOW FAR ARE YOU WILLING TO GO TO MAKE THAT HAPPEN? AS FAR AS YOUR FATHER DID?

I don't know what you're talking about. "I believe everyone should have a home to call their own. I've been researching what the other states are doing to aid the homeless population, and I am formulating a plan to initiate some of those same concepts in our state."

GET OUT WHILE YOU STILL CAN.

Chills swept over her arms. Her pulse pounded in her chest. A knock sounded on the door. Kathleen screamed. *That'll give the viewers something to talk about.*

After regaining her composure, she plastered her fake smile on her face, bid the viewers a good night, and shut off the live video feed.

The office door opened, and Dennis stuck his head in. "Mayor Phillips?"

"You startled me. I thought you left."

"I was on my way out, but Pastor Whitestone is here. He wants to speak with you."

Ryan? Why is he here? "Tell him to go away." *He's the last person I want to see right now.*

"Yes, ma'am."

The door started to close, then burst open. Ryan filled the doorway, wearing a determined expression. Dennis stood behind him, hidden from view by the much taller man, his voice babbling as he fretfully rebuked the pastor.

Ryan closed the door, leaving the timid man standing in the hallway, and as he turned from the door, she saw something in his eyes. Something she hadn't seen directed at her in a long time. Tenderness. Compassion.

Her back stiffened. If Ryan was coming here to talk her into accepting Paige, he'd be sorely disappointed. She wasn't going to budge. She turned her back to him. "Go away."

"No, I won't go away."

When she looked back, he'd moved directly beside her. His nearness sent butterflies fluttering in her chest. Memories of his arms around her brought a warmth to her neck. Would he notice? He always had before. It was like he sensed her discomfort or embarrassment, and he'd been there no matter what she'd needed. It was one reason she'd fallen in love with him.

She lifted her face and made eye contact. He leaned over her, and his gaze dipped to her lips. In the blink of an eye, he pulled away and stepped back. The distance was palpable. Had he wanted to kiss her? Did she want him to?

Where did that thought come from? Kathleen cleared her throat and shattered the moment. "Is there something I can do for you, or are you just here to get in my way?"

"Why do you want to be governor?"

Kathleen froze. "What did you say?" This was about her campaign for governor? Certainly not what she'd expected. Wasn't that what the person on social media had asked just minutes ago? "I don't see how that's any of your business." She didn't have to schmooze Ryan like she did the voters.

"I want a straight answer, Ann—Kathleen. It's important."

She took a deep breath. "Okay. I believe I can make a difference." It was the safest answer she could think of. She mentally patted herself on the back.

"Everyone says that. It's the *right* answer, but there are many ways you can make a difference, why be a politician?"

Should she tell him the truth? Would he understand? "It's the one thing Dad and I had in common. He was my hero, but after you and I messed up, he didn't speak to me for twenty years. I failed him, and he hated me for it. If I can do this one thing right, maybe I can make it up to him, and he will be proud of me."

"Annie, he's dead."

Ryan's words punched Kathleen in the stomach. She narrowed her eyes. "Did you just come here to remind me my father is dead, or did you have another purpose?"

Ryan's Adam's apple bobbed as he swallowed. "Annie, I'm so sorry. That's not…"

He'd called her Annie. Wasn't that what the caller that day in the café had called her? She'd thought it odd that he knew her old nickname. Was Ryan the menace? Was he angry enough to make threats?

He had shown up right after the truck had tried to run her over. And the person online tonight had asked about family. "Someone has been threatening me. Is it you? Are you so angry about Paige that you've resorted to harassing me?"

The veins in Ryan's neck popped, and his face turned red. "That's absurd. Why would you think—"

"Just tell me what you want."

His face relaxed. "I heard you need a new headquarters. Remember the barn at my parent's place. I'd like to offer it to you—free of charge."

She raised an eyebrow. What was Ryan's interest in her campaign? "Why?"

"It's sitting empty. I thought you could use it."

Memories of the old barn raced through her mind like a forest fire. No. She couldn't. She crossed her arms and averted her gaze. The look in Ryan's eyes was too kind. Too genuine. Why did he have to be so lovely? Why couldn't he hate her? She deserved it. Hate she could bear. This—this affection was foreign and disconcerting. It knocked her off balance and left her defenseless.

Her vision blurred. "What do you want from me?"

Ryan took her hand in his. His thumb stroked her skin. "I want you to be Annie again. The girl who loved the Lord and loved me. I miss you."

Why did he have to keep bringing that up? "Annie is gone. I'm all that's left. And if that's not good enough? If I'm not good enough? We have nothing more to talk about."

"Annie, I care about you. Those people—the voters—they'll never love you."

"No, but they'll admire me. Look up to me."

Ryan's lips turned down. "That's not true love."

Kathleen withdrew her hand. "I know, but it's the best I've got."

She turned away and walked toward the credenza and the bouquet. She touched the petals. Something stuck out from between the stems. *What's this?* She hadn't noticed it before. Kathleen removed a small envelope and opened the flap, withdrawing a florist card. Her brow furrowed, and her hands trembled.

If you prick us, do we not bleed? If you tickle us, do we not laugh? If you poison us, do we not die? And if you wrong us, shall we not revenge?

19

Kathleen closed her eyes and rubbed the ache in her forehead. The florist was closed when she tried to call last night. She phoned as soon as they opened this morning. The florist remembered that a man had come in, and picked the bouquet from the shelf, wrote out the note himself, then paid in cash.

"If you wrong us, shall we not revenge?"

When she opened her eyes, her gaze instantly fell on the lines of blue ink on her legal pad. How many people had she trampled over the years? The list was far longer than she'd imagined it would be. Who, out of these people, hated her enough to want revenge and was willing to go to such extreme lengths to get it?

What frightened her most was the possibility she'd forgotten someone in her attempt to recall.

Kathleen reclined in the leather executive chair. It wasn't *all* her fault—she'd only been invoking Dad's advice. His constant admonition had been her guide and echoed now through her thoughts. *Do whatever it takes to win, Annie. Never apologize. Apologies are for weaklings and fools. Simply put it behind you and move on.*

And she'd done just that. Repeatedly.

Have I been wrong? What if Dad gave me lousy advice? But it worked for him. Why wouldn't it work for me?

She rolled her shoulders, loosening the tension, and looked at her list again. The name at the top stood out like it was bordered with neon flashing lights.

Ryan.

She'd hurt him most of all.

What kind of monster lied to a man for twenty-five years, keeping him from knowing his child? How could he ever forgive her? She didn't even have the right to ask.

But I'm not a monster, am I?

Her cheeks steamed hot. If anyone deserved vengeance, Ryan did. Was he that sort of man? Would he take his revenge on her? She scoffed. *How would I know?* It's not like he'd put any effort into contacting her over the past twenty-five years. Maybe if he'd come after her, she would have changed her mind. Stopped the adoption and become a family: *Ryan, Paige, and me.*

Maybe her life could have been different.

Could? Her life *would* have been different. *Completely different.*

Kathleen glanced at the framed photo on the corner of the desk. The blond girl in the graduation cap and gown grinned back. *My precious Kylie.* If she'd married Ryan when he'd asked, she wouldn't have Kylie—the only good thing to come from her marriage to Lionel Phillips.

Lionel had loved his race car and his fans more than he'd ever loved them, and he'd never failed to let them know. Kathleen ran her finger over her forearm. The physical injuries had long since healed, but the emotional scars she would bear forever. Even his death didn't erase the pain he'd caused her.

A timid tap sounded on the study door and jerked her

from her thoughts. She flicked away the tears that had started down her cheeks. "Come in."

The door eased open, and Dennis's head appeared. "Excuse me, ma'am. I have the information you asked for."

She scrunched her forehead. What information had she asked Dennis for?

"I looked up that address from the safety deposit box."

Right. The address. The key with the tag. Kathleen straightened in her chair, pulse picking up. "What did you discover?"

"May I come in?"

Excitement surged through her veins as she gestured toward the chair opposite hers. "Of course. Please. Have a seat."

Dennis entered and sat, holding a steno pad. He'd taken notes. "The address belongs to a cabin in the Eagle Cap Wilderness. I found it on the county assessor's website." He handed her a printout of photos of the cabin and surrounding property. "It remained private after the area was turned into a protected park. Originally built in 1939, the builder was also the first owner, a man named Charles Staten. In 1986, he transferred the property to Richard Staten and… get this, Kenneth Chatham. That's the senator, right?"

Kathleen nodded, her mind processing Dennis's words. Dad and Kenneth Chatham owned a property in the Eagle Cap Wilderness. *Together?* "Is that everything?"

"Yes, ma'am."

"Thank you, Dennis."

He rose from his chair and left the room, closing the door behind him.

Kathleen leaned back in her chair and tapped her pen against her lip. The name Charles Staten sounded familiar. Grandfather, maybe? Dad hadn't spoken of his father often, but grandfather's name wasn't Charles though, it was… Harry… or Henry…

So then, who was Charles? He must be a relative—they shared the same surname. Charles Staten had built a cabin, then given it to Dad and Kenneth Chatham.

Why? Was this a joke? Dad had never mentioned owning property in the mountains. Not that she could recall. And it hadn't been in Dad's will. What had happened to her father's holdings? In all their meetings, the lawyer never mentioned a cabin, either. Was he aware it existed? Was it merely an oversight?

Kathleen picked up her cell from off the desk and tapped Don's name in her contacts. Hopefully, he was in the office. It rang twice before the secretary answered. "Don Wall, attorney-at-law. How may I direct your call?"

Sounded like Dr. Seuss. Did the secretary rhyme on purpose? A smile tinged Kathleen's lips, then faded. "This is Kathleen Phillips. Is Don available?"

"He is. Just give me a moment to transfer your call."

She stood and used the scooter to roll to the window. A minute later, Don's voice came over the line. "Kathleen. What can I do for you?"

Dark storm clouds gathered over the mountain range. "Do you know anything about my father owning property in the Eagle Cap Wilderness?"

"Where?" A tapping noise echoed in the background. Was he looking up Dad's information?

"Eagle Cap Wilderness."

A moment of silence passed. "I don't have anything. Where did you see this?"

"My assistant looked up the address attached to that key from Dad's safety deposit box. The one with the tag. According to the country assessor's site, someone named Charles Staten transferred the deed to Dad"—she swallowed the bitter taste in her mouth—"and Kenneth Chatham."

"The senator?"

"Possibly." Could it be a different Kenneth Chatham? Maybe it wasn't the senator, after all. How many Kenneth Chatham's were there in the world?

"I can do some digging if you want."

"I'll let you know. Thank you for your assistance." She pushed the end call button, then scooted to the internal door to the attached meeting room and opened it.

Dennis sat at a makeshift desk. He raised his head. "Yes?"

"Clear my calendar. I'm going to check out that cabin for myself."

"Yes, ma'am. Here are the directions. Cell signal might be spotty up that direction."

Kenneth ground his teeth and cracked the walnut with his bare hands. He opened the shell, chucked the nut into his mouth, then added the broken pieces to the litter on the floor. The newspaper clippings had arrived earlier that day in a manila envelope with no return address.

He raised one of the clippings and held it to the light. The ink was faded, but legible—*Chatham Withdraws Candidacy from Gubernatorial Race.* A photo followed. A younger version of himself stared back.

He laid the clipping back on the desk and picked up the other. *Staten Wins.*

The man is dead, and he's still a thorn in my side.

Two weeks before the 1992 election, Staten had shown up at his doorstep unannounced, claiming to have photographic evidence of covert meetings between Kenneth and Iraqi leaders.

Merited claims.

Staten's demand was simple. Kenneth had to withdraw. If not, Staten would send the photos to every newspaper and TV station in the country, no matter the outcome of the election. Panic had swept Kenneth into overdrive. But in the end—Kenneth couldn't risk exposure. He withdrew. Staten was elected governor. And those photos never saw the light of day.

With a scowl, Kenneth tossed the faded newspaper clipping onto the desktop. Where were those photos now? Had Richard destroyed them? Unlikely. They were just waiting to be discovered. *And ruin me.*

Kenneth slammed his fist on the desktop. Walnuts scattered. Those photos would jeopardize his political career, leading to impeachment… and imprisonment for treason. The laws had been amended so he couldn't be put to death, but life in prison wasn't a pleasant thought, either. His life would be ravaged, not only his, but also that of his wife and daughter. He couldn't let that happen. He wouldn't let that happen.

Iago lit a cigarette and plopped down on his couch, feet on the coffee table. Just one of the joys of being single—no one could tell him where to put his feet. He sucked in a draw, then blew out, laying his head against the cushion. His stomach churned. Maybe his dinner hadn't agreed with him, but he knew it was more than that. Tybalt pounced beside him and curled near his leg. He rubbed the cat's soft fur. Purring vibrations traveled his arm.

He'd hated to do it. That woman didn't deserve to die, but the aconite he'd purchased on the black market had done the job. According to the obituaries, Patti Hayes had died of a heart attack.

He could breathe easy.

And go back to making Kathleen as miserable as possible.

Iago leaned forward, set his cigarette in the ashtray, then pulled the buffalo leather messenger bag into his lap. He dug inside to find his USB drive. Where was it? It didn't seem to be here.

He frantically pawed through the satchel, then turned the bag over and dumped the contents onto the floor—papers, pens, and a tape recorder scattered across the carpet, but no thumb drive.

No. I can't have lost it.

He scooted back on the couch, bent forward, and cupped his face with his hands. His facial hair brushed his palms like sandpaper, and hot breath rebounded into his face. Thinking back over his day, he tried to recall the last place he'd taken the satchel. *The bookstore.*

His eyes widened. What if Paige found it?

Worse. What if she opened it?

His phone rang. *Why is Chatham calling on the weekend?* Iago waited until the third ring before answering. He cleared his throat, then tapped the screen. "Sir?"

"There's something I need you to find."

Kathleen had never been more grateful for Dennis's initiative. As predicted, her cell had lost signal several hours ago, and without the directions, she'd have been lost for sure. The view was stunning as she wound her way through the wilderness. The open window allowed the smell of pine after rain to envelop her senses. The world was peaceful up here. She hadn't come across another vehicle all day.

She rolled up the window as the blacktop changed to dirt. A dark cloud billowed around the car as night began to fall. She flipped on her headlights and turned down her music to concentrate on the road. She didn't want to be caught off-guard by deer or any other creature.

By the time she found the property, darkness had covered the mountain. Her headlights fell on a mailbox with the numbers 100 painted on the side. She turned into the fenced lot and followed the driveway through the thick forest until a clearing opened. High beams illumined a rustic one-story log cabin with an open porch.

Kathleen parked and exited the car. An owl hooted from somewhere in the dark tree line, making chills run down her spine. A creature with a long tail scampered across the front porch.

She left the headlights on to see the keyhole on the front door, then struggled to carry her overnight bag and purse. Stupid walker boot hampered her mobility, but she'd refused to ask for help. She could do this on her own.

The boards on the porch creaked but appeared steady enough to support her. She unlocked the solid wood door, pushed it open, and wriggled her bag into the dark room. A stale, musty odor struck her in the face. Wrinkling her nose, she set her suitcase on the floor, then turned on the flashlight app and looked for a light switch. Did the place have electricity? It was too dark outside to make out power lines.

After several minutes of searching, she found a switch. Light flooded the main room. Her gaze roved the space, taking in the sturdy, handcrafted log furniture, woven Indian rugs and blankets mixed with Buffalo plaid, and a massive stone fireplace. She set her purse on the polished hardwood kitchen counter, then searched for a switch to the outside light. Once she found it, she went outside and turned off her car lights. The bulbs in the lantern-style sconces lit the way back to the cabin.

After closing the door, Kathleen looked around. There were no signs of technology, just an over-sized radio from the 60s. Cobwebs stuck in the corners, and a thick layer of dust coated everything. The walls were bare except for a stuffed elk head mounted over the fireplace. Clearly, no one had been there in years.

She checked the rest of the house, finding a bedroom with a bed and a dresser. A painting hung on the wall over the headboard. A smaller room held a toilet, sink, and shower. *Thank goodness this place has running water.*

Kathleen brought her overnight bag into the bedroom, then set about finding sheets for the bed. A skinny door in the hallway looked like a linen closet. She opened it, and something scurried past her feet. She screamed as a disgusting mouse ran into the living room and disappeared under the couch. "Great. I'll never get to sleep now."

Taking a set of sheets from the closet, she pressed them to her nose. Musty, but clean. She made the bed, then returned to the living room and sat in the rocker, avoiding the couch. Now what? Kathleen drummed her fingernails on the wooden armrest. *Okay, Dad, why did you keep this place a secret?*

What didn't you want me to know?

A scratching noise came from the front porch. Startled, Kathleen jumped to her feet. A dull ache shot through her leg at the movement. With a wince, she limped to the door and opened it, shining her phone flashlight into the darkness. A badger peeked out from under the porch stairs, its eyes blinking in the bright light before it scuttled away. She blew out a breath, then closed the door and leaned against it.

What was she doing here? She hated the outdoors. The clock on her phone read 9:30. *I guess I'll try to sleep.* She pushed from the door and went into the bedroom, turning off the lights as she passed the switches. In the bedroom, she turned on the light and perched on the edge of the bed. After changing into a T-shirt and shorts, she crawled under the covers. She glanced at the overhead light—she'd forgotten to shut it off.

Should she struggle across the floor in her bare feet? *What if the mouse comes in here?* No way. She'd just sleep with it on. Kathleen rolled to her side and closed her eyes. Something thumped outside the bedroom window. Her eyes flew open. What was out there? *The badger?* That was it—just a harmless badger.

Iago cringed as another spider crawled across a sticky web strung between the two by fours. Digging through a garden shed in the middle of the night wasn't exactly his idea of fun. How long had it been since anybody had been in here? Cobwebs choked the air, and a thick layer of dust covered the boxes like snow.

He'd been through each one and hadn't found Chatham's photos. Where else would Staten have kept them? Maybe they were long gone.

The corner of Iago's mouth twitched. The articles he'd sent Chatham had done the trick.

The senator carried a much bigger secret than Iago had

hoped. S*candalous photos.* He would find them. And when he did, he'd tell Chatham they'd been destroyed, but then he'd keep them to blackmail the future President of the United States. How much would a president pay to avoid treason?

Iago stepped out of the shed and coughed. As he brushed a cobweb from his arm, he maneuvered from behind the shed door and looked toward the cabin. A light shone through one of the windows. The place had been dark when he'd arrived. He hadn't even heard a car approach. Iago cursed and turned off his flashlight. His pupils adjusted to the dark. *Who's in there? Chatham said the place had sat unused for decades. How am I going to search inside now? I'll have to come back later.* For now, he'd look elsewhere. The Staten house, perhaps?

20

At dawn, Kathleen stumbled out of bed, back aching, and in desperate need of caffeine. How far down the mountain would she have to go before she'd find a decent cup of coffee? She surveyed the room before her feet touched the floor. Was that mouse still out there? She put on her shoe and her brace, then left the bedroom, stretching her arms over her head. A yawn escaped her lips.

As she entered the central area, her eyes fell upon the kitchen cabinets. What was the chance there was a coffee tin inside? *Probably not.* Burying her disappointment, she crossed to the kitchen, opened a cupboard, and took down a glass. She checked the area for a bottle of soap. None. How was she going to wash the glass? Apparently, she wasn't. She filled it with lukewarm tap water, leaned against the counter, and took a drink. *It'll do, but it's not coffee.*

During the night, she'd decided to head home as soon as possible. There was nothing here. If she were going to find answers to her questions, she'd have to ask Senator Chatham.

Bile rose in her throat at the thought.

Kathleen rinsed out the glass and set it on the counter, then walked toward the bedroom, pulling her cell phone from her pocket. No signal. Right.

She stepped inside the room and lifted her eyes. The mouse! It scampered across the headboard. "Oh, no, you don't." Kathleen yanked off her shoe and hurled it at the trespassing rodent. Missing the creature, the footwear slammed into the painting hanging over the bed. It swayed, then crashed to the floor.

A small recessed blue panel appeared on the wall. Kathleen crossed the room and ran her fingertips over a small safe.

She traced the numbers around the dial. *Could it be that simple?* Kathleen retrieved her keys and looked at the address tag. 5 28 17. She limped back to the bedroom and carefully rotated the knob right, then left, and right again. She turned the handle, and the mechanism clicked. As she pried it open, the metal door squeaked.

A wooden box sat inside. Kathleen removed it from the safe and turned it to get a better look. The contents made a rattling noise. She sat on the edge of the bed and raised the lid. The box was full of Polaroid photos taken ages ago. Some had begun to yellow and fade. Why would anyone keep pictures in a safe?

She pulled out a handful and set the box aside. Flipping through carefully, she tried not to get the oil from her skin on them. How long had they been locked away? Most of the photos looked like they'd been taken at the cabin, showing an elderly man and woman doing various things around the property—fishing and whatnot. Some looked like family picnics?

Several of the photos had two boys playing together in the pond or shooting bows and arrows. She turned the snapshot over—handwriting marked the back. *Papa and boys fishing.* Who were the boys?

She picked up a photo with the same two boys around

twelve years old or so, their arms draped over each other's shoulders, sporting giant smiles. Why did they look familiar? She held the photo closer, her mind racing with the possibilities. She flipped it over and stopped cold. No. It wasn't possible. But the truth was written in plain ink.

Kenny and Ricky, cousins. Another great summer at Papa and Maw Maw's cabin.

Kenny? As in Kenneth Chatham? No, how was this possible? They were cousins?

As she sorted through the photos, they told the story of two young boys who'd played together on their grandparent's property every summer, or at least most summers—they'd practically grown up together.

By the time she'd come along, Richard Staten and Kenneth Chatham were arch enemies. At least that's what her father had told her. Had something happened between them?

But Senator Chatham had attended her father's funeral, offered his condolences… did he regret the chasm between their families? Did Chatham desire to make reconciliation? What was it he'd said at the rally in Salem? *He came to support an old family friend. Am I that family friend?* He'd allowed her to use the extra bedroom in his suite. Had he been reaching out, and she'd gotten it all wrong? Could she trust him?

Her gut said no, but maybe she should give him a chance.

Beneath the photos, she found two faded newspaper articles. The bold headline read: *Chatham Withdraws Candidacy from Gubernatorial Race.* The *Oregonian* article was from the early nineties when her dad had run for Governor. Her eyes skimmed the text.

In a surprising turn of events, State Representative Kenneth Chatham withdrew from Oregon's gubernatorial race, leaving Richard Staten, mayor of Whitman, in the lead. The representative had held an enormous edge over the other candidates through the spring primaries. His withdrawal has shocked the state. When asked his reason, Chatham made no comment…

She turned to the second article: *Staten Wins. By a landslide, Richard Staten elected the new governor of Oregon…*

One thing was certain. Kathleen didn't know her father as well as she'd thought. What else was he hiding?

She was almost afraid to find out.

Paige finished loading the dishwasher with the breakfast dishes and started the machine. Jessie entered through the back door carrying her Bible and a notebook. She set them on the counter, then set about making a cup of tea. Paige wiped her hands on a dishrag. "Jessie," she reclined against the refrigerator. "Mr. Bryant, your accountant, needs your permission to share the bookstore's financial history with me. Would you be willing to sign an affidavit granting him your permission? It has to be signed by a notary public."

Jessie poured a stream of hot water over the herbal teabag in her ceramic teacup. Steam rose, then dissipated. Mild tones of lemon and ginger wafted through the air. "I'll make an appointment and take care of that later today. Have I told you how much I appreciate you taking over the bookstore? It does my heart good to see all of Lawrence's hard work extend to a new generation. You're doing a wonderful job. Thank you."

Paige's skin grew warm at the compliment. "Thank you, Jessie. You took a chance on me, and that means more to me than you'll ever know." She paused. "Speaking of Lawrence. I'd love to take a look at the old ledgers just to see the history of the bookstore. When did Lawrence open The Bookshelf?"

Jessie stared off in the distance. "It was the mid-fifties or so. After we married, Lawrence and I bought this house. He opened the bookstore, and I worked as a midwife until the hospital opened."

"Do you know where I can find his books?"

Jessie sat at the table and added a spoonful of sugar to her tea. "I remember he kept a storage unit for the bookstore over on Fifth street. The same place you have yours. I haven't been there in years. Technically, everything in there belongs to you now. Though I think there might be some personal stuff in there, too. The key should have been with the one for the filing cabinet."

"Thank you, Hamilton. I'm sure this wasn't how you planned on spending your day off, but I'm grateful for the help." The afternoon sun beamed, making Paige's hair stick to her face—perspiration soaked her neck and back. She sputtered and swept a strand from her cheek. As the days approached August, the temperatures soared. She rolled the storage unit door out of the way.

"As long as I get to spend my day off with you, I couldn't care less about what we do. Besides, I'm getting accustomed to moving boxes for you. I'll be a pro by the time you move in with me." He made a strangled noise. "Not move-in move in. When we get married. I mean… well, that took an unexpected turn. Shutting up now." He moved to start looking through the boxes for the one they needed.

Paige's face grew warm. She leaned over a cardboard box to hide her embarrassment. Her hair tumbled forward, shielding her face from his view. Through the dangling strands, she admired the handsome man checking permanent marker labels on the boxes. Butterflies fluttered in her stomach. *He believes we'll get married someday.*

When she and Hamilton had first met, he'd been opposed to romantic relationships. He'd lost his best friend in the line of duty, and after seeing what his friend's widow suffered, he'd vowed never to put a woman through that same heartache. *I'm glad I've changed his mind.*

"Here's a box labeled *Ledgers.*" Hamilton's voice sounded muffled—he'd gone deeper into the unit. "Want me to open it and check?"

Paige straightened, then followed the light from his cell phone. "I've got it." She popped open the blade and sliced through the tape. They unfolded the flaps, and Hamilton moved his flashlight over the opening so they could see the contents—piles of loose pink and yellow papers. She dug into the box and felt thicker books underneath. After pulling it out, she checked the pages inside. Columns and rows of numbers. "That's what we're looking for. Will you carry it to your truck?"

"Sure." Hamilton handed Paige his phone, then lifted the box with a grunt and carried it out. Paige took another look around. Shining the flashlight through the dark, the beam traveled over stacks of boxes and old dusty furniture. Toward the back, the light fell on a box labeled *Old Books.*

"There's a box over here labeled 'photo albums.' Are you interested?" Hamilton's voice carried from outside.

Photo albums. That could be fun. "Bring those, too. Jessie might get a kick out of reminiscing about old times."

Paige put the knife in her pocket, then climbed onto a high back chair, holding onto the phone tightly. From there, she could reach the book box. Taking the knife from her pants, she sliced through the tape, then laid the blade aside, opened the flaps, and shined the light inside. The box was full of books sealed in plastic coverings—only one reason to protect them in this fashion. Her pulse quickened. These weren't just any old books.

First Editions.

She read the title off the top of the stack, then opened the web browser app on Hamilton's phone. The app opened but didn't connect. The metal building must be blocking the signal. Removing the book from the box, she carried it into the sunlight.

Hamilton stepped close and looked over her shoulder. "Whattaya got there?"

"I'm not sure yet." The app connected to the internet. Paige typed the book's title into the search engine with her thumb, then scrolled through the suggested websites. After a few more clicks, her eyes widened. *What? How?* The book she held was worth eleven thousand dollars.

Where did Jessie get these? Ms. Jessie Faye had some serious explaining to do.

21

"Jessie, where did your husband get these?" Paige held up the book she'd found. "This one is worth over ten thousand dollars." She hadn't totaled the entire value of the contents of the box, but it was going to be a significant number.

The old woman, sitting at the kitchen table across from her, remained unfazed, while Aunt Hattie dropped into a chair. "Ten thousand dollars, is it?"

"And that's just what I discovered doing a quick search. No offense, but you aren't swimming in money. How did Lawrence afford all those first editions? Was he secretly in the mafia, or a gambler, or a hidden millionaire?"

Jessie guffawed, then rose, her old bones cracking audibly. She shuffled to the counter and poured another cup of hot tea. "Tea, Hattie?" How could she remain so calm?

"No, thank you. I don't drink grass. My coffee is just fine."

Paige chortled.

Jessie rolled her eyes, then returned to her chair. Steam rose from the china cup. "My Lawrence wasn't any of those things. As far as I remember, Richard Staten gave them to him."

Richard Staten gave those books to Lawrence Faye? Some gift. Concern niggled Paige's conscious. Maybe as a former thief, she thought like a villain, but something was off. But Jessie's explanation would have to do for now. Better to change the subject than upset her friend by accusing Jessie's husband of a crime without evidence to support her charge.

"Speaking of old memories." Paige held up her finger. "I've got something to show you." She jogged into the living room and opened the box of photo albums. Lifting one, she carried it back to the kitchen and set it on the table. "I thought you might like to look at these old photos. I know *I'd* love to hear your stories about the old days."

Jessie's wrinkled hands took hold of the cover and opened to the first fragile, yellowed page plastered with square black and white photos. Jessie pointed at a tall woman wearing an outfit from the Great Depression era. A toddler stood at her side. "This is my mother, and the little one is me." She moved her finger to a photo of a man in a World War II Army uniform. "This strapping young man was my father. He was a doctor during World War Two. He died when I was thirteen years old."

Jessie turned the page, and Aunt Hattie leaned closer to get a better look. "This is my brother Bernard, and this is Harriet, my best… friend… from…" Jessie didn't finish her sentence. She lowered her chin, averting her gaze to the floor.

Aunt Hattie's face turned ghostly white, and her hands trembled. She stared at the photograph, speechless.

Paige touched her aunt's arm. "Aunt Hattie. Are you OK? You don't look so good."

Aunt Hattie didn't answer.

Jessie raised her head. "Paige, there's something you should know—"

"Josephine Rushing?" Aunt Hattie's voice squeaked. She

glanced from the picture to Jessie and back again. "It's you?" She didn't sound happy to see her old friend—in fact, quite the opposite. "I won't live here." Aunt Hattie pursed her lips and folded her arms. "Either she goes, or I go."

Paige's eyes widened at Aunt Hattie's response. "We can't kick Jessie out of her own house." The two women used to be friends? *I never saw that coming.*

"It's not her house. It's yours. You bought it."

"Yes, but—"

"I won't live under the same roof as that backstabber."

With those words, Jessie sprang to life. She jumped from her chair as fast as her aged legs would move. "Backstabber! That's not how I remember it."

Aunt Hattie stood. "That's exactly how I remember it."

"What's going on? Can't we at least talk about this?" Confusion swallowed Paige's mind. No wonder the two hadn't been able to get along. Had Jessie known Aunt Hattie was her old friend this whole time? What had happened between them to create such animosity toward each other?

Aunt Hattie stuck out her lip and humphed. "There's nothing to talk about. I won't stay another minute."

"Jessie?" Paige turned her attention to the other woman. Her eyes pleaded with her to explain what all the fuss was about.

Jessie closed the photo album. "Harriet and I used to know each other. I recognized her the minute she stepped out of her station wagon with all those ridiculous animals." She didn't look up. "Harriet always did love God's creatures."

Paige turned back to her aunt, who was pouting like a child. "We've lived here for eight days. How did you not recognize Jessie before this?"

"We haven't seen each other in sixty years," Jessie answered. "A lot of water has passed under that bridge."

"Not enough," Aunt Hattie snapped.

"Your aunt knew me as Josephine—Josie for short. My Lawrence nicknamed me Jessie. I haven't been Josie for a long time."

Paige's eyes flickered to the photo album on the table. "Sit down. Both of you. No one is leaving." Both women eased into their chairs without breaking eye contact. "Will you please give this a chance? I bought this home to take care of both of you, but you're acting like children. Whatever happened between you is long in the past. Let it go."

"I—" Aunt Hattie started, her tone revealing her displeasure at Paige's suggestion.

Paige held up her finger, and Aunt Hattie fell silent. "This is my house. I bought it, and I'm allowing you both to live with me. If we can't make this work, I'm sure I could find you both a room at the senior living center."

Jessie took a sip of tea and sighed. "Seeing how it's in everyone's best interest to make this work, I can put the past behind us. If she apologizes."

"If *I* apologize? You're the one who needs to apologize. It was all your fault."

Paige put her head between her hands—these two were giving her a headache. She stood and left the kitchen. Their squabbling faded. Sitting on the couch, Paige pushed Delilah from the top of the dusty box and pulled it closer. She held back the flap and gazed inside—plastic-wrapped first editions winked back. "Where did you all come from?"

Why did Lawrence store them away rather than sell them? He did own a bookstore after all. He could have been a collector, I guess.

And why would Richard Staten give Lawrence Faye a book worth eleven thousand dollars, much less an entire box with a value of approximately 100,000 dollars or more? No one's that good of a friend.

What did Paige know about her birth grandfather? Not much. She took her laptop out of the bag, opened the lid, then opened the web browser on her computer and typed *Richard Staten* into the search engine. Several thousand links appeared. *This could take a while.* She opened an online encyclopedia, and typed *Richard Staten* in the search box, then leaned back in her chair while it loaded. When it finished, she read over the paragraphs. *Mayor, Governor, State Attorney General…* her grandfather had lived a full life. She scrolled down to the section labeled, *Family Life.*

Richard Staten and actress Dawn Winters were together for thirty-five years before their marriage ended in divorce in 2010.

The Hollywood celebrity had been married to Paige's grandfather? Paige kept reading: *They had two children, Kathleen Staten Phillips, mayor of Whitman, Oregon, and Erik Richard Staten, a Portland businessman.*

As she slumped against the back of the couch, her eyes bulged. No wonder she and the actress resembled one another. Dawn Winters was her grandmother. *Why didn't she tell me?*

Her phone chimed. Kylie's number showed at the top of the screen.

NEED TO TALK. MEET ME @ SQUARE. LATE. AFTER MOM IS ASLEEP. KYLIE.

Paige packed her laptop into its bag and set it behind her. Her eyelids grew heavy. It was getting late. She glanced at the clock on her phone. Almost midnight. Where was Kylie? Hadn't Kathleen gone to bed yet?

She laid her head against the headrest and let her eyes drift closed. Aunt Hattie's car was growing warm and stuffy with the engine off. The streets were quiet. Is this what it was like to be on a stakeout? *How boring.*

Something tapped the glass. Paige rolled her head to the left. A face pressed against the glass. Paige screamed and scrambled back. Her hands searched for something to use as a weapon. The figure stepped back from the window. Features came into view. "Hamilton?" Her relief relaxed her tense muscles.

Hamilton signaled for her to roll down the window. After she lowered it, he laid his bare arms on the frame. "It's the middle of the night. What are you doing out here?" He sounded worried, confused, and slightly annoyed.

"You scared me to death." Her heartbeat pulsed in her throat. "What are you doing?"

He tapped his badge. "My job." He reached through the window and laced his fingers with hers. "What are you doing?"

"I'm waiting for Kylie."

"What? Why?"

"She needs to talk." She showed him the text.

He took her phone and read over the message. "What's so important it can't wait until morning?"

Paige shrugged. "I don't know. She didn't say."

"You shouldn't be out here. It's late. Text Kylie and tell her you'll meet tomorrow."

Why had Kylie suggested this? Paige felt like a total fool. "I'm just trying to be there for her."

"Trying to be the big sister, huh?"

Yeah. Something like that.

"Paige, I know you want—but you can't… put … yourself…" His voice slowed, and his gaze shifted. Paige looked in that direction. A vehicle pulled along the curb on the side of the courthouse. Someone leaped out—a man, judging by his size and build. He crossed the yard toward the building with wide steps.

Hamilton pushed away from the car and tapped the side. "I'll check it out. Stay here." He crossed the street with his hand on his weapon and shouted. At the sound of Hamilton's voice, the man turned, hands in the air. The two men spoke. Hamilton's hand relaxed. *What are they saying?* Paige leaned across the seat and rolled down the passenger window, hoping the night air would carry their voices. Nope, too far away.

She leaned back into her seat. Movement flashed in her peripheral—a hand shot through the open window. She gasped. Soft fabric closed over her mouth and nose. A sickeningly sweet smell enveloped her senses.

The world went dark.

"Paige. Paige. Are you all right?"

A shaking sensation pulled her from her slumber. A bright light shone in her face. Paige squinted. *What is going on? Did an elephant stomp on my head?* After a moment, her vision cleared then centered on Hamilton's worried expression. The car door was open, and he squatted at her side. He lowered the flashlight. "Good. You're awake. I was just about to call the medic."

Paige straightened in her seat. "What happened? Did I fall asleep?"

"I don't think so. I smell chloroform."

Her eyes widened. *The hand through the window!* "Someone knocked me out while you were over there." She swung her head around to look in the direction of the courthouse. A wave of nausea gripped her stomach. She clapped her hand over her mouth.

"What's wrong?"

Paige shook her head and leaned out of the car.

Hamilton grabbed her hair. "It's the aftereffects of the drug. You'll be okay in a minute."

"That's rough." Paige sat up and wiped her mouth with a Kleenex.

"Yeah, it is. I'm sorry."

"What happened with the guy?" She glanced at the building again, this time more slowly. The area was vacant, and the car was gone. "Where did he go?"

"Who? Roy?"

"The guy breaking into the courthouse."

"Paige." He squeezed her shoulder. "He wasn't breaking in. He had a key. He works there."

"But what was he doing in the middle of the night?"

"He was working late at home and realized he'd left some important files. He went back to retrieve them. He has a big project due in the morning."

"Oh."

"Yeah. Did you see who drugged you?"

Paige slowly shook her head, then laid it against the headrest. "It was weird. I leaned over to roll down the window." She gestured toward the opening. "When I sat back, a hand reached in and stuck a rag over my face. That's all I remember until you shook me awake."

"All of that happened while I was over there?"

"Apparently."

"Is anything missing?"

"Well, I still have my radio and my tires."

"This isn't New York City. I doubt they were after your treads."

She glanced around the car, then turned around in her seat. *Where's my laptop bag?* She arched and searched the back. "It's gone."

"What's gone?"

"They—someone stole my laptop."

22

The next morning, Paige entered the café. If her sister had sent that text yesterday, why had she never showed? Had something happened to hinder her arrival? Kylie stood behind the counter, drawing in the white foam of a customer's cappuccino. She caught sight of Paige and waved. "Hi. I'll be with you in just a minute." She gave the waiting customer his drink, then swiped his card. "Thank you for coming in. Have a nice day." Kylie turned to face Paige, grinning from ear to ear. "So, what would you like?"

"I'm not here for coffee. I need to talk to you. When is your break?"

Kylie's smile faded. "Is something wrong? Did I do something to make you mad? I'm so sorry. I didn't mean to—whatever it was. I can take a break right now, I think. The café is pretty empty. Do you want to sit?"

Paige reached over the counter and touched Kylie's arm. "Calm down. I'm not mad. Just confused."

Jenn McMillan exited the kitchen carrying a tray of fresh-baked brownies.

"Jenn, may I take my break now?" Kylie batted her eyes and frowned like a sad puppy. "Please."

Jenn's eyes flittered between Kylie and Paige, then she slowly nodded. "That's all right with me. I can help any customers that come in. You girls want a brownie?"

"Thank you, Jenn." Kylie's mood shot back up. She grabbed a brownie, then skipped from behind the counter, and dropped into a booth.

Paige rolled her eyes at Kylie's antics, then took the offered brownie, and sat across from her sister. She pinched off a bite and stuck it into her mouth. The chocolate melted over her tongue. She moaned. "That's delicious."

Kylie's brownie was already half consumed. "I know. Jenn's amazing. What's going on with you?"

Paige took a paper napkin from the dispenser, laid it on the table, then placed the rest of her brownie on top. "Did you text me yesterday?

"No. Why?"

A knot formed in Paige's stomach—with that one answer, she knew the rest. Kylie hadn't sent that message. *Someone must have spoofed Kylie's number.* "Yesterday, I received a text… here it's better if I show you." Paige took her phone from her pocket, entered her password, then laid it on the table in front of Kylie.

Kylie's lips moved as she read the text. She raised her chin, eyes bulging. "I didn't send that."

"While I was waiting for you, someone drugged me and stole my laptop. I'm guessing it was the same person who sent this message. They lured me to the square for some reason." *But how would they know I would bring my laptop? Unless… they'd planned to do more but were interrupted by something. Hamilton?*

"Why would someone do that?" Kylie's voice cracked. "What if you had been killed? Why would someone pretend to be me?"

That's precisely what Paige wanted to know. "It's not

your fault. I wasn't hurt. I have a backup of all my computer files. No harm. No foul." *At least, not yet.*

"I'm really sorry, Paige. I'm glad you're okay. I don't know what I'd do without you." Kylie took a shuttered breath and finished her brownie in one bite. She stood and picked up her trash, wiping brownie crumbs into her open palm. "Jenn McMillan, my boss, teaches a Bible study at church. Do you want to go with me tonight? We have lots of fun, and the studies are good. Jenn's a really good teach—"

"Kylie." Paige interrupted. "I'd love to."

Later that afternoon, the bell on the front door of the bookstore jingled, and Paige raised her head. The glass entry closed behind a man, tall and tanned, with graying chestnut hair and a beard. He wore sunglasses, which he removed and hung on the collar of his button-down shirt. His eyes were like dark, empty wells, giving her an uncomfortable feeling. Paige swallowed, wishing Nori wasn't on her lunch break.

She shut her book and set it on the checkout desk. "Welcome to Paige's Second Chance Books. May I help you?"

He moved toward the counter with long, determined strides, bringing the odor of tobacco and cologne with him. "I heard about The Bookshelf's remodel and wanted to check it out. I'm a bibliophile myself."

"It was getting pretty run down." She reached under the desk, pulled out her cell, and set it on top. *Just in case. He sounds friendly, but something about his demeanor feels off.* "I'm Paige. What's your name?"

"Iago. You're the owner, I presume."

"I am." Paige tilted her head. "Iago? As in the villain from Othello?"

Iago raised an eyebrow. "Someone knows their Shakespeare. Most people assume I'm referring to Jafar's annoying parrot." He moved from the counter toward the shelves and ran his fingers along the spines. "You have a beautiful collection here."

"Thank you. Books are my passion."

"Favorite author?"

"I'm a Brontë fan. You?"

"Shakespeare. No one writes like the bard. Anyway, if someone left something in the store, how might they go about getting it back?"

Paige's ears perked. Did the flash drive belong to him? "I have a lost and found. Did you lose something in particular?"

He turned to face her. "My wife and son were in here the other day for the storytime. Would you mind if I take a look?"

"Of course." Did the USB belong to the family? Should she mention it was in her office? *I'll wait to see if Iago asks about it.* Paige removed the bin from underneath the counter and set it on top. Iago crossed with quick steps and dug through the contents. He raised an Oregon State Beaver's ball cap and made a triumphant noise. "Aha. Here it is. My son's been looking all over for this. It's his favorite. Thank you."

"You're welcome. Glad I could help. I hope your wife brings your son to storytime again. We're planning for it to be a monthly event."

"I'll remind her. Have a nice afternoon." Iago put the hat on his head and his sunglasses on his face, then left, the bell signaling his departure.

Paige placed the box underneath the counter, then walked back to the office, and removed the flash drive from the drawer. She twirled the piece of plastic and metal between her fingers. It had been several days since it was left, and no one had come to claim it. Maybe the files would give her a clue, and she'd be able to return it to the rightful owner. *Should I look?* Guilt plagued her stomach. Was this considered prying or snooping? But it wasn't for personal gain; she only wanted to know who to give it back to. A quick peek wouldn't hurt. She'd apologize for intruding when she returned the drive.

She leaned forward, aiming the drive for the USB port on the desktop computer, then hesitated. What if Nori was right and it was a virus? Better safe than sorry. She backed the computer up to her external hard drive, then stuck the USB into the port and clicked *open* when the system prompted. A series of icons appeared.

Paige double-clicked the icon, and it opened on her screen. Her eyes widened. *I know that place.* Powell's City of Books stood in the background—the bookstore she'd worked at while living in Portland. She squinted. Someone was leaving the building. She zoomed closer. And gasped.

It was her.

Strange. Paige closed the photo and opened the next one. It was a snapshot of her and Aunt Hattie's home. She zoomed in again, and sure enough, she was pushing her bike up the driveway. Hands trembling and heart racing, hardly able to control the mouse, she clicked on the next photo—the Thorne's garage apartment. She was standing at the top of the fire escape.

She swallowed the lump in her throat. These photos were all of her. One photo remained.

Paige clicked.

The file opened.

Tears stung Paige's eyes. *Heavenly's. The day Kathleen rejected me. Someone knows I'm Kathleen's daughter.*

Her phone rang, startling her. She glanced at the caller ID and answered. "What's up, Kylie?"

The sounds of the coffee grinder, clinking of ceramic mugs, and a hum of voices echoed in the background. "You promised you'd go to Bible study with me tonight. Did you forget?"

Bible study. With Kylie. Nausea tormented her stomach. Could she decline? Paige removed the drive from the computer, dropped it back into the drawer, and locked it. "I'm coming."

At nine o'clock, the two girls left the Whitman Baptist Church, climbed into Kylie's car, and began the drive to drop off Paige before Kylie went home. Kylie turned off Church St and onto Nutwood. *Thump. Thump.* The vehicle rocked awkwardly. *Thump. Thump.* "Kylie. Stop over here. I think you have a flat tire."

Kylie turned the wheel and parked the car along a grassy ditch. "I've never had a flat tire before. I don't even know how to change a tire. What are we going to do?"

They exited the car. Paige squatted and checked the tires for a flat. A rusty nail stuck out of the back left tire, and the air pressure was down to nil. She straightened. "Don't worry. If you have a jack and a spare, I'll fix it up, and we can be on our way before it gets dark."

Kylie opened the truck. Paige helped her retrieve the spare tire, then they searched for the jack. She located the black bag, but when she took out the jack, something didn't look right. "We've got a problem. You're missing the lug nut wrench. Without it, I can't take off the tire."

Kylie let out an exasperated sigh. "Now, what are we going to do?"

Paige glanced around. The road out to the church wasn't a high traffic area. "Let's walk to the bookstore. At least we can wait in comfort while we call someone to change the tire."

"Works for me." Kylie spun on her heel and began walking away. Paige shook her head, then shut off the car, took the keys from the ignition, and grabbed both purses.

"Hey, Kylie. Forgetting something."

"What?" Kylie stopped and turned to look over her shoulder.

Paige caught up and handed Kylie her purse and keys. "You might need these." Kylie laughed at herself, then started toward the bookstore. As they walked, the sun lowered behind the mountains, filling the sky with rich tones of fiery oranges and shadowy clouds. Kylie hummed one of the songs they'd sung at the Bible study. All evening, Paige had had trouble keeping her mind on the lesson and not on those photos. She chewed her lip. Her insides quivered. Who was watching her? And why? Was the USB connected to her laptop being stolen?

Kylie stopped humming. "Did you like the Bible study?"

Paige pulled her thoughts to the present and nodded to answer Kylie's question. She appreciated the warm welcome the other ladies had given her. They seemed genuinely happy to have her as part of their little group. The singing was unlike anything she'd ever heard, and Jenn McMillan did an excellent job explaining things in her lesson, especially to a newbie like Paige.

Jenn had shared a story about a boy who had taken his inheritance and spent it all on parties and luxuries. But when his money was gone, so were his so-called friends, and he'd had to resort to eating pig slop, which, apparently, was a bad thing during those times. Eventually, he came to himself or something like that and went home. The most incredible part was when the boy's father had welcomed him home and forgave him.

Paige mentally replayed Jenn's words, which had spoken directly to her heart. *"What if the prodigal son had never gone home because he believed his father would never forgive him? How different would his life have turned out? We all mess up. We all make mistakes. We all sin willfully and unknowingly. It's what we do with our sins that defines who we are. Seek forgiveness and move forward. Let go of the past. Don't let your mistakes define you. See yourself as the Heavenly Father sees you. His child."*

As the girls passed the alley between Junk Monkey Antiques and the nail salon, the hair on the back of Paige's neck stood on end. A cold chill swept down her arms, leaving goosebumps. Across the street, the volunteer fire station was dark, but a shadow moved at the edge of the building. Was someone there?

Paige blew out a series of short breaths to calm her nerves. *I'm just skittish because of those photos. No one is there. It's only a few more blocks.* Maybe it was a figment of her imagination. Just to be safe, Paige picked up her pace, and Kylie lengthened her strides to keep up.

As they approached the intersection, Paige cut a darting glance over her shoulder. A man followed. He slipped into the deepening shadows. Had he seen her spot him? "Kylie, let's cross the street here."

Kylie followed without question.

Don't follow us. Stay on that side.

To her dismay, he crossed the street. Pulse pounding, Paige quickened her steps. Kylie huffed. "Paige, we're moving awfully fast. Is everything okay? Is it something I said?"

Footsteps echoed behind them. Closer. Closer.

Paige slipped her hand into her purse, then put on the brakes, spun on her heels, whipped a can of mace from her purse, and sprayed it in his eyes. "Kylie, run!"

Kylie's screams mixed with the man's. As he covered his face with his hands, Kylie charged down the sidewalk. Paige whipped around and grabbed Kylie's hand as she passed. The hammering in her chest matched the pounding of their feet.

When they reached the bookstore, Paige unlocked the door. They hurried inside. She bolted the front door behind them, then tugged Kylie into the office and locked them inside. Still breathing heavily, Paige dialed Hamilton's number. "Paige." His voice sounded so sweet, she hated to ruin his evening. "What's up?"

"We're being followed. I sprayed the man with mace, then locked Kylie and me in my office."

"Hang on, Paige. I'll be right there."

"We canvased the whole block. No one's out there." Hamilton held her close to his chest. Paige pressed her face into his uniform. "Are you and Kylie okay?"

"I think so."

Kylie sat in the office chair, shaking like an autumn leaf. Paige slipped from the safety of Hamilton's embrace and knelt. "Are you OK, Kylie?"

Her sister lifted fear-stricken eyes, hands clenched in her lap. Her face was as pale as the moon. "I was so scared. How-

how did you stay so calm?"

Paige lifted her shoulders. "I learned a long time ago not to panic. It's easier to determine the best course of action if you're thinking straight."

Kylie's lip trembled. "I've never had anything like that happen before. Was that man going to hurt us?"

Don't answer that. You'll scare her more. "I'm just glad you ran when I told you to." *His intentions really weren't all that important. What matters is that we got away.*

Kylie wrapped her arms around Paige's neck. "Thank you for saving me. Without you, I would have been a goner."

Paige accepted the embrace, then peeled her sister's arms back so Paige could breathe again. She stood as Officer Jesse Martin stepped forward with an official notepad in hand. "Do you know anyone who would want to harm you, Miss Phillips?"

Kylie raised her doe eyes to the officer. "Do you *really* think he was after me?"

Officer Martin nodded. "Your mother is running for governor. Someone has tried to harm her multiple times. It's reasonable to suspect they'd go after her only child."

Only child.

A brick dropped into Paige's stomach, stealing her breath. *As far as they know, Kylie is Kathleen's only child. But what if that man knew the truth? What if he was after Kylie and me? Or... just me?*

What if this didn't have anything to do with the election? What if it had to do with Kathleen being her mother? Paige considered the flash drive with the photos she'd found. Would he have abducted her to try to get a ransom from Kathleen to keep her secret hidden?

Paige blinked back the tears that pooled and moved to Hamilton's side, tucking her hand in his elbow. He glanced down at her and frowned. "What's wrong?" His breath was warm against her ear.

"I'm not sure he was after Kylie."

Hamilton quirked an eyebrow. "What do you mean? Why

not?"

Paige jerked her chin toward the back of the office and urged him to follow her. Unlocking the drawer, she handed Hamilton the flash drive.

"What's this?"

"I found it a couple days ago and put it in here to hold until someone turned up looking for it." She told him about finding the photos. "There's more."

"More?"

Paige dug into her purse and pulled out the note she'd received.

Hamilton unfolded the paper, and as he read aloud, his eyes flickered back and forth. "All the world's a stage, And all the men and women merely players; They have their exits and their entrances, And one man in his time plays many parts." He furrowed his forehead. "I'm confused. What is this?"

"It's Shakespeare."

"Right. Still not following. You're going to have to explain."

She told him about the man at her door and the manila envelope. Flush reddened the space behind Hamilton's ears. "And you opened it? What if it had been something dangerous? That was really stupid." Frustration built up in his voice. "When were you going to tell me about this?"

"I'm telling you now."

"Why did you hide this from me?"

"I didn't…" She couldn't answer. "I…" What could she say? "Hamilton. I—I'm used to taking care of myself. This…having someone who cares about my well-being…it's a new experience for me. It's going to take some time. I'm sorry I kept this from you. I know I shouldn't have. But I can't promise it won't happen again."

A shadow passed over his face, and his jaw hardened. Paige had seen that look before—Hamilton had reverted to cop mode—his safe place. "What did he look like?"

"I didn't get a good look."

"How did he leave? In a car? Truck? Did you see the

license plate? Can you describe the vehicle?" He looked at the paper in his hand. "You've probably already smudged any fingerprints." His voice lowered to a mumble. "Should have put this in a plastic bag."

A tear ran down Paige's cheek and dripped onto her blouse. "I doubt he left fingerprints—he wore gloves."

Hamilton pivoted. "Officer Martin will give you a ride home."

"Hamilton, please…"

Ignoring her, he walked away before she could finish. He whispered to the other officer then stalked out the door. Paige drew her arms to her body as a tightness squeezed her chest.

Officer Martin laid his hand on her shoulder. "If you'll come with me, we'll go down to the station and take your official statement. Then I'll drive you home."

23

Kathleen threw the car into park, then climbed out of the seat, slamming the door behind her. She hobbled into the police station. The lobby was empty, and so was the reception desk. She hit the intercom button on the wall.

"Hello? How can I help you?" A staticky voice came through the speaker.

"This is Mayor Phillips. I got a call about my daughter."

The buzzer sounded. Kathleen hauled the heavy metal door open and entered the bullpen. Where was Kylie? She spotted her through the open doorway of Chief House's office. Ignoring the others, she headed straight back, wending her way between the desks. Chief Mark House stood when she entered the room. "Kathleen. Thank you for coming. I know it's late."

Kylie sprang from the couch and threw her arms around Kathleen's neck. "Mom!"

Kathleen patted her back, then pried her arms away before they strangled her. Kylie continued to blubber incomprehensibly. *What is she trying to say? What happened here?* "Will someone tell me why my daughter is at the police station?" Kathleen addressed Mark, raising her voice to be heard over Kylie's crying.

"A man was tailing the girls on their way home from a Bible study…"

Girls? What girls? Is Kylie in danger now?

Mark was still speaking. "…They ran to the bookstore, locked themselves in, and called us. If it weren't for Miss McDonald's quick reflexes, tonight might have had a vastly different outcome."

Miss Donald? As in Paige? Kathleen surveyed the bullpen through the window. Paige spoke with one of the uniformed officers near the water cooler. He patted her shoulder and handed her a Styrofoam cup. Kathleen stiffened. "Where was your car, Kylie? Why were you on foot?"

"My car got a flat tire. Paige wanted to change it, but a tool was missing. She said we'd go wait in the bookstore instead of the car, while we called someone to change the tire."

So, it was all Paige's fault. If she hadn't suggested walking, Kylie would have waited in the car. Paige put Kylie in danger. "I wasn't aware Paige attended the Bible study."

Kylie sniffled and dabbed her eyes with a balled-up tissue. "This was her first time. I invited her to go with me."

Kylie invited Paige, but not me? Kathleen pressed her lips flat and clenched her teeth. *Why am I jealous? I don't have anything to do with God or the church. I wouldn't have gone even if she'd asked.* She shook her head, driving away the guilt that suddenly filtered into her thoughts. "Did you arrest the perpetrator?"

Mark shook his head. "My officers combed the area but didn't find anyone matching the girls' description."

Just great. So, that man's still out there. "Do you believe the pervert was after my daughter?"

"We don't know that for sure. He could have been tailing either one of the girls. Or both. With the other attacks on your campaign, we assumed—"

"What about Miss McDonald? Could he have been after her, and this had nothing to do with my daughter or the election?"

Mark cleared his throat. "It's possible, of course, but it makes sense to presume Kylie was the target. She *is* your only child, and this man may have wanted to use her for leverage. We try not to read too much into these things without evidence to support our theories. Why would anyone have a reason to go after Paige?"

Only child? Mark didn't know about Paige then. Kathleen pinched her lips against the smile that threatened. This was good. Her secret hadn't spread. "Do you need anything else from us?"

"No ma'am. You and Kylie are free to go."

Paige slammed the police cruiser door closed, then jogged up the stairs to her house. The headlights disappeared as Officer Martin backed out of the driveway, leaving Paige in the dark. The inside lights were all off. Aunt Hattie and Jessie had gone to bed. Paige didn't blame them—it was after 11:30.

She let herself into the bungalow, dropped her purse on the floor, then kicked her shoes off one by one. Starting for the couch, she stopped, turned back, and put everything away neatly. Even upset, she couldn't leave a mess for someone else to clean up.

With a sigh, she plopped on the center couch cushion and buried her face in her palms.

This night had not gone well. Hamilton's disappointment bothered her far more than the stalker. Would he forgive her? Was their relationship over? *If only I'd called him as soon as I received that note.*

Something warm and soft rubbed against her ankles. She uncovered her face and scooped Delilah, setting the cat in her lap. Low purring vibrated her legs and brought a sad smile to her lips.

"You should have seen Hamilton's face, Delilah. He was so hurt that I hadn't told him about that message. I wish I understood why I kept it from him. I don't know if I was scared or if I thought it would change things between us. I'm still learning what it's like to have someone care about you. I know I had Benjamin McDonald and still have Aunt Hattie, but it's different. I knew—know that they love me, but I thought they're required to love me because they're family. Having someone chose to love me—it's a new experience and a little intimidating."

As she swiped a tear from her cheek, Delilah raised her head and meowed. Someone shuffled down the hall, and the kitchen light turned on. Jessie stopped at the sink and filled a glass with water.

When she turned, she spotted Paige on the couch, shrieked, and the water splashed over the edge of the cup, spilling onto the tile floor. The old woman put her hand to her chest. "You startled me. What are you doing still awake?"

Jessie set her glass on the counter, then took a dishrag, dropped it on the floor, and mopped up the spill with her foot. She picked up the cup again and shuffled into the living room. Her gaze dropped to Delilah. "Would you mind putting down the fuzz ball?"

Paige pushed the cat off her lap and brushed off the unwanted hair. Jessie sighed, then joined her on the couch.

"Why do you dislike animals so much?"

Jessie plucked a stray hair from the sofa cushion and dropped it on the carpet. "You haven't answered my question."

Paige wrinkled her brow. "What question was that?"

"Why are you still awake?"

"I just got home."

Paige recounted the events of the last couple of hours, starting with the photos on the flash drive and ending with Hamilton's response.

"Oh, dear." Jessie gripped Paige's hands and squeezed. "I'm so sorry."

"I didn't mean to hurt his feelings or break his trust. I just hadn't found the best time to tell him."

"Love covers a multitude of sins."

Huh? "What did you say?"

"First Peter chapter four verse eight says, 'for charity shall cover the multitude of sins.'"

"That sounds like the verse Jenn asked us to memorize. 'He that covereth a transgression seeketh love; but he that repeateth a matter separateth very friends.'"

Jessie's eyes widened. "You just learned that tonight? You have a sharp memory."

"It's a blessing and a curse." Her ability to memorize things with speed also made Paige a good criminal, a life she was working overtime to leave behind. "But what does that verse mean for me?"

"Hamilton loves you more than you could ever know. He's hurt because he's scared. He could have lost you—did you think about that? Just give him time. He'll be ready to forgive and put it behind him before you know it."

"And if he doesn't?"

"He will." Jessie patted a pile of clean bedding lying on the couch arm. "Now get some sleep. I'll see you in the morning. Everything will look better when the sun comes up. Good night."

The old lady disappeared around the corner, and her bedroom door clicked shut.

A wave of tiredness rolled over Paige. Covering a yawn with her palm, she stood and stretched her back, then pulled out the hide-a-bed. The old rusty springs protested. She unfolded the frame and rubbed her hand over the thin mattress that reminded her of her days at the Juvenile Detention Center.

After picking up the fitted sheet, she started to stretch it across the mattress, but a soft rapping on the window drew her attention. Letting go of the cloth, it snapped back.

She crossed the room, flipped on the porch light, and peaked out the window. Hamilton stood outside, holding a blanket and a thermos, and looking like a little lost puppy. She opened the front door.

"Join me?" He jerked his chin toward the porch swing.

"OK."

The night sky was clear with a million stars twinkling overhead. The temperature had cooled until there was a slight nip in the air. They sat together on the wooden swing, and he laid the blanket over their legs. After opening the lid of the thermos, the rich, earthy smell of coffee drifted to her.

He poured some into the lid, handed it to her, then took a swig directly from the thermos. She laid her head on his chest, and Hamilton draped his arm over her shoulders, tucking her to his side.

Without a word, he kissed the top of her head. She met his eyes and rubbed his scruffy face. A smile spread over his lips, and he dipped his head toward her until their foreheads touched. His eyes flickered back and forth. "I shouldn't have gotten upset before. I… the thought…" His voice choked up. "I don't know what I would do if I lost you. Are we okay?"

"We're fine." *Everything's fine.*

Iago scowled into the bathroom mirror. His reflection echoed his sentiments. The stinging in his eyes had subsided, but they were still bloodshot. He angled his face one way and then the other. Overall, he looked severely sunburned.

She'd sprayed him with mace—he hadn't been expecting that. His plan had seemed so simple, but Paige McDonald was tougher than she looked. He should have seen it coming, given her history with Erik Staten. The man didn't hire wimps.

Now, his face hurt, and he still didn't have his USB.

His cell phone chimed. *Missed call?* Who would call at two in the morning?

He put the phone to his ear and listened to the voicemail.

"It's Chatham. Call me."

Iago scrambled to the living room, nearly tripping over Tybalt in his haste. "Sorry, boy."

Taking a seat on the couch, he put on his socks and shoes, then headed out the door.

First, he'd call Chatham back and find out what he wanted. He'd then send Kathleen another little reminder of the danger she was in if she didn't withdraw from the election.

Something that would spook her good. He was playing with her like a cat plays with a mouse. And when the time was right, the trap would snap shut.

A high-pitched scream woke Kathleen from a deep sleep. Her eyes sprang open, and her heart slammed against her rib cage. A second scream ripped her from her bed. She threw on a robe and tied the sash, then struggled down the stairs, her booted foot hindering her progress.

The front door hung open. Kylie, in her pajamas, stood in the foyer, blocking the entry and screaming. The security alarm wasn't beeping—Kylie must have turned it off before she opened the door.

As Kathleen's feet hit the cold tile floor, Kylie turned her head, ghostly white, and with trembling fingers pointed toward the entry. Kathleen circumvented the open door.

Joe! Kathleen put her hand to her mouth. His clothes were torn and muddied. A gash dripped red down his face, and his bare arms and neck bore welts and bruises. "What happened to you? Come inside." Kathleen stepped back, allowing Joe to enter. "Kylie, get some warm water, bandages, and antibacterial cream. Quickly."

Kylie darted down the hallway, half sliding in her socked feet.

Joe followed Kathleen into the kitchen and sat at the table with a groan. "What happened?" She took a water bottle from the fridge, opened the lid, and set it on the table in front of him. Kylie returned with the first aid kit and a wet rag.

"I was attacked." Joe snatched the rag and gingerly dabbed at the gash on his head.

"Attacked? By whom?"

"I didn't see his face. He wore a mask and jumped me from behind as I was walking to my car."

Kathleen opened the first aid kit and began sorting through the bandages. "Where did this happen? What were you doing?"

Joe grabbed the water, then drank for several seconds. He gasped. The bottle popped. "Would you mind if I cleaned up in your bathroom first, then we can talk?"

"Of course. You know where it is. I'm going to call the police."

As Joe stood, he moaned and shook his head. "There's no point. The guy is long gone. I can't give them a useful description. It was too dark."

He carried the rag, still pressed against his head, and the first aid kit into the bathroom.

While she waited, Kathleen sent Kylie back to bed, then scooped coffee into the filter, poured water into the reservoir, and turned on the coffee maker. Soon the comforting aroma filled the room. *Why would someone attack Joe? And what was he doing out this late at night?*

Had her nemesis taken to harming those on her campaign committee? Was stealing from her campaign and threatening her life not enough for him? Was that why Patti was killed—died? Had Joe barely escaped with his life?

The bathroom door opened. Joe had removed his torn coat. Bloody spots stained the collar of his white dress shirt and the sleeves that he'd rolled up. Band-aids stuck to his arms, and a bandage covered his temple. He set the kit on the island, then winced as he returned to his chair. "Nothing like a kick in the pants." He chuckled, then took another swig of water.

"Coffee?"

"Thank you."

She carried two mugs to the table, then sat kitty-corner to Joe. "Tell me what happened. Where were you? Can you remember anything about the attack?"

He took a drink of coffee, then licked his lips. "None of that's important. What matters is that he had a message for you."

A message? This couldn't be good. Not if the sender was willing to beat a man to a pulp to relay it.

"What's the message?"

Joe took a folded scrap of paper from his pants' pocket.

She snatched it from his fingers. "Did you read it?"

"No."

Nausea strangled her stomach, and her temples throbbed. Kathleen unfolded the paper.

Get it now? Withdraw from the election or someone you love is next.

24

The next morning, Paige parked in front of the bookstore and jogged up the sidewalk. Nori Pham leaned over the public trashcan, pawing her way through the garbage. "What are you doing?"

Nori raised her head. "Trying to find my keys. I threw away my breakfast trash in here and dropped them in too."

Paige stepped closer. "Need some help?"

"No, I think I see them." Nori stood on her tiptoes and reached into the bin with a grunt. Paige's gaze followed and fell on black fabric. After Nori retrieved her keys and stepped aside, Paige reached down and pulled an OSU Beavers cap from among the trash. The one Iago had claimed. *No. What are the odds?* What was the chance this hat belonged to someone else, and they just happened to throw it away outside her bookstore? *Even I don't believe that.*

She was starting to put the pieces together. Iago had come for his flash drive, and when he hadn't found it, he took the hat to cover his true intentions. Iago was her stalker.

Had he stolen her laptop? *But who is Iago? Is that his real name?* Was she being followed because she was Kathleen's daughter?

Later, the front door bell jingled. Paige looked up from the cash register and closed the drawer. Hamilton, wearing jeans and a white T-shirt, crossed the threshold into the bookstore. His weapon wasn't visible, but she didn't doubt it was somewhere on his person. He leaned over the counter and gave her a quick peck on the lips. "Morning, beautiful. You busy?"

She glanced around the room and gestured with her hand. "The store's been empty all morning. What's up?"

He fiddled with a paper clip, then raised his head to meet her eyes. Her heart skipped at the intensity in his gaze. "With everything going on, I need you to be safe. I'm going to buy you a gun."

Paige chuckled and shook her head. "Hamilton, I don't want a gun. I'll be fine. You worry too much." Did he? The photos came to mind and the stalker—she swallowed and silenced her apprehensions. She hadn't received any more threatening notes, and could it really be classified as a threat? A quote from Shakespeare's *As You Like It* wasn't very frightening when you thought about it.

Hamilton caught her chin in his fingers, pulling her thoughts back to him. "Please. I insist."

Her smile faded—he was serious. A cold chill swept her spine. Goosebumps raised on her arms. "OK. Let me get my purse and let Nori know I'm leaving."

Fifteen minutes later, Hamilton parked his baby blue 1962 Chevy pickup in front of the gun shop, then jogged around to the passenger side and opened Paige's door. "Thank you." *I don't need a gun. The mace did its job.* But she'd humor him if it made him feel better about her safety. *I've never owned a gun before.*

As they entered the store, he held the door. The smell of

leather and oil permeated the showroom. Paige wrinkled her nose, but Hamilton took a deep breath and pounded his chest like a gorilla. "Nothing like the smell of safety in the morning."

Paige rolled her eyes and headed for the glass display cases of smaller handguns and knives. The store had a concrete floor and a wall to wall display rack of rifles and shotguns. Metal shelves held targets and hunting gear. Rotating racks displayed different types of holsters, and several sizable shiny gun safes stood off to the side like sentries. The preserved heads of an elk, pronghorn, and bighorn sheep were mounted on the walls.

Her eyes scanned the glass shelves, reading words like *caliber, automatic, semi-automatic, mag, Ruger, Sig, Beretta, 9mm, .308, G3, G4… I have no clue what any of that means. Glocks, pistols, revolvers, snubbies—why do they have different names? They all look the same to me.*

The gunsmith welcomed them. "What can I do for you, Officer Bryant?" The two men shook hands.

"Hey, Harley, I want to get my girlfriend something for self-defense. It's a crazy world out there." He didn't mention anything specific about the danger she'd been in. "What do you have for rookies?"

Harley unlocked the back of the cabinet, slid the glass aside, and pulled out a black handgun. "Glock nineteen, compact, semi-automatic, nine millimeter. Great for beginners. Fits easily in a small hand. Not too much kickback."

Hamilton took it from the seller and looked it over, weighing it in his hand. He pointed at the wall and looked down the barrel. He turned toward Paige. "What about this one?"

"I told you, I don't need a gun." *I've been in far worse danger than this before. I think he forgets what I used to do for a living. I was always aware of the potential consequences of my actions.*

Hamilton placed the small handgun on the counter, then captured Paige's arm and pulled her to the windows. He intertwined their fingers. "Look, Paige. I can't be with you every minute, and I'm not always available if you call. I'm concerned that something is going to happen to you. You've already been in danger since you moved here, and it's only been a couple of weeks."

Paige cocked an eyebrow. "It's turning into a real dangerous place around here. The police should do something about that."

He didn't smile. "It's not funny. I'm serious. You need to be able to protect yourself."

"If it makes you happy." She slid her hands from his and walked back to the cabinet. Hamilton followed. She scanned the case until she spotted a tiny hot pink pistol in the corner. "I'll take this one." She pointed, then glanced over her shoulder to see Hamilton's reaction.

His mouth dropped open, and his eyes widened. "You're joking."

"Nope. I want that one."

Hamilton shook his head. He obviously didn't believe her. "Kylie might carry one like that, but you don't even like pink."

She grinned and leaned her hip against the cabinet.

"Not going to budge, are you?"

"Nope."

With a roll of his eyes, Hamilton addressed the gunsmith. "We'd like to purchase the pink pistol, please." He nearly choked on the words. She touched her knuckles to her lips to hide her pleasure in his discomfort.

Harley slid a paper and pen toward them. "All right. Fill out the lady's information, and I'll run a quick background check." He moved to help another customer.

Paige frowned, bit her lip, and tugged on Hamilton's sleeve. "If I fill that out, he's going to find out I've been arrested."

"You'll be fine."

"If you say so." She picked up the pen and filled out the request.

The cash register dinged. The door closed behind the other customer. "Are you ready down there?"

Paige nodded.

Harley returned to where they stood and picked up the paper. "I'll be right back. This only takes a couple of minutes."

While they waited, Hamilton and Paige strolled around the store. Paige ran her finger over a leather holster. "You know, I don't even know how to shoot. I've never used a gun before."

"I'll teach you." He grinned mischievously at her. "We'll go to the shooting range,"—he pulled her back against his chest and wrapped his arms around her, sliding his palms down her forearms— "and you'll be an expert shot in no time at all."

His breath tickled her neck. Her face tingled. "Is this why you wanted to get me a gun?"

"Maybe." He pressed his lips to her collar bone.

"All right. Everything checks out." Harley entered the showroom.

Hamilton jumped back like a kid caught with his hand in the cookie jar. He coughed and moved toward the counter, but his cheeks had turned several shades of red. "How much do I owe you?" He pulled his wallet from his back pocket.

Harley slid the boxed weapon toward the cash register then set a box of ammunition next to the other container. "Ammo's on the house, Officer Bryant. You take good care of that sweetheart of yours." He winked, and Paige's cheeks grew warm.

"Thanks, Harley. Appreciate it."

Harley scanned the bar code and rang up their purchase. When he told them the amount, Hamilton handed the man his credit card. The gunsmith put it through the scanner and gave it back.

On the way out the door, Hamilton checked something on his phone, then paused on the sidewalk. Paige stopped beside him. "Got a couple hours before my shift. You want to head over to the range and try out your"—he swallowed—"pink pistol?"

Paige chuckled at his reaction to the florescent weapon. "Sure." Nori wouldn't mind watching the store for an hour or so.

"Thank you for speaking with me, Ms. Jessie." Ryan held the door for the elderly woman. She entered his office at the church, then settled into the chair he offered.

"You're welcome, Pastor. What can I do for you?" Jessie set a large handbag on the floor, then patted her thinning white bun. "I wasn't expecting your call."

Ryan sat in his chair behind the desk, facing her. "I'd like some advice. Relationship-wise." He intertwined his fingers and laid his hands on the desktop. No one in town had known his Annie longer than Jessie Faye. There must be a way to get through to Annie. Maybe the wise woman could give him some pointers on how to reach Annie's heart.

Jessie covered her mouth and coughed. "I'm not sure I'm the right person to ask. I'm having some relationship trouble of my own." Her cheeks flushed.

"Hattie McDonald?"

Jessie nodded.

"Paige told me. What's wrong?"

"Hattie just gets under my skin. She's my opposite in every way."

Ryan arched his eyebrow. Interesting that Jessie didn't mention the two of them had once been friends. "I heard there's a bit of unresolved history between you two as well."

"I thought we were here to talk about you, Pastor."

Ryan chuckled—he got the hint. The topic was off-limits. "We are. But I'm also your pastor, and I'm concerned about you." He paused. When Jessie didn't respond, he changed subjects. "It's Annie, I mean, Mayor Phillips. After everything that's happened, I should be angry with her, but the truth is,

I'm not. I've never stopped loving her. However, she doesn't want me in her life, and I don't know what to do."

"She broke your heart."

Ryan nodded. Wasn't that obvious?

"She lied to you. Betrayed you."

"She did." Where was Jessie going with this?

The old woman shifted in the chair. "Sounds like she's your Gomer."

"Gomer Pyle?" He smiled, and she chuckled. She wasn't referring to the old TV show, but the wife of Hosea from Scripture. God had commanded the prophet to marry a known prostitute. Although Hosea had obeyed God, his wife still betrayed him.

Despite the pain she had caused him, he still loved her. Ryan sighed. "I want my Annie back. However, she claims *that* part of her is no more."

Jessie locked onto his eyes. "Annie's not the same woman she used to be. Something happened after she left home. A lot of suffering, I suspect. Your job is to help her heal."

Help her heal? "She said, 'I'm'— meaning herself—'all that's left. And if that's not good enough? We have nothing more to talk about." *What did she mean by that?*

"Then, you have your answer."

Ryan pinched his eyebrows together. "I don't understand."

"You're not the same person you were back then. Why do you expect her to be? My question is, can you love Kathleen as much as you loved Annie? She needs someone to love her for who she is, not who she used to be. Can you do that?"

Ryan walked Jessie to her car parked in front of the church, then returned to the foyer, their conversation still ringing in his ears like he'd fired a gun without wearing earplugs.

Can I love Kathleen as much as I loved Annie?

He hadn't been able to answer Jessie's question. Kathleen was the opposite of everything Annie represented. But other than her obsession with becoming the governor of Oregon, what else did he know about her? *Not much. And that's my fault.*

He headed for the office, then changed directions and entered the auditorium. The afternoon sun shone through the window over the platform where he preached each Sunday. A cross-shaped podium stood just above the carpeted stairs. He scanned the wooden pews, and a head of silver hair caught his attention. *Who's here?*

The woman sat with her head bowed toward the floor. He moved closer, then tipped his head to view her face. "Dawn?" His eyes widened with recognition. "What are you doing here?"

Kathleen's mother raised her head. "Oh, Ryan… I didn't expect to see you here." She brushed at her eyes, but not before he'd caught a glimpse of her glistening tears. "I'll get out of your way." Dawn gathered her purse and stood, stuffing it under her arm. "I'm sorry to bother you."

Ryan laid his palm on her forearm. "You're not bothering anyone. What's wrong? You seem distraught."

With a sigh, Dawn sank into the pew, purse clutched in her lap. Ryan knelt with one leg on the bench in front of her. "Do you want to talk about it? I've been told I'm a good listener."

Dawn gave him a half-hearted smile. "If only Kathleen listened half as well as you do."

He'd never heard what had happened after he left the night they found Dawn making coffee in Kathleen's kitchen. "Have you spoken with her since that night?"

Dawn shook her head and moved her purse to rest beside her leg. "Kathleen isn't interested in anything I have to say. She has her own preconceived ideas and won't budge."

"What *are* you doing here in Whitman?"

"I want to meet my granddaughters."

"Is that all?"

Dawn cocked her eyebrow. "Is that so hard to believe?"

Ryan scrunched his forehead. "When you say 'meet'…" He paused. "Are you saying you've never been introduced?"

Dawn's face flushed. She lowered her eyes. "Unfortunately, yes."

"Kathleen never told you about Paige? Her own mother."

"No."

"And you've never met Kylie either?"

Dawn shook her head, and her shoulders drooped. She began to cry again.

The poor woman. Has Annie harbored so much bitterness she won't even let her mother be introduced to Paige and Kylie? Paige, I can understand, I guess, but Dawn's never even gotten to meet Kylie. Why would Ann—Kathleen do this?

"Will you answer a question for me? Honestly." Ryan shifted positions and sat on the hard pew. "How long have you known about Paige's existence?"

Dawn dabbed at her tears. "Richard telephoned a couple weeks before he died."

"He did? I know it's none of my business, but why?"

"You won't believe me if I tell you."

"Try me."

"He called to apologize."

Ryan's eyes widened. Dawn's disclosure left him speechless. Richard Staten apologized to his ex-wife? The Richard Staten he'd known hadn't handed out apologies voluntarily.

Dawn chuckled. "I see you're as surprised as I was when I took his call."

He could only nod.

"I didn't believe him at first, of course, but my goodness, he was insistent. Richard asked me to forgive him for being a horrible husband and father, then he told me what he'd done with our granddaughter. He said to speak to his lawyer, and Don would arrange a meeting when I was ready. Richard had never apologized to me before. When I questioned his sincerity, he told me how he became a Christian. If God could change someone like him, it had to be real."

"Why didn't you come to Richard's funeral?"

"Richard said it was all right if I didn't come. He understood. I had to process it all. My only daughter had hidden her first pregnancy from me, her mother. I was heartbroken—she didn't trust me with her greatest secret."

She continued, "Kathleen's just like Richard. Too proud to admit failure. They'd rather charge into battle like General George Armstrong Custer at the Battle of Little Big Horn than count the cost before they begin. Richard loved being mayor of this town. It was the happiest time of his life, but then his cousin began running for governor, and he let jealousy consume him. He wanted what Kenneth had, and he found a way to get it."

Kenneth? His cousin? "Who—?"

"How did *you* learn about Paige? You are her father, aren't you?"

"I am." Ryan spent the next several minutes recounting Paige's discovery of Annie's Bible, which led her to the town of Whitman, of how Paige had asked him for assistance. As soon as he'd seen Annie's handwriting inside the Bible, he knew.

"Kathleen kept Paige from you all those years?"

He nodded.

"Ouch. I'm sorry. But—" Dawn made eye contact and held it. She narrowed her eyes like she was reading his mind. "You still love her, don't you?"

"I do. But Kathleen doesn't want me. She's stated as much."

"My daughter is too hurt to know what she wants and too stubborn to admit when she's made a mistake."

"Who hurt her?"

Dawn raised her eyebrows, then frowned. "You don't know, do you?"

Ryan shook his head.

"Ever heard of Lionel Phillips, Formula One driver?"

"No." He scratched his head. "Should I have? Wait,

Phillips? That's Kathleen's last name. Were they married?"

"You really don't know anything about her, do you?"

Jessie was right—he'd been so distracted with his memories of Annie, he'd paid no attention to the woman she'd become. "What happened?"

"Lionel Phillips was a monster, on and off the track."

25

That afternoon, Ryan knocked on the front door of Annie's home then stepped back. *Not Annie. Think of her as Kathleen from now on.* He shifted the bouquet to his left hand and wiped the sweaty right hand on his trousers. The vase in the study had had roses in it—maybe those were her favorites now. It was worth a try. He breathed a prayer, hoping he would make a better impression than he had the last several times they'd interacted. *I've got to show her I'm nothing like her husband was. Show her she can trust me. I would never do anything to hurt her.*

His conversations with Jessie and Dawn tumbled through his thoughts. All he could do was try. Try to understand. And try his best to love Kathleen for who she was and not who she used to be—not an easy task with reminders of the past swirling around him.

He had stood on this same stoop over twenty-five years ago, waiting to take Annie on their first date, feeling just as nervous as he did right now. He'd taken her to The Golden Spoon—a greasy roadside diner that shut down years ago.

This time he had something different in mind—something more fitting the sophisticated Madam Mayor.

The door creaked, and Matilda's brown face and gray hair appeared around the jamb. She made a noise, clasping her hand to her chest, then opened the door wide. "It's you. What a relief. All the loco around here, I'm almost afraid to open the door."

What craziness? What's she talking about? "What happened, Matilda?"

The old lady stepped aside and gestured for him to enter. "That man who works for Kathleen shows up here the other night all beat up. He brought Kathleen a message."

Ryan crinkled his forehead. "What man? What message?" Fear gripped his chest. What was going on? *I thought the police arrested the hostile. Is Kathleen still in danger?*

Matilda shook her head. "It's better Kathleen explains. I only know what she said. She's in the study. Go on up."

Ryan turned to jog upstairs but paused and laid his hand on Matilda's shoulder. "By the way, it's nice to see you again, Matilda."

Tears brimmed the old woman's eyes. "I'm glad to see you too, Ryan. You've grown into a good man." She patted his cheek with her calloused palm.

"Thank you." Coming from her, that meant a lot. If she trusted him, maybe Kathleen would, too. Eventually.

Ryan took the stairs two at a time, then slowed when he approached the study door. It hung ajar. Kathleen's voice carried into the hall. As fast as she was monologuing, she was either on the phone or dictating to her assistant. Should he interrupt?

He took a quick breath to quiet his nerves, then pushed the door open. The hinges creaked. Kathleen paced with her back to him, hobbling on her booted ankle. She pressed her cell phone to her ear, and her tone sounded angry. "I don't care what it takes. I want those files on my desk by Monday morning."

She spun on her good heel. When their eyes met, she

froze. "I'll have to call you back." She lowered the phone. "What are you doing here?" Her eyes fell on the yellow roses. "You brought flowers?" Her voice faded from mad to uncertain. "Um, thank you? I guess."

He pointed toward the credenza. Droopy blooms hung over the edge of the vase. "Looks like you could use some fresh ones." He held the bouquet toward her.

She tentatively took them. "Is there something I can do for you?" Her tone was far softer than the last time he'd visited.

Ryan nodded, then let his eyes momentarily scan the bookshelves. Richard Staten had books on every subject known to man it seemed. How Ryan's hands itched to dig into some of those volumes. Maybe Paige had received her love of books from him. Were things like that passed through DNA?

He peeled his gaze away. Kathleen stood quietly, eyes wide, still waiting for him to answer. "Will you have dinner with me?"

A beat passed. "Where would we go?"

It was his turn to be surprised—she hadn't instinctively brushed him off. Maybe he was making more progress than he thought. "I have reservations at the lodge on Wallowa Lake, if you're interested."

"Really?" Her voice brightened, then she cleared her throat. "It's difficult to get reservations there. Thank you for asking." She paused a moment. "Yes, I'll join you."

Yes! Ryan imagined fist-pumping the air. Not wanting his enthusiasm to anger her into changing her mind, he simply nodded. "The reservation is at eight. Does that work for you?" He deferred the decision to her, letting Kathleen know he cared about her opinion rather than order her around. She'd had enough of that with Lionel. And her father.

It seemed to work. Kathleen laid her palm on her flushed cheek, looking slightly off-balance. "Thank you. Eight is fine. What time will you pick me up?"

As soon as Ryan left, Kathleen sat at the desk to center her nerves, the bouquet still in her hand. She pressed her other hand to her cheek. The skin warmed her fingers. What had she been thinking? Why on earth had she agreed? Holding the roses under her nose, she took a deep breath and drank in their intoxicating scent. Was she so easily swayed by a pretty bouquet?

She stood and carried them to the credenza, preparing to switch them out with the dying ones, then changed directions. At the study door, she called downstairs. "Matilda."

Matilda appeared at the bottom of the staircase. "Yes?"

Kathleen touched a soft petal. "Do we have any more vases? I'd like to put these in my bedroom."

"Yes, of course. I will find one."

"Thank you." Kathleen limped down the hall. She laid the bouquet on her bedspread, then crossed to the closet to find something to wear to dinner, feeling almost giddy. How long had it been since she'd been on an actual date?

Her hands froze. *A date?* Was that what this was?

She eased onto the bed, pressing her hands into the soft material. Why had she agreed to go on a date with Ryan Whitestone? This was sure to end badly. *I should cancel.* Kathleen patted her pockets, looking for her cell phone, which reminded her—she still needed to call the office back. Later. Her pockets were empty. She'd left the phone in the study.

She lay back on the mattress, hands on her stomach. Butterflies flittered beneath her fingers. A date with Ryan Whitestone. The two of them hadn't dated in over twenty-five years… *This isn't a date.*

Just two friends sharing a meal—oh, who was she kidding? They weren't friends.

Friends didn't treat each other like they had. They didn't betray each other, lie to each other… but… did Ryan want to be friends? What if he wanted more than friendship?

A cannonball replaced the butterflies. Memories of Lionel's cruelty chased away the good feelings like the running of the bulls in Spain. Would she ever trust another man enough to enter the marriage covenant a second time?

She rolled to her side, her sight falling on the roses.

And if she did, could Ryan be that man?

"I found a vase underneath the sink." Matilda's voice preceded her as she entered the bedroom. Kathleen sat up and brushed tears from her eyes. She hadn't thought about Ryan in years. Why was she suddenly letting her daydreams run away with her?

It was one dinner. Not a marriage proposal.

Kathleen slid from the bed, picked up the bouquet, then dropped it into the vase Matilda set on the dresser. "Thank you, Matilda."

"You're welcome. Beautiful."

Had Matilda been referring to the flowers or to Kathleen? She peeked over her shoulder at the smiling old woman. "Penny for your thoughts?"

"Pastor Whitestone is a good man." Matilda patted Kathleen's arm, then turned toward the door. "You could do worse."

"I know."

Because she had.

Promptly at 7:30 that evening, the doorbell rang. Kathleen, mouth dry and heart palpitating, opened the front door. Ryan, wearing a tailored gray suit and necktie, stood on the front porch. His stance was rigid with his hands jammed into his pockets, making the coat flaps bunch at his waist. His graying hair was parted to the side, beard trimmed. Appreciation flickered in his eyes, and his jaw dropped.

Kathleen's lips quirked in the corner. She had dressed in a sleeveless Tommy Hilfiger jersey crepe black dress that went from collarbone to knees. The skirt flared at her hips with white stripes. She carried a gold clutch purse and wore a gold sandal on her good foot while trying to ignore how badly the gray boot clashed with her outfit.

Ryan blinked twice, then held out his arm. "Your carriage awaits, my lady." His voice cracked. He cleared his throat. "I mean, are you ready?" *He's as nervous as I am.*

At that moment, she almost expected to see a horse-drawn carriage in her drive. Instead, Ryan's Kia sat on the asphalt, waiting for its passengers. He helped her into the car, then jogged to the driver's side, and settled into the seat. Ryan started the engine, then they drove to the restaurant in relative silence.

After passing through town, they headed toward the lake. The setting sun cast pink and orange tendrils across the sky and reflected in the calm waters of Wallowa Lake. Kathleen spotted the rustic lodge through the evergreen trees—the parking lot was full.

"I'm going to have to park in overflow. I'll let you out at the door, so you won't have so far to walk."

Kathleen glanced at Ryan from the corner of her eye. *That was thoughtful.* He stopped the car in front of the double door entrance, came around to her side, then helped her to the sidewalk. "You're welcome to wait or go on it and let them know we're here."

With that, he returned to the car, then drove toward the overflow parking lot down the road. Warmth expanded in her chest, and her midsection jumbled. As a sting prickled behind her eyes, she bit her lower lip. How long had it been since someone had considered her needs before their own? How long had it been since anyone, besides Kylie and Matilda, had treated her with kindness or compassion? Fear, even respect, she comprehended, but this—this was new. *And appreciated.*

Kathleen opted to wait for Ryan outside the lodge. A slight breeze sent goosebumps up her arms as it cooled the evening temperatures. When her foot began to ache from standing, she moved to a cast iron bench. The bars chilled the backs of her legs. She checked the time on her watch. They'd be late if Ryan didn't hurry.

A minute later, he hustled toward the building, coat flaring, tie over his shoulder, hair windblown. He stopped beside Kathleen, bending at the waist, hands on his knees. As he caught his breath, Ryan coughed. "I'm getting too old for that."

"No mentions of getting old. We're the same age."

Ryan laughed and held out his arm. "Shall we?"

Arm in arm, they entered the lodge, crossed the lobby to the restaurant, and were promptly seated on the outside deck overlooking the lake. The host went over the specials and asked what they'd like to drink. They both ordered water and coffee, then the host left them to peruse the menus.

"Thank you, Ryan. I'm—this is nice." Anxiety bubbled in Kathleen's chest. She reached out and began rearranging the sugar packets in the ceramic box. The simple task eased the tension in her shoulders.

"You're very welcome." He paused. "Paige—never mind. Have you decided what you'd like to eat?"

Kathleen drew her eyebrows together. He'd started to say something about Paige but had changed his mind. What was it he'd planned to say? "The special sounded good. I think I'll have that."

The server arrived with their drinks, then took their orders. As they waited, they chatted about inconsequential subjects. They'd both grown up in Whitman and now held positions of leadership in their community. They shared many of the same acquaintances and memories. Every other sentence began with the words, "Do you remember…"

Minutes passed, and the recollections deepened. Kathleen's present stress and current crises faded.

Kathleen wiped away the tear that ran down her cheek and put her hand on her knotted stomach. Ryan's story of Mr. Haberdeen's bulldog, Puggles, smashing through the Keiths' wedding cake and running off with the bride and groom topper had her gasping for air.

How long had it been since she'd laughed this hard? Too long, that was for sure. She felt freer than she had in years. No judgment. No expectations.

Ryan took her hand from across the table. "Would you mind if I asked you a question?" His tone sobered.

Uh, oh. Something tells me I'm not going to like this.

"What happened to your faith? You used to be a dedicated Christian, but Kylie said you haven't been to church in years. Why?"

Kathleen rolled her head as her shoulders tightened once again. The evening was going so well. Why did he have to bring that up? She closed her eyes, trying to block out the memories. When she opened them, Ryan was staring at her, waiting for her answer. "Look, Ryan, it's not something I like to talk about."

"Kathleen—"

She jerked her hand from his. "I don't want to talk about it." She snapped, louder than she'd expected. Other diners looked their way. "Can you please just drop it?"

Ryan nodded. "Of course. I'm sorry for upsetting you. That wasn't my intention." He fell silent and looked down at his hands.

Kathleen fiddled with the silver napkin ring. She shouldn't have gotten upset. He'd asked a legitimate question, but one she wasn't ready to answer. Not to him. Only God knew the real reason she'd quit church. Quit her faith.

She glanced at Ryan. His head hung like a reprimanded child. "How is Paige doing?" Not exactly a subject she wanted to traverse, but at least Ryan's eyes lit up at the mention of their daughter.

"Good. She's doing good. How— how's the campaign?"

"Good. It's good," Kathleen lied—it wasn't. When she'd gotten home from the cabin, she'd learned half the volunteers had quit without a word. How much longer could she press on?

The server interrupted, bringing their plates of grilled

salmon, rice pilaf, and buttered asparagus.

Kathleen drew in a breath and sighed. It was easier to eat than converse. As she parted her fish with a fork, a melody slipped into her thoughts, and she found herself humming the familiar tune. Her head shot up. Her eyes widened. "You sent me that sheet music, didn't you?"

Ryan swallowed. "I did."

"Why?"

"It doesn't matter anymore." Ryan lowered his eyes and played with the end of his tie.

"It does. Why did you send me that song?"

"To remind you of who you used to be."

"Who I used to be? You mean, Annie." He didn't answer—he didn't have to. Kathleen read it in his expression. "Do you want to know why I stopped being Annie?" When he didn't respond, she continued, "My husband was an abusive alcoholic. It didn't matter if he won or lost his race; he got drunk either way. But if he lost, the evening always ended badly. One time, in a drunken rage, he smashed my collection of Precious Moments.

"Then one night, ten years ago, he—" The memory choked her throat. "I ended up in the hospital where I miscarried. I prayed and begged God to spare my child. And He didn't. When I went home, I started using my middle name. I couldn't stomach 'Annie' any longer. I didn't want to be Annie. Annie was weak. Annie was helpless. Annie couldn't stand up for herself.

"Kathleen—on the other hand—Kathleen was strong. Kathleen didn't take nothing from nobody. Kathleen didn't need God; she could handle it all on her own. Five years later, Lionel was killed in a freak accident on the racetrack. When my father called me after his cancer diagnosis, I moved home, so Kylie and I could have a fresh start. So, I could put all my mistakes in the past. It worked until you came back into my life. Then Paige."

Kathleen took shaky breaths. She hadn't meant to reveal all of that. It had just slipped out. But at least Ryan now knew the truth. He slouched in his chair as if it suddenly took too much effort to sit up straight. His hand lightly held his throat. "You can't blame God because your husband was an evil man." Ryan's voice warbled with emotion.

"Why not? He could have stopped Lionel at any time, but He didn't. He could have spared my child, but He didn't. Why shouldn't I blame Him?"

Ryan reached across the table and cupped her hand. A tingle climbed her arm at his touch. "I know you're hurting, but you've shut everyone out, even God, and look at what that's gotten you."

Numbness swept over her and fortified the cracks in the walls around her heart. Kathleen ripped her hand from his. "It got me everything I ever wanted." She shoved the chair back from the table, grabbed her purse, and turned toward the exit. "Thank you for dinner. Please take me home."

26

To say her *date* with Ryan had been a disaster was an understatement.

A wildfire was a disaster.

A landslide was a disaster.

Dinner last night was a fallout of nuclear bomb proportions.

Kathleen, with eyes puffy and tension knotting her neck, instructed Kylie to drop her off at the airport to fly to Portland for the gala at the Treasury Ballroom. She hurried to catch her plane, lashing out at everyone and making a fool of herself.

When the puddle jumper landed in the city an hour late, she rented a car and drove to the Hotel De Luxe, then checked into her suite and logged onto her laptop at the rectangular writing desk. Kathleen slouched in the wingback chair, too distracted to focus on work. Her blood boiled. What business was it of his if she'd pushed others away? He would never understand her pain—her regret. And if she chose to blame God for the way her life had turned out, that was her business.

Ryan Whitestone could stick his Bible-thumping opinion into someone else's problems.

He only broached the subject because he cares. Kathleen swallowed the lump in her throat. Of course, he did. But why? He shouldn't. They could never be together, not after the things she'd done.

He'd never forgive her if he ever learned the truth.

Letting her guard down had been a colossal mistake. She never should have agreed to go out with him. Kathleen squared her shoulders. It wouldn't happen again. She had built walls around her heart for a reason, and no one, not even Ryan Whitestone, could be allowed to tear them down.

A knock sounded on the door. Kathleen startled. *Who could that be?* She wasn't expecting anyone. After limping across the room, she unlocked and opened the door. Joe Donahue, wearing a polo shirt and khakis, stood on the other side. Ugly bruises still marred his features, and his nose angled, slightly crooked. "May I come in?"

Kathleen stepped back. "Oh, sure. What can I do for you?"

Joe crossed the threshold and folded his arms over his chest. "I don't think you should go to the gala tonight."

Her eyes grew wide as she closed the door behind him. "Excuse me?"

"You've been threatened multiple times. Your volunteer coordinator is dead. I was beaten to a pulp… should I go on?"

Kathleen mirrored his stance. "Forget it. I'm going. Do your job or get out of my way." Why did everyone think they could push her around?

"Fine. If you're going to be obstinate, I'm not going to argue with you. I'll do my job. But don't say I didn't warn you."

Warn her? She tilted her head and made eye contact. She hadn't made a campaign appearance yet that hadn't ended in disaster. But she couldn't miss the gala, not after finding those photos of Chatham and her dad.

Joe walked to the hotel closet and removed a garment bag hanging inside. "If you insist on going, wear this." He unzipped the zipper. Bright red fabric peeked out from between the teeth. He removed the dress and held it for her to get a better view.

"I'm not wearing that. I'll look like a—a coquette."

"A coquette? Really? Isn't that word a little old fashioned?"

What kind of person did he think she was? She wouldn't voice any of those other words aloud, and she wasn't going to dress like one either.

"Just wear the dress. Your numbers in the polls are dropping. Voters are saying you're stiff and unlikeable."

Kathleen huffed and put her hands on her hips. "I'm not stiff. I'm mature and professional—"

"And you dress like a man. Use your womanhood. Don't hide it behind a pantsuit. You'll catch more flies with honey than vinegar."

How did he know what she'd planned to wear tonight? "I'm not trying to catch flies."

"No. You're trying to catch voters, which is harder."

Fine. Kathleen jerked the dress out of his hand. It was entirely outside her typical style, but if Joe thought she needed to change her look to garner support… she'd do it.

Just this once.

Several hours later, Kathleen entered the Treasury Ballroom, catching her reflection in the mirrored walls. She wore the dress Joe had chosen, ruby-red with a sweetheart neckline and off-the-shoulder sleeves. The pleated skirt fell to just above her knees. Her brunette hair tumbled in soft curls and brushed against her bare shoulders as she crossed the marble floor with one open-toed pump and one full shell walker boot. Men, dressed in tuxedos, turned to stare. *Could this be any more awkward?*

Politicians and influentials from all over the state populated the warm room. Servers walked between them, carrying trays of aperitifs. One offered her a drink, but she waved her hand. "No, thank you."

Joe leaned against a pillar across the room, sipping a glass of champagne. He was alone at the moment. Kathleen stalked his direction, only stumbling once in the icepick heeled shoe. His eyebrows raised to his hairline as she approached.

"I look ridiculous." She hissed as she tugged at the low neckline.

Joe set his empty glass on a passing tray. "Are you kidding me? You look stunning."

"All right, then I *feel* ridiculous. How did you convince me to wear this? I can't decide whether to pull it up or down."

"The point is for you to be unforgettable." He ran his eyes over her with a look of appreciation. "And you, Madam Mayor, are definitely unforgettable." With that, he walked off, chasing a waiter carrying a tray of bubbling glasses.

Kathleen growled, feeling more like a seductress than a political candidate, and as unprofessional as answering a cell phone during an interview.

Isaiah Orozco, her political opponent, approached champagne in hand. Unmistakable interest lit his eyes. "Mayor Phillips. You look lovely this evening."

She grunted in response. Who cared what Orozco thought?

"May I get you something to drink?" He raised his glass.

"No, thank you, I don't imbibe."

Orozco lowered his glass and cleared his throat. "How's the campaign trail treating you?"

Terrible. But Kathleen wasn't going to admit that to him. "It's going well. Thank you."

Orozco swallowed a mouthful of beige liquid. "Crazy about that shooter at the debate. Do you think he was aiming for the incumbent governor and hit your podium instead?"

He was aiming for me, you idiot. Kathleen shrugged. "I

suppose any one of us could have been the target. Even you."

Liquor spewed from his lips, barely missing her couture gown. Orozco yanked a handkerchief from his pocket and wiped his face clean. "I—I guess that is possible. Enjoy your evening." He folded his handkerchief and slid it back into his pocket, then hurried away.

That was almost humorous. Poor man. Had he never considered the gunman could have been targeting him? Or was the idea utterly too preposterous?

Kathleen scanned the crowd. A group of women stood together, off to one side. The only one she recognized was Patricia Chatham. *Avoid that.* She turned, running smack into Joe's chest.

"Go. Talk to them." He whispered, waving his hand toward the group of women.

Had he lost his mind? "No."

"Every vote counts. Theirs are just as valuable."

Who cared about their opinion? They could say what they wanted. It didn't matter what they thought of her. "What are they talking about? Shoes?" *Or feelings?* She shuddered.

Joe put his hand on her shoulder and gave her a shove. "Go."

"Fine." She headed toward her worst nightmare. "You're rather pushy today."

The group of women stopped talking. Patricia Chatham smiled. "Kathleen. So good to see you. How have you been?" She pulled Kathleen into an embrace.

Kathleen's body went rigid. Hugs? Really? She tried not to grimace. Patricia released her, and the other women greeted her with handshakes and…air kisses. Worse than hugs. So fake and superficial.

"What happened?" Patricia motioned toward the ankle boot.

Should she lie or tell the truth? Kathleen opted for the lie. "I stumbled over a stray cat and fell down the courthouse stairs. The doctor says it's just a sprain. It should heal in another week or two." There. These biddies didn't need to know what had really happened. She'd rather them think her a klutz than know someone was threatening her life.

After a round of "oh, you poor dear," one of the representative's wives, who'd introduced herself as Sarah Arnold, spoke up. "We've been discussing the inequality between men and women in the workplace. You're running for governor. Do you have a plan on how to deal with this?"

She'd rather talk about shoes. "I suppose it depends on what you mean by inequality."

"You're not an advocate for women's rights?"

"I'm an advocate for all rights."

The group fell silent. Kathleen could have bowled any one of them over with a feather. With a shake of their heads, the women moved away.

"Aren't you the Queen of Tact tonight?" Joe. What was he going to make her do now?

"They asked for my opinion, and I gave it to them. Why should they be offended just because it differs from theirs?"

"I sent you over here to woo them, not alienate them."

She waved her hand as she took a glass of water from a passing tray. "Who cares what they think?"

"You should. You should care. Do you know how influential those women are?"

Kathleen narrowed her eyes. "I don't need their approval." She took a sip of the chilled beverage.

"You may not *need* their approval, but there might come a day when you wished you *had* it." Joe spun on his heel. She fought the urge to stick out her tongue.

She glanced over to where the women had moved. They huddled close and whispered to one another. Were they talking about her? Sarah looked her way. When their eyes met, Sarah jerked back, and Kathleen's confidence slipped. Had she made a mistake? Had she done irreparable damage to her campaign?

Suddenly, her stomach didn't feel so well. *Where is the bathroom?*

She walked forward, eyes searching for an exit—her body

connected with a solid. Air puffed from her lungs. Water splashed from her glass. What had she hit?

A hand grabbed her forearm. "Evening. Ms. Phillips. You look prettier than a sunset over Mount Hood." False enthusiasm laced the deep voice. Senator Chatham, of course.

She lifted her eyes. This man was Dad's cousin. Family. "I appreciate the compliment. Congratulations on your candidacy for president."

"Thank you, Ms. Phillips. Isn't it a lovely evening? I hope you aren't planning to ruin it by announcing your surrender."

Announcing her surrender? Why would he think that? Her stomach roiled. She scrunched her face. "Why would I surrender? I didn't know we were at war." She gave him a fake laugh to cover her irritation.

"I heard through the grapevine your campaign is struggling. I assumed you'd be announcing your withdrawal soon."

Where had he heard that? Kathleen steamed like a kettle of hot water. "You heard wrong. I have no intention of withdrawing from the election. Your grapevine is clearly misinformed." The longer she looked at him, the harder it was to keep calm. She jerked her arm out of his grip. "If you'll excuse me, I'm looking for the ladies' room." The knots in her stomach worsened.

"Ms. Phillips." Senator Chatham stepped out of her way and dipped his chin.

Without a backward glance, she headed for the exit, leaving her glass on a table as she passed. At the top of the stairs, she spotted the restroom sign. Voices carried to where she stood.

"Did you ever meet Richard Staten?" The deep voice spoke of Kathleen's father.

"No, I never had that pleasure. Staten was gone before I entered the political arena. Cancer, wasn't it?" Another man answered.

It's rude to eavesdrop. Should she step out and reveal herself or stay hidden to hear more? Kathleen paused to listen.

The first man spoke again. "You know how he got the nickname Minotaur Staten?" When the second man shook his head, the first continued. "The Minotaur is a symbol of power. Richard Staten was power-hungry. He did whatever it took to get what he wanted and didn't care who he hurt in the process."

That's not true. How could those men believe that?

Dad had been ruthless, she wouldn't deny that, but to say he'd purposefully harm someone… his actions were justified. The political arena was more brutal than the Roman Colosseum.

"I heard his daughter is just like him." The second man spoke.

Me? From the man's tone, she gathered it wasn't a compliment.

"Oh, absolutely. Phillips hasn't even been elected, and they're already calling her the Ice Queen of Capitol Hill. She's a heartless, unfeeling woman. The voters are starting to notice."

Tears stung her eyes and nose. How could they say those things about her? Ice Queen? Heartless and unfeeling? An ill-timed sob slipped from her lips.

The men stopped talking. They'd heard her. Saw her. Together, they walked away without an apology.

A warm drop trickled down her cheek. She sniffled and quickly brushed it away. She wouldn't let them see her cry. Wouldn't give them the satisfaction.

Kathleen spun on her heel and left the ballroom. The doorman tipped his hat and held the door as she swept through, mimicking the winter breeze to which the men had alluded.

She stalked down the street as quickly as her boot would allow, then paused. Hadn't she parked the rental car in the other direction? Irritated with herself, she pivoted and ran directly into a broad chest. Again. *I should start looking where I'm going. Who did I hit this time?*

"Annie—Kathleen—I mean, Mayor Phillips. What are

you doing here?"

Ryan. Of course. She'd know that voice anywhere. And the way he adorably stumbled over what to call her. *It's not adorable. Stop calling me by the wrong name.* "I could ask you the same question." What was he doing in downtown Portland? Was he stalking her?

"I'm not stalking you if that's what you think. I had errands to take care of." It freaked her how well he could read her thoughts.

She cleared her throat and touched the ends of her hair, suddenly uncomfortable in his presence dressed this way. "I was attending a political gala."

He studied her face in the slanted light from the streetlamp. "Have you been crying?" He brushed a wayward tear from her cheek.

She shrank back under his touch. "It's nothing. I was just leaving."

"May I walk with you?"

His concern aggravated her. Why should he care? "I'm more than capable of walking to my car alone."

"I wondered if we might speak about yesterday."

Kathleen darted around him and marched down the sidewalk, hoping he wouldn't follow. He matched her stride for stride. "I've already expressed my feelings on the matter. We have nothing more to talk about."

"You're being unfair. She deserves to know her parents and be loved by them. She missed out on so much."

She? He was referring to Paige? Kathleen froze on the sidewalk so quickly he passed her and had to take a few steps back. "*She* missed out on so much. Did you ever think about what I missed out on?"

"Kathleen—"

"I missed everything. Paige's first steps. Her first words. Her first day of school. I didn't even get to name her." The words stuck in her throat—she couldn't continue.

"You let him take her from you."

As his words cut her like a knife, she gasped. Images

flashed through her mind for the umpteenth time since Paige had reentered her life. "I didn't have a choice." He didn't understand.

"Yes, you did. You chose to push Paige away. Just like you're doing now. Again. To her. To me."

"I did what I thought was best. For all of us."

He circled around and blocked her path. "Kathleen. Stop. Look at yourself. Look at what you've become. He's dead, Annie. You can't please him. This isn't what he'd want for you. You broke my heart. You allowed your daughter to grow up without her family. None of our lives were ever the same. Don't you see that? You're willing to sacrifice your own children to get ahead. But even if you win the election, where will you be? You'll have everything, and yet, you'll have nothing. Absolutely nothing."

Of course, she knew that—but she couldn't change the past. The pain in her heart was unbearable. She had to get away, and she did it the only way she knew how. "And I'd do it all over again."

He recoiled under her frostbite, and she set off at a rapid pace. Nearing the parking garage, she slowed and looked back over her shoulder. He was gone. Her ribs grew tight, restricting her breath—but she hadn't wanted him to follow her, had she? Wasn't that why she'd run away? Shouldn't she be glad he was gone?

She finished the walk to the rental car, then unlocked the doors, and dropped into the driver's seat. She set her clutch purse beside her, then reached under the steering wheel and removed the ridiculous high heel shoe from her sore foot. After she closed the car door, she laid her head against the headrest. How could she get Ryan to understand how she felt when she barely comprehended it herself? Whatever they'd had in the past, it was gone.

Kathleen let hot tears roll down her cheeks uninhibited. His words hurt more than she could have imagined. She hadn't wanted to break his heart, but what other alternative did she have? They were all wrong for each other. Their dreams led them in different directions.

To this day, she couldn't picture herself as the dutiful pastor's wife, taking casseroles to sick people and letting snotty-nosed babies drool on her in the nursery. Ryan was called to preach. He never would have been happy as the husband of a politician.

With a sigh and a shake of her head, she shifted, put the key in the ignition, and turned it. Nothing happened. She tried again—still nothing.

She pounded on the steering wheel and pressed her forehead to it. How could this be happening? Could this night get any worse?

Kathleen reached under her seat and popped the hood, then climbed out of the car. The concrete floor was cold under her stockinged foot. She raised the metal covering, used the bar to hold it up, then leaned forward and poked around. Did she even know what she was looking for? When she removed her hands, dark sticky grease had coated her fingers.

She dropped the hood with a bang, then climbed inside the car, looking for something to clean her hands. Not even a tissue was available. With an eye roll, she wiped them down the front of her dress. Piece of junk was going in the garbage as soon as she got to her hotel. She preferred her pantsuit's practicality to dressing like a Barbie doll.

Kathleen picked up her cell phone. *Call Ryan.* No way. Absolutely not. He'd come running to her rescue like Prince Charming with the Paul Revere Reveille playing in the background. She didn't need his chivalry—she could take care of herself.

She used her phone to look up the closest rideshare service, then arranged for a pickup, paying no attention to the photo of the driver or the description of the car. If they got her to her hotel room in one piece, what did it matter what the driver looked like? She dropped her phone into her purse and glanced over at her shoe. No way was she putting that ankle breaker back on. She'd rather be barefoot.

Kathleen grabbed her purse, then walked out of the parking garage and stood on the sidewalk, waiting for her ride.

Kenneth paced his personal study. The glittering soiree had turned out to be a total bust. Kathleen had no intention of dropping out of the election. He poured a glass of whiskey and downed it in one gulp—something to clear his head and calm his nerves.

Kenneth slammed his fist on the mantle of the fireplace. A sharp pain radiated through his wrist and arm, but he ignored it. Memories burned like fire in his soul. With one phone call, Richard's daughter could squash his entire presidential campaign. But it appeared the woman had no idea the power she possessed. And he intended to keep it that way, no matter what it took. No Staten would thwart his plans ever again—one betrayal was enough for a lifetime. He'd never allow a second. Protecting his own interests was suddenly more important than getting revenge on Richard Staten.

He returned to pacing the length of the patterned carpet. How long would that fool keep him waiting? He should have responded by now. He dropped into an armchair and scrubbed his hand across his face. If this kept up, he'd need an antacid for the heartburn building in his stomach. The Fillet Mignon and Duchess Potatoes sat like boulders in his gut. A knock drew his attention to the door. "Come in."

It quickly opened and shut. Bridge stepped inside the room.

"Did you send someone?"

"He's on his way now."

27

The night air sent chills up Kathleen's bare arms. She should have brought a jacket. All she could think about was taking pain medicine for her headache and getting off her aching feet. A long soak in the tub sounded lovely. Maybe when she pulled the plug, her troubles with Ryan would swirl down the drain with the water.

A black Suburban pulled along the curb and stopped. This must be it.

Kathleen opened the front passenger door and hopped onto the faux leather seat. "Thank you for picking me up." She kept her eyes on her phone and didn't look at the driver.

"My name is Nigel. Where would you like to go?" A gruff voice spoke from the other side of the SUV.

"The Hotel De Luxe."

The driver pulled into the late-night traffic. Kathleen flipped down the visor and used the small mirror. Her hair hung to her shoulders in flat clumps, and she had a smudge on her cheek where she must have touched her face. Black streaks ran down the front of her dress, and she was shoeless, except for the walker boot.

She should have called a taxi. Then she wouldn't have had to give her name or be rated as a passenger. Oh well, it was too late to worry about that now. Maybe the driver didn't even know who she was or care that she was running for governor.

Of course, if that was the case, she should be trying to sway his vote in her direction, but it's not like one vote made that much of a difference, did it? Joe's words from earlier ran through her mind. "*Every vote counts.*"

Fine. I'll ask.

She returned the visor to its place and turned to look at her driver. He wore a knit cap pulled down over his ears. He had flipped up his coat collar to hide his face. *Wait. Coat collar?*

According to the temperature reading on the dashboard, it was a balmy 64 degrees outside. A jacket, yes, but a winter coat? Fear rolled over her and settled in her belly. Something wasn't right.

Kathleen looked out the window. Headlights illuminated bridge trusses as they flashed past, and the Willamette River flowed beneath. Wasn't the Hotel De Luxe in the opposite direction? Her pulse picked up speed. "Hey! Where are you going? My hotel is the other way."

Something sharp stuck into her ribs. She gasped and glanced down. The tip of a knife glinted in the light from an oncoming vehicle.

"If you want to make it to our destination alive, I suggest you sit back and enjoy the ride."

Nigel, if that was his real name, snatched her phone from her lap, rolled down the window, and tossed it into the river. Strange hands appeared on either side of her head from the back seat. Her heart pounded in her chest. Someone else was in the vehicle. As soft fabric covered her face, her view went dark. *This can't be happening to me. Where are we going? What are they going to do with me when we get there? Am I going to die?*

If she called out to God for help, would He hear her this time?

After what seemed like hours, the car slowed, then rolled to a stop. They'd made so many turns, Kathleen had lost track. Were they still in Portland? *In Oregon*? How long had it been since she'd first been picked up?

The car door opened, and chilly air raced over her arms. Rough hands grabbed and pulled her from the vehicle, and the cold concrete chilled the bottom of her stockinged foot. It was still dark out. Something sharp poked her side—the knife. She moved forward, unable to see where she was going. Her toe kicked against something, and she stumbled.

"Steps," Nigel muttered.

The other person hadn't uttered a word, but Kathleen sensed his presence behind her. She concentrated on climbing the stairs then halted when the men stopped.

A doorbell echoed, faintly. Was this someone's private residence? Where had they taken her?

The door opened. No one spoke. Bright light permeated Kathleen's blindfold. Silhouettes moved. Someone led the way across an expansive foyer and into a room with the faint stench of aftershave, cigar smoke, and whiskey. Nigel pressed firmly on her shoulder. "Have a seat. He'll be with you in a moment."

"Who? Where am I?" She lowered to the seat. The cushions were soft beneath her legs. The two people chuckled but didn't answer her questions.

A door closed, and she was alone. Or, at least, she assumed she was. Nigel and his accomplice hadn't bothered to tie her hands. Kathleen yanked off the blindfold, dropping it to the floor, then surveyed her surroundings, searching for a way to escape. Office furniture, belonging to someone with expensive taste, filled the room. White suede sofas faced each other. A crystal chandelier hung from the ceiling. Wall to wall bookshelves. A 50-inch flat-screen TV. Massive executive desk.

A telephone sat on the edge of the desk. *Telephone! I can call for help.* Kathleen limped across the room and grabbed the receiver. Nothing. No signal. Was the phone even plugged in?

She squatted, looking for the cord.

Or maybe the phone had been disconnected so she wouldn't be able to make a call.

"Ms. Phillips? Whatever are you doing?"

That voice. Kathleen scrunched her forehead. Senator Chatham? She lifted her eyes. His large frame plugged the open doorway. She stood.

"You! What's going on here?" Shock and confusion colored her words. What was he doing here? Was this *his* house?

Chatham stepped across the threshold and gestured toward the couch. The door closed behind him, but not before she spotted a guard standing in the foyer. "Please have a seat. May I get you a drink?"

He moved through the room to a cabinet, poured a shot glass full of an amber liquid, then chucked it down his throat at breakneck speed.

"I don't want anything until you tell me what's going on." Of all people, Chatham had abducted her? It didn't make sense. They'd just spoken at the gala. Her father hadn't trusted the man, and neither did she, but he couldn't hurt her. He was family.

Curiosity won over her anger, and Kathleen returned to the very white sofa. The grease on her hands and dress begged to soil the expensive fabric. "Is there somewhere I can clean up? I'd hate to stain your furniture."

"Of course. Through that door."

Kathleen darted in the direction he pointed. The bathroom was small with only a commode and sink, no windows, and no exit other than through the office. She couldn't hide her disappointment. *How am I going to get out of here?*

What did Chatham want with her? Did this have to do

with withdrawing from the election? Had he been the one threatening her?

At the gala, he'd asked about her plans and had assumed she would be announcing her departure. How did he know about her recent setbacks? Was someone reporting to him? A mole? A spy? In her campaign team? Ridiculous. This wasn't the Cold War.

"Ms. Phillips. Is everything all right?" Chatham's voice traveled through the door.

"Just a minute." She turned on the sink and washed the remaining grease from her hands. Then she cleaned the smear from her cheek and straightened her hair. What to do about her dress? Did Chatham keep extra bath towels under the sink? She opened the cabinet door. Score! She took one of the cloths, wet it, and dabbed at the grease stains on her clothing. It wasn't perfect, but she felt more presentable—more in control.

Kathleen glanced at her feet. Her stocking was torn, but there was nothing she could do about that. She removed the hose and dropped it into the garbage, then she opened the door, carrying the dirty towels. "I wasn't sure what to do with these."

"Leave them."

Kathleen shrugged, tossed them into the sink, then limped to the couch and sat. Chatham roosted in a matching armchair kitty-corner to the sofa. He set the empty shot glass onto a rounded accent table. Did he need the drink for fortitude? Surely, she didn't intimidate him. What could she possibly do to such a powerful man? She wouldn't even be able to report the abduction to the police because it'd be her word against his. She knew that. He knew that. So, what was this all about?

"I'm sure you have many questions."

Many questions? That's the understatement of the year.

"We're two peas in a pod, you and I."

Nothing could be further from the truth. Kathleen and Senator Chatham were nothing alike. *But aren't we?*

"I'm hoping we can come to a truce."

Surrender? Truce? What was it with the war analogies? But she might as well hear him out. Would he let her go if she didn't? Doubtful. "I'm listening."

Chatham rocked the glass in a circle. "It's no secret that your father and I had our differences, but it doesn't have to be that way between us."

Kathleen cocked an eyebrow. "Why is that?"

The glass stilled. "Why your father and I didn't get along, or why you and I could?"

"Why were you and my father at such odds with each other?" Should she let Chatham know she'd discovered their family connection? Kathleen opted to wait for his answer first.

Chatham tugged at his bow tie, then lowered his hand to his knee. "Your father and I played together as boys. We were good friends once if you can believe it."

She'd seen the photos. So far, Chatham told the truth. Though he didn't mention that the two men were cousins.

"In high school, Richard and I were as competitive as two boys could be. When I was chosen as quarterback for the football team instead of him, he spread a vicious rumor about me. Coach kicked me off the team, and my girlfriend dumped me. His betrayal severed our friendship. When it was time for us to attend college, I applied to Harvard. Your father did, as well."

Harvard? Dad didn't go to Harvard. He graduated from Stanford. That's why I chose it for my alma mater.

"I assume you weren't aware."

Had her facial expression given her away? Kathleen shook her head.

"There were only a few openings in the program. And to secure my place, I forged a letter from our school principal, slandering Richard in every way I could. Then I sent a second letter praising my accomplishments and my character."

How ironic.

"I was accepted. Richard was not."

"But what does all this have to do with me?" Really? He'd abducted her in the middle of the night to confess fifty-year-old crimes? Wasn't he afraid she'd go to the police? But again, who would believe her? It was still her word against his.

"I'm getting to that. Are you sure you don't want some water?"

"I'm sure. Please continue."

"When Richard learned I was running for governor, he immediately started his campaign. To my chagrin, he garnered enough support to make it onto the ballot. To make matters worse, we both passed the primaries and eventually stood head to head in the polls. Only this time, Richard stooped to his old tactics." Chatham shifted in his chair, crossing his foot over his knee. "Let me get right to the point."

About time.

"Your father possessed some critical photographs that would spell ruin for my political career and shame my family. He blackmailed me, and I withdrew from the election. He went on to win by a landslide. As far as I know, those photos still exist. I'd like to offer you a deal."

Alarms went off in her head. "What kind of deal?"

"You hand over those photos, and I will appoint you to whatever position you desire in the federal government once I'm elected president."

What photos is he talking about? He can't mean the ones from the cabin. How could those pictures ruin anything? It's not like they contain government secrets.

"You seem overly confident. What if you don't win?"

Chatham cleared his throat. "I will see to it that you are well compensated for your trouble."

A bribe? He was offering her a bribe. A large one with many perks, which brought up the question, why? No one made deals in the other person's favor. And an appointed position was far more tempting than a governorship. What was in it for him? *Why are those photos so valuable? This doesn't make sense. He has to mean a different set of images. But how can I find them if I don't even know what they contain?* "If I don't turn over the photos?"

Chatham rose. His imposing stature cast a shadow over her. His jaw hardened, and his eyes steeled. "You'll find me those photos, or I'll make sure everyone in Oregon knows your little secret."

So much for reconciliation. But this wasn't war—it was a game of chess. And Chatham had just made a fatal move.

28

A half-hour later, a taxi dropped Kathleen at her hotel. Chatham's home had been just outside Portland proper in Hillside, near the historic Pittock Mansion, a mere ten minutes from the ballroom. As she rushed inside the lobby, the awning sheltered her from the pouring rain.

She swept through the double doors, then came to a halt. Where was her clutch? Had she lost it in all the craziness? No ID. No hotel key. She wouldn't even be able to get back into her room. And the hotel would want to see her ID before giving her a replacement key.

The lobby stood deserted. The restaurant, dark. What was Kathleen going to do? The bar was the only thing still open.

Kathleen wrinkled her nose and quieted the roiling in her stomach. She stepped through the open doors. As soft jazz played over the speakers, the bartender wiped down the counter.

He lifted his head, and his gaze traveled from her tangled hair to her bare feet. Was he deciding whether her presence was worth acknowledging? He cleared his throat. "Can I get you anything?"

Shaking her head, Kathleen moved to a corner table. A couple sat at the counter, toasting and flirting. At the other end, a lone man nursed a glass of liquor. She didn't even know what the drink was called, but the smell took her back to a time she'd rather forget.

Instinctively, she rubbed her cheek. The bruise had long healed, but she'd never forgotten the feel of Lionel's palm against her skin, no matter how hard she tried.

No man would ever be allowed to treat her that way again. Not Lionel Phillips. And not Kenneth Chatham. Did he really think she would just keel over because he pushed? She was made of tougher stuff than that.

Kathleen rubbed her tongue across her lips. Dry and chapped. She signaled the bartender.

"Yes."

"May I have a coffee, please? Black?"

"Coming up."

Several minutes later, a steaming cup appeared on the table. Kathleen nodded her thanks, then picked it up and blew into the dark liquid before taking a sip. The coffee warmed her from the inside out.

Chatham had to figure she'd found photos of something other than his childhood summers out at the cabin. She couldn't see any reason they would damage his campaign for president, even if he had been friends with his *archenemy*, Richard Staten. It's not like Dad was a fugitive or a terrorist.

So, where were these photos that Chatham was so deathly afraid of becoming public? Had that been what was in the envelope the stranger had given Dad that night in his office? The one that he claimed would ruin Chatham?

If she found those photos, she could turn them over to the police and take him down. Or… She took a sip of coffee and licked her lips.

She *could* give them to Chatham and get insanely rich or receive an appointment in the federal government where she could skip straight to the top, working alongside the President of the United States. It was a tempting offer. *Very tempting, no matter my personal feelings for the man.*

But those things Chatham had said about Dad. Had he really used extortion to become governor? What about his position as mayor and state attorney general? Had he gained those honestly? Was he guilty of other white-collar crimes?

And what of Chatham? Wasn't he guilty? If he was worried about the media or the police getting ahold of those photos, they had to be incriminating. He was awfully trusting to assume she'd just give him the pictures and not use them to further her own aspirations. What was to keep her from turning around and blackmailing him?

Except, he knew about Paige and wouldn't think twice about ratting her out to the media and the public.

Kathleen took a drink, swallowed hard, then pinched her lips shut. The bitter coffee burned her throat. Chatham had said they were two peas in a pod.

Was she headed down that path?

She'd already bribed the city treasurer to lie about the missing funds, and she'd paid off the coroner, almost without blinking.

Had she really become that person? The Ice Queen of Capitol Hill?

I don't have a choice. If I'm soft, the media and the voters will eat me alive. It takes a hard person to make tough decisions.

Kathleen stood. She wouldn't let their comments bother her. She was everything her father had raised her to be—a strong, independent woman who wouldn't let anyone walk over her. Chatham had no idea who he was messing with, and if she got elected, Capitol Hill would see a blizzard they wouldn't soon forget.

She signaled the bartender again.

"Yes." Annoyance laced his voice.

"Please charge this to my room. 410."

"Sure, lady." He looked over her again. "Rough night?"

"You have no idea." Kathleen left the bar.

When she entered the lobby, the night attendant waved at her. "Are you Ms. Kathleen Phillips?"

"I am."

He pulled something from under the desk. Kathleen's purse. "Someone just dropped this off."

Kathleen crossed the lobby as quickly as possible and scooped up the handbag, clasping it to her chest. Relief washed over her like an ocean wave. "Thank you." She opened the snap and checked the contents. Everything was still inside. Her ID. Her credit card. Her car keys. And thank heavens, her room key. She didn't know how much actual sleep she would get tonight, but at least she would be comfortable.

The next morning, Kathleen checked out of the hotel, then took a taxi back to the parking garage where she'd left the rental car. She tried to start the vehicle. When nothing happened, she called the rental company and reported the incident, then cleaned out the inside of the car, adding her pump from last night to her luggage.

It seemed like forever before the tow truck arrived, and even longer before she reached the Portland airport. The flight home went smoothly, and Dennis had her car waiting for her when she landed.

Kathleen drove home and parked in the garage, then entered the house and deposited her purse and keys on the sideboard along the wall. She would make a cup of coffee, then crash into bed.

Chatham's photos would have to wait—she was dead on her feet. And she had to wake early tomorrow to start prepping for a press conference in a few days.

The aroma of freshly brewed Colombian Roast greeted her when she entered the kitchen. The coffee pot sat half-full on the warming plate. She set her hand against the carafe and glanced at the clock on the stove. 8:30. It was still warm. Kylie must have made a cup when she got home from work.

Taking a mug from the cabinet, Kathleen poured a stream of steaming black liquid into it and breathed in the earthy scent. A light came from under the sliding doors into the living room. She crossed to the door and slid it open.

Mother reclined in the armchair under the reading lamp, a copy of West Side Story in her hands.

Kathleen's eyes widened in shock. "Mother!"

Mother raised her head. "You're home." She didn't sound surprised nor embarrassed to be caught in the house for the second time.

Kathleen set one hand on her hip. The other clenched the handle of the mug. "What are you doing in my house? Again."

"You still haven't changed the locks." Mother closed her book, then set it on the table beside her. "How was the gala?"

Kathleen's pulse pounded in her temples. "Whether I've changed the locks or not doesn't give you permission to break into my house."

"I didn't break in. I unlocked the door. Entirely different."

"No, it's not." Okay, so maybe it was, but Kathleen wasn't thinking straight. She struggled to control her temper. "What do you want? Why are you here?"

"Here, as in your house or here, as in Whitman."

"Both."

Mother stood and closed the distance between them. "I've already told you."

"And I already told you no." Kathleen stepped back, widening her personal bubble.

"You can't just say no without giving me a viable reason. We need to talk about it."

Kathleen didn't want to talk about it. Not now. Not ever. She had too many other things on her mind. If she were going to talk about anything, she'd rather find out how much her mother knew about the history between Senator Chatham and Dad. Maybe Mother could shed new light that would direct Kathleen to those photos. "Are you aware Senator

Kenneth Chatham ran against Dad for governor?"

Mother faltered. Obviously, the abrupt change in the conversation had thrown her. "Yes." Her eyebrows drew together. "Why—"

"Did you know Dad used extortion to force Chatham to withdraw?"

Mother sighed and lowered her gaze. "Kathleen—"

"So, you did know. That makes you an accessory."

"No, I didn't know. But I'm not surprised. Your father was—"

"Was what?" Kathleen's temper flared.

Mother tucked her hair behind her ear and fingered her earring. "Not exactly known for being upright and honest. It's why I divorced him. A scandal would have destroyed my acting career. I had to distance myself from his actions. I had no proof that anything he was doing was criminal, just unethical."

Kathleen had known her father was calloused, but this was taking his behavior to a whole new level entirely. "Speaking of being upright and honest, how did you learn about Paige?"

"Richard told me."

Dad? "When?"

"A couple of weeks before he died."

"Why?"

"Why did he call?"

Kathleen nodded. Her leg ached. She moved to sit at the antique Windsor writing desk in the corner.

Mother returned to the chair she'd vacated moments ago. "He called to apologize. Said he wanted to make things right. He also told me about Paige and his part in the whole mess."

"Did he tell you he didn't speak to me for twenty years? I'd humiliated him, and he—"

Mother shook her head. "It wasn't you. He was so ashamed of what *he* had done—abandoning the baby at the fire station. He'd lied to his only daughter, and it tore him up inside."

Ashamed of himself? "I thought he was ashamed of me. He never once apologized." *Or even told me what he'd done.*

"He'd regretted his actions for years but couldn't voice his feelings aloud. He said he'd written you a letter explaining everything and hoped you would find it in your heart to forgive him."

A letter? *Dad left me a message?* Kathleen's memory triggered. *The letter in the desk!*

She headed upstairs. Mother's footsteps clomped on the flooring behind her. "Let me be." Kathleen picked up her pace, and in an awkward, rocking gait, went straight to the study. She opened the drawer where she'd stashed the letter, then lowered into the chair, removing the folded sheet of paper.

My dear Annie,

If you are reading this letter, I have passed into eternity—an eternity, by the grace of God, of peace and happiness. I wish I were brave enough to say these things to your face, but I've never been good with emotions. You are everything your mother and I raised you to be. Fierce, ambitious, driven… but we were wrong to make you that way.

You, my dear daughter, don't feel. You don't let love into your heart. I know Lionel hurt you deeply, but not all men are like him. My heart's prayer is that you will not only find humanly love someday but that you will open your heart once again to the love of the Heavenly Father.

I regret not seeking the Lord sooner in my life—my illness has reminded me of how frail I am. I was a merciless man and hurt a lot of people with my words and actions. I have done many things I'm not proud of. Some of them, criminal. In the safe, you will find a record of all my wrongdoing. Please turn it over to the police, and allow justice to be served.

My greatest regret of all is letting you give up your baby girl. You should have raised her, and I should have helped you. But I was too blinded by my own ambitions to see clearly, and I let those ambitions run my life. I repeatedly chose power over my family, and by my example, I taught you to do the same.

When I received a blackmail note, I felt I didn't have a choice but to lie about having contacted an adoption agency and arranging an adoptive family. I was afraid your mistake would ruin my chances of becoming governor, and I wasn't going to let anything spoil those goals. I was only trying to protect you, too.

I drove to Portland that night and drove around the city for hours, deciding what to do. I almost threw her in the river, ending her life. Then I saw the fire department and the safe haven sticker. I took the baby from her car seat and placed her along with your Bible in an apple crate I found in an alley, then left her on the steps.

I drove home with my eyes fogged with tears. It is my prayer that you will be reunited with your daughter someday. I have located her, and my lawyer is keeping an eye on her until you are ready to meet. She's had a rough go of things, but with some motivation, she's trying to give herself a better life. I hope she will come to know Jesus as her Savior. She will be a good big sister to Kylie if you give her a chance. I have left both girls an inheritance that they may use for their futures.

Lastly, I want to ask your forgiveness for the man I was. I regret not being a better father to you and Erik. My selfishness destroyed my marriage and my family. I've begged God to heal the wounds I have left behind. Come home to the Father, my dear daughter. He's waiting with open arms.

Dad

Kathleen read over the letter again. Her vision blurred. She sucked in her cheek and bit down until she tasted blood. *I don't understand. You were my hero. I always looked up to you.* The pain that built up in her soul was more than she could bear. Had everyone known what he was really like except her? Had she been blinded by her desire for his affection? She knew he had enemies and was hated, but she'd always thought it was because he was tough, not because he was crooked. *You really did a number on me, Dad.*

All her life, he'd told her to do whatever it took to be the best. To get ahead. Even if it meant cheating on tests in school or rigging the election for student body president. When she became a Christian, those things didn't feel right anymore, but she'd wanted to please him and make him proud of her. She was more concerned with what he thought than what God thought, and that desire fueled her every decision.

Dad claimed she didn't feel, but he'd made her that way. He'd told her to hide her emotions. Not to cry and not let anyone get an advantage over her by using her feelings against her.

Now, here he was changing course, admitting everything he'd said was a lie, and expecting her to believe him. How was she supposed to trust him now? How could she know if he was genuinely remorseful, or merely sorry he'd gotten caught in the spider web of God's judgment? Had he really changed?

After professing Christianity, Dad had started attending church, reading the Bible, and praying. He'd spent more time with Kylie, his demeanor had softened, and he'd given up whiskey, tobacco, and cussing.

He claimed God forgave him, and if that was true, shouldn't she? He was sorry and regretted his actions, and he apologized for not being the father he should have been.

But, according to the letter, her father *had* actually abandoned Paige. Hearsay was one thing, but to see it written in her father's own handwriting was another. He hadn't just left her baby. He'd almost taken her life—thrown her in the river like a piece of garbage.

Her nails dug into her palms. Tears burned her eyes. It didn't matter if he'd been blackmailed. His actions were unforgivable. He'd lied to her. Let her believe she was doing a good thing by giving up her baby, only so he could protect his own interest. Had he even once considered what it would do to her? How much guilt she would carry for the things she'd said to Ryan at his suggestion? How the hate she had for herself would lead her to marry a man like Lionel Phillips?

Forgive him? After everything he'd done? Never. He didn't deserve her forgiveness. Just like she didn't deserve God's mercy. Or Ryan's. Some things just couldn't be forgotten.

"What did he say?"

Kathleen's chin shot up. Mother—she'd followed her upstairs. Hands shaking, Kathleen folded the letter and returned it to the envelope. "None of your business."

"It's about Paige, isn't it? Did he ask your forgiveness?"

Paige.

If it weren't for Paige, Kathleen wouldn't be in this mess. Paige had caused the chasm between Kathleen and Dad. Paige had put Kathleen's career in jeopardy—her very existence made Kathleen vulnerable to extortion and scandal. If Chatham or whoever these other threats had come from informed the media, her future would be destroyed. It was all Paige's fault.

Kathleen set her jaw. "I don't know who you're talking about."

Mother raised an eyebrow. "Don't say that. She's your daughter."

My daughter. "I know she's my daughter. But I don't want her here. I don't want her in my life. I wish she'd never been born."

29

Knock. Knock. Knock.

Paige's eyelids opened wide, her pulse racing. Who was banging on the front door? It was still dark outside the windows. *What time is it?* She rolled over on the hide-a-bed, grabbed her phone off the floor, and checked the time. *Four o'clock. It's too early.*

She groaned, sat up, and rubbed her eyes, then walked to the door, running her tongue over her teeth. *Yuck.* She had terrible breath this morning but no time to brush. *Oh well. Hope they don't mind pajamas and halitosis.*

Paige flipped on the porch light, then peeked through the peephole before opening the front door. Kylie stood outside, wearing a jacket over her pj's. Her eyes were red and puffy. "What are you doing here? Do you know what time it is? Have you been crying?"

"I'm sorry to wake you, but I had nowhere else to go. I don't know what to do." With a wail, Kylie fell against Paige's chest.

"Come on in. What's wrong?" Paige wrapped her arm around Kylie's back and led her to the sofa bed. "Sit here. Can I get you something to drink?"

Kylie nodded but didn't specify what she wanted. *OK. Coffee it is.* Paige went into the kitchen and turned on the coffee maker. The sounds of sniffling carried from the other room.

Jessie appeared in the doorway in her robe and slippers. "What's going on?"

"I don't know. Kylie's upset about something, but I've got it under control. You can go back to bed."

Jessie yawned and blinked. "I'm awake now. I'll just get my coffee and do my devotions on the back porch. At least then, I won't bother your aunt with my Bible-thumping."

Paige's lips tilted in a sad smile. "I'm sorry, Jessie. Do you want me to talk to her about it?"

"No, dear. I understand. I've added Hattie to my prayer list. She needs the Lord."

Paige turned back to the coffee pot. The water made a dribbling sound as it ran through the grounds and filled the glass carafe with black gold. She'd never thought of her aunt needing to be saved, but she supposed it was true. Aunt Hattie had never taken her to church or talked about religion at all. Paige should pray for her aunt, too.

When the coffee maker clicked off, Paige poured two cups. One for her and one for Kylie. She'd need it if she wanted to get through the day after being awakened at four in the morning.

Jessie got a mug out of the cabinet, and Paige headed for the living room. Seconds later, the back door closed.

Paige joined Kylie on the bed and handed her a steaming mug. "What's going on? Why did you say you have nowhere else to go? Has someone hurt you?" She sat cross-legged on the mattress and let her gaze wander over her sister. She looked OK. No bruises or lacerations. At least, physically.

Kylie sniffled. "Remember the silver-haired lady from the café. I came home from work last night and went upstairs, and she was standing in the hallway outside my grandpa's old study. Before I could ask her what she was doing in my house, I heard my mom's voice coming from inside the room. Mom said—" Sobs broke into her words and racked her shoulders.

Paige held Kylie's hand until the crying slowed. *Kylie doesn't know that the silver-haired woman is Dawn Winters, our grandmother. Kathleen hasn't told her either. Why is she keeping it a secret?*

Kylie drew a deep, shaky breath. "I knew she was mad at me for wanting to quit college, but I didn't know she was that angry." Kylie raised her head and met Paige's eyes. "Mom said she didn't want me."

Paige lowered her eyebrows. Something wasn't right about Kylie's story. Kathleen was cold, but she'd never say she didn't want Kylie. There had to be something Kylie wasn't saying or something she hadn't heard correctly.

Paige shifted on the mattress, unfolding her legs, and tucking her hair behind her ear. "Your mother loves you. She would never say that. Tell me exactly what you heard."

Kylie huffed, then took a drink.

Paige waited as patiently as she could.

Kylie smacked her lips and stuck out her tongue. "This coffee is kind of bitter. Do you have any cream or sugar?"

"In a minute. First, tell me what your mom said." Paige's heartbeat thumped against her ribs.

Kylie lowered the coffee mug to her lap. "She said, 'I know she's my daughter. But I don't want her here. I don't want her in my life. I wish she'd never been born.'"

Paige mentally replayed the words. Her vision blurred, and blood pounded in her ears. She knew exactly who her mother was referring to, and it wasn't Kylie.

It was me.

Kathleen slouched in her chair and let her gaze travel the

room. It felt good to be back at City Hall. Her first day since the accident. She still needed the boot, of course, but she could get around well enough. Working at home had kept the paperwork from piling up, and Dennis had stayed on top of things. She'd scheduled an afternoon meeting with Joe to talk over plans for the campaign, and when she got home tonight, she'd tear the house apart, if need be, to find those photos of Chatham's.

A knock sounded on the door. "Come in."

The door opened, and Dennis stepped inside, followed by two men in suits. "Mayor Phillips. These gentlemen would like a word." He slipped out again, leaving the two men behind.

"Yes, gentlemen, what can I do for you?"

"Mayor Phillips. Agent Carlisle." The agent flashed a badge in her direction, then gestured to the other man. "This is Agent Daniels. We're from the FBI. We have a few questions we'd like to ask you about your missing campaign funds."

Paige drove Aunt Hattie's station wagon to the courthouse and marched into her mother's office, spine rigid and blood pressure roaring. Kathleen's assistant tried to block her path, but she skirted around him, grabbed the door handle, and threw open the door. It banged against the wall. The occupants startled and rose to their feet. Two men in suits stood next to their chairs, frowning. Kathleen stepped from behind her desk. "What is the meaning of this?"

"We need to talk."

Her mother gestured to her guests. "Can't you see I'm in a meeting? I'm asking nicely for you to leave. Don't make me call security."

Paige's eyes flashed. She would not be turned away. "I'm not leaving. This is important."

"So is this." Kathleen pursed her lips and narrowed her

eyes. Paige held eye contact and wouldn't give in.

Kathleen's face relaxed, and a false smile spread over her lips. "Fine. If you'll excuse me, gentlemen, I won't be but a moment. Something has come up. Dennis!"

Wide-eyed, Dennis skip-hopped across the room to Kathleen's side. "Dennis, why don't you take these nice men down to the break room and get them some coffee while I speak with Miss McDonald?" She pulled his ear down to lip level, whispered something, then let him go and turned to her guests. "Please, if you'll follow my assistant. This won't take long."

As soon as the men left, Kathleen discarded all pretense. The fake smile faded. "What do you want?" She dropped into her chair, hand on her chin.

"You have to tell Kylie about me."

"Absolutely not."

Paige lowered into the chair that one of the suited men had vacated and took a deep breath. Maybe if she calmed down and explained, she could get Kathleen to see reason. "Please. She needs to know." Kathleen didn't say a word—just sat, shaking her head. The woman was unreasonable. "She overheard you last night."

Kathleen leaned forward again, taking a sudden interest. "What exactly does she think she heard?"

"You said you didn't want your daughter in your life. That you'd wished she hadn't been born. Kylie thinks you meant her."

A heavy silence hung in the room, except for the drumming of Kathleen's fingernails on the desk.

Paige shifted as the awkwardness grew. *Say something.* "Why didn't you tell me my grandmother was in town?" Maybe the sudden change in subject would shock Kathleen into responding.

Kathleen flinched, and her hand stilled. "How did you find out?"

"I looked her up on the internet, but Ms. Winters doesn't know I know." Paige's thoughts whirled and knots bunched in her stomach. Was Kathleen going to comment on what Kylie had overheard? Was Kathleen considering telling Kylie the truth? Would she see reason when she realized Kylie thought her own mother didn't love her?

Paige swallowed and took a deep breath, then parted her lips to speak.

"I wasn't talking about Kylie—I was talking about you."

Words died in Paige's throat. Kathleen's admission was weighted, calculated, and hurt like a fresh waxing. Paige's flesh burned as if her mother had peeled the skin right off her body.

Help me, Lord, I don't know how much more I can take. I just want her to love me, is that too much to ask?

The pain in Paige's heart was nearly overwhelming. But to win this argument, she'd have to remain as emotionless as the woman before her. She stuffed down her pain and met Kathleen's stony gaze. "You know that, and I know that. But Kylie doesn't know that. As far as that poor girl's concerned, she's the only daughter you have. Imagine her feelings—if you can."

Is that even possible? Does Kathleen have emotions? Is her heart completely frozen? "Kylie showed up at my house this morning, balling her eyes out. She's hurt. Very hurt. She needs to know you love her. The only way to do that is to tell her about me."

Kathleen laughed.

Paige's stomach tightened. *I don't think it's funny at all.*

"You think I can fix this by telling Kylie she has a sister?"

Paige didn't answer. *Is this a trap?*

Kathleen's smile faded. "I lied for nineteen years and kept her only sibling from her. I'm supposed to tell her that it's that sister that I don't want to have anything to do with."

Some people might have spoken those words with inflection and dramatic gestures. Her mother had said them like she was ordering take-out from a Chinese menu.

"Besides, I don't want Kylie spending time with a criminal."

As Paige sucked in a sharp breath, her skin tingled.

Kathleen's words cut like a knife.

"You're a bad influence on Kylie. From now on, stay away from her."

The metaphorical knife twisted. Paige's hands shook. *How can she say those things? What have I done to deserve such hatred?* Her chest tightened, and she struggled to breathe. "I'm sorry I bothered you." She stood unsteadily. "I'll—I'll get out of your hair." What else could she do? What else could she say? Kathleen was never going to change her mind.

As tears threatened to spill down her cheeks, Paige pivoted and trudged to the door. She reached for the handle, but something grasped her forearm. She half-turned and came eye-to-eye with her mother. Kathleen squeezed. A sharp twinge traveled up Paige's wrist. "Don't you dare tell Kylie she's your sister. Do you hear me?" She let go and stepped back.

Paige rubbed the red marks on her skin. "Loud and clear."

Kylie and Aunt Hattie played checkers at the kitchen table. Paige stood in the doorway and watched for a moment. She wanted to burn this image of her sister forever into her mind. *What if we can never be friends again?*

The two women stopped their game and looked up. "Did you finish your errands?" Kylie asked, her smile lighting the room like the sunrise illuminates the darkness of night.

A knot formed in Paige's throat—she might never be the recipient of that smile again. "We need to talk."

Confusion clouded her sister's face and broke Paige's heart. She hated to do this, but what other option did she have? Kathleen hadn't given her one. Paige glanced at Aunt Hattie and met her eyes, hoping the elderly woman would understand the need for them to talk alone.

Aunt Hattie stood and straightened her day dress. "I think I'll go outside and help Jessie pull weeds."

Thank you, Paige mouthed the words. Aunt Hattie hated

to pull weeds… or spend time with Jessie.

When the back door closed, Paige moved to sit in the chair her aunt had vacated. "I'm sorry, Kylie, but you have to go home. You can't stay here."

"Oh." Kylie angled her eyebrows. "If you're worried about space, I don't take up much room. Your aunt said I could share her closet if you don't mind sharing the hide-a-bed. I don't snore. I promise. Or at least, I don't think I do." She chuckled. "It's not like I've ever woken up to check."

Aunt Hattie was going to share her closet with Kylie? Aunt Hattie didn't even share the closet with Paige. "It's not space that's the problem. Kathleen doesn't want us spending time together. You can't stay here because we can't be friends anymore."

Silence. The corners of Kylie's lips turned down. Her eyes shimmered. "But you're more than my friend. You're like a sister to me. I don't understand. Why would she say that?"

Like a sister. That phrase hurt Paige more than smashing her thumb with a hammer or stepping on a plastic building block. Should she just tell Kylie the truth? She wanted to, but she couldn't go behind their mother's back, no matter how hateful she'd been. However, she could share the rest of *her* story and let Kylie decide if she wanted to be friends with a *criminal.* Paige swallowed as tears burned her eyes. After this, Kylie might never speak to her again. Kylie's own words haunted her thoughts. *"I don't think I could be friends with a criminal."* "There's something you need to know about me… I'm a thief."

Kylie's face turned ashen. "You're—you're a crook?"

Paige squeezed her eyes shut then reopened them. "Yes. When I was a kid, I started shoplifting. I got caught a couple of times, but in high school, one of my so-called friends stole money and hid it in my backpack, and I was arrested. I was innocent that time, but because of my prior violations, they sent me to juvenile hall for six months. When I got out, instead of going straight, I got worse. I started stealing and then selling the items. Sometimes, I would meet up with other thieves to transfer the stolen goods."

She continued, "One night, I met a guy and was given a sack of diamonds. I didn't know the police were watching him. They caught me with the diamonds, and I was arrested again. But instead of serving time, I was given mercy and released with a promise to meet with a parole officer and get my life on track."

"But you're not a thief anymore, right? You said you were innocent when the pawnshop got robbed."

Paige rubbed at the scar in her hand that itched when she got nervous. "I'm not an active thief anymore, but I'm not sure it's something you ever escape. The stigma, that is. Jessie told me about this thief next to Jesus when he died on the cross—the one Jesus took to Heaven with him. That event took place over two-thousand years ago, and yet, people still refer to that poor man as the thief on the cross. I'm a redeemed thief, but yes, a thief nonetheless."

"I'm confused. Why would anyone get involved with criminals if they knew they were bad?"

Paige had asked herself that question so many times over the past couple of years. "When you don't feel like you belong, you'll join with anyone who makes you feel important. Even if that group is a notorious crime ring."

Kylie fell quiet. Paige hurried to continue. "But I don't feel that way anymore. I belong to Jesus now." *I know I am loved and accepted, even if my mother never loves or accepts me.* "I've got Aunt Hattie and Jessie…" *My father.* "And Hamilton. And I've got y—" Paige caught herself. Technically, she didn't have Kylie anymore.

As Kylie stood, chair legs scraped the floor. "Thanks for listening this morning. I—I think I'll head home."

No, don't go. Paige's vision clouded.

When the front door closed behind Kylie, Paige folded her arms on the table, laid her head on top, and let the tears flow. *Oh, God, what am I going to do?*

30

The chairman of the pulpit committee and head deacon were already waiting for him. Ryan could kick himself for not beating them to his office. He should have been waiting for them—not the other way around. As soon as he'd arrived home from Portland yesterday, he'd called and set up the meeting.

He passed through the doorway, and the two men stood. "Pastor Whitestone." Nathan Keith, Sr dipped his chin, and Ryan shook the chairman's hand first.

Then he turned to the head deacon, Wade Bryant. How much of the situation had Paige shared with Hamilton? How much information had Hamilton passed to his parents?

"Please be seated." Ryan put his fedora on hat rack hook as he passed, then sat, folding his hands, and laying them on top of the desk calendar. "I appreciate you gentlemen meeting with me today."

Nathan flipped out the tails of his suit coat and lowered into the fabric-covered armchair. "I will say I was intrigued by your call. What do you need to talk about? You're not thinking of quitting on us, are you?"

Quit? No. Get fired. Quite possibly. Ryan ran his finger between his collar and his neck. Had his shirt shrunk since he'd entered the room? No small talk. Nathan Keith was the type of man who jumped right into the meat of a matter. Ryan still wasn't sure how to begin this conversation, even after rehearsing this moment a million times in his head. The pulpit committee deserved the truth. He'd have to leave the consequences up to God. "No, I don't plan on quitting unless you men ask me to resign after I say my piece."

Nathan leaned forward, bending at the hips. His lips pursed in a frown. "Resign? This sounds serious."

Ryan took a deep breath. "You are both aware of a young woman who recently bought the Faye's used bookstore."

"Of course. Paige McDonald. Seems like a nice girl. Except for that unfortunate event surrounding the pawnshop robbery. What about her?"

Wade had yet to say anything. What was going through his mind? Did he know where this conversation was headed? If he did, why hadn't he addressed the matter before? Had he just been waiting for Ryan to come forward with the truth?

"Paige McDonald is my daughter."

Wade's face remained unchanged. Nathan, however, could have been knocked down by a bunny rabbit. He blinked rapidly as the color drained from his face. "I—I apologize." He stammered. "I didn't realize you were ever married. You made no mention of it during your interview. Please accept my condolences. What was her name?"

Ryan picked at a hangnail on his thumb. This was the tricky part. Though he had to give Nathan credit for his expression of sympathy. The man genuinely cared. If only Ryan didn't have to crush Nathan's faith in his pastor. He cleared the lump forming in his throat. "Thank you, I appreciate that, but I'm not a widower. Paige's mother and I were never married."

Nathan's eyes widened as he put two and two together. "I

don't mind saying that I am stunned, Pastor. Do you have anything to say in your defense?"

"Only that this transgression occurred in high school. If I had known about Paige, I would have disclosed that fact at the candidacy meetings as I did my other failures. I had no desire to hide anything. I ask that you consider the mercy God grants you when you fail Him and reflect that same grace onto your pastor."

Through it all, Wade remained quiet. Ryan sent prayers up to Heaven that these men would understand his heart and not fire him. He loved this church and wanted to stay the pastor until he died, or God gave clear direction elsewhere.

"If you can give us a few minutes, we'd like to discuss this."

Ryan nodded and stepped out of his office into the auditorium—the place where he bore his heart and shared God's Word with the people of his community. Would that be ripped from him? He mentally pictured his congregants in the pews—each member meant so much to him.

In the short time he'd been their pastor, they had touched more than his heart. They'd changed his life. His gaze flickered to the stairs at the bottom of the platform. He crossed the carpet, then knelt, placing his hands and face prostrate.

Father. Speak to the hearts of Wade and Nathan. Give them Your wisdom as they make this decision… As Ryan prayed, words failed him. A low groan escaped his lips. *You know my heart. Give me the strength to accept Your will.*

The door opened. When Ryan raised his head, Wade hooked his finger. Nathan was standing when Ryan re-entered the office. "Please sit. This won't take long."

Oh no. They are going to fire me.

"Nathan and I have talked this over," Wade began, "Our Savior said, 'He that is without sin cast the first stone.' We've all done things we shouldn't. Not one of us is without sin. We've made mistakes in our past that we'd hate if people held them over our heads. We appreciate your honesty. And we've decided not to take action other than assuring you your position as pastor of Whitman Baptist Church is not at risk. We thank God for returning you to our little church and look forward to seeing how He's going to use you in our community."

Ryan couldn't help the tears that brimmed. *Oh, thank you, Lord.* He stood and shook both men's hands. "Thank you. So much."

I'm losing my mind.

Kathleen yanked open another desk drawer in the study at home and dug through the contents. She'd left work early, so she would have time to look for Chatham's photos. *I don't know what I'm going to do with them once I find them, but locating them is the first step.*

Where was that film canister with the photo negatives? She'd put it somewhere in the desk. But the plastic cylinder didn't seem to be there. *I've got to find it!* The more she'd thought about it, the more confident she grew that Chatham's scandalous photos were on those negatives. It made perfect sense. Why else would Dad have kept them in the safety deposit box?

I can't believe I'm entertaining thoughts of Dad having committed extortion.

Footsteps pounded on the staircase. Orange fabric flashed down the hallway past the open doorway. "Kylie," Kathleen called out. A second later, stepping backward, Kylie moved into view. She kept her eyes trained on the floor. Tears dripped from her chin. Kathleen's heart did a flip. *Kylie overheard my conversation with Mother last night.*

Did her precious daughter really believe her mother didn't want her? Kathleen left the drawer open and walked to the couch and sat. She patted the cushion beside her. "Have a seat. We need to talk."

Kylie shook her head, not making eye contact. "I can't."

Her voice cracked.

"Why not? You've been inside every other room in this house."

What wasn't Kylie telling her? A sense of dread niggled at her thoughts. Kathleen stood from the couch, moved toe to toe with her daughter. She reached out and touched Kylie's hair and lowered her voice. "Did something bad happen in this room?"

"I overheard." Kylie's voice squeaked.

"Overheard what? When?" Kylie had avoided the study long before last night.

"Right after we moved here. Grandfather, he was… he was on the phone. I don't know who he was talking to, but it was loud and mean. Whoever it was, he threatened to ruin them."

Kathleen brushed a tear from Kylie's cheek. She didn't say anything—just waited. This was probably the first real heart to heart conversation they'd ever had. She couldn't risk messing it up.

Kylie continued. "I'll never forget the look on his face. He—he had this fire in his eyes like he meant every word he was saying. Then he saw me listening. I thought he'd hurt me for eavesdropping. Every time I think of this room, I remember that look."

"Your grandfather would have never done anything to hurt you. He loved you."

"It reminded me of Dad."

Kathleen's eyes dropped to Kylie's crooked finger. If only she hadn't been out of town dealing with a case, she could have gotten Kylie to the doctor before the bones had set. "I'm sorry he frightened you. I wish you would have told me years ago."

"I tried," Kylie whispered.

Kathleen barely heard the words, but they struck her heart like lightning. She swallowed. Her sinuses burned. She balanced with her hand on the door jamb. "You tried? What do you mean?"

"I came to talk to you about it a couple of days later. But you were working. You were always working. When I tried to talk to you, you got mad and sent me to my room for the rest of the evening."

"Kylie, I—"

"Last night, I heard you tell that old woman that you don't want me in your life. That you'd wished I'd never been born. I'm sorry I'm such a disappointment."

I never meant you. I'd never mean you. Oh, my precious Kylie.

"Do you know why I don't want to be a politician?"

Kathleen shook her head. *I'm not going to like the answer.* Still, she needed to let Kylie speak her mind, no matter how much it pained her to hear it. "Why?"

"I don't want to be like you or grandfather. I don't want to trample people to get what I want in life. I don't want to make so many enemies that I'm always looking over my shoulder to see if one will try to run me over while I'm out jogging." Kylie's eyes dipped to Kathleen's boot.

Kylie knew the truth about the accident. Kylie's words smote her heart. *Is that how she sees me?* "I didn't want you to worry."

Kylie stuck out her lower lip. "Maybe I wouldn't worry if you didn't keep things from me."

Kathleen blinked. "Why would you think I'm keeping things from you?"

"Remember the day I helped out at headquarters, and the lights went out… You asked me where I'd been." Kylie pulled a crumpled piece of paper from her pocket. "Someone turned out the lights so they could pass me this note."

Kathleen took the balled-up sheet, peeled it open, and read the typed words. *False face must hide what false heart doth know.*

"I showed Paige. She told me it was from *Macbeth* by William Shakespeare."

Kylie had received a Shakespeare note, too. This one was from a play about a man who'd murdered the king to take over the throne, then had to keep killing people to hide his deception.

"You hate when I keep things from you, and yet you do it to me all the time. How is that fair?" Kylie jabbed her hands onto her hips.

Kathleen swiveled away from the doorway, her hand connecting with the vase of dead roses on the credenza. The vessel hit the floor and the glass shattered. Kylie yelped. Brown rose petals sprinkled the carpet.

This was the perfect opportunity to tell Kylie the truth about Paige. Kylie had always longed for a sister, and Kathleen had kept her deepest desire from her. Concealing the truth was destroying their relationship, but if she told Kylie, her daughter would never look at her the same way again. How could Kathleen sever the last fragile strand that bonded them to each other?

Kathleen closed her eyes. *If I tell her the truth, she won't love me anymore. I need her to love me. What if she never forgives me? How can I live with that?*

The doorbell rang. *What now?* Kathleen limped down the stairs, Kylie behind her.

In the foyer, she opened the door. Empty. *Strange. Neighborhood kids playing Ding Dong Ditch, I suppose.* She started to close the door. The sound of a vehicle backfiring drew her eyes to the road. A black pickup truck turned onto the main thoroughfare from her driveway. *That truck looks familiar. Could that be the same one that tried to run me over?*

As she lowered her eyes, she spotted something on the porch. Kathleen stepped outside and picked up a piece of paper held down with a rock. She unfolded the piece of paper—another Shakespeare quote.

Time shall unfold what plighted cunning hides, Who covers faults at last with shame derides.

31

"And in conclusion, I want my supporters to know we are not out of this race, not by a long shot. These obstacles can and will be overcome. With your donations and your help, we can win this thing!"

Scattered applause came from the press representatives. Kathleen frowned at the lack of enthusiasm. Joe stepped forward, placing a hand on her shoulder. "Thank you, Mayor Phillips." She moved from the microphone, and he took her place. "Thank you again for coming. Ms. Phillips will take follow-up questions at this time."

Dark clouds gathered over the mountain peaks. The wind picked up, swaying the trees. The flags on the flagpole snapped and waved. A reporter near the base of the courthouse stairs raised her hand. Joe gestured in her direction, and she stood. "Violet Xavier, Salem News. What setbacks have your campaign sustained?"

Kathleen had expected that question would come. "Just the usual things. Nothing we can't handle." She kept her answer as vague as possible. The journalist sat down, apparently satisfied.

Another stood.

"Yes, you," Joe called on him.

Kathleen made eye contact. The reporter from the debate—her pulse skipped—the one who'd given her chills when she'd looked into his eyes.

"Geoff Palmer, Channel Nine News. Is it true you've brought in over nine million dollars for your campaign?"

Kathleen cut her eyes at Joe. How should she answer? Where was Palmer going with this? "Yes. In a word. But—"

"Then, Ms. Phillips, would you please explain why you require more donations?"

"I—we—can always use—"

"Is it true that, two weeks ago, three million dollars went missing from your campaign account?"

"How—"

"Is it also true that you bribed a municipal employee to lie about missing city funds? And that you paid off your local coroner to rule the death of your volunteer coordinator, Patti Hayes, as a heart attack and forgo an autopsy?"

A gasp descended like a cloud, and a rumble of whispers came from the members of the press. Cameras flashed. Kathleen licked her lips. Her legs ached to flee to the safety of her office. How did the journalist know these things? No one was supposed to know.

Veins protruded from Joe's red face. "These are serious accusations. Do you have any evidence to support your claims?"

"I do not." Palmer conceded but didn't appear one bit repentant for stirring up trouble. Kathleen's heart pounded. If he didn't have evidence, why bring it up? *Unless he was merely planting seeds of doubt in the minds of the others.*

Joe's voice echoed, "Then I suggest you keep your allegations to yourself. You'll be hearing from our lawyers. We'll sue you for defamation. Security!"

Two security officers made their way toward the reporter.

He slipped a pen behind his ear and raised his suit jacket to drop his notebook into his shirt pocket. Palmer cleared his throat. "I've just one more question before I go."

"I think you've said quite enough." Joe set his jaw.

Kathleen's teeth ached from clenching. Her pulse raced, and her temples thrummed. Tremors ran through her limbs as her stomach roiled. *What's he going to ask? These questions could ruin me. Someone stop him!*

The officers hooked their arms through each of Palmer's elbows and pulled him away. Kathleen relaxed. *That's right. Get him out of here before he says something I can't go back from.*

"Is it true, Mayor Phillips, that your platform stands on the motto, A Vote for Phillips is a Vote for Family, yet you disowned your own child?" Palmer yelled from a distance.

Gasps and a murmur of voices rumbled through the crowd gathered in the town square. Lightning flashed across the western sky. A clap of thunder followed. Kathleen couldn't breathe. An electrical current surged through the air. Kathleen's hair on the back of her neck stood on end. She looked at Joe, her eyes pleading for his help. This was his area of expertise. It was his job to fix this mess.

A phone dinged. Then another. And another. As one, the press members answered their mobile devices. A gentle murmur quickly rose to a cacophony of voices. *What's going on? What's happening?*

Joe's expression reflected her confusion. A security officer moved through the crowd, stopped at the base of the steps, and signaled for Joe to approach. Joe stepped down the stairs. As the officer spoke, Joe's face paled. He nodded, then climbed the steps to where she stood. The officer disappeared into the agitated mass of bodies.

"What is it? What's happened?" Kathleen asked.

Joe raked his fingers through his hair, leaving furrows. He raised his eyes, locking onto her face. *Say something. Anything. You're frightening me.*

"Senator Chatham is dead."

Smoke from the fire pit curled toward the night sky. Shades of red and yellow danced together, matching the fire burning in Paige's heart. Hamilton's nephews, Tyler, Tony, and Timmy, danced around the yard, hooting and hollering. Each had a s'more in one hand, and the crumbs of their previous ones were stuck to their faces.

How could Kathleen tell me to stay away from Kylie? It's not fair.

"Marshmallow's on fire." Something bumped her side. Hamilton's voice broke into her thoughts.

Paige blinked. "Huh? What?"

"Your marshmallow. It's on fire."

"Oh." Paige removed the straightened coat hanger from the flames licking the metal rod, and wrinkled her nose at the charred glob of sugar and gelatin. *That marshmallow looks like my heart.*

"If you don't like them burnt, I'll eat it." When she shook her head, Hamilton took two graham crackers and scrapped the blackened stickiness between them. "Want to try again?" He reached for the bag of fluffy marshmallows at his feet.

"No thanks." She leaned the stick against the picnic table that held packages of graham crackers and chocolate bars.

Hamilton lowered the s'more he'd been about to put in his mouth. "Hey, you okay?" He squeezed her hand. "You were a million miles away."

"No. I'm not OK." What good was it keeping this to herself? She laced her fingers through his—they were sticky with marshmallows remnants. "My mom…"

What was the point in calling Kathleen *mom*? She had never been a mother to Paige, and she obviously had no desire to fulfill that role—ever. "Mayor Phillips ordered me to stay away from Kylie. She says I'm a bad influence, but I know she's afraid I'll tell Kylie we're sisters."

"Why don't you just tell Kylie the truth? Kathleen is so self-serving, she doesn't deserve your respect."

Kathleen may not deserve to be obeyed, but that didn't

give Paige the right to retaliate. Tears welled in her eyes. "She called me a criminal."

Hamilton set his s'more on the log they occupied and took Paige's hands in both of his. "I'm sorry she said that. Your past is under the blood of Christ. *He's* forgiven you, but unfortunately, that won't stop other people from throwing it in your face whenever it suits them. All you can do is pray for her. God loves you, and I love you. Nothing in this world will ever change that."

Her cheeks grew warm under the intensity of his gaze. His hand released hers and moved up to her face. He cupped her chin, gently pulled her close, and leaned in. His eyes flickered to her lips.

"Eww. Gross. They're about to kiss." Timmy broke the moment with a pointed finger and a disgusted expression.

Tyler grabbed Timmy and clamped a hand over his brother's mouth. The small boy continued to express his displeasure in muffled tones. "Sorry, Uncle Ham. Way to ruin the moment, dork."

The screen door of the Thorne's old farmhouse squeaked open. "Time for bed, boys." Hamilton's sister, Becky, called from the deck. Tyler released his hold on his brother.

"Good night, Uncle Ham. Good night, Miss Paige." The three boys spoke in unison, then scampered across the yard to the back door.

Just before ducking inside, Timmy shouted over his shoulder, "I'll be the best ring bearer in the whole wide world." He disappeared into the house, and the door closed behind him. Hamilton and Paige chuckled at Timmy's antics.

Hamilton pulled his phone from his pocket and checked the time, then stood and dusted tree bark from the back of his pants. "Sorry, wish I could stay, but I've got to head out. Working the early shift tomorrow. Good night, Paige." He pulled her into his arms.

"Good night." Paige murmured against his shirt.

Slowly, he released her and brushed a tear from her cheek. "Call me if you need to talk."

"Thank you. I will." Paige stepped back and folded her arms. Hamilton waved to his sister and walked to his truck. The engine turned over, and he backed out of the driveway and disappeared down the dark county road.

Becky approached, carrying a bucket. "What was that about a ring bearer? Did Ham propose?"

Paige's neck warmed. "No."

"Then what was that all about."

"Just Timmy being Timmy." Paige waved her hand like it was no big deal, but her pulse leaped at the thought of marriage to Hamilton. *It's too early in our relationship to begin thinking about marriage. We've only known each other for a couple of months.*

Becky turned the bucket upside down and poured water over the fire. It hissed, and steam rose from the wet wood. "Do you want to come in for some coffee?"

"That's OK. I should head home. Thank you for inviting me, though. I had fun."

Becky set the bucket on the ground and hugged Paige. "Anytime. You're always welcome."

"Thanks." At least someone wanted her around. *Why can't that someone be my mother?*

Jessie was seated on the porch swing, a blanket over her legs, and a cup of tea in her hands, staring into the distance when Paige arrived home. Insects chirped from the fields surrounding the bungalow. Paige climbed the wooden steps, her footfalls echoing on the boards. The elderly woman lifted her head and patted the empty space. "Join me?"

"Whatcha doing out here?"

"Hiding." Jessie sighed, then set her teacup on the wooden railing.

Paige sat on the swing, then propelled it backward with her foot. "Hiding from whom?"

"Hattie."

From Aunt Hattie? "What's going on?"

"While you were gone, she let her dogs run free inside the house. They knocked over an antique lamp of my mother's and broke it."

"I'm so sorry. Do you want me to talk to my aunt?"

Jessie shook her head. "The lamp was ugly. I only kept it for sentimental reasons. The point is, at every turn, Hattie McDonald does her utmost to annoy me. It's like she takes pleasure in getting on my nerves."

"You get on her nerves, too, you know."

Jessie fell silent. She picked up her teacup, took a sip, then returned it to the railing. "Did you have fun at the Thorne's?"

Obviously, she didn't want to talk about Aunt Hattie anymore.

"I did. We made s'mores."

Jessie shifted positions and straightened the blanket. "There's something I've wanted to ask you." She took hold of Paige's hands, then set them in her lap. "Have you forgiven your mother for giving you up?" She ran her thumb over Paige's knuckles and met her gaze.

A sharp breath puffed from Paige's lips. *Have I?* She thought back over the past couple of months. "I'm waiting for her to apologize. I want to hear her say she's sorry for giving me away."

"And if she never does?"

At that moment, reality struck Paige's heart. Her mother might never apologize. Might never accept Paige as her daughter. Might never tell Paige she regretted her decision. And Paige couldn't change that. The only thing she could change was her own perspective.

And I say unto you, love your enemies, bless them that curse you, do good to them that hate you, and pray for them that despitefully use you, and persecute you.

The Bible verse certainly fit her circumstances. Had Paige ever prayed for *her mother's needs*? "No, I haven't forgiven her."

"Hurting people hurt people. Forgive her for your sake.

Carrying bitterness will destroy you from the inside out. Once you forgive her, then love her. No matter what."

Dear God. Help me forgive my mother for the wrongs she has done me. Help me forgive her for the hateful things she's said and for keeping me away from my father and sister.

As Paige prayed, peace settled over her. *She must be hurting so much to treat other people this way. Help her heal from the pain she has endured. Open her eyes to Your love and forgiveness. Not for my benefit, but for hers. Fill her with Your peace.* Paige raised her head. "What about you and Aunt Hattie?"

The old woman startled. Her eyes widened. "Excuse me?"

"You can hardly stand living in the same house. When are you going to forgive each other?"

Jessie stood, her knees cracking and popping, and shuffled across the porch without a word.

"Jessie—" The screen door slammed.

I can't figure Jessie out. She's the same sweet lady I've grown to love until Aunt Hattie is around, or I mention her name. What did they do to each other? Whatever it was, the hurt runs deep. Lord, I love them both, and I don't like seeing them in so much pain. Guide them to work out their differences, forgive each other, and restore their friendship.

Hinges squeaked. Jessie stepped onto the porch and closed the screen door. She joined Paige on the swing, setting a ceramic figurine of two girls picking flowers into Paige's lap. The piece was inundated with cracks as if it had been broken and glued back together.

"Growing up, Hattie and I were the best of friends. We lived on the same street and spent our days and often our nights in each other's company. As inseparable as salt and pepper—until we entered high school. Hattie, in all her quirkiness, became an outsider, while my own popularity grew. In her jealousy, Hattie plastered my most personal secrets all over the school. And in retaliation, I stole her prom date. She came over to my house to confront me, and in anger, hurled this symbol of our friendship into the wall. We never spoke again."

Paige traced the figurine. Broken, but not beyond repair. Maybe Jessie's relationship with Aunt Hattie wasn't beyond repair. And maybe Paige's relationship with Kathleen wasn't beyond repair either. "I'm sorry, Jessie. Do you think you two will ever make up?"

"I don't know. That was a long time ago. It's hard to believe something that happened in high school could have such a lasting effect."

Paige stood and handed the ceramic figurine to Jessie. "I guess we never really know how much our actions can affect the lives of those around us. Are you ready to head inside?"

"Yes, I am."

Paige took Jessie's hand and helped Jessie to her feet, then together, they went inside the bungalow. Aunt Hattie sat on the couch with Delilah in her lap, her eyes glued to the glowing TV screen. "This is Barbara Kelley with Channel Nine News. Earlier today, US Senator Kenneth Chatham was found dead in his home office from what appeared to be blunt force trauma to the head. Hair and blood found on the corner of the executive desk matched the senator's wound. The senator's blood-alcohol level was elevated, and an empty whiskey decanter was found open on the coffee table. We're here with Senator Chatham's executive assistant, Mr. Mason Bridge, who, along with Mrs. Chatham, discovered the deceased. Mr. Bridge, could you tell us what happened?"

The TV camera turned. Barbara Kelley extended the microphone. A man stepped into view. *That's the same man who came to my store looking for the OSU cap. Chatham's assistant, Mason Bridge, is Iago.*

32

Paige paced the living room long after the two older women had gone to bed. She couldn't stop thinking about Iago—Mason Bridge. That day in the bookstore, Iago—Mason—spoke of his love of Shakespeare. "Iago" was the name of the villain in Shakespeare's *Othello*—a man who manipulated everyone else out of jealousy and revenge.

"No one writes like the bard."

Had Mason sent the Shakespeare notes? But why? What was his purpose? Psychological intimidation?

Kylie had received a Shakespeare note, too. Was Mason Bridge the man who'd been following them after the Bible Study? Was her sister in danger? Was Paige? And how did the Shakespeare notes connect to the pictures of Paige on the flash drive? Especially the one of Paige and Kathleen at Heavenly's. Had he been hoping to use those photos to blackmail Kathleen? Had Mason stole Paige's computer? Had he thought she might have downloaded the images, and he was hoping to destroy the evidence?

What about the attacks on Kathleen's life? Could they be connected to all of this, too?

Paige left the house and drove to the bookstore. In her office, she booted the computer and logged in. She opened the internet browser, and at a public record's website, she typed *Mason Bridge* into the search box. It was an uncommon name—only one result appeared on the screen. She paid the $1 for the trial access. The records showed his last six addresses, but no phone number. No marriage license. No warrants, civil judgments, or lawsuits. *Man, this guy is clean.* She snatched a slip of paper and a tiny pencil and scribbled the address, then leaned back in her chair.

Like the literary Iago, was Mason Bridge after revenge? And if so, revenge on whom? Kathleen? Did Mason have a personal vendetta against Kathleen?

Did Kathleen receive any notes with Shakespeare quotes or just her and Kylie?

I've got to warn Kylie. She dialed her sister's number. It rang three times. Voicemail answered. "You've reached Kylie Phillips. Well, you haven't actually reached me, just my phone, but you can leave a message, and I will call back whenever I get it."

"Hi, Kylie. It's Paige. Call me as soon as you can. It's important."

Paige lowered her phone and scrolled her contact list for Hamilton's name. She paused with her finger over the entry. What could she tell him? What evidence did she have that Mason Bridge was connected to any of this? Even if Hamilton believed her, the authorities would never take her seriously. Mason Bridge was the former senator's executive assistant. Unquestionably, they would accept his word over that of a former thief. They might even suggest she was involved. *What can I do?*

Paige glanced over at the sheet of paper where she'd written down Mason's address. It was risky. Hamilton had warned her about putting herself in danger, but did she have another option? If she were going to incriminate Mason

Bridge, she'd have to have concrete evidence of his wrongdoings.

Forgive me, Hamilton. I've got to do what I've got to do. Tomorrow morning, she'd drive out to La Grande. She needed proof. And the only way to get it was to search Mason Bridge's apartment. *Mason Bridge, you messed with the wrong girl.*

It had been an accident. Iago hadn't intended to kill Senator Chatham, but the stubborn man wouldn't listen to reason. Iago had done everything Chatham had ever ordered. And still, the man only viewed him as a lowly puppet to be used at his command. Iago's anger had built until he shoved, and the heavyset man had toppled like a Jenga tower. One too many whiskeys, Iago suspected. The senator's head had connected with the corner of his desk. When Iago saw the blood, he fled.

And Iago had been the last person to see him alive.

Iago pulled the roll of film negatives from the canister, dropped them into the garbage disposal, and flipped the switch. A grinding noise filled the apartment. Minuscule pieces of plastic film shot in every direction. Iago flipped off the noisy machine, then ran the tap, flushing the remaining shreds down the drain. The photos were useless now that the senator had met with an unexpected end.

If only Chatham had been willing to bend, but he'd chosen his own skin over revenge and offered his enemy—Iago's enemy—a presidential appointment. An appointment that should have belonged to Iago.

He checked his phone battery. *Dead.* He swore in frustration. He'd have to leave it plugged in.

Iago straightened his tie and buttoned his jacket. He had a date with destiny. Because after tonight, everything would change. Iago would be top dog, and Anna Kathleen Staten Phillips would slink away, tail tucked between her legs.

Hopefully, someone had snapped a photo of the horrified look on Kathleen's face yesterday. He'd frame it and hang it on the wall, so he'd never forget. Kathleen could not have the last laugh.

Then he'd get rid of her… permanently.

"Mr. Bridge, are you here?"

Paige knocked one last time. No one answered. Adrenaline pulsed through her veins. She battled with the guilt building in her chest. Maybe this wasn't such a good idea. The air in the dark hallway was stifling. The sounds of traffic carried through the small window that overlooked the busy main street. The odor of garlic and tomatoes from an Italian Restaurant on the corner mixed with the smell of old cooking grease leaking from one of the other apartments compounding her nervous nausea.

Paige slipped on a pair of leather gloves, then used lock picking tools on the deadbolt. Her pulse skipped when the mechanism on the inside clicked. The subtle sound brought back a hoard of memories. *I thought I'd never hear that sound again.* Tears pricked her eyes. She'd promised herself she wouldn't go back to this life. Still, she didn't have any other choice—the police would need evidence to support her accusations. But if Hamilton learned she was here, putting herself in danger… *I have to. My family needs me to set things right.*

Carefully, she pushed open the door. No alarm to shut off. Mason Bridge's apartment unfolded before her. Typical beige walls and carpet. A tall bookcase stood in the entryway directly opposite the door. The stench of cigarette smoke smacked her in the face. A tickle irritated her throat, and she coughed.

Holding her breath, she peeked around the door jamb and scanned the walls for security cameras. If she got caught on video, she'd go to jail for breaking and entering. No security system.

Paige released a shuttering breath, scrunched her nose, and crossed the threshold. She closed the door then covered her sandals with disposable shoe covers. A coat rack bolted to the wall, hung empty. She scanned the bookshelves—a set of the complete works of William Shakespeare in their original bindings. She brushed her gloved fingers over the leather spines. One was missing. But which one? She racked her brain, trying to remember all of Shakespeare's plays, but couldn't recall which one was not in Mason's collection.

Leaving the foyer, she moved into the living room. The sparse furnishings were neat and organized, which meant if she left with one thing out of place, Mason would know someone had been in his home.

An ashtray sat on the scuffed coffee table in front of a tattered couch. Paige took a plastic bag from her pocket and dropped one of the cigarette butts inside. Hamilton could match it to the ones he'd found in the bushes to prove whether Mason had been the one watching her apartment on the Thorne's property.

She traversed the living room, stepping lightly, and entered the small kitchen with laminate countertops and linoleum flooring. The trashcan overflowed. Dishes were piled in the sink—what a contrast to the other room. Apparently, Mason Bridge hated doing dishes and taking out the trash.

A muffled noise sounded down the hall. *Someone's here.* Paige's heart leaped into her throat. She scrambled backward, her hands searching for something to use as a weapon. Her fingers tightened around the handle of a metal skillet with flecks of scrambled eggs sticking to the enamel. Her knees shook. What if he had a gun? *Why didn't I bring mine? Because I can't shoot it straight, silly.*

A minute passed. Deep breaths.

With a grunt and a meow, a gray-striped tabby with three legs hopped through the doorway. He lazily loped across the floor, seemingly undisturbed by the presence of a stranger. "Hello, kitty. What's your name? You scared me." Paige squatted and stroked the cat's soft fur. It tried to rub against her jeans but tumbled over. "Are you the only one here?"

Paige moved into the bathroom and checked the medicine cabinet. The first thing her eyes fell on was a bottle of chloroform—not a common household item. Hamilton had said he smelled chloroform the night she'd been drugged.

And sitting beside the bottle of poison was a package of Zolpidem sleep aid.

How had Kathleen been drugged the night she drove off the road? Kylie said the doctor mentioned something specific, not just that Kathleen had fallen asleep. Could this be what had been used?

Paige took photos with her phone, closed the medicine cabinet door, and moved into the bedroom. She surveyed the small space. The bed was unmade, and piles of dirty clothes dotted the stained carpet. The bedside table held a flute glass and an empty bottle of champagne. *Someone was celebrating. But what was he toasting?* A newspaper clipping was taped to the wall beside a desk. Moving closer, she read the bold headline: *New Mayor in Whitman.*

There's a new mayor in Whitman. Kathleen Phillips, daughter of former mayor Richard Staten, wins mayoral bid in Tuesday's election. When asked, her opponent, Mason Bridge, had this to say, "Ms. Phillips was the better man. She had the backing and support to get her to where she is. I wish her the best." Kathleen took the win by an overwhelming majority…

Mason Bridge had run opposite Kathleen for mayor of Whitman and lost. *And apparently, he's been stewing about it for the past three years. Could that be why he wants revenge?*

A second clipping hung beside the first. *Kathleen Phillips Announces Intentions to Run for Oregon Governor.* So, this *did* have to do with the election.

Paige turned from the newspaper articles and lowered herself into the chair at the simple desk. After tapping the mouse, a password-protected login screen appeared on the computer. Glancing around the desk, she quickly determined she wasn't going to find the password on a sticky note. She'd have hack into the computer the hard way. But she'd anticipated this problem and had memorized the online directions before leaving her house.

Using sticky keys, Paige tricked the computer into making her the administrator, then changed the password. When Mason went to log in, the previous password wouldn't work, but hopefully, he'd think he'd forgotten the correct one. Mason's desktop background appeared on the monitor. A lovely photo of an island somewhere.

Paige ran the mouse cursor over the icons. She clicked the logo for accounting software. *OK, Mr. Bridge, what other nefarious deeds have you been up to?*

She worked her way down the columns, making notes and taking screenshots with her phone. Paige paused and ran her finger across a particular transaction. The entry was in abbreviations, but the amount of money moved was three-million dollars. *That's a lot of money. Where did it come from?*

As she scanned the rows and rows of numbers, her analytical mind went to work. The letters R.S. appeared under income. She clicked to separate the entries from R.S. from the others, then ran her finger down the date column. R.S. had consistently paid Mason Bridge 9,900 dollars each month. Paige's fingers froze over the keys as she reached the initial payment. *10 August 1992.*

That's five days after I was born.

R.S. as in Richard Staten? Had her grandfather been paying a bribe or blackmail since her birth twenty-six years ago? *My birthday's tomorrow. Grandfather passed away four months ago.* She scrolled back to the top of the page. The payments had continued since Richard's passing. So, who was still paying it? Kathleen? Richard's accountant?

There were other entries marked the same way with someone's initials. And always the same amount. $9,900. Just low enough to stay under the radar of the IRS and the FBI.

Mason Bridge is a professional blackmailer. Or somehow he manages to witness a lot of secrets.

At any moment, Mason could return. Paige closed out of

the financial program and logged out of the computer. She had to get out of here before she got caught. A large book lay open on the dresser—the missing volume—Shakespeare's *The Tempest.* Yellow highlighter marked a short line on the page. She leaned forward to get a better look. *At this hour Lie at my mercy all mine enemies.*

Paige hurried from the apartment building. Torrential rains poured on her head as she dashed for Aunt Hattie's car, getting soaked in the process. She climbed into the driver's seat, buckled her belt, then dialed Kylie's number. Voicemail answered. She hung up and tried Kathleen's number. It rang. Once. Twice. Three times.

Pick up. Pick up. Pick up.

"I have nothing to say to you." Kathleen's voice was curt, her tone harsh. "Goodbye."

"No, wait— please."

Nothing. Kathleen had ended the call.

Paige turned the key in the ignition, started the engine, then dialed again. Straight to voicemail. She groaned and smacked her hand on the steering wheel. "Come on!" She put the car in gear and started toward the highway. *Lord, don't let me be too late.*

33

Iago propped his laptop bag against the bookcase in his foyer, then froze—a trace of female perfume filtered into his nostrils. *Someone was here—a woman.* His pulse picked up as a knot formed in his stomach. *Who was here?*

He stepped into the living room and turned on the overhead light. His eyes swept the furniture, looking for anything out of place. Everything seemed in order. Tybalt slinked out from under the couch and meowed. He rubbed against Iago's ankles and fell over. Iago lifted the cat and stroked his head. "Who was in my house, Tybalt?" Had the intruder left? Was she hiding somewhere in the apartment?

Iago returned the cat to the floor, then moved to the coat closet, and opened the folding doors. The gun case still sat on the upper shelf. Iago took it down, then removed the Glock 17, and snapped the magazine into place. He held the gun extended and tiptoed into the kitchen. A quick glance, then he moved into the hallway and cleared the bathroom. The shower curtain hung open, revealing an empty tub. His eyes fell on the medicine cabinet. What if the intruder had looked inside? He growled. *Should have dumped that stuff immediately.*

His bedroom door stood ajar. He peeked around the door jamb—the room was empty. In two long strides, he reached the closet and threw the door open. "Ha," he shouted at nothing but his clothes. His shoulders relaxed. What an idiot. The intruder was long gone. He lowered his gun.

But who'd been here and what did they want? The camera, hidden in the electrical plug. Of course. The intruder's every move would have been recorded. The memory card would reveal all.

He laid the gun on the desk, extracted the SD card from the camera, then dropped into the chair and touched the wireless mouse. The monitor lit up and asked for his password. Iago typed and hit enter. Access denied. *What? That's not right.* His fingers fumbled with the keys as he tried the same password a second time, being more careful to press the exact combination of letters and numbers. Access denied. *What's going on? That's my password. Why won't it work? It's not possible to…*

He swiveled around and worked his jaw. Iago fetched the laptop from the foyer, entered the password, then stuck the memory card into the port. A few clicks more and he was viewing the day's footage.

An empty office. Fast-forward. A woman appeared on the screen and flipped the light switch. *Paige McDonald.*

She sat in his chair and typed on his keyboard. *That's why my password won't work. But how did she get into the apartment?*

Of course. Iago face-palmed his forehead. *Paige can pick a lock. Who knows what other skills she possesses?*

As a full-frontal view of her face filled the frame, he paused the video. Her eyes were wide with fear. He started the video again, and she stopped next to the open book on his dresser. She'd seen his final note.

What had she learned from his private computer files? He shook his head. What did the specifics matter? That nosy girl could have found any number of things that would ruin him. But he wasn't going to prison. He had to stop her before she revealed his secrets.

He checked the time stamp on the video. His lip curled and spread into a smile. Perfect. Miss McDonald had left his house only twenty minutes ago. His blood pressure rose, and he snapped the laptop closed. It didn't matter how he did it, Paige McDonald had to go. Hopefully, she'd head straight for Whitman. There was only one road from here to there.

If he hurried, he could catch her.

Paige's line of sight blurred as sheets of rain pounded her windshield. She turned on the wipers, but they did little to clear the downpour. The yellow line down the center was barely visible. With the press of a button, she turned on her emergency flashers. Maybe she should have waited. A strong wind rocked the car. Thick clouds blocked the sunlight, and darkness pressed down on the deserted mountain road. *Hard to believe it's the middle of the afternoon.*

Lightning split the sky, and thunder quickly followed. A weight pressed on her chest. *I'll be all right if I take my time.* Her head ached from the unrelenting noise. She passed a green mile-marker. The slope of the road shifted, and as her speed naturally increased, she tapped her brakes. *Lord, get me home safely.*

High beams appeared over the ridge behind her, approaching fast. *Slow down!* A dark pickup materialized and pressed close to her bumper. The engine roared above the rain's pelting. Paige squinted. The blinding light compounded the pain in her temples.

A passing lane was coming up. Paige pumped the brakes several times and slowed even more, hoping the driver would switch lanes and move along. Relief lessened the tension in her shoulders. Undoubtedly, the driver would go around.

A jolt shot through her neck. What! The truck had

slammed into the back of the car. The station wagon swerved from the impact, slipping on the wet road. Paige tightened her fingers on the steering wheel and managed to stay in her lane. "Hey, buddy. Watch what you're doing."

The dashed line appeared, barely visible in the deluge. The other vehicle pulled alongside, then crossed the line and slammed into the broadside of her car. Paige jerked the wheel to the right and fought to maintain control. The truck moved over again, pinning her to the railing. Screeching filled the air. Sparks flew.

When the truck veered to the left, Paige steered back into the lane and increased her speed. *I've got to get away from this maniac.* The pickup sped, closing the distance between them. The passing lane vanished, but the driver stayed beside her.

Paige raised her cell phone to call for help. A split second later, the truck smashed into her doors. She jerked sideways and lost control. The added speed propelled the vehicle into the rail—metal crunched and gave way. The whole world tilted sideways, then upside down. As trees flashed past the windshield, Paige closed her eyes. The car plunged down the embankment. A scream tore from her throat. Glass shattered. Her head slammed into the steering wheel. Her consciousness faded as everything went black and silent.

34

Ryan leaned forward in his chair and picked up the small gift box on his desk. The red velvet was soft beneath his fingers as he flipped open the lid. A gold locket peered out. He lifted it, and the delicate metal looked odd against his calloused skin. The jewelers in Portland had done a fantastic job mending the broken clasp. It was the perfect gift for Paige's twenty-sixth birthday next week. He opened the small heart-shaped pendant. Inside, he had pasted a tiny photo of him on one side and another of his parents on the other. Paige ought to know where she'd come from. He snapped it closed, then turned it over and read the inscription engraved in the back.

To My Loving Daughter. Happy Birthday. Dad.

Nothing could prevent them from building the relationship they both desired.

His cell rang. *Who's calling?* The number didn't look familiar. He picked up the phone, swiped the screen, and held it to his ear without taking his eyes from the locket. *I hope she likes it.*

"Pastor… Sir… Reverend… accident… hurry… hospital…"

A frantic female voice came over the line—heavy breathing and sobs broke up her words. Ryan laid the necklace on his desk and shifted the cell to his other ear. "Please, calm down. I can't help you if I can't understand you. Who is this?"

"Hattie McDonald." The voice broke into sobs again.

A voice in the background spoke, "Here, let me talk to him." There was a short pause, then— "Pastor Whitestone, it's Jessie Faye. Paige has been in an accident. She's alive, but barely. That's all we know—they wouldn't tell us anything more. We're on our way to the hospital now. Can you meet us there?"

Ryan's eyes stung as his gaze cut to the golden locket. The overhead light shimmered off the shiny metal. *Dear God. Not my little girl.* Emotion choked his throat. "I'm on my way."

He pressed the screen to end the call, then stood, grabbing his keys and wallet from a drawer beside him. With long strides, he left the church building and headed for his car. Hand on the handle, he froze. *Who's going to tell Kathleen?*

"What did you do?" Joe Donahue burst through her office door, looking slightly disheveled and soaking wet.

Kathleen shook her head. "I don't know what you're talking about."

Angry red veins popped from her manager's throat. "Oh, really? You don't know anything about those accusations that reporter tossed around like candy."

Kathleen swallowed and averted her eyes from the wild look on Joe's face. "I did what needed to be done."

"Did what…" A curse and a groan finished his sentence. "Do you have any idea how much trouble you could be in? Bribing civil employees? Interfering with police investigations? You didn't kill Patti Hayes, did you?"

Kathleen raised her chin. "Of course not. Don't be ridiculous." She tried to laugh off his suggestion. "Did you?"

Joe stumbled backward. "Excuse me? Did you just accuse me of murder?"

"I asked a simple question." Patti's frightened expression when Kathleen had mentioned she'd rehired Joe came to mind. "She seemed afraid of you."

Joe raked his hand through his wet hair, making it stand on end. "I threatened if she didn't get her numbers up, I'd fire her. I didn't kill her."

"Well, I didn't either."

They both fell silent, staring at each other like two cats preparing to fight. *I did what I had to do. Doesn't Joe get that? We've got to repair the damage Geoff Palmer has done. He should be helping me figure out how to keep this out of the media, not shouting accusations at me.*

Kathleen crossed her arms. "What were you doing the night you were attacked? You showed up at my house at three in the morning."

"I was following a lead, not that it's any of your business."

Following a lead? "What, you're a detective now. Don't quit your day job."

A knock vibrated the office door—Kathleen jumped at the sound. Dennis stepped inside. "Yes. What is it?"

He held out a manila envelope. "Th—this came for you. Just now." His voice trembled, and his face was pale. His eyes darted between Kathleen and Joe. Had he overheard?

"Thank you. You may go."

Dennis rushed out of the office like he was swimming to shore with a shark at his heels. The door slammed.

"What is it?" Joe took a step closer.

"I don't know." Should she open it? She shrugged and picked at the clasp. It couldn't be worse than the rest of the messages she'd received. She raised the flap and withdrew several sheets of copier paper. On top was a typed note.

At this hour Lie at my mercy all mine enemies.

Like the other notes, there was no attribution, but it looked like another Shakespeare line. But this time, the message didn't stop there.

$7 million 24 HRS OR ELSE.

That was it. No signature. Just a tersely worded threat. *Why would I pay someone that kind of money? Where would I even get that kind of money?*

"What do you think they meant by 'or else?'" Joe asked over her shoulder. *That's exactly what I want to know.*

The second page was a newspaper article, complete with photo. The title read: *Two-faced Phillips—Best for Oregon?*

While toting the benefits she'll provide Oregon families, Mayor Kathleen Phillips has disowned her own blood. Brooklyn Paige McDonald, the owner of Paige's Second Chance Books, arrived in Whitman in April, looking for her birth mother. The latter abandoned her on the steps of a fire station. Phillips has failed to recognize McDonald as her progeny, choosing instead to conceal her past actions from the public. Should a woman as devious and deceptive as Phillips be trusted with Oregon's future?

Kathleen gasped. Her eyes burned with unshed tears. *No! I'm ruined!*

"Who wrote this?" Joe asked.

"Geoff Palmer—the news anchor from the press conference." Geoff Palmer was blackmailing her. He must have sent those odd notes with the quotes from Shakespeare, too. *How did he uncover all that stuff about me?*

"Look at the date. August 6." Joe pointed at the top of the paper. "This hasn't been published yet."

Kathleen's cell phone vibrated. Caller ID showed a number, not a name. "Hello?"

"Kathleen. It's Ryan. Your daughter's been in a car accident…"

She didn't hear anything else—the blood drained from her face, leaving her lightheaded. She lowered the phone.

"What is it?"

She raised her eyes to meet Joe's. "Kylie's been in an

accident."

As Ryan hung up the phone, guilt gnawed at his gut. He shouldn't have bent the truth, but if he told Kathleen it was Paige who'd been in the accident, she might not come.

Jessie and Hattie paced the waiting area, looking like two worried mother hens. Hattie muttered and wrung her hands.

Ryan stepped toward the two women and set one hand on each of their shoulders. "Ladies. I know you two haven't gotten along in the past, but you need to set aside your differences and focus on the one thing you have in common. You both love Paige. She needs you now more than ever."

Jessie nodded. "I'm ready to forgive. Hattie, will you forgive me? I never should have let something so petty come between us. I was wrong."

Hattie raised her wrinkled, tear-streaked face. "I'm so sorry, Jessie. I was so jealous. It's silly now that I look back on it. I forgive you." The two women embraced. "I want to help Paige, but what can we do?"

"We can pray," Ryan answered, looking from one woman to the other.

"I don't know how to pray."

Jessie took Hattie's hand. "I can teach you. We'll pray together."

As the women settled into chairs, hands clasped, and heads bent toward each other, tears stung Ryan's eyes. *My dear Paige. If only you could see this.*

He was witnessing a miracle.

Dear God, I hope you have more than one miracle in mind for us today.

"Where's my daughter?" Worry shook Kathleen's voice as she limped toward the reception desk.

"Excuse me?" The gray-haired receptionist wrinkled his forehead and adjusted his glasses. "How may I help you, Mayor Phillips?"

Kathleen fought to steady her tone as her blood pressure rose. "Where's Kylie? She was in a car accident this afternoon. I want to see her."

The receptionist typed on his keyboard. "I'm sorry, but I don't show Kylie Phillips in the system. When was she brought in?"

"I don't know. A few minutes ago, maybe."

"Kathleen!"

Who was calling her? She scanned the waiting area and spotted Ryan waving his arm to get her attention. She rushed forward. "What happened? Where's Kylie? How is she? Is she okay?"

Ryan rested a hand on her shoulder, but she shrugged it off. She didn't need sympathy. If only someone would tell her where to find her daughter.

"Kylie is fine. It was Paige who was in the accident. She's in critical condition. They won't let anyone back yet, but it doesn't look good."

Paige? Paige was in an accident? You said, my daughter? Her eyes widened, and she planted her hands on her hips. "You lied to get me here."

"I'm sorry. I wasn't sure you'd come otherwise. But I didn't lie. Paige is your daughter."

Kathleen clenched her jaw. "I was in an important meeting when I got the call." Not really a meeting, but Ryan didn't have to know that.

Ryan's forehead wrinkled. "Aren't you the least bit concerned about—" he dropped his voice to a whisper—"our daughter?" His voice cracked, and his eyes glistened with unshed tears.

Our daughter? What if someone overheard him? "What are you doing here? Why did the hospital call you? Do they know you're her father?"

Ryan shook his head. "Hattie McDonald, Paige's aunt,

called me in hysterics. I came right away. I wanted to make sure you were here too in case Paige—" His voice caught. He closed his eyes, and a tear squeezed out from under his eyelid.

I shouldn't be here. Kathleen felt herself drifting backward. "I—I've gotta go."

"Kathleen!" His voice rose. Veins popped out of his neck. His face flushed. "She might be dying. You should be with her."

"I can't. Mayors don't just visit anyone in the hospital, and they definitely don't wait for news of their condition. People will start asking questions. The media will want to know my connection to the patient. I have to go." She bolted from the waiting room as fast as her booted foot would carry her, her purse swinging in sync with her steps. Ryan's stare on the back of her head made her hair stand on end, but she didn't look back.

Footsteps pounded the pavement behind her. "Kathleen. Stop."

Kathleen turned to face Ryan. "You don't understand. I have to go."

A news van pulled up in front of the hospital. Carmela Carlson jumped out, followed by a camera crew. *I've got to get out of here before they see me.*

Ryan stepped closer and clasped his hand around her upper arm. "You're really going to choose your career over your daughter? I don't even know you anymore."

Kathleen jerked out of his grasp. "Don't you see? It's not about Paige. It's not about the election. It's about weakness. I can't be weak. No one wants a weak leader. No one can know the truth. Every time I look at her, I am faced with my own weakness."

"Weakness? Why are you weak? Because you didn't say no. Because your father forced you to give away your baby, and you didn't stand up to him. Because your husband was cruel and abusive? Why?"

Tears burned Kathleen's eyes. "You still don't get it, do you? My father didn't force me. Giving up Paige…" Her voice faltered. "…was my idea."

35

Ryan stared after Kathleen's vehicle as it drove away, a paralysis spreading over his body. He hadn't the strength to keep her from leaving. Her confession had hit him like a hurricane on the Florida coast. Giving up Paige was her idea? He'd thought her father had coerced her into it, but in reality, she'd thought of it first.

But she must have had a moment of doubt. She'd tried calling him the day after he returned from visiting his grandparents in Texas, but they'd gotten disconnected. What had she planned to tell him? Was it about the baby or something unrelated? If only he'd come home sooner, maybe things would have been different.

Don't blame yourself. It wasn't your fault.

Familiar guilt jabbed his conscious. He'd known it was wrong the night he'd taken Annie's virtue. Still, he'd let himself get caught up in how she made him feel, and never once considered the potential consequences of their actions. Sure, the consent was mutual, but he should have done the right thing, instead of feeding his fleshly lust. Still, God had allowed good to come from their immorality. He'd given them Paige. *Dear God, don't take her from us now. I know we don't deserve her, but please allow us another chance to be a family.*

Ryan lifted his eyes to the hospital windows. Which room was Paige's? He closed his eyelids and let his shoulders rise and fall as he took a deep breath. *Lord, give me the strength to face whatever happens tonight. Please let my daughter see the dawning of a new day.* He opened his eyes, straightened his shoulders, then headed back inside. The doctor greeted him in the waiting area. "Pastor Whitestone. These ladies tell me you're Paige's father. I have an update on her condition…"

Ryan would hate her now that he knew the truth. Richard Staten hadn't forced her to give up her baby. It had been her idea, so her goals and plans could stay on track. Dad had only kept her from changing her mind when she'd faltered her resolve.

Kathleen threw open the study door and crossed the threshold. *I've got to come up with seven-million dollars.* Her phone rang. She barely stopped long enough to answer. Mother. "I just saw the news and talked to Ryan. Kathleen. Go be with Paige in the hospital."

Kathleen narrowed her eyebrows. "You know why I can't do that." *I have to stop that article from releasing if its the last thing I do.*

"Just go see her."

"But—"

Mother's voice grew insistent."Go. At least see how she's doing, even if you don't hang around. If she doesn't make it through the night, you will regret not saying goodbye."

Say goodbye? Make it through the night? Kathleen hung up and lowered her phone. Had she underestimated Paige's condition?

Her words replayed in her mind. *I don't want her here. I don't want her in my life. I wish she'd never been born.* A sharp exhale escaped her lips. What if Paige died? Could she live with herself knowing she'd never given Paige the one thing she wanted? *I have to go see her for myself.*

Kathleen peeked around the corner into the hall. Good. The nurses' station was empty. She couldn't believe she was slinking through the hallways of a hospital like a criminal, even knowing that the security cameras were catching the whole thing. As a nurse passed, Kathleen ducked out of sight. Once the nurse turned a corner, Kathleen released her held breath, then craned her neck to glimpse the patient board for Paige's room number. She scurried down the hallway and slipped inside the open door.

A male voice drifted from inside the room. Kathleen hid behind the modesty curtain. Officer Hamilton Bryant sat in a chair next to the bed with Paige's pale hand clutched in his. He pressed her knuckles to his lips. "Heal her, dear God, please heal her. Bring her back to me. I love this woman, and I want to spend my life with her. Please, wake her up."

Kathleen's gaze traveled from Paige's arm to her face, and her breath caught in her throat. Her stomach tightened. Bruises and lacerations darkened her daughter's face. A bandage wrapped around her head, and a brace covered her neck. She was intubated, with a ventilator breathing for her. An intravenous drip stretched from its pole to her other hand.

As lightheadedness overshadowed her, Kathleen closed her eyes. Her chest tightened, restricting her breathing. *Dear God. How did I let this happen?* A wheeze squeezed from her throat.

The officer's head shot up, and he grabbed the weapon from his holster. "Come out where I can see you." He stood and pointed the gun in her direction.

Kathleen pushed the curtain aside and folded her arms across her chest. She arched her eyebrow. "Are you really going to shoot the mayor?"

Officer Bryant holstered his weapon. "What are you doing here? You don't care about her."

His words stabbed her heart, even though what he said was true. Wasn't it? Or was it merely a cover for her guilt and grief? "How-How is she?"

Officer Bryant shook his head, lowered into the chair, and took hold of Paige's hand. He closed his eyes and bowed his head as if he were going to begin praying again.

"Don't bother. God's not going to hear you." Why did she say that? The bitterness in her soul had seeped out. "He doesn't care what happens to any of us."

Officer Bryant lifted his head and made eye contact. "Pardon, Madam Mayor, but I beg to differ."

"You think by whispering words into the air, she'll be miraculously healed?"

"I'm not whispering words into the air. I'm having a conversation with the God of the Universe."

"Believe what you like, but if He cares, He does a lousy job of showing it. He never bothered to answer my prayers."

Officer Bryant laid Paige's hand on the bed and stood. He faced Kathleen. "Did you ever think that maybe He did?"

"What?" When had God ever answered her prayers? It always seemed like the times she needed Him most, He was most elusive.

"I don't know much about your life, but I know God promised to be there for His children. A verse in Isaiah says something like, why do you say your way is hidden from the Lord? It goes on to mention God as giving us wings like eagles when we're weak. When life is at its worst, He gives us the ability to go on. And if we keep our focus on Him, He gives us the strength to soar."

"He was never there for me." Memories scorched her mind. Tears attempted to put out the burning flames. "You have no idea what I've been through."

"Paige said—"

She jutted her chin toward the bed. "That girl knows

nothing about me."

Officer Bryant crossed his arms. "And who's fault is that? You never gave her a chance."

A nurse entered the room, cutting off their conversation. Kathleen ducked behind the curtain again, then slipped out of the room. The nurse's voice drifted down the hall behind her. "Alright, lover boy, I need you to leave so I can tend to the patient. Go get something to eat, or, better yet, go back to work. We'll call if anything changes."

If anything changes? Nothing would ever change. This is all my fault. I did this. I have to get out of here.

Ryan strode toward her, carrying two paper coffee cups. Was he heading for Paige's room?

"Kathleen, what are you doing here?" He froze mid-step.

She didn't answer but pivoted and skirted around him. *This is all my fault.*

"Kathleen," Ryan called, his voice fading down the hallway.

The exit sign signaled her escape. Just a few more steps and she'd be free. She burst through the side door and inhaled, letting the fresh air fill her lungs. Her eyes stung, and her vision blurred. Images of Paige played on a loop through her mind. *Is she going to die? This is all my fault. I told God I didn't want her in my life. He's taking her away.*

A lump clogged her throat. She coughed.

"Kathleen." Ryan's voice was closer again. She turned. He stood directly behind. "What are you doing here?"

Words failed her. What could she say? She glanced toward the front door. The news van from earlier had left. "I—I wanted to see Paige for myself."

A scream pierced the evening sky and carried across the parking lot. Kylie closed the distance in a matter of moments and shoved a piece of paper in Kathleen's face. "You lied to me!"

Kylie held the fake newspaper article. Kathleen had forgotten them on the desk at City Hall, but how had Kylie gotten it? "Kylie! What are you doing here?"

"I came to see Paige, but I didn't expect to find you here. I saw the news story about Paige being in an accident. Is it true? Is Paige my sister?" Kylie's voice quivered and broke.

"Kylie, I…" What could she say? What viable excuse could she give to convince her daughter she'd done the right thing, that it had all been in Kylie's best interest? Every reason that filtered through her mind fell as flat as a soufflé after someone slammed the oven door. She felt deflated and crushed under her daughter's withering gaze. Had Kylie ever looked at her that way before? No. It was the exact look she'd been trying so hard to avoid—an expression of utter disappointment and betrayal. Hadn't that been what she'd been afraid of all this time? And here it was—nose to nose with a hungry lion waiting for just the right second to devour her.

Ryan stepped around Kathleen and put his hand on Kylie's shoulder. "She is."

"Is… she going to be okay?"

His movements nearly imperceptible, but he must have shaken his head because another of Kylie's wails pierced the air. The sound penetrated to the deepest depths of Kathleen's soul and cut her to the quick. Mere words could never express the despair that settled over her entire being.

Kylie crumpled against Ryan's chest, like a child to a father. He wrapped his arms over her shoulders and let her cry against his shirt. Soft whispers came from his lips. "Would you like to see her?"

Kathleen swallowed.

Kylie leaned back. A parking lot light glittered off her wet cheeks. She brushed her tears with her knuckles, then slowly nodded and licked her lips. "Yes, please."

Ryan draped his arm over Kylie's shoulder, protectively drew her to his side, and led her to the automatic doors.

Kathleen wanted to call out after them, but words failed her. She wasn't invited. They disappeared inside the hospital. She brushed her hair back behind her ear. It was soaking wet. She lifted her eyes to the sky. It was raining? Cold rain seeped through her stockings and touched her feet, soaked her head, and ran down her neck. She shivered, standing alone in the parking lot. Her hair hung in soggy ropes, and her clothes clung to her frame. The fake newspaper lay in a puddle. Her lies rang in her head like a bell that wouldn't quit. All her attempts to hide the truth had been exposed. *"I don't want to be like you or grandfather. I don't want to trample people to get what I want in life. I don't want to make so many enemies that I'm always looking over my shoulder."*

All this pain. All this heartache was her fault. Hers and hers alone.

36

Kathleen smashed the beer bottle on top of the tombstone. Brown glass littered the ground. She screamed and kicked at the marble stone. She stomped back and forth, shouting at the top of her lungs. "How could You do this? You claim to answer prayer, but You never answered mine. You claim to love, but You've never cared about me? Do I mean nothing to You? Am I a joke to You? Am I Your plaything? Do You sit up in Heaven and say, 'Let's see what torture I can inflict on poor little Annie today?'"

Annie. Her steps faltered. She hadn't referred to herself that way in years. *I'm still Annie deep inside. Why can't I rid myself of her influence? I don't want to be Annie.*

Her soul felt raw and exposed. "What do You want from me?" She screamed into the night sky, fist raised. *I don't have anything left to give You. You've already taken it all.*

A flashlight beam crossed her face, momentarily blinding her. She squinted but couldn't make out the person approaching. "Kathleen. Whatcha doing out here?" Chief

House. He strode closer and wrinkled his nose. "Have you been drinking?"

She lifted her chin. "So, what if I have. It's a free country."

"You're drunk, Kathleen, and you're disturbing the peace. I'm gonna need you to come with me."

"What if I don't want to?" She grabbed the tombstone to keep from falling over. Why was everything spinning?

"You can come peacefully, or I can handcuff you whichever you prefer."

Kathleen bit her lip until she tasted blood—*I think it's blood.* Bitterness filled her mouth. The liquor that had seemed appealing moments ago turned sour in her stomach. "I'll come." She stumbled toward the officer. He caught her before she fell.

At the station, she dropped into a chair. The room swirled around her as her belly knotted. A sour taste crawled her throat, and she gagged. Chief House grabbed a trashcan. Why had she thought this was a good idea? Never drank before in her life. Because of Lionel, she despised liquor, and yet here she sat. She wiped her mouth on her sleeve. "Thank you."

Chief House perched on the edge of a desk. "Who do you want us to call? I don't think you want to spend the night here."

"You're not going to arrest me?"

Mark shook his head. "Want me to call Kylie?"

Not Kylie. The thought of her daughter seeing her like this. She cringed. There was only one other person she trusted. "Ryan. Call Ryan Whitestone."

The bullpen's buzzer helped wake Ryan further. He rubbed the sleep from his eyes. His lower back pinched, and he twisted to stretch out the knot. Sleeping in Paige's hospital room hadn't done him any favors. Then getting the call from the Whitman Police Department—the pain in his body was nearly as bad as the pain in his spirit. What was Kathleen thinking? Why would she do this?

Chief Mark House met him as he came through the secure door. The bullpen was eerily quiet at this time of night.

Mark clapped him on the upper arm. "Thanks for coming down here. She's in pretty bad shape." He motioned for Ryan to follow.

As they entered the chief's office, Ryan looked around. He'd expected to find Kathleen locked in a cell, but she lay on the couch in a fetal position, covered by the chief's jacket.

"I'll leave you two alone." Chief House exited the office and closed the door behind him.

Frowning, Ryan stood over her and stared at the sleeping form, afraid to open his mouth. He fought against the anger boiling in his gut. His fist clenched and unclenched. What had she been thinking? Getting drunk and disturbing the peace? Had she completely lost her mind?

Kathleen shifted in her sleep, rolled over, and opened her eyes, blinking rapidly as if she was having trouble focusing. "Ryan?" Her voice was crusty with sleep and dryness. "What are you doing here?" She moved her feet and slowly eased into a sitting position. He sat beside her as her hands pressed against the sides of her head. She must have a massive headache.

"You asked Chief House to call me."

"I did?" She looked around as if trying to remember where she was and how she'd gotten there. A dark cloud passed over her face. "Am I a horrible person?"

Ryan wrinkled his forehead. "What?"

"Am I a horrible person?"

"You're not a horrible person, but what were you thinking? What if you'd gotten behind the wheel of a car? You could have hurt yourself or someone else." He should know.

Kathleen's face reddened. Veins popped out of her neck. She threw off the jacket, and it fell to the floor. "I don't want to talk about it."

But he had to talk about it. Terrible images had flashed through his memory the moment the police had said Kathleen was drunk.

There was a light tap on the door, then it opened. The chief addressed Ryan. "We won't be pressing charges. Take her home, pastor."

"Thank you, Chief House." Ryan stood. "Come on. Let's get you home."

Kathleen dropped her head, and demurely allowed him to lead her from the office.

"Here's her personal effects."

Ryan took the purse and passed it to Kathleen. They walked out to the car, and he helped her into the passenger seat. He climbed into his side, buckled his seatbelt, and then made sure she had. "You want to go home?"

"Anywhere but home. Kylie can't see me like this."

Ryan twisted the key, and the engine turned over. He put the car in gear and pulled out of the parking space, then onto the road. "Everything else is closed. We'll go to my house and get some coffee in you before you go home."

"Fine with me." She laid her head against the window and closed her eyes.

Ryan turned onto the street leading to his apartment, then changed his mind and headed out of town to the old farmhouse. He parked on the dirt driveway, then shook Kathleen's shoulder.

"We're here."

Kathleen blinked and groggily lifted her head. "This isn't your apartment."

"Nope." Ryan helped her out of the car and into the house. She slumped into a chair and laid her head on the kitchen table. He made a pot of coffee then poured it into two mugs. "Do you still like your coffee sweet enough to rot your teeth?"

"Black, please."

He glanced over his shoulder. Kathleen still looked like

the girl he'd fallen in love with, but so much had changed—little things. Unexpected things. In many ways, he hardly recognized her. He brought the steaming mugs to the table and set one in front of her before taking a seat.

She took a long drink, then set the cup down and licked her lips. "That's good. Thank you."

"You're welcome.

Her gaze dropped to her coffee mug, and her fingers rubbed the handle. "I'm being blackmailed."

"What?"

Ryan listened as she told him about the Shakespeare notes from the reporter, Geoff Palmer. "If I don't come up with seven-million dollars—" She looked at the watch on her wrist— "in fifteen hours or so, he's going to tell the whole nation about Paige."

"If you tell the world about Paige first, he's got nothing on you."

"I can't. I'm in too deep. Everyone will know I'm a liar. They'll think every one of my campaign promises is a lie. If people know about Paige, they'll know how I failed, and they won't love me anymore."

"I guess you could just let her die. That would solve your problem."

Kathleen's eyes grew wide. "Excuse me? What kind of preacher are you? Shouldn't you be encouraging me with some pointless Scripture, not telling me to off my own children?"

"I'm trying to make a point. Is winning worth losing everything? If you win all alone, did you really win at all?"

She bowed her head. The ticking cuckoo clock and Kathleen's heavy breathing were the only sounds cutting the silence. A tear slipped from her eye. He caught it and rubbed it between his fingers. Without looking up, she said, "Ryan, why don't you hate me?"

"Because I've forgiven you."

"Why?"

"Because God has forgiven me. When I fail Him, he

forgives me, again and again. How can I not offer you that same mercy?"

Ryan took Kathleen's hand in his and laced their fingers together. His thumb rubbed over the smooth palm. His story needed to be told—he couldn't run from the truth. Couldn't pretend the past hadn't happened. Annie needed to know. "We all make mistakes."

She raised her chin and combed her fingers through her hair, but she didn't release his hand. "What did you do? Steal a pen from work? Or forget to give back the change when the cashier gave you too much?" Sarcasm laced her voice.

If only it were that simple. The events that took place that night after Annie's going away party had forever marred him. "I killed someone."

She paled, the laughter died in her throat, and her eyes froze on his. A gasp slipped from her lips as her hand moved to cover her mouth.

"Do you remember the night before you left for college?"

She nodded.

"It had been two weeks since you tried to tell me something, and the call got disconnected. Every time I tried to call or visit, you pushed me away, so I confronted you that night. I still remember every word you said. You told me I was holding you back. That you didn't want me in your life."

Kathleen's eyes brimmed with tears. "Ryan. I'm so sorry, I—"

"Please, this is difficult. Let me get it out before you speak."

"All right."

"I left the party and drove around for about an hour, sulking and stewing. I stopped at a red light. When I turned my head, I saw the brightly lit signs of a bar. It called to me. Told me I could drown my sorrows and forget how much you hurt me. I went inside. And that's all I remember of that night."

Ryan continued, "I woke up two days later in the hospital with a concussion. A detective came to my room and told me

I'd left the bar stone drunk. Somewhere around midnight, I struck another car." His voice cracked.

The next part was the most difficult. "I killed the driver, and I was charged with underage drinking, reckless driving, driving under the influence, and secondary manslaughter. I spent the next ten years in prison. When I was released, I came here to my parent's farmhouse, where I spent six years alone, begging God to forgive me. But receiving God's forgiveness was the easy part. Forgiving myself—that was hard." He fell silent. The weight of his confession hung in the air.

Ryan's voice reached her ears and penetrated her heart. Kathleen lifted her chin to meet his eyes. "How could God allow this to happen to my daughter? What does He want from me?"

"He wants you, Annie. He wants all of you. He wants your heart. And your soul. You can sit there, shaking your fist at God all you want, but He's still waiting with open arms to welcome you home."

"Annie is gone."

"No, she's not. She's still inside you. She's who you really are."

"You don't understand. God can never forgive me. I can never go back."

"Yes, you can. You think *I* don't understand. I *killed* a man. I've proven that nothing is unforgivable with God. He is waiting with open arms. He loves you. You haven't done anything you can't come back from. Don't you think if I could go back, I would choose a different road?"

"God is punishing me because I said I didn't want Paige in my life. I don't deserve his forgiveness."

"God isn't punishing you. You're punishing yourself. You've never forgiven yourself for giving her up."

"He's taken everything from me."

"No, Kathleen. You've done this to yourself. It's no one's fault but your own. The only dragon you need to slay here is yourself. Get out of your own way. It's not a weakness to do the right thing."

"What about my father? All I ever wanted to do is please him. To make him love me."

"You've become so focused on pleasing him, you've forgotten about pleasing *Him*." Ryan pointed upward. "You can't blame your parents. You can't blame your husband. And you can't blame God. He never promised a life of happily ever afters. To wish it so is to build your life on a faulty foundation."

Ryan continued, "Don't be the beasts they were. Choose who you were meant to be. Annie wasn't weak. She is everything good about you. Your father's gone. Lionel's gone. You can choose not to let them hurt you anymore. Choose those who love you for who you are. Me. Kylie. Dawn. Paige. Choose faith. Choose your Heavenly Father."

Kathleen mentally replayed the officer's words from earlier. *When life is at its worst, He gives us the ability to go on. And if we keep our focus on Him, He gives us the strength to soar.*

"Do you remember the story of the prodigal son?"

Kathleen nodded.

"There's a line that gets me every time. It says, 'when he came to himself.' Nothing could be done for him when he thought he could take care of everything himself. He had to come to the end of his own strength. And when he returned home, do you remember where his father was? While he was still a long way off, his father saw him and ran to him. That means his father was watching and waiting. God is like that father. He's waiting for you to come home. He's waiting for you to come to yourself. It's time to wake up."

Wake up. All this time, Kathleen had never asked God what He wanted her to do. She'd never sought His will or wisdom but had simply done what she wanted and whatever it took to get ahead. She'd believed a lie.

Do whatever it takes to win, Annie. Whatever it takes… whatever it takes.

Look where that had gotten her. She'd done whatever it took, and it had led her down this road away from God. Apart from His love and care. She was the one who'd moved. Not Him.

It's my fault I'm in this mess. If Kathleen continued down this path, she'd lose everything. It was time to close this chapter of her life. Make amends for the hurt and pain she'd caused. Starting with the One she'd hurt the most.

I'm tired of running, Lord. I'm tired of trying to handle everything on my own. I'm sorry I pursued my own dreams instead of seeking Your plans for me. Please forgive me for turning my back on You. Have mercy on me. I want to come home.

I'm coming home.

37

Ryan drove Kathleen home, parked in the driveway, and helped her from the vehicle. "Are you going to be okay?"

"I'll be fine. Thank you." Her heart weighed lighter than it had in years. She leaned forward and lightly kissed Ryan's cheek. His eyes widened in the porch light. "Thank you… for tonight."

He squeezed her hand. "You're welcome. Will I see you soon?"

"I hope so."

He drove down the driveway until the headlights faded into the distance, leaving her alone in the dark.

Kathleen reached for the door. *Unlocked? Kylie's car isn't here. She must still be at the hospital. Did I forget to lock it on my way out?* She flipped on the foyer light switch. Kathleen drew a breath and immediately smelled cigarette smoke. *What in the world?*

She took a step deeper into the house. *Is someone here?*

The front door slammed shut and locked.

Kathleen whirled, stumbling.

Someone aimed a gun at her chest. "Who are you? What are you doing in my house?"

"Hello, Kathleen." He stepped closer but didn't lower the weapon.

"Do I know you?"

"You should. It's Mason. Mason Bridge."

"What are you doing here? What do you want?" *Mason Bridge? Why does that name sound familiar? I wish I wasn't so bad with names and faces.*

"You've walked over so many people, you don't even remember me, do you?" He locked eyes with her.

The mayoral election three years ago, Mason Bridge ran against me. I won. "I remember. We both ran for mayor of Whitman. Don't you also work for Chatham? Or did, I guess." *He attended Dad's funeral and was at the rally in Salem. Always two steps behind Chatham.* "You were his assistant, right?"

According to the news reports, Mason had been the one to discover Chatham. *Discover or murder?* Her eyes cut to the Glock in Mason's hand. *If Mason killed Chatham, will he kill me too?* She cut her eyes toward the sideboard drawer. *If I can just get to my gun.* "What do you want?"

"Where's my seven-million?"

"Your—But I thought—" She'd thought wrong. Geoff Palmer hadn't sent the threat. *But somehow he's wrapped up in all of this.*

She inched toward the sideboard. "Are you the one who's been threatening me?"

Mason didn't answer.

"Did you send those Shakespeare quotes? To me? To Kylie?"

Mason smirked.

I guess he did. "What about everything else that's happened? Were you behind the ending of my lease? And my volunteers quitting? Did you steal my campaign money? Did you try to run me over?" Kathleen inhaled sharply. "Did you kill Patti Hayes?" Her eyes misted at the possibility that sweet

Patti had been murdered in cold blood. "Why?"

"Madam Mayor, we don't have time to rehash everything I did or didn't do. Now, where's my money?"

"I don't have it. I can't possibly come up with that much cash." Her fingers closed the last few millimeters between her hand and the drawer.

"I thought you might want to do this the hard way. You seem to enjoy making things difficult." Mason gestured with the gun toward the back of the house.

She grabbed the handle and jerked the drawer open. Empty. *No! Where's the gun?* Had Ryan not put it back like she thought? Did he put it in one of the other two drawers?

Mason's hand slowly closed the drawer. She turned. His dark eyes stared hard, and he scowled. Mason didn't say a word, just gestured down the hall with his chin.

Kathleen released the handle and moved forward, repeatedly glancing over her shoulder. *Would he shoot me in the back?* Her heart pounded against her ribcage. Quivers ran up and down her limbs, making it difficult to walk. *What's he going to do to me?*

Mason halted in front of the closed sliding doors to the living room. "In there." He motioned with the gun.

Kathleen took a deep breath and slid the doors open. Mother sat in the armchair, blindfolded. Hands and feet tied. "Mother!" She shrieked.

"Kathleen?" Sobs choked her voice. "Kathleen, what's going on? Who is this man?"

"Mother, what are you doing here?"

"I just wanted to ask if I could see Paige in the hospital. She's dying, Kathleen."

Mother just wanted to meet her granddaughters. That's all. And I prevented it. Now, she might never get the chance. "I'm so sorry, Mother." *God, forgive me. How many lives have I destroyed with my selfishness?*

"Quiet." Mason snapped from behind Kathleen. "Both of you shut up." He shoved Kathleen's back, and she stumbled forward, falling to her knees. Pain shot through both legs.

"What do you want from me? What are you going to do to us?"

Mason squatted, level with Kathleen's face. "That'll be up to you, won't it?"

"Why are you doing this? What do you have against me? What did I ever do to you?"

Mason's face grew red, and his veins popped out of his neck. "You stole the election from me, Kathleen. You didn't win fair and square. Your father bought those votes for you. You don't deserve to be mayor."

"I won on my own merits. My father didn't buy the votes. How dare you say that."

Mason stood. "I guess we'll never know, will we?"

Kathleen needed a plan. She lowered her eyes, and it fell on the walker boot. "I'll find a way to get your money. Just help me up. I can't get up on my own. Stupid boot."

Mason narrowed his eyes then reached out to give her a lift. Kathleen grabbed his hand, then used her weight to launch into his chest, struggling to snatch the weapon from his other hand. Her fingernails dug into his arms as he blocked her reach.

"No, you don't." Mason gave her a hard thrust and propelled her backward into the wall, arms flailing. The jolt knocked the breath from her lungs. Her head hit the corner of the window ledge, sending sharp pangs through her skull and momentarily blackening her vision. When her eyesight cleared, Mason stood on the other side of the room, pressing the gun to Mother's forehead.

Ryan pulled into the parking space in front of the hospital, shut off the engine, then leaned his head back. His emotions were a scrambled mess—gratitude for the change in Kathleen and the breakthrough she had made tonight, but still wondering if they could have a future together, and worried about Paige's health. She was in a coma last he'd checked. The doctor didn't know if she would wake up, and he'd admitted that if she did, she'd be in terrible pain. His last admonition was to prepare for the worst.

Ryan was exhausted, but he would stay by his daughter's side until God healed her. *One way or the other. Thank you, Lord, that I know where she's going to spend eternity if she doesn't make it through the night.* Kylie and Hamilton were with Paige now, and one of them would have called if anything had happened—good or bad.

As he opened the door to exit his vehicle, he looked over at the passenger seat and noticed something on the floorboard. Ryan leaned over and picked up a set of keys. Kathleen must have dropped them. How did Kathleen get into her house without her keys? He dropped them into the cupholder, then shut the car door and restarted the engine. *I better take them over now and not wait until morning. I know it's late, but I'd hate for her to spend the night on her porch. But if she couldn't get in the house, wouldn't she have called by now?*

Dear God, if I get out of this alive, I'm going to hold onto that girl and never let go. Please heal her, so she and I can have the relationship we were meant to have. Give us a second chance.

In reality, it would be her third chance. Paige's arrival in Whitman four months ago had been her second chance.

But if she and Mother weren't going to get out of here alive, there was at least one thing she could make right, even if she never got to tell Paige how much she loved her.

"I'd like to talk to my mother."

"Fine." Mason growled. "Make it quick."

"Mother?" Kathleen called.

Mother turned her head toward Kathleen's voice. "What is it?"

"I just wanted to say how sorry I am for not telling you about Paige. I thought you wouldn't understand. I thought it didn't matter since I was giving her up for adoption. And I apologize for giving you a hard time about meeting the girls when you got here. I never should have stood in your way. I'm sorry."

"That's enough." Mason shoved the mouth of the pistol against her mother's skin. She screamed.

"Leave my mother alone. She had nothing to do with this. Do whatever you want to me, but please don't hurt her."

A wicked grin spread over Mason's face. "Look at that. The Ice Queen has melted. Too bad you won't be around to convince the voters of that. Stand up."

"I can't. Remember. Plastic boot. I guess you gave me that little present, too."

He didn't deny it, just aimed the gun at her, and frowned. "I said, stand up."

Using the wall and the window ledge, Kathleen managed to scramble to her feet and turn with a hop. "Sit." He ordered, pointing to the stool by the antique writing desk.

She took the seat. "What now? Are you going to kill me too?"

"You're going to write a letter."

"On the computer?"

Mason shook his head. "Of course not. A typed letter isn't reliable evidence. I want you to write this letter in your own hand."

"What do you want it to say?"

"Confess to all your crimes. You, madam mayor, are guilty of extortion, fraud, and murder. Then I'm going to disappear, and you're going to rot in a prison cell for the rest of your miserable existence."

"Murder!"

"You killed Patti Hayes and Senator Chatham."

"I did not!" She wasn't guilty of any such thing, but she had no choice but to comply until she thought of a better plan. She softened her voice. "I guess I'll need paper and a pen. I think there's some inside the desk." Kathleen pulled open the drawer. Sure enough, the desk drawer had a few remaining sheets of Richard Staten's stationery in it.

"Hurry up."

"I've got it." She grabbed a pen and pushed the drawer closed. "You'll have to tell me what to write."

As Mason dictated her confession, each word brought her closer to the end of the letter. Who knew what Mason had planned for them once she finished? Was he going to kill them both and make it look like a murder/suicide? *If we're going to survive this night, I've got to get that gun away from him.*

The doorbell rang.

Ryan tried the doorbell a second time, then knocked. Light shone through the curtains of the parlor windows, but no one answered. "Kathleen." He called out. *She was probably so tired, she forgot to turn out the lights. I should let her sleep.* He'd return her keys first thing in the morning, so she wouldn't worry. He turned to leave. The door creaked behind him.

Ryan pivoted. Kathleen's head peeked around the door. "Ryan! What are you doing here?"

He held up her keys. "You left these in my car. I didn't want you to ransack your house looking for them."

"It's fine. Thank you." She took the keys from his fingers, then turned her head.

Something wet and sticky matted her hair. *Is she bleeding?* "Kathleen, are you all right? Did you hit your head?"

"My leg is feeling much better." She raised her voice. "Thank you for asking."

Her leg? She must have hit her head harder than she wants to admit. "Kathleen—"

"Good night." She shut the door, and the lock clicked.

That was strange. Why did Kathleen think I asked about her leg? She got the sprained ankle when someone tried to run her over. Was she trying to tell him she was in trouble? Ryan hurried to his car, pulling his cell phone from his pocket.

Dispatch answered. "Nine. One. One. How may I direct your call?"

"Hey, Kelly, I think we've got a hostage situation over at Mayor Phillip's mansion."

As Kathleen returned to the desk to finish the letter, her body trembled. Mason had stayed out of Ryan's line of sight, but she'd sensed the gun on her the entire time. *My head's bleeding?* She hadn't noticed, but the way it throbbed, she wasn't surprised.

She picked up the pen. "What do you want me to say next?"

I don't know what to do. If I challenge Mason, he'll kill Mother. If I do what he wants, he'll kill me and then Mother. If I run, he'll kill Mother.

Dear Lord, I don't know what to do. Please show me. She glanced at the letter she was writing. Mason was going to kill her when she finished, she had no doubt of that.

Ryan's words came to mind. "*If you tell the world, he's got nothing on you.*" If she told on herself, she'd remove Mason's leverage, and he'd kill her.

I'm going to die anyway. If only I could make things right beforehand. Would Mason let me confess live?

"What are you doing?" Mason pressed her shoulder with the gun barrel. "You're supposed to be writing."

"You haven't told me what to write."

Mason stomped away, hand on his chin.

"You know, if you were any good at your job, you'd realize there was a better way for me to confess. Anyone can forge my handwriting. I bet the defense lawyer would even suggest that to the judge and jury. A recorded live stream of my confession would have a lot more standing in court."

She glanced over her shoulder. Mason's face had turned red. Would he take the bait?

"What if I don't like what you say?"

Kathleen shrugged. "Then, you can shoot me."

Within minutes, Kathleen was seated in the middle of the

room, her back to the sliding doors. Her laptop sat on a TV tray in front of her, with Mason standing out of view. Logged into her social media account and prepped to record, Kathleen clicked the button to stream live.

Ryan paced the driveway outside. Why were the police taking so long? He glanced at his watch. Okay, so he'd only called a couple minutes ago. But this was a small town, and they should be here by now. If they came with sirens and lights, they would alert whoever held Kathleen hostage. Would they think to come silently? He couldn't just stand here when Kathleen could be in grave danger. He had to do something, but what?

He raked his fingers through his hair and groaned in frustration. Was there any way he could storm the castle like a knight in shining armor, rushing to the defense of the maiden in distress? He shook his head at the silly image—this was no castle. He was no knight. And Kathleen was no maiden in distress. She was a strong woman, who'd probably not appreciate him coming to her rescue.

He sat on the front stoop and rotated his neck to release the tension in his shoulders. Something stuck out of the flowerpot. Ryan reached out and withdrew it from the dirt. A key? What was a key doing in the flowerbed? That night Dawn was in the kitchen; how had she gotten inside? She'd mentioned something about Kathleen not having changed the locks. He'd assumed that meant Dawn still had a key to the house. What if she'd gotten in using a spare key hidden here? It was worth the try.

He leaped up, stuck the key into the lock.

It fit.

He turned it.

The bolt clicked.

He twisted the knob, opened the door, and stepped inside the foyer. Treading lightly, he crossed the floor and removed

Kathleen's gun from the drawer in the sideboard. He loaded a bullet into the chamber and cocked the hammer.

Kathleen's muffled voice carried from somewhere in the house.

"… In high school, I gave birth to a baby girl. But I was selfish and believed this child would ruin my future goals, so I gave her up for adoption. In pursuit of my dreams, I have climbed the ladder of success on the backs of others. I was more concerned with power than what was right. To protect my reputation, I did what I thought necessary, including covering up the theft of municipal funds, bribing a city employee, and interfering with the investigation into Patti Hayes's death."

She paused. Mason lifted an eyebrow. If he spoke, his voice would be heard by thousands of viewers. Someone was sure to recognize him.

Kathleen continued, "Recently, the child I abandoned found me, but I rejected her and prevented her from connecting with her birth family. I deceived my family, and I deceived the voters."

She took a breath. *I can do this—Mason's going to kill me anyway.* "If you believe this makes me unfit for the office of governor, you're right. Kylie, if you're listening, please know how much I love you. I should never have lied to you, and I'm sorry. Please forgive me. Kylie, you once asked if I would withdraw from the election if you asked me to."

Mason frowned and scrunched his forehead.

"As of this moment, I officially withdraw from the election. I am no longer a candidate for governor of Oregon. This decision was made of my own accord."

She stopped. Said nothing about committing extortion or murder.

"I won't confess to crimes I did not commit."

Mason slammed the laptop shut. The gun's handle

cracked her skull. Pain split her head. A deep voice filtered through the fog as she flickered in and out of consciousness. It wasn't Mason's. It was Ryan's. *Help me, please.* Darkness pressed into her vision—*my dear daughters. Please forgive me.*

Shots fired. Everything went dark. *I'm going to die.*

38

Her vision grew lighter, and the darkness faded. Kathleen blinked. Her head pounded. With a sharp inhale, she opened her eyes. Nothing, but white. Wincing against the pain, she rotated her neck. Her living room slowly emerged through the cloud. *Why am I on the floor?* Sticky red puddled beneath her hair. Something squeezed her shoulder.

"Kathleen!"

Ryan. Kathleen turned in the opposite direction. A wave of nausea rolled her stomach. She closed her eyes, then opened them again. Ryan knelt beside her. A smile spread over his face, and his eyes lit. Tears wet his cheeks. He leaned forward, pressing his lips to her forehead.

"Hi." He whispered.

"Hi." Her voice cracked. "What happened?" Her tongue stuck to the roof of her mouth. She tried to swallow.

"How do you feel?"

"Not good. Will you help me sit up?"

Ryan put his arm behind her shoulders and lifted. As

Kathleen forced herself to sit up, her head swelled. She touched her hair. When Kathleen pulled her fingers away, they were red with blood. Voices traveled to her ears, and she looked around. Blood soaked the carpet.

Mother, her face pale, spoke to an officer with her arms clenched across her abdomen.

A medic knelt beside Kathleen. "Welcome back, Mayor Phillips. My name is Marci Jarvis. Do you mind if I check you over?" She touched Kathleen's arm.

"No."

The medic shone a flashlight into Kathleen's eyes, then checked her pulse and listened to her lungs. "You've got a concussion, but you're going to be okay. Do you want to try to stand?"

Kathleen nodded, then instantly regretted it as a sharp pang stabbed her skull. Her heart thumped in her neck. She inhaled slowly, then exhaled. "Yes, please."

Ryan and Marci helped her to her feet. As Ryan cupped his arm around her back, she leaned against him for support. Marci moved away and knelt beside a duffel bag.

Memories filtered into Kathleen's thoughts. *Where is Mason?* "What happened? Did the police arrest Mason?"

Ryan's Adam's apple bobbed as he swallowed. "Yeah, they got him. Justice will be served."

He groaned and moved his arm. For the first time, Kathleen noticed the bandage. She widened her eyes, and her lips parted. "Did he do that to you?"

"It's all right. I'll heal. I gave him a little something to remember me by."

Kathleen stared. "Huh?"

"I shot him."

She sucked in a breath. Ryan was still speaking, probably explaining, but she couldn't focus her thoughts. *Mason shot Ryan. Ryan shot Mason.*

Marci returned. "If you sit here, Mayor Phillips, I'm going to bandage your head."

Ryan helped lower Kathleen into the chair from which

she'd recorded her live confession. What would happen now? Would she go to jail? She scrunched her eyes closed as a stinging ran through her skull.

"Sorry. I know it hurts." The medic's hands worked carefully. Moments later, she said, "All done." She stepped back. "Take it easy, okay."

Minutes passed. The officers finished their interviews, and Chief House stepped up to the chair. He held a pair of handcuffs. "I'm sorry. I have to do this."

"I understand."

"Kathleen Phillips. You're under arrest for bribery and obstruction of justice. You have the right to remain silent. Anything you say can be used against you in a court of law. You have the right to an attorney. If you cannot afford an attorney, one will be provided for you. Do you understand these rights?"

"I do."

The handcuffs snapped around her wrists. Chief House helped Kathleen to her feet.

A musical tone sliced the quiet. Ryan pulled his phone from his pocket. "Hello. This is Ryan Whitestone… Thank you… Thank you. We'll be right there." He hung up.

"What is it?" Kathleen asked.

"It's Paige. She's awake."

Chief House agreed to wait in the hall. When he removed the handcuffs, Kathleen rubbed the red marks on her wrists. "Thank you."

"Of course."

"Are you ready?" Ryan asked Kathleen.

"As ready as I'll ever be."

A nurse held the door, and they entered together. Kathleen took a deep breath—she could do this. She had to do this. Officer Bryant stood on the opposite side of the bed. He gave Kathleen a curt nod as she approached. The tubing had been removed from Paige's mouth, though an oxygen cannula was still in her nose. A faint beeping pulsed from the monitor.

Paige's eyes were closed, but her chest rose and fell on its own. As Ryan squeezed Kathleen's hand, she stepped closer to the bed. Behind her, the doctor spoke with Ryan. "She still has some major healing to do, but now that she's awake, she's out of the woods. We'll give her a few more days to make sure everything is stable, then we'll release her." She kept her eyes on her daughter.

Paige's eyes flickered, then opened. "Mom." Her voice was deep and scratchy—the most beautiful sound Kathleen had ever heard.

A sob caught in her throat. "Hello, daughter." She sat on the edge of the bed and took hold of Paige's hand. "I'm here."

"What happened?"

"You were in a terrible accident."

A look of recall crossed Paige's face. She slowly shifted her head and glanced around the room. "How long have I been here?"

"Just since yesterday." *Has it only been that long?*

Paige narrowed her eyes and frowned. "What are you doing here?"

Kathleen squeezed Paige's hand. "I'm here to ask for your forgiveness. I have treated you abominably, and I'm so sorry. I love you. I want you in my life. I want to be your mother, and I want you to be my daughter."

"Won't that ruin your chances of becoming governor?"

We don't have to worry about that. "I've already withdrawn."

Surprise widened Paige's expression. "You withdrew?"

Kathleen nodded and swept Paige's hair out of her eyes. "You, my daughter, were more important. Will you forgive me for how I treated you? For giving you up all those years ago?"

Paige's lips tugged into a smile. "I already have." Her eyes shimmered.

Kathleen closed her eyes and took a deep breath as the weight lifted from her heart. *Forgiven.* What a beautiful word. She opened her eyes. "If you're up to it, someone is dying to meet you." Dying might not have been the best word choice in the situation, but no one seemed to notice. Kathleen stood and strode into the hallway.

Kylie waited, hands shaking, eyes glimmering.

"Are you ready?"

Kylie nodded. A smile spread over Kathleen's lips—her little chatterbox was too overwhelmed to speak. She took Kylie's hand, then led her into the room and up to the bed. "Kylie. I'd like you to meet your sister."

Kylie took her place on the bed, sobbing and crying. Paige held out her arms, and Kylie bent into her embrace.

Kathleen stepped back. There was one more thing she had to take care of. "Ryan?"

He closed the distance between them. "Yes."

She brushed a tear from his cheek. "You've never stopped loving me even when I didn't deserve it. You helped me see who I was becoming and helped me return to who I was supposed to be. You reminded me who I was, who I still am. I've never stopped loving you either, and I know I don't deserve anything from you, but I have a question."

"What's that?"

"Will you give me a second chance?"

"Absolutely."

Kathleen sighed as he pulled her into his arms and lowered his lips to hers. The journey ahead would not be without its bumps and detours, their future uncertain. But she was confident in this one thing.

No matter who I am. No matter what I've done. Your mercy calls for me to find You there. Your grace is ever new. Your love is ever true. Who am I, but what You see in me?

I'm forgiven. Forgiven again.

Epilogue

One Year Later

The August sun beamed overhead as Kathleen entered Paige's backyard, carrying a pan of brownies. Paige met her at the gate, wearing a cute, yellow sundress, with a partial embrace and a kiss to the cheek. In the accident, Paige had broken several vertebrae. Her gait was still stilted, but she had improved so much over the past few months and had graduated from physical therapy and no longer had to wear a back brace. "Happy birthday, daughter."

"Thanks, Mom." Paige reached for the dessert. "Those look delicious. Did you make them?"

Kathleen's face grew warm. "I did. Hopefully, they're edible. I'm still getting used to doing everything myself." Matilda had retired in June and moved to Arizona with her children. It had been hard to see the old woman go. "I brought Matilda's last postcard for everyone. She seems really happy."

Paige took the brownies and the postcard. "Thank you. I'll put these on the food table, and pass this around." She looked at something past Kathleen's shoulder. "Hi Grandma, come join the party."

Kathleen rotated to let her mother through the gate. Mother wore Bermuda shorts, a tank top, and Hollywood style sunglasses. "Welcome home, Mother. How was your flight?"

"It was good. Thank you."

She and Mother embraced. Unshed tears stung her eyes. It hadn't been easy, but with counseling and long heart-to-heart conversations, she and Mother were finding their place in each other's lives. Mother had come to accept the truth about Erik. And in no uncertain terms, she told him he deserved his punishment, and she wasn't going to bail him out. Never again.

"When do you close on your new house?"

"Monday. If everything goes according to plan. I'm looking forward to being in Whitman again. This little town holds a lot of fond memories. And everyone I love is here." She smiled at Paige. Kathleen's daughter and mother embraced, then headed toward the tables.

Kathleen followed them deeper into the yard, where the others had gathered. The Thorne boys chased Galahad and Lancelot around a flower bed. One of the dogs plowed through the rose bushes, crushing the fragile petals. Becky Thorne turned and shouted at the boys to behave. She met Kathleen's eyes and smiled as she held out her hand. "Mayor Phillips, it's good to see you."

Kathleen shook her head. "I won't be mayor much longer. I've decided not to run again."

Becky's eyes widened. "Wow! What are you going to do instead?"

Kylie skipped up and threw her arm over Kathleen's shoulder. "She's going to invest in new businesses, starting with mine." Kylie grinned. "I got my business license approved yesterday. Hill O' Beans will officially open this fall!"

"Congratulations, Kylie. I'll be your first customer." Ryan stepped forward and planted a quick kiss on Kathleen's cheek. Her neck grew warm, and butterflies fluttered in her stomach.

"Kylie! Catch!" The Thorne's littlest boy, Timmy, called from the other side of the yard. He flung a whiffle ball in her direction. Kylie ran off to catch it in her scoop.

"I wish I had half their energy." Jessie carried a plate of deviled eggs to the table.

Paige's aunt, Hattie, followed at her heels. She stepped carefully to avoid spilling the bowl of pasta salad she carried. "I made this all by myself," she said, glowing. "Jessie's been teaching me how to cook, and I'm getting a lot better."

Jessie set her plate down on the table, then took the bowl from Hattie. "Yes, you are. You're a good student. I think we'll tackle lasagna next."

"Oh, Italian!" Hattie's joy at the simple things made Kathleen's lips tug into a smile.

Paige sat in one of the lawn chairs, crossing one leg over the other, and straightened the hem of her dress. "It's too bad we had to return all those first editions. Did you get everything sorted with the FBI?"

Kathleen nodded. "I did. I will stand trial for the part I played in covering Mason Bridge's crimes and Nelson's. The DA has decided not to press postmortem charges against your grandfather."

"Steaks are ready!" David Thorne stood by the grill, wearing an apron that read: *My Dad grills better than yours.* "Get it while it's hot!"

Everyone gathered around, filling their plates, then took seats at the wooden picnic tables. Hamilton stood and tapped his fork against his glass. "Um, before we pray, I have something I need to ask an extraordinary woman in my life. Paige, when I first met you, I was determined to remain single for the rest of my life. I was controlling my destiny rather than allowing God to be in control. I had to learn that loving someone for even a short time was better than never loving at all, and it was out of my control how much time that would be. I had to give it over to God. I don't know the future, and as a law enforcement officer, my future is even more uncertain. But I am certain of one thing. I love you, and I don't want to live my life without you, no matter how long God allows."

Kathleen's eyes misted.

Hamilton knelt on the grass and pulled something from his pocket. "Brooklyn Paige McDonald. Will you marry me?"

"Yes!" Paige screamed, threw her arms around his neck, then kissed him full on the lips. When she released him, laughing and crying, he held her hand and slid the ring onto her fourth finger. Sunlight glinted off the diamond and sent a rainbow of color shimmering across the table. Hugs and congratulations showered the happy couple.

A hand pressed on Kathleen's shoulder. She looked up into Ryan's teary eyes as he put his arm around her. She didn't flinch or move away. The past 12 months had been spent in therapy, where she learned to forgive Lionel for her own sake. She learned that not all men were like him. Ryan had been with her every step of the way. His gentleness and patience had won over her heart. It hadn't been an easy road, not at all. Healing from physical and emotional abuse didn't come from a magic pill. It wasn't over either; she still had a long way to go, but she was getting there.

As the sun began to set, Ryan took her hand. "Would you take a drive with me?" Ryan asked. Kathleen nodded and climbed in the car while he held the door. He drove through town and out to the overlook at Sacajawea Peak.

They left the vehicle and climbed onto the rocks, Ryan holding onto her hand so she wouldn't slip. Kathleen sat, expecting Ryan to join her. She looked up. Ryan was down on his knee. She gasped and put her hand to her lips.

"Anna Kathleen, I have loved you as long as I can

remember. We've had a bumpy road, but God saw fit to lead us back to one another. You are the love of my life, and I can't imagine being without you. Annie, will you make me the happiest man on earth by consenting to be my wife?" He held out a white gold ring with a heart-shaped solitaire diamond.

They'd been through a lot in the past year. They'd been through a lot in the past 27 years. And whether she had realized it or not, God had brought them through it all. They still had difficult roads ahead. She expected to serve time for her crimes. But over the past year, she had faithfully attended family counseling with both Paige and Kylie. She had also got help working through her hurt and bitterness and had been able to forgive Dad and Lionel for their emotional and physical abuse. She was ready to move on, but in a much better way than before. She still had a long way to go, and while trusting someone else would never come easy, she was confident she had at least two she could always lean on—the Heavenly Father and the man at her side. They had both seen her at her very worst, and yet for some unknown reason, loved her anyway. "I love you, Ryan Whitestone. I will marry you."

As Ryan took her into his arms and kissed her, Annie's heart filled to bursting. She may not have gotten everything she wanted, but the Lord had given her everything she needed.

"When life is at its worst, He gives us the ability to go on. And if we keep our focus on Him, He gives us the strength to soar."

In God's everlasting strength and the unfailing love of her family, she was finally ready to soar.

Shadows Over Whitman #1

No Greater Love

Gina Holder

She's looking for her birth mother.
He's looking for a thief.
Will each find what they are truly seeking?

Acknowledgements

First, I want to thank my Lord and Savior Jesus Christ for calling me to write stories. It's His love and mercy that I want to shine through everything that I write, and I want it all to bring glory to His name.

Thank you to my husband, Daniel, and daughter, Lydia, your love and support keeps me going when it gets difficult.

Thank you to my beta readers, Kathy, Amy, Chris, Anne, Joni, Vicki, Claudia, Wendy, and Alysha. The input you gave me has helped to make this story what it is today.

Thank you to my critique partner, A.D. Lawrence. Your insight, grammar fixes, and brain-storming help was a blessing to me. I'm looking forward to working together in the future.

Thank you to Amy Perkins for naming the Dalmatians—Galahad and Lancelot.

Thank you to Mavis Duke Hinton for naming Kylie's coffee shop—Hill O' Beans.

Thank you to the members of my launch team for spreading the word and sharing my book with the world. You all are a blessing to me!

Gina Holder lives in Colorado with her husband and daughter. She is a stay-at-home mom and homeschooler. She is a member of ACFW (America Christian Fiction Writers). She enjoys writing her blog, where she reviews Christian fiction. She has also served on launch teams for several other authors.

She dreamed of being a writer from her early teen years and graduated from the Long Ridge Writer's Group "Breaking into Print" program in 2004. She graduated from Faith Bible Institute, a three-year Bible correspondence course in 2005. She began her career as a writer crafting non-fiction articles for several online newsletters and websites, but her heart has always been to write fiction. In 2017, she finally saw this dream fulfilled when she indie published her debut novel.

When she's not working on her next book, Gina loves to watch cheesy romance movies, cook dinner for her family, and play the piano and organ and sing for worship services at her church. She loves to read Christian fiction and has a never-ending "to be read" pile.

Blog: storiesbygina.wordpress.com
Facebook: storiesbygina
Instagram: @storiesbygina
Twitter: @storiesbygina
Amazon: B074HC9SHX
Bookbub: gina-holder
Goodreads: Gina Holder

Made in the USA
Monee, IL
07 November 2020

46880245R00208